WHEN ANGELS
FAIL TO FLY
A STEVE CASSIDY MYSTERY

WHEN ANGELS
FAIL TO FLY
A STEVE CASSIDY MYSTERY

SCANNER PUBLISHING

WINDSOR, ONTARIO, CANADA

COPYRIGHT 2009 BY JOHN SCHLARBAUM

Library and Archives Canada Cataloguing in Publication

Schlarbaum, John, 1966-
When angels fail to fly / John Schlarbaum.

ISBN 978-0-9738498-4-4

I. Title. II. Series: Schlarbaum, John, 1966- . Steve Cassidy mystery.

PS8637.C448W45 2009   C813'.6   C2009-902455-1

SCANNER PUBLISHING
5060 Tecumseh Road East, Suite #1106
Windsor, Ontario, Canada N8T 1C1

Cover design: Hawksworth Designs © 2009
www.hawksworthdesigns.com

Acknowledgements

With each book release, I am amazed how much goodwill I continue to receive from family, friends and new readers of my work. I appreciate the encouragement and thank you all.

Since the publication of the first Steve Cassidy Mystery – *Barry Jones' Cold Dinner* – I have had the pleasure of meeting hundreds of book lovers at various events. Without exception, it appears no matter what the economic forecast or new technologies available, the enjoyment of getting lost in a good story will remain a mainstay in our lives for many years to come.

This novel presented several new challenges from a creative stand-point, the most pressing, of course, was keeping the fans of P.I. Steve Cassidy intrigued and engaged a second time around. To help in this endeavour, I would like to give special thanks to:

All of those who took the time to read preview copies of the book and give me valuable feedback.

Laura Borland for helping to bring my original free-flowing storyline into focus.

Susan Forrest for her considerable insight and helping to edit my manuscript. Your many hours of hard work are greatly appreciated.

Jennifer Hawksworth for her graphic design expertise, as well as her limitless patience when it comes to my requests for changes, changes, and more changes.

Jenne D. whose fabulous friendship and unconditional support has always been without compare. You are truly an original.

John Schlarbaum
November 2009

DEDICATION

For Jessica

A true friend
and incredible Muse.

"Seriously . . . I'm just saying."

ONE

"So who's the lucky guy tonight, Steve?"

"Must you say that so loud, Nancy?" I protested as I placed my gym bag on a nearby bar stool.

"Afraid someone will get the wrong idea about you?" Nancy replied with a smile.

"The short answer? Yes."

"You private dicks can sure be touchy sometimes." Nancy, the attractive forty–something bartender with short dirty blonde hair and haunting brown eyes, slowly began checking out the dinner crowd. "Just between us, do I know him?" she asked in a low conspiratorial tone.

"That depends," I said. "Are you acquainted with many fifty–six–year–old overweight plumbers from Plymouth, who like to lay a little extra pipe when they're out of town attending a plumbing convention?"

"Did you say plumbing convention? They have those?"

"It's big business. I was there this afternoon sizing up tonight's target."

"I bet those guys are a laugh a minute," Nancy said, shaking her head in disbelief.

"Oh yeah, you'd be surprised how many *tools* there are at those things."

Nancy and I locked eyes and both laughed.

"So who's the lucky girl?" Nancy inquired a few moments later. "Does she know what you've planned for her? For a chunky plumber past his prime, I hope you're giving her danger pay."

"You'll like Samantha," I said. "She recently dumped her fiancé after finding out he'd been cheating on her. She wants to see every no-good boyfriend, husband and lover go down in flames."

Nancy rolled her eyes. "I've been there and all I can say is Heaven help Peter Plumber."

"Exactly."

I checked my watch: 5:29 p.m. Sam and "Peter" were scheduled to arrive here for an intimate dinner in thirty minutes. For marital cases I often use Randy's Saloon and Grill, an outdated restaurant located in the east end of the City of Darrien—my new home. This cozy get-together would hopefully be followed by a visit to Room 215 at the nearby Tecumseh Motel, all of which would be captured on video by yours truly. I glanced at the predetermined rear booth where my cute couple would be seated and noted the RESERVED sign. A few feet away, there was a similar sign atop a smaller table for two, where I would enjoy a steak dinner paid for by the client, Mrs. Plumber. On the vacant chair across from me, I would position my gym bag so the pinhole camera within it could record both video and audio of the soon-to-be lovers.

"Don't these guys get suspicious when your girl takes off her blouse to reveal wires running from her bra, down her stomach and into her waistband?" Nancy asked, breaking my concentration. Before I could answer she added, "Who knows—maybe for a twisted, cheating husband that could be a turn-on."

"Maybe," I concurred, "but that would never happen."

"Why?"

"Because within two minutes of Samantha entering the motel room, I'll page her. She'll then say there's an emergency and ask the guy to leave."

"Are his pants already down around his ankles?"

"On occasion."

"How embarrassing."

"Not as embarrassing as when he's sitting across from his wife, giving a deposition at her divorce lawyer's office," I smirked.

Nancy gave me a dirty look. "How can you take pleasure in destroying a marriage like that?"

"I get no delight. I get paid for a job well done," I countered. "I don't instruct these fools to break their wedding vows—they just do it. I am paid by the hour, regardless if they go to the motel or not. If the wife's right, I confirm her suspicions. If she's wrong, I alleviate her anxiety about her soul mate when he's out of town."

Nancy bent forward across the bar, reached both hands out above my head and then turned her arms slightly. "There," she said, "your halo was a bit crooked."

"Thanks," I laughed. "I keep forgetting to check it when I go out."

After I downed a shot of whiskey with Nancy, I went to the rest room to make a final check of my new digital video camera. Once in a stall, I opened the pullout screen, which revealed a beautiful shot of my feet resting on the tiled floor, with today's time and date in the lower right-hand corner. Next, I turned on my wireless audio recorder and fit a discreet earpiece in my left ear. I pressed the TEST button on the recorder, which emitted a low-pitched squeal. When Samantha and her date showed up, I'd be able to hear everything they said. With my equipment in good working order, I zipped the gym bag closed and proceeded into the dining room.

No sign of Samantha and Peter. I looked up at the clock above the jukebox: 6:02 p.m.

I grabbed another drink and decided to take a seat at my table. Within a few minutes, I heard Sam's heavenly laugh in my earpiece.

They had arrived.

Showtime.

You could tell from Peter's demeanour that this was not the first time he had taken a woman out for dinner without his wife present. In this dimly lit atmosphere, he actually appeared to be a successful businessman. He was six feet tall, clean-shaven, with a full head of black hair. Earlier in the day, I had categorized him as being stout but on second look, I realized that wasn't the case; he simply had a "middle-aged gut," as my dad would say. Gone were the rumpled suit, unkempt hair and glasses I had seen him sporting at the convention centre. Tonight his hair was slicked back, his contacts were in place and he was wearing a low-end Brooks Brothers suit. To top off the transformation, a high school ring was now on his left hand, where his wedding ring once proudly sat.

As I watched this makeover success brush by me, I wondered

which of these "changes" his wife had discovered first, setting this file in motion.

As usual, Samantha played to perfection the part of a sexy businesswoman visiting a strange city looking for a discreet romantic encounter. Her dark blue sundress, seductively hugging her curvaceous frame, gave the illusion she had just stepped out of a swimming pool. As she got closer to the booth, I forced myself to concentrate on the menu, to avoid any unintentional eye contact. I then made a quick scan of the room and saw that every other male in her vicinity was also feeling Sam's considerable presence.

"Trust me, guys, she's the last woman you want to be caught out on a date with," I said under my breath, intoxicated by her perfume as she shimmied her way into the booth.

During the next hour and a half, Samantha and Peter did all the predictable first date things: made small talk, joked around, laughed too quickly at each other's amusing observations on life, flirted, lied, flirted some more and lied, lied, lied.

Our plumber friend, however, was participating with one major disadvantage: I hadn't provided him with a full dossier of his date's actual vital statistics. Listening to him brag about his university education, football career (cut short due to a blown-out knee during THE BIG GAME), the timeshare condo in Mexico and most interesting, his wife's tragic death on their honeymoon no less, I was amazed at how Samantha could keep a straight face. Throughout the meal, she countered each exaggerated untruth with one of her own, speaking as casually as a telemarketer trying to sell you life insurance over the phone.

During this time, I partook of a caesar salad, a large New York strip streak, loaded baked potato and steamed vegetables, while appearing to read a new Howard Hughes biography. The conversation behind me soon turned to the topic of what to do after they left the restaurant. As their dinner banter consisted almost entirely of sexually charged innuendos, I figured old Plumber Pete would be primed to jump Samantha's bones the moment they reached the parking lot. Of course, she had other plans.

Marital cases are much like police sting operations; for them to be a complete success, you must avoid an "entrapment" rap from the target at all costs. Yes, you supply all the temptations (girl/drugs) and enticements (sex/big bucks), but in the end, you can't force someone to do something against their will.

In a court of law, the prosecution has to prove several things in regard to the defendant's actions:

1. That he knew why he had attended that specific sting room.
2. Why he brought a briefcase full of money.
3. Why he gave the nice drug dealer his hard-earned cash.
4. Why he then left the room carrying a knapsack of cocaine.

A P.I., on the other hand, only has to get his subject up to a woman's hotel room for a "conviction." As a former cop, I always like a clean conclusion to each cheating spouse case I take on. That's why you'll never hear Samantha suggest they go to her room. To me, that is entrapment. If however, Peter Pipe Layer brings it up first, he has only himself to blame.

For better or worse, that's the way I operate.

"Are you finished, sir?"

I looked up from my book to see Nancy standing over me with a huge grin on her face.

"I am. The meal was excellent, as always," I said handing her my plate.

She looked at the booth behind me. "Did you leave enough room for dessert or would you like the bill?"

"Dessert, huh? I think I can stick around a few more minutes. I hear the cherry pie is quite good."

"I made it fresh this morning."

"You don't say."

As Nancy walked away, I heard our friendly neighbourhood plumber make his last play for the fiery red-haired babe sitting across from him. During my dessert order, I registered only bits and pieces of Sam and Peter's discussion. There was something about him not wanting to go to his hotel, as he was afraid his accountant friends—also in town for a business convention—would hit on her.

5

"Maybe . . ." he started tentatively, yet to my trained ear confidently, "we can head to your room. Where are you staying again?"

"The Tecumseh Motel," Samantha replied, "but there's really nothing to do there. I don't think they even have pay-for-view movies," she said, a bit embarrassed. "My employer is pretty cheap."

Just wait until you see your pay slip, I thought, amused by Sam's declaration.

Peter Plumber then laughed nervously as he asked, "Did he at least spring for a room with a king-sized bed?"

GOTCHA!

Five minutes later, Nancy was surprised when I declined the piece of pie she was holding and requested the bill.

"You're still paying for the pie, right?" she asked playfully.

"My gift to you," I said, giving her my credit card.

She looked at the plate in her hand. "This isn't my tip, is it?"

"Not by a long shot."

Before heading to my van, I gave Nancy her usual $100 "hospitality tip" and scribbled, "See you soon," on the top of the receipt. Outside, I hailed a nearby taxi and paid the driver $40 to wait for Samantha and Peter.

"No problem, pal," the cabbie said coolly.

When they stepped out into the early evening sun, I snapped some good identification shots. As the last thing we wanted was for Samantha to get into a strange man's car, she suggested they take a cab, which caused a brief argument to erupt. Peter was adamant he was fine to drive but soon realized his protests were futile when my cab driver pulled up to whisk them away.

I followed at a discreet distance, recording the plumber's verbal flirtations with Samantha, who continued to play it cool, before zipping past them to established a surveillance position at the motel.

The Tecumseh Motel is an older-style building with all the unit doors facing the parking lot. I set up in an adjacent convenience store lot, jumped in the backseat and awaited the taxi's arrival. The beauty of this location was it gave the target ample opportunities to change his mind, to save his dignity, and to rescue his faltering marriage.

The short cab ride from the restaurant fell into the *This is dangerous but fun* category. However, once buddy was actually at the motel the reality of the situation set in: "Oh my God, I'm going to have sex with this woman! Should I really be doing this?" Some guys actually sprinted up the exterior staircase, trying to get down to business as soon as humanly possible. Don't get me wrong, occasionally there are would-be-cheaters who suddenly have looks of terror wash over their features. Maybe images of their wife or kids pop into their mind—who knows. Despite the consequences, one by one almost all physically will themselves forward, across the parking lot, up the two flights of stairs and finally to Samantha's room, or as she calls it, The Loser's Love Den.

I videotaped more close-ups of Peter's face and saw only joy; no trepidation at all. A player, pure and simple. He was alone, out of town, horny and about to make it with a beautiful young woman who wouldn't charge him a dime.

How lucky could one plumber get?

Once inside the room, Peter immediately tried to kiss Samantha. I could hear the microphone being jostled as their chests collided with one another.

"Hey, slow down," Sam said.

"I'm sorry," Peter stammered. "It's been awhile. I guess I'm out of practice. I didn't mean to . . ."

"It's all right," Sam cut him off. "I'm kind of new at this too."

Good girl, I thought. *Keep him cool. We're almost there.*

"Why don't I freshen up? The cigarette smoke was pretty thick in the restaurant and I hate the smell."

"So do I," Peter replied.

There was a long period of silence in the room that made me uncomfortable, but then our plumber playboy said something that would be the final nail in his marital coffin.

"Would you be opposed to getting cleaned up . . . together?" Long pause. "You know . . . have a shower, or bath, if you prefer?"

"Let me think about that," Samantha replied, as she entered the bathroom and closed the door. "Let's rock and roll," she said in a low whisper to me.

This was my cue. I auto-dialed Samantha's pager and a minute later, I could hear Sam's distinctive pager tone go off in my earpiece. I heard the bathroom door open and Sam give out a short cry as she read the message.

"My father's had a heart attack."

"You're kidding?" I heard Peter say.

Wrong reaction, friend.

There was authentic fury in Samantha's response. "Do you think I would kid around about something like that? What does this message say?"

I visualized poor Peter's expression as he read my message: *Urgent. Dad's had a heart attack. Call me. Sara.*

"Sara is my sister," Samantha snapped, venom dripping from each syllable.

"Geez, I'm sorry . . . I didn't mean to imply . . ."

"I have to pack," Sam cut him off again. "I'm the one who should be sorry. You've been so nice and we were getting along so well."

"No, these things happen." He was good at hiding his disappointment but what choice did he have?

Samantha continued to sob into my ear as the exterior room door opened and I saw Peter looking out.

"I'll grab the taxi we came here in. It's still out front." He turned to Samantha and enveloped her in a big bear embrace. "Everything will turn out okay. Trust me." He looked at Samantha's tear-stained face and kissed her on her right cheek.

Samantha stepped away and smiled weakly. "Maybe we'll meet again."

As Peter put on his coat, his attention returned to the bed. "I attend these conventions twice a year. With any luck we'll be able to make some beautiful music together next time." There was another awkward pause before he added, "I'll get out of your way so you can pack. It was very nice meeting you."

"Again, thanks for dinner, it was lovely."

Peter walked down to the parking lot and then looked up to Sam's

8

room, where she remained standing in the doorway. They waved to each other as he entered the back seat of the taxi, which was driven off the lot. Five seconds after Samantha closed the door my phone rang. I couldn't even get, "Hello," out before she started screaming at me.

"Did you see what he did? That perv kissed my cheek so he could taste my tears! What kind of sicko does that?"

"If your father had cut out those fatty foods, maybe you'd have found out."

"I don't think so," she hissed. "Are you coming up?"

"Be there in a sec. I'm going to follow the taxi, to make sure our mutual acquaintance gets to his hotel in one piece."

Unfortunately, due to slow traffic flow on the main drag, I lost sight of the taxi a short time later. As it was heading in the right direction, I made the executive decision to pull the plug and return to the motel.

I opened the door with my key and was immediately struck by how gorgeous Samantha was. That she was stretched provocatively across the bed in only bra and panties was also mighty appealing to my old eyes.

"Now what would your significant other say about us hanging out together under these circumstances?"

Before a response could be uttered, I found myself joining Samantha on the bed, where she gave me a long sensuous kiss.

"How'd I do tonight? Were you jealous?"

"You were wonderful," I replied as Samantha began to unbutton my shirt. "As for being jealous—I don't get jealous. I'll admit I was a bit envious when plumber boy wanted to take a shower with you."

"Do you want to take that shower with me now?"

"I thought you'd never ask."

As the room was already paid for in full, we decided to use all the amenities provided for a few more hours. The in-joke was I would then bill the client for the time it took to *debrief* the other investigator on the evening's events. Some female clients actually praised me for such a thorough job and said *the other woman's* comments had been very enlightening.

If only they knew just how enlightening those sessions were for

Samantha and me.

Around ten–thirty, I offered to make a quick dessert run, as we were both hungry after our very physical interview session. I drove the van off the lot, hoping to find the ice cream stand up the road open. I thought a banana split would hit the spot. Bananas, whipped cream, three scoops of ice cream, two spoons and one Samantha.

What I hadn't counted on was having the tables turned and now being the one under surveillance. Like most of my targets, I was completely oblivious to being watched. I hadn't noticed that our jilted plumber friend had returned in his dark green Saturn rental car and saw me exit the room kissing Sam in the doorway on my way out.

Apparently, he had been waiting to make his move for some time, seething over our little deception. A taxi driver would come forward to say he had driven the former Plymouth resident—who appeared agitated at the time—to the Holiday Plaza Hotel around 7:45 p.m. "He was, you know—frustrated," the driver was quoted in the newspaper the following morning.

What this scumbag cabbie failed to mention was he'd told Peter the Plumber about our $40 arrangement outside the restaurant. Mr. Plumber, always good with numbers while on the job, had no difficulty putting two and two together.

When I returned fifteen minutes later with the banana split on the passenger seat, the only thing left for the police officers to do was fill out the proper paper work. They had already responded to a 911 call about an enraged couple screaming at each other in a cheap motel room. They had already shot and killed a man covered in blood and brandishing what looked like a gun (but turned out to be a hammer). And they had already determined the naked woman on the bed inside Room 215 had been bludgeoned to death with the aforementioned household tool.

As I looked up to our room and then at the plumber's dead body on the pavement below, I could only think of the question Samantha had posed to me earlier:

Now what would your significant other say about us hanging out together under these circumstances?

10

Of all the questions I would have to answer, that would be the toughest. I could handle the cops, the lawyers and even Samantha's family, but I had no clue how my lovely Linda would react. Her move from our small hometown to the big city was meant to be a fresh start for us. Now I had royally and tragically screwed things up.

As the media would play up for weeks, the irony of this whole debacle was that my mistress, Samantha, had been killed due to a suspicious wife. I wondered how Linda would feel knowing a home-maker from Plymouth had suspected her husband of cheating, yet she hadn't suspected me.

Or had she?

I figured I'd never find out. If I were in her position, I knew I would hit the road and never look back.

In life there are certain lines you should never cross: as a kid, you're programmed to colour inside the lines. In wartime, there's always a line drawn in the sand. And in committed relationships, the line you never step over is to cheat on your partner.

Devoid of any meaningful emotion, I got out of the van and started toward the officer in charge, inadvertently stepping under yet another taboo line: the yellow police tape that surrounds a crime scene. In that instant, I knew that morally I was no better than Peter Plumber.

Pathetic.

"What's your business here, sir?" the officer asked as I approached.

"My name is Steve Cassidy. I'm the P.I. and resident dirt bag responsible for this mess."

TWO

After a night of questioning at Police Headquarters, I arrived home to find Linda gone. On the coffee table I found a note and her set of keys.

As the old song goes: Life is made up of Hellos and Goodbyes.

This is Goodbye.

Linda

I made a pointless tour through the house, hoping to find something that would confirm Linda had once lived here. Sadly, no traces of our relationship had been left behind. Gone were the pictures of us together, as well as her clothes and makeup. Most disheartening was the loss of a packet of love letters we had exchanged prior to Linda's move to Darrien. My letters to her were still neatly stacked on the fireplace mantle but her notes to me were missing. She had been so thorough in her departure the only personal item I found, aside from her note, was the start of a grocery list in her handwriting:

Milk

Good old wholesome milk. If that was all I needed, my life would certainly be less complicated, or so I imagined.

I took a seat on the living room couch and tried to collect my thoughts. I badly wanted to believe I had been the perfect cheater; that prior to last evening, no one had been hurt by my lack of control; that no one knew about Samantha and me, right up to when the "Breaking News Report" aired.

Who was I kidding? The dapper plumber believed he was invincible and look where it got him: a one-way ticket to the morgue.

I figured I could locate Linda in three phone calls, but decided against such a plan for the moment. She wouldn't want to talk and I doubted the words, "Oops, you caught me," would restore my credibility in her eyes. I was also too exhausted to attempt such calls. Instead, I unplugged the phone and collapsed into bed. When I awoke a few hours later, I found I had missed fifty–six calls, most of which I believed would be from media outlets, looking for a comment to accompany their scandal-tainted storylines.

With pen in hand, my expectations were soon met, as an astounding forty–three of the calls were from TV, newspaper, magazine and radio reporters. Even the great local columnist, Jeremy Atkins of the Darrien Free Press, made an impassioned plea, leaving me his personal cell number for twenty–four hour access. He'd written a nice piece on me in his "World According To Me" column, after the successful conclusion of a missing person case in my old hometown. I wrote down his information for future reference and erased the others.

Of the thirteen remaining calls, five were hang-ups and six were from male jokers wanting to hire me. "Is it possible to get my wife to a hotel room to get laid and then have her killed?" one smart aleck asked. "I heard that was your specialty." Not surprisingly, none of these comedians left return numbers.

The final two calls intrigued and worried me.

"Ah . . . hi . . . Linda, are you there?" an older female asked in an unsteady voice. "It's Dolores from the library. We were wondering if you'd be coming in today? With everything that's happened, if you want to take the day off go right ahead. Could you give us a call when you get this? Thanks."

The machine's time display read 11:01 a.m., which meant Linda was two hours late for her regular Thursday shift. I assumed after leaving here that she would have gone straight to work. Even if she had decided to take a personal day, it was unlike her not to inform her supervisor.

Before I could reflect further on Linda's current whereabouts, the fifty–sixth message began to play.

"Hey, Steve and Linda. It's Maria. Long time no hear. The reason I'm calling is I need Steve's opinion about a strange call I received from an old friend of ours. Give me a shout when you have a minute.

14

Take care."

I stared at the machine as my high school sweetheart, Maria Antonio, left her home and work phone numbers, which I failed to write down. I replayed the message to verify what I had heard was for real. On the second pass I detected something in Maria's voice that bothered me: there was an undercurrent of concern which she had tried to cover up with her usual bubbly, friendly tone. Something was definitely wrong. I tried unsuccessfully to figure out what could have caused her to become anxious. Until recently the only person capable of such a thing was me, but we hadn't talked in a couple of months. It was obvious my latest indiscretions had yet to reach the lovely back-woods community of Delta. I wondered if Maria would still want my advice when the news broke. I doubted it.

I erased the messages, which reset the machine's counter to zero. I toyed with the idea of calling the library but decided I would only further embarrass the two of us if she didn't pick up. I did the next best thing and called Linda's cell phone, which automatically went to voice mail.

"Hi, it's me. I know you don't want to talk to me right now—and justifiably so—but could you please call Dolores at the library, she sounded a bit worried that you hadn't come into work." I paused and then said, "I hope you're doing okay . . . and I'm sorry for being such an ass."

I hung up, not knowing what more I could say at this juncture. As I stood from the kitchen table to grab a drink from the fridge, I sensed my legs shaking slightly and felt a tad light-headed. I steadied myself against a nearby wall and concluded my nervous system must be on the verge of collapse; too many conflicting emotions were about to trip the final safety fuse in my strained brain.

Until this moment, I'd had a very laid-back, no-ulcer attitude about the events that had followed Samantha and the Plymouth plumber's dinner date. Now the reality of the past eighteen hours flooded my entire being.

Your mistress is dead. Your fiancée is gone and your first love needs your help.

Taken separately, these situations would have been stressful enough. Having to deal with them all at once was overwhelming.

I was so disoriented, I barely registered that someone was knocking loudly on the front door. When a second person simultaneously began to knock at the back door, the brain fog I'd been experiencing began to lift. When a man on the front porch yelled, "Darrien City Police. Open this door or we'll break it down!" the fog completely dissipated.

I made my way through the front room shouting, "I'm coming! Just hold on!"

I opened the foyer door and found myself facing three officers. All had their guns drawn, the barrels aimed directly at my heart.

"Cassidy, show us your hands and slowly step onto the porch," an officer instructed.

I recognized him as the one who had taken my statement at the motel. "I don't know what this is about, Sergeant Anderton," I said while walking very slowly out the front door. "I have no problem answering any follow-up questions you might have but this show of fire power is a bit much, don't you think?"

"We'll see," Anderton replied coolly. "Up against the wall."

"Are you out of your freaking—"

"Shut up and assume the position!"

I glanced at the steely faces of the two younger cops and then saw a fourth officer—probably the back door knocker—come around the side of the house.

"No problem, guys," I said as I placed my hands against the porch wall. I spread my legs as Anderton holstered his weapon and stepped toward me.

After an unproductive pat-down, he spun me around by my shoulder. "I want you to sit on that chair right there and don't make a move."

Like any law-abiding citizen, I followed the nice officer's orders and sat in one of two lawn chairs Linda had bought in the spring.

"Want to clue me in on what this is about?" I asked.

Before answering Anderton turned and barked, "Dwyer, Salem— go inside and do a search."

"Hey, you can't just enter my house," I objected. "Where's your search warrant?"

"We don't need one when there's a reasonable belief a crime is in process," Anderton said with a devilish smirk.

The brain fog began to roll in again.

"What are you talking about?"

"We received a call from Linda Brooks' employer, who felt your fiancée may be in danger after she didn't show up for work this morning."

"I would never hurt Linda. This is ridiculous."

Anderton cut me off. "Plus, we were in touch with her brother in Bismarck, Chief of Police Burkhart."

Okay, here we go, I thought. "Acting Chief Burkhart," I corrected him. "With all due respect, Keith is a moron and would love to pin anything on me. He still thinks I killed his mentor, Chief Gordon, while I was locked up in a prison cell earlier in the year. Did he mention Gordon died from a gunshot wound and that I was unarmed at the time?" Anderton gave me a blank stare. "Of course he didn't. What a tool."

"Enough chit-chat, Cassidy. Is Ms. Brooks in the house or not?"

"No," I answered. "After finding out I'd cheated on her, she left me."

"And when was this?"

"I don't know—sometime during the night. When I got home she was gone."

"When was the last time you saw her alive?"

"What do you mean, *saw her alive*? Unless you know something I don't, she's still very much alive—somewhere."

"Answer the question."

"Fine. If you must know, we talked on the phone yesterday after-noon for about ten minutes. Are you happy now?"

"Not until I see Ms. Brooks alive."

Officers Dwyer and Salem returned to the porch.

"Nothing," Dwyer stated.

"No sign of the girl anywhere," Salem chimed in. "We did find

17

this on the coffee table, alongside a set of keys." As Salem showed Anderton the song inspired kiss-off letter, I was stunned to see he was wearing a latex glove to hold it.

"What is this?" Anderton asked me.

"Don't they teach newbies the significance of *Dear John* letters at the academy any more?"

He ignored me and turned to Salem. "Bag it as evidence."

"I wouldn't do that if I were you, Officer Salem," I spoke up in a surprisingly easy tone that belied the rage welling inside me. "It's evident your superior skipped the Rules of Search and Seizure class."

Salem, a young copper I pegged to be about twenty–three, looked to Anderton for some much-needed guidance, which I provided.

"Even though your search of my house was technically legal, having found no evidence a crime was being committed or has been committed here, you must now leave everything exactly as you found it. You can't take my personal correspondence or any other items— that's stealing. Furthermore, from what I can recall from my days on the force, stealing is against the law. It would be like attending a noise complaint call, finding no problems at the given address and then confiscating the owner's CD collection for the heck of it. Just from looking at you, Salem, I can tell you graduated near the top of your class. Think about what I'm saying."

I sensed I shocked Salem by stating I had once been an officer.

"But this letter could be part of his plan to cover up his crime," Salem stammered to Anderton.

"And what crime would that be—infidelity?"

"Enough!" Anderton screamed at both of us. "We'll get a warrant and then bag it," he addressed Salem sternly.

I hated senior officers like Anderton. He was probably a twenty-year veteran, each year promoted to a higher rank based on "time served" instead of merit. Today, he was trying to impress his young, wet-behind-the-ears officers, for which I gave him full marks. His problem was that from a legal standpoint, his overblown porch bluster would not have a snowball's chance in hell in a court of law.

"With all due respect, it's bloody near impossible to get a judge to sign off on a search warrant of a private citizen's residence, on the basis a librarian failed to show up for work approximately four hours ago. Trust me on this one, boys," I said to the rookies.

That brain fog I had mentioned previously was now apparently invading the space between the ears of the officers in front of me. The youngsters looked dazed and confused, as their fearless leader stood red-faced with anger. He glared at me, while silently conveying his desire to crack my skull open with his nightstick.

"Why don't you just tell us where she is then?" Dwyer asked, exhibiting some courage.

"If I knew I'd tell you. Right now, I don't have a clue. If I did, I could apologize for turning out to be such an idiot." I paused and added, "But I'm sure you'll communicate those sentiments for me when you speak to her in the near future." I looked at each officer present and asked, "So, are we finished here?"

After an impassioned, yet useless, "We're not finished by a long shot," speech, Sergeant Anderton and his minions begrudgingly departed, much to the neighbourhood's relief.

Show's over. Everybody inside, I wanted to tell all of the sidewalk gawkers.

I carried Linda's letter into the house and bolted both doors. As I walked toward the fridge to get a cold beer, I noticed my answering machine light blinking.

"Hey Steve-O, it's your buddy Doogie, the world's ultimate pig farmer. I was surfing the web and saw an interesting story on the Darrien Free Press page. Do you have a death wish or what, buddy? Anyway, call me on my cell. Do not—I repeat—do not call me at home. Wifey will go ballistic when she finds out about this. Don't delay, call today. Talkatcha."

19

THE WORLD ACCORDING TO ME
WHEN A GOOD P.I. GOES BAD

Jeremy Atkins
Darrien Free Press
August 14, 1997

A little more than six months ago, Private Investigator Steve Cassidy returned to Darrien a hero—but just barely. Today he is being investigated in a bizarre love triangle gone bad. Very bad.

Cassidy had been hired to learn if a visiting plumber from Plymouth was cheating on his wife. To do so, Steve hired a female accomplice to pose as a willing single businesswoman looking for love in all the wrong places. After dinner the couple returned to the Tecumseh Motel, where the plumber was hoping to have consensual sex with his attractive date. That is when a problem arose: the woman was paged and informed her father had taken ill. She would have to leave soon. The plumber would have to leave even sooner.

By all accounts, that's exactly what he did. He left his distressed fake date alone in her room, and returned to his hotel on the other side of the city. Somewhere along the line, however, the Plymouth plumber decided he had to see this wonderful gal one last time.

Now you may be asking yourself, *Where was the P.I. during all this activity?* Well, after secretly videotaping the couple at a local grill, Mr. Cassidy followed them back to the motel, still recording their every move from the comfort of his heavily tinted van.

When the night's scheduled fun and games were over, the real show began—this time unscripted. You see, Samantha Jennings was not only good at playing a man's mistress during work hours but also long after her intended mark left her side.

Maybe that's why Steve Cassidy hired her in the first place. What better way to cheat on

20

your fiancée then to say, "Of course nothing is happening between Samantha and me. Our relationship is strictly professional. Trust me."

Regardless of how Mr. Cassidy's and Ms. Jennings' relationship began, it ended abruptly with several swings of a hammer and a hail of police bullets.

A few years ago, while employed as a patrol officer, Cassidy turned on several of his fellow officers, in an attempt to save his own hide during a scandalous corruption case, from which that force is still smarting.

Earlier this year Cassidy returned to his old hometown to locate a missing person. Not only did he determine family man Barry Jones had been dead for seven years, he also got the killer to confess to the murder on tape. The killer is now spending the next twenty–five years as a guest of the Sandwedge Penitentiary.

Did I mention that during the same investigation Mr. Cassidy had been arrested for Mr. Jones' murder? Or that the local police chief was shot and killed by one of his own during a verbal confrontation with Cassidy? For more on that, buy the recently released true crime book *Late For Dinner*, as newsprint costs don't allow me to give up the juicier details just now.

Should we feel bad for Steve Cassidy? I don't think so. Should we feel sad for the homicidal cheating plumber? Nah. The ones for whom we should really feel sorrow for— pity even—are the women involved in this tragedy, who trusted Cassidy: the plumber's wife, the mistress, and finally his poor fiancée, who was probably the last to know.

At present, Steve Cassidy's P.I. licence has been suspended by the proper authorities, and the local police continue to probe his involvement in this sordid affair.

THREE

Personal privacy is one aspect of a private investigator's life taken very seriously. My driver's licence lists the address of a private postal depot where I rent a mailbox. Even the telephone number for Cassidy Investigations does not list an actual street location in the phone book. If someone requests a meeting, I have it at a neutral location like a donut shop. All of these measures are to protect me from disgruntled clients or subjects knowing where I eat and sleep. Unfortunately, there are no safeguards against a neighbour calling the local television station about a SWAT-like situation next door. I glanced out the front window of my house and wondered when the media would arrive to stake claim to my yard. So far, they had either ignored the tip altogether or figured it wasn't worth getting involved in dangerous police business. At least something was going my way.

Before calling Maria, I tried to get hold of my former best friend, Wayne "Doogie" Dugan, hoping he might know about her strange phone message.

After two rings Wayne picked up and stated quite forcibly, "I don't know how you got this number but I'm not giving any interviews about that loser Steve Cassidy. So stop calling!"

"Mr. Dugan, please don't hang up. We're willing to pay $50,000 for your story." My offer was met with a long, thoughtful moment of silence.

"You know, Steve," Wayne began to laugh, "for fifty grand I'd give up details of my grandparents' sex life."

"Call display takes all the fun out of life, Doogie."

"Tell me about it. It sure comes in handy though when Trudy is trying to track me down."

We both let out a quick, awkward laugh, each knowing what was coming next.

"So, has anyone called you?" I began.

"Not yet."

"I'm sorry about any inconvenience this will cause."

"Hey, no biggie. I will only give 'em my rank and serial number. Trudy on the other hand . . ."

"Does your lovely wife know yet?"

"She went to work at the flower shop early, so I doubt it."

"But when she finds out, Maria will find out, right?"

"That's the way it goes when you work side by side." Another deadly pause. "What about Linda? How's she taking this?"

"Not well," I sighed. "She's gone. Took everything belonging to her and left me a note." I wanted to tell Wayne about the police visit but couldn't find the strength. There was no use bringing up Linda's apparent disappearance if she was just cooling her heels out of town for a while.

"You haven't talked to her?"

"I didn't have the chance," I offered. "I'm hoping to though."

"I don't know what to say, Steve. I'm kinda in a rough spot— you're my friend but I also like Linda a lot. My kids still talk about her since she left the library."

"I screwed up, Wayne. That's what I do," I admitted. "Regrettably my moral breakdowns end up hurting a pile of innocent people, like Linda and Samantha."

"Who's Samantha?" Wayne asked, before it dawned on him. "You can't blame yourself for what happened," he added quickly. "From what I read, you were doing your job. Who knew that guy was going to go psycho?"

"That's easy for you to say. If I hadn't been fooling around, we would have left the motel as soon as buddy got in the taxi. That's the way it worked in the past and no one got killed. Anyway, what's done is done. I'll have to live with the consequences. As for those reporters, tell them whatever they want to know," I said. "And if they want to contribute to your kids' college fund, go for it. There will be no hard feelings."

"I wouldn't rat you out."

"Not even for fifty thousand big ones?" I kidded him.

"Trudy'd kill me if I turned down that kind of dough," he admitted.

"Make sure you tell the Global Scoop reporter some of my good points, okay?"

"As soon as I think of one, I'll pass it right along."

"That's all I can ask of you. Now . . . the real reason for my call is—"

"Maria."

"Yes, Maria. Do you know anything about a phone call she received? She left a message on our—I mean, my machine."

"You must be talking about the call from the penitentiary," Doogie said.

"What penitentiary? Sandwedge?" I began to fear that somehow the killer from my celebrated missing person case was trying to threaten Maria from the big house.

"Too small. Think B-I-G. Think of sandy beaches and palm trees."

"The Farmington Penitentiary?"

"Boy, you're good," Wayne replied. "You've been watching Jeopardy, haven't you?"

"More like Court TV," I said. "So who does Maria know at The Farm?"

"You mean who do *we* know?"

"Wayne, you're slaying me here."

"Okay, okay. Do you remember Max Feldberg, class of '84?"

"Of course I do. We were like brothers," I said. "The last I heard he was on the run for passing himself off as a shrink and disappearing with his patients' cash. I guess they caught up with him then."

"To the tune of seventy–four years."

"For fraud? Isn't that a bit harsh?" I recalled a conversation with my former Delta lawyer, Francis McKillop, who had updated me on my friends' whereabouts since graduation. "Hold on—aside from being a thief, didn't a disturbed woman jump to her death from his office window or some such thing?"

I heard Wayne laughing. "You're half-right. He did milk his clients for big cash but the woman was pushed—she didn't jump. The stolen money got him six years. The other sixty-eight was for the manslaughter conviction."

"So, getting back to Maria's mystery call, do you know why he contacted her?" I asked, growing more perplexed.

"No. She told Trudy there was a message saying Maxwell Feldberg had requested to speak with her and that she should contact the penitentiary."

"Did they say if it was an emergency or anything?"

"Nope—just that she should call."

"Has she?"

"I don't think so," Wayne said. "She wanted to talk to you first."

"I'll try her at work. The sooner the better. She may not want to speak to me after she hears what I did to Linda."

"Your secret is safe with me but I don't think it'll be a secret for long, once a reporter or two or twenty descend on Delta."

"You'd think they would have uncovered all my dirty secrets from the last go-round."

"Then again," Wayne said in a more serious tone, "you'd think you would have learned a lesson or two from the last go-round."

Touché, I thought. "I wish I could be as good a friend as you, Wayne."

"I call 'em like I see 'em. Anyway, give Maria a shout. I'll get all the gory details during supper tonight."

Before hanging up, Wayne told me not to be a stranger and asked if I was planning to visit Delta in the near future. We'd actually discussed going home for the next long weekend, however under the current circumstances, a trip didn't look practical. I said he'd have a better chance of seeing Linda than me.

"I highly doubt the police would be too pleased if I skipped town, even though I haven't been charged with anything." I let out a laugh. "With my licence suspended and no new work coming in, it would be a great time for a mini-vacation, although there would be no point. Once this new scandal goes public, everyone in town will hate me."

"Actually," Wayne broke in, "don't be so hard on yourself. The fact is most everyone with kids already hates you."

"Why?"

"For making Linda leave her library job."

"I didn't make her leave."

"That's not what I've heard."

"Thanks for that update, pal. I feel so much better now."

"That's what friends are for, right?"

When I got off the phone with Wayne, I felt depressed and pissed off with myself. Once again I had let my old friends down with my self-ishness. Although no one in Delta knew, Linda and I had been having a difficult time adjusting to our life together. After years wrapped in the comfy warmth of a small town where everybody knew your name, Linda wasn't prepared for the coldness of Darrien. She was also ill-prepared for my long days on the road and the ever-changing plans. And let's not get into those overnight marital cases.

In a nutshell: Linda was living in a strange city with no friends and a boyfriend who may or may not be home for dinner.

Even then I think this new lifestyle arrangement was more stressful for me. You see, I loved having someone to come home to, but my job ultimately dictated my arrival time. This concept was foreign to Linda. As a librarian she was used to saying, "The library closes at 6:00, so let's meet for dinner at 6:05, okay?" It's for this very reason many police officers marry fellow cops. Both understand the fluid nature of the job; that the last call you're dispatched to may involve hours of overtime filling out paper work. No huge deal. No guilt trips. (Of course, I had also managed to screw up that arrangement. More on that later.)

I should have stopped Linda from moving, but at the time I too was thinking with my heart instead of my head. Our ill-advised quickie engagement only made matters worse as we were still getting used to each other's habits and personalities. Then came Samantha. When I hired her part-time, I'd actually convinced myself I was on solid ground and nothing would happen between us. She was in a committed relationship and proudly showed off her engagement ring to everyone, including our subjects, who thought nothing of bedding another man's woman. With Linda now living at my place, we were also very serious. Sam and I had no plans of screwing things up—

literally or figuratively.

For the first couple of months, we had a great employer-employee partnership and were a successful team. There was flirting involved; harmless verbal fun in the context of the sleazy work we were doing. Then things began to go sideways for us: Linda and I argued about my insane work hours, while at the same time, Samantha's fiancé accused her of sleeping with me, which she rightfully denied. On a stake-out one day, I told Sam I had often accused my lover of cheating in order to cover up, or later justify, my own extra-curricular activities.

A few days later, Samantha arrived at the office in a very foul mood.

"Her name is Lucy and she lives in the east end on Myers Avenue."

Having no idea what she was talking about, I asked, "Who is this Lucy person and why should I care?"

Samantha stopped in mid-stride and glared daggers in my direction. "You should care because she's the little tramp Richard is doing behind my back!"

"As in, Do you take Samantha to be your lovely bride, Richard?"

"That's the one," she said, as she made her way to her desk, where she let out an angry grunting sound. "To love, honour and cherish— my ass! He's a dead man."

"I agree," I quipped. "Any man who doesn't love, honour or cherish your ass must be dead."

"You got that right."

It was this type of goofy flirtation which passed as typical conversation between the two of us. In the true business world, my comment would have landed me in jail for sexual harassment. My office however, doesn't actually exist or operate in the real world; it's located somewhere on the underbelly of the real world, out of sight and out of mind. When I hired Samantha, I did so for three reasons: she was smart, attractive and engaged to be married. It was only when we became more comfortable working together, her politically incorrect self emerged. To an observer, our constant sexually charged come-ons and put-downs meant only one thing: we desperately wanted to get into each other's pants. I again state categorically that was not the case—at least not until Richard began to see other women and Linda began to hate me. (Note: Unlike Richard, Linda never accused me of shagging my work partner, although I'm certain the idea crossed her mind a time or two.)

"So, did you catch them together?" I asked.

"Not in the physical sense."

"Then how can you be sure Richard is having an affair?"

Samantha opened her purse and pulled out a stack of papers. "You're an investigator—investigate these." She handed me a pile of e-mail messages written between Richard and Lucy.

"Did you find these filed under 'Tramp' in his desk?" I asked as I began to read the forbidden love letters.

"He's smart," Samantha admitted, "just not that smart."

"Then how?"

"Ever hear of an e-tracker?"

"Enlighten me."

"An e-tracker is a program that records every keystroke a person types when using a computer. They could be writing a letter to Grandma, playing a game, or working on a cost datasheet for their business. Regardless, this program stores every hit on the keyboard."

"I'm impressed," I said, looking up into Samantha's now triumphant face. "And what government agency did you go through to get this top-secret software, which essentially bypasses every privacy law ever written? And what was the agent's name? We might need to use him in the future."

"The agency goes by the name of The Computer Emporium on Ouellette Avenue—next to the Burger King. As for the agent, I don't know what his real name is but his little yellow nametag had 'Willy D' typed on it."

"Probably his undercover alias."

"Yeah, probably."

"So let me get this straight," I started, after a humorous beat passed between us. "Richard composes his little letter, not knowing that every key he taps is being secretly recorded?"

"Right."

"You being little Miss Innocent then tell Richard there is a report you need to type up on his laptop."

"Something like that."

"But instead of writing up the Delphi case I've been asking for, you access your covert program and come up with these e-mails." I waved the stack of papers in my hand. "Am I close?"

"Basically," Samantha said with a grin. "I didn't have much time as *loserboy* was having a shower, so I figured out his e-mail password and then shut everything down."

"With his password you then broke into his mailbox later on and read everything, right?" She nodded her head. "Very resourceful."

"If you like that, check out the last e-mail dated yesterday."

I flipped through the pages and began to read the final message when Samantha stopped me. She pointed to the top of the page where the 'To and From' addresses were printed. As a computer novice it took me several seconds to realize what was different from the others I'd read.

"How is it your e-mail address is listed here?"

"You're going to love this," Samantha chirped giddily. "The beauty of free e-mail networks is they understand a person may have two or three different addresses—like a work one or one that came bundled with their internet provider. So, as a courtesy, they offer a forwarding option to send messages to a second address."

"But wouldn't Richard realize he isn't getting his messages?" I inquired.

"No, because unlike a single letter which is forwarded to your cottage during the summer, in this case a second duplicate message is generated and sent out."

"Which means Richard gets one and you get one, right?"

"Exactly."

"I'm still a bit fuzzy on the details here. Again, won't Richard realize or be notified his love notes from Lucy are also being sent to you?"

"Only if he decides to change his personal options—which no one ever does once their address is up and running. Anyway, by the time he figures it out he'll be six feet in the ground."

I looked at Samantha, in awe of her talent and cunning.

"You realize that when you confront Richard he'll think I was behind this, as part of my plan to steal you away from him? Then he'll come after me."

"Not after I tell his Mom on him. She absolutely loves me and couldn't wait until I became her daughter-in-law."

"The news is going to break her heart."

A week after kicking Richard to the curb, Samantha and I had to go out of town for one night on a case. After doing all the wrong things, our guy was busted and soon left, perplexed by the evening's strange ending. After his departure, Samantha and I found ourselves alone in the hotel room. She was still provocatively dressed and lying on the bed, watching me pack up the camera equipment we had installed earlier in the day. Without warning, I realized she had gotten off the bed and was now standing directly behind me. Not knowing exactly what was going through her mind, I didn't immediately turn to face her.

"Remember yesterday when you said now that Richard was out of the picture, all we needed was for Linda to find a new boy toy?"

"I was kidding around," I said, slowly turning to face her. "Unless you know something about Linda's love life I don't."

"All I know is this . . ." Samantha placed her hands on my cheeks and briefly pressed her soft lips against mine.

"I've never been much good as the rebound guy," I offered. "And besides—"

"I know—Linda," Samantha interrupted. "Here's a news flash: she thinks you and I are getting it on already. So what's the difference if we are or we're not, right?"

"After what you've gone through with Richard, that's quite possibly the most hypocritical statement I've ever heard in my life."

"I realize that," she replied, "but I also now know life is too short to be stuck in an unloving relationship. Richard and me. You and Linda. Being unhappy and sexually frustrated is not the kind of life I

WHEN ANGELS FAIL TO FLY

want to be living and neither do you."

I was about to defend my position, when Samantha followed up her first kiss with an even more sensual one. She then took hold of my belt buckle and led me like a lamb to the bed.

There is no good reason for infidelity. Either you're committed or you should be committed. It's that simple. Like the yearnings for drugs and booze in a former existence, the fire that began to burn inside me was simply one of overwhelming desire for something that was forbidden for good reason. Sexy and single Samantha was only part of my downfall. Another female in another city would have caused the same reaction. As much as I cared for Linda, I wasn't strong enough to say no.

There were a million reasons this arrangement wouldn't work, yet somehow my brain was convinced there were a million and one reasons it could.

Fifty percent plus one wins every time.

Once an addict, always an addict.

Once a loser, always a loser.

Once corrupted, always corruptible.

What we could not know, or even comprehend on that fine spring evening, was the start of this misguided fling would in due course destroy our lives.

It would be Richard who would attend Samantha's funeral and not the other way around.

As for Linda and me, it was now going on two days since she'd left our house and I still hadn't heard a word from her.

Then again, neither had anyone else.

FOUR

After speaking with Wayne, I decided to wait a little longer before reaching out to Maria. If I called acting like my life was peachy and she then learned about Linda, I'd look like the dolt I was. I figured it was better to talk after the news hit Delta. That way it would be her decision to discuss the "Max Feldberg" situation with me or not.

Instead of staying cooped up, I took a tour to the lake where I found myself alone in the parking lot off our small beach. Although it was a bit cooler than the previous week, I was surprised there were no rollerbladers, bicyclists or moms with strollers on the boardwalk. Even the waves couldn't muster much energy, with the water lazily lapping the edge of the shoreline instead of cresting, then crashing, as was the case most days.

Relocating my body and thoughts here turned out to be another bonehead idea. When Linda was debating if she should move to the big bad city, I'd brought her to this very beach, built a fire, poured some wine and tried to convince her evenings like this could be repeated nightly—if only she'd move in with me. "It is nice at night," she'd said, "but what about during the day?" I remember looking her straight in the eye and saying, "Like paradise," and then kissing her, as the fire softly popped and crackled nearby. For the remainder of her three–day visit we practically lived at this beach—swimming, sun tanning and participating in impromptu volleyball games with the local teenagers and college kids. At dusk, I would build another fire and we'd talk, snuggle and make out when the coast was clear.

As I vacantly watched the calm water stretched out in front of me, an attractive couple in their early 20's walked past my van. The girl casually glanced in my direction and for a millisecond I saw that *new-in-love* sparkle in her eye. I prayed it would never diminish for her but knew it would eventually. It always does. Being *new-in-love* meant you felt giddy all the time. When you've decided you're actually *in love* however, giddy is replaced by a higher level of comfort and trust with your partner. In time though, even these feelings change.

I know now Linda and I never truly crossed the threshold between *new-in-love* to being *in love*. Maybe that's why I hooked up with Samantha; she was my *new-in-love* conquest (or was I hers)? Not that it matters anymore. Both are gone because of my involvement with them.

It dawned on me what a shame it was that self-pity was so useless, as it is one of the few things at which I excel in this life.

As I started the van's engine, I noticed the two cute lovebirds searching the beach for dry pieces of wood to build a fire.

Enjoy it while you can, kids, I thought wistfully.

I returned to my house pleasantly surprised to find it quiet. No SWAT teams. No TV trucks. The answering machine had a few new messages from persistent reporters and there were a couple of hangups. Maria hadn't called or if she had, she hadn't left a message. I punched the erase button at the same time the phone rang, which gave me a bit of a start.

"Hello," I said.

"Go outside and check your garbage can."

CLICK.

I stared at the phone for a second. I couldn't determine if the caller had been a man or a woman, as the voice sounded like it had been electronically altered. Seven words isn't a lot to go on in the first place. Figuring I wasn't in any physical danger— believing someone could have easily offed me at the beach—I went into my backyard and retrieved a sealed manila envelope. Inside I could feel the unmistakable outline of a VHS tape.

"What's this?" I wondered aloud.

I went back to the living room ripping the package open, finding a video and nothing else. Maybe my mysterious courier would show himself or herself on the tape. I popped it into my VCR, sat in my recliner and pushed PLAY on the remote.

"On with the show," I commanded.

I honestly didn't know what to expect but the sight of Samantha and I checking into The Loser's Love Den on that fateful afternoon, sent a blistering shiver down my spine. There was Samantha, full of life and vitality and myself getting out of the van and walking to the office. Then we were both laughing and smiling like honeymooners, as we made our way to our room without a care in the world. Next were the kisses—I had forgotten about them: one as we strolled across the lot hand in hand and a second longer sweeter one as we crossed the threshold of Room 215.

This wonderful scene however, was just a mirage.

The TV screen's image switched to a night shot, with the camera operator zooming out from our room's door to a close-up of Linda's stoic face. I didn't recognize the dark-coloured sedan in which she was seated. It was then I realized the footage had been shot from yet another vehicle, far away from Linda's car in the Tecumseh Motel parking lot.

Did she know about this other vehicle?

Were they working together?

And if not, how did the camera operator know Linda?

As I continued to watch that evening's events play out like some dramatic film flashback, I felt ill. Moments later, I was again brutally slammed back to reality as I watched Linda's tears cascade down her cheeks. Her facial expression was a combination of grief, anger and resignation.

What had I done?

I sat transfixed as I saw the bewildered Plymouth plumber exit the room and give Samantha a kiss on the cheek. There were shots of me following the taxi off the lot, only to return a short time later to enter the second level room. Next was a shot of me looking out toward the parking lot, as I placed a Do Not Disturb sign on the outside door handle. Again, Linda's sobbing face was full frame. I felt as if someone had punched me in the stomach.

"Please stop," I yelled at the television.

But it wouldn't.

Soon came footage of me exiting the room, freshly showered, with a huge smile plastered on my face, departing the area on a banana split run.

Aside from Linda's attendance, to this point the video had documented the inauspicious events in a faithful manner. I vividly remembered everything. Yet, as any good filmmaker will attest, the best part of shooting real people in real situations is that something happens—a plot twist—that changes the viewer's perception. In this case, I assumed the next footage would be of plumber-boy returning to Samantha's room, then the arrival of the police and finally the shoot-out. This would be followed by my return from the ice cream stand.

Instead, I watched Linda make her way to the second floor of the motel and head to Room 215. My heart was now pounding wildly. *She was coming to confront us. Catch us in the act.*

Linda was three doors away from The Loser's Love Den when she was startled and abruptly stopped in her tracks. An expression of terror could be seen clearly on her face as she jerked her head to the left to look over the balcony railing. It was then the video operator zoomed out and panned the camera to catch the arrival of a dark green Saturn in the parking lot.

The plumber had returned to exact his revenge.

Without warning, the screen went black and I was left stupefied, unsure of what I had viewed. I felt as though I had watched a snuff film, knowing what took place following the plumber's arrival. Yet I really knew nothing of what happened next; all of my information had come from the police. Watching the tape, however, I now knew the cops' facts were not only inaccurate—they were possibly completely wrong. There were no reports of a woman near the victim's door prior to the alleged argument, yet Linda had been there. Had she called 911 about the argument in Room 215 after I left? Had the person in the surveillance vehicle called? Had they been in on it together?

My mind whirled relentlessly. The tape had produced more questions than answers, which I presumed was the sender's intention.

The ringing of my telephone temporarily put a stop to my confusion.

"Hello!" I snapped, believing my Secret Santa was making a follow-up call.

"Steven? Is that you? Are you all right?"

The genuine concern in Maria's voice instantly melted away my fear, anguish and anger. She was the one person I'd tried to avoid thinking about today and the only one I wanted—or needed—to talk to now.

"Yes, Maria, it's me," I replied apologetically. "Sorry about that, I was expecting another call." A long pause followed.

"I can call later," Maria offered hesitantly.

"You don't have to do that. I've been thinking of calling you about the message you got from Max."

Another long agonizing pause, during which I wondered if Maria had picked up on my little white lie.

"I heard about what happened."

Silence.

"I'm sorry to hear that," I finally said.

"Not as much as I was."

"What can I say? As I told Wayne, I screwed up. There is nothing more I can offer. I can't find Linda to apologize and Samantha . . . well . . ."

"I don't remember asking for an apology," Maria said, cutting me off.

"Not yet, but in time you would have. Linda was your friend and I broke her heart because I'm a self absorbed a-hole."

"Even though I wholeheartedly agree with your self-diagnoses, you should know by now I'm not the 'I-told-you-so' type." She paused, then added, "For which you should be eternally grateful. As for you and Linda, I'm probably one of the few people who knew things weren't working out the way you hoped it would."

"Did she tell you or was that just your womanly intuition?"

"We had a few telephone conversations over the past several weeks."

"I didn't know you two had become so close—especially with *our* past."

"You mean that little high school, puppy-love, crush thingy we shared fourteen long years ago?"

I could picture the wide smirk on Maria's face and laughed. "Yes, that's exactly what I meant."

"In all honesty, I think aside from books, you were the common denominator between us. I loved you then, she loved you now and thankfully she didn't feel threatened talking to me about you."

"I'm sure you had a lot of nice things to say about me, didn't you?" She didn't reply to my sarcasm. "I guess I'm fortunate she didn't bond with Trudy."

"You'd be in real trouble there," Maria chuckled.

"But seriously, Maria, did Linda suspect I was fooling around? If you don't want to tell me I'll understand."

Without hesitation she replied, "She never came right out and said so but I think phrases like, 'He works long hours' and 'He's often out of town,' were her code words for 'That rat bastard is cheating on me with his slutty assistant.'"

Before I could stop myself, I blurted angrily, "Samantha wasn't a slut. Not that anyone cares, now that she's dead and all."

"Steven, I didn't mean to . . . I never met her . . ." Maria started.

"Stop, Maria. I know you didn't mean anything by that." I glanced over at the blank TV screen. "I've got a lot going on right now. A set of new problems I'm trying to figure out. I didn't mean to shout like that." I took a deep breath. "I'm pretty sure you didn't call to get yelled at by a low-life like me."

"I called to see how you were doing," Maria replied. "That's all. No hidden agenda. When I heard about what happened, I didn't know if I should be furious with you or sad for you."

"So you took the pity route over the pissed off route?"

"Neither," she said defiantly. "I went the concerned route! I was worried about you and thought you might need someone to talk to— besides news reporters and homicide investigators. And even though Linda is a friend and didn't deserve any of this stupidity, I don't have a history with her like I do with you." She stopped, maybe waiting for me to say something. Getting no response, she added, "And if you don't think I'm emotionally conflicted, you're wrong."

"Maria—"

"Maybe calling you was a mistake."

"It wasn't a—"

"Right now it feels like it is, so I'm going to hang up and get some dinner."

"What about Max's phone call?" I asked, trying desperately to keep her on the line.

"I'll call him tomorrow. Good night, Steve."

The line went dead.

In my notorious past, I might have ripped the phone out of the wall and smashed it into a hundred pieces on the floor. Not today. As I unclenched the receiver and placed it in its cradle, I asked myself the question that had been echoing through my brain for the past two days: *Why bother?*

I grabbed my coat and walked out the front door, leaving the TV on and my frozen dinner in the microwave. As I proceeded to the nearby Sunsetter Pub & Eatery (a little watering hole I hadn't frequented in months), I was hoping an alien life form would notice me, decide I was the best human specimen on Earth and beam me up—never to be seen again by friend or foe. Without a doubt, the news stories of my disappearance would focus on the TV and my uneaten meal. *What a story they all would tell.* I imagined columnist Jeremy Atkins writing that after destroying so many lives, I had ended my own in order to stop the madness once and for all.

On the other hand, like me, Mr. Atkins and his ilk might discuss my plight at the morning pitch meeting and collectively say, "Why bother?"

Unable to interest any extraterrestrials in my intergalactic kidnapping scheme, I entered the nearly empty pub and barricaded myself in a corner booth. An attractive new waitress was soon standing before me asking if I'd like a drink. When I looked up I saw she was staring at me. *This can't be good*, I worried.

"I know you from somewhere," she said, tilting her head a bit to the side.

I met her quizzical gaze and also felt a sense of familiarity. She was in her early 20's, with a petite curvy frame and dark curly brown hair, which bounced on her shoulders as she walked. "I live in the neighbourhood," I answered, hoping she wasn't a news junkie.

Her face quickly lit up. "I know—you were sitting in a van down at the lake today, right?"

Her joyful smile and little laugh transported me back to the beach. "That's right. I was down there."

"We didn't talk or anything. I'm just good with faces."

"I'm sure that comes in handy working here," I said. "You don't want to give the wrong order to the wrong customer."

"I never thought about it that way but it makes sense, I guess." She pondered this revelation as she took her order pad out of her pocket. "So, do you go to the beach often?" she asked in a tone that was slower and softer than before.

At this moment I didn't know if I should be surprised, confused, or flattered that my "new-in-love-sparkle" girl was flirting with me, right here, right now.

"Every once in awhile," I offered. "What about you? Do you and your boyfriend hang out there much?"

"No, he hates the beach."

"What about this afternoon? What made him change his mind?"

The sunny expression on my waitresses' face dimmed a couple of watts and was slyly replaced by a devilish expression.

"Like I said, my *boyfriend* hates the beach."

Our eyes met again in an *I won't tell if you won't tell* conspiratorial way.

"Your secret is safe with me," I said.

This time when she smiled, I realized she still possessed that elusive sparkle which I had so envied earlier in the day. *We have more in common than you would ever know,* I mused to myself. Her walk on the beach with her boy-toy was a mirror image of Samantha and I walking across the parking lot at the Tecumseh Motel. We were both just selfish horndogs, with no sense of decency or respect for others.

"By the way, my name is Dawn."

"I'm Steve."

"Well, Steve, would you like a drink tonight?"

In my fragile state, I knew if I started to drink I wouldn't be able to stop. That scared me. Alcohol is a depressant and I didn't think I needed to be more depressed right now.

Why bother? the rational side of my brain asked.

"Why not?" I said to Dawn the waitress. "What do I have to lose?"

After taking my order, I watched Dawn saunter toward the bar. I knew I was in the midst of making a huge mistake but was unable to stop myself. I had long ago lost the phone number of my AA sponsor and didn't think Wayne or Maria would want to hear from me again today.

When Dawn returned, she placed two cardboard drink coasters on the table and put my beer on one of them. I looked at the second coaster. "Is someone going to join me for a drink?"

"Maybe," she laughed as she turned away. "That's a commemorative coaster. Make sure you don't lose it."

I picked the coaster up and noted Dawn had graciously written her cell number on it. I watched her take an order at another table and wondered how many *souvenirs* she handed out each night; how many different collectors had taken a moonlit walk on the beach with her. Probably more than her boyfriend at home would care to know about.

I took a large swig of beer and placed the personalized coaster in my jacket pocket.

This is going to be a long night, I thought.

"Steven, he wants to talk to you."

It was almost noon the next morning and my brain—now embalmed with beer and tequila shots—understandably took several seconds to kick into gear. When it did however, panic soon followed.

The voice coming from the next room was definitely female but what did she mean by *he wants to talk to you*? Dawn's boyfriend? Her father? A Sex Crimes Investigator? I forced myself upright and took in my surroundings. I was fully clothed on my own bed and there were no signs I'd had any company the previous evening.

Then who was in the living room?

"Steven, pick up. This is important."

Realizing the voice was coming from the answering machine, I sprawled across the duvet and grabbed the phone.

"Hello? Who is this?" I asked.

"Thank goodness you're home," the woman's voice replied. "I already left you two messages and was getting worried."

"Maria?"

"Of course it's me. Who did you think it was?"

"I'm not exactly in the thinking mood yet."

I knew her brief silence was an indictment of sorts; she was too classy to pursue the issue.

"I'm sure I don't want to know, right?" she finally asked.

"Right."

"Anyway," she started with a disapproving sigh, "I called the penitentiary and spoke with Max."

"And how did that go?"

"Okay, I guess."

"Meaning what exactly?"

"Meaning the person he really wanted to speak to was you."

I adjusted the pillow under my now throbbing head. "Then why call you?"

"Because he figured I was the one person from high school who might know your current whereabouts."

"They don't get newspapers or cable in the big house?"

"Apparently not."

"Did he say why he was looking for me, because when felons want to get together it's not usually for a surprise party."

"He said he needed your help but couldn't go into detail over the phone."

"Did you get the impression this was a personal matter or a professional one?"

"All he said was it had to do with his case."

"Did you tell him I was a P.I.—or at least used to be?"

"I was going to, when the operator came on. She said we only had sixty seconds left before the phone would automatically cut us off. Max then asked if I could get hold of you and have you call him."

I mulled this over a moment. "Don't you find it odd that after all this time he wouldn't try to contact me directly? What if you had married and changed your surname? Then what? Even getting hold of Doogie would be easier—he's at least listed in the Delta phone book."

"That is strange," Maria said slowly. "I wonder how he got my number? It's been unlisted for years."

It was my turn to reassure Maria. "There are plenty of ways you can get an unlisted phone number—most of them legally. Companies sell customer lists to one another all the time. A magazine subscription or charity you've donated to in the past might have your home number on file."

"Still . . . like you said, tracking down Wayne would have been simpler, don't you think?"

"For all we know Max gave his lawyer a list of names from the old days and yours was the first and only one he checked."

"I guess you're right."

"If it makes you feel better, I'll ask him when we talk, okay?"

"If you don't mind."

"Anything for you, Maria. You know that," I said.

I hoped she knew I was being sincere but I'd understand if her trust level was not very high. She gave me the phone number and explained the procedures she'd had to go through to talk with Max.

"Did Max ask you about anyone else from our class?"

"Not really. He wondered what I was doing and if I was happy still living in Delta," Maria replied. "We didn't really get into why he was calling from a federal penitentiary. All he said was he hadn't made the best post-secondary choices and I didn't ask."

Classy, classy, classy, I thought.

"Have you heard from Linda?" Maria inquired, changing the subject.

"Not yet. Truth be told, I don't think I'd be on her people to call list," I said. "I take it she hasn't contacted you either?"

"No and that's got me worried."

The silence that passed through the line was accompanied by a dose of bitterness. Although I wanted Maria to yell, 'Why did you do this?' I knew she wouldn't—it wasn't her style. Still, I wished she would, just this once. I needed someone to put me in my place.

"I have to go," Maria said. "If you hear from Linda, please tell her to call me."

"I'll do that." I wanted to add some sort of apology for the hurt I'd caused, only she hung up before I had the chance.

I staggered out of bed and checked the answering machine, which had Maria's two previous messages on it. I was about to erase them but stopped myself. It might have been the alcohol still flowing through my brain, but all I could think was, *That might have been the last conversation you'll ever have with her. The last time you'll hear her voice. You don't want to erase her voice, do you?* An optimist would have quickly deleted the messages. Being a seasoned pessimist, I saved both calls.

By mid-afternoon I started to feel better—the coffee, sandwich and a refreshing shower had helped immensely. Figuring there was no time like the present, I dialed the penitentiary's number and waded through the many automated options, until the operator came on the line.

"Which inmate are you calling?" the woman asked curtly.

"His name is Max Feldberg. I don't know where—"

"And your name is?"

"Steven. Steven Cassidy. I used to go to high school—"

"Can you be reached at this number?" She then rattled off my phone number.

"Yes."

"Is this number registered in your name?"

"Yes, it is."

"Will you be at this number between 3:00 p.m. and 3:15 p.m. today?"

"I can, I guess."

"Very well. An attempt to contact you will be made later today between 3:00 p.m. and 3:15 p.m. If there is no response, a second attempt will be made tomorrow and if necessary, the following day, during the same time period. If we are unable to contact you on the third attempt, you will be deemed unresponsive and your name will be permanently removed from Mr. Feldberg's call list. Is that clear, Mr. Cassidy?"

"Yes," I stammered, trying to digest everything she'd said.

"Thank you for calling The Farmington Penitentiary."

Like my previous day's mystery caller, I was so emotionally unbalanced upon hanging up, I had doubts I'd just spoken to a living, breathing human being.

With nothing but time on my hands, I plopped down on my well-worn couch and looked around for the TV remote. It was then I remembered how I had left for the pub with the television and lights still on. Now however, I realized both were off. I turned on the TV and VCR expecting to see images of the Tecumseh Motel massacre but the screen remained blank. I crawled across the floor to the entertainment unit, where I pressed the Eject button on the VCR. Again, nothing happened.

Where was the tape? I was sure I hadn't taken it out of the machine. *Then who had?* I wondered.

I went to the phone and called the pub.

"Hello."

"Dawn, it's me—Steve, from the bar last night."

"So you survived to see another day?" she asked playfully. "I was worried you might pull a Keith Moon or a Bon Scott—you know—the rock stars who choked on their vomit and died in the '70's."

"Yes, I got the reference," I admitted, somewhat baffled how a girl so young would know such classic rock folklore. Before I could ask, she was telling me.

"I figured an old guy like you would remember them. A friend of mine is this huge music fan and he's always telling me these morbid tales about bands my parents used to listen to."

"Is this your boyfriend?"

"No, he hates music," came the reply.

"So, this is the guy from the beach?" I ventured.

"Are you kidding?" she laughed. "He only likes techno music.

45

No, this friend is much older."

"How old?"

"I don't know—thirty–five, thirty–six. You know—your age."

"Ouch."

"I didn't mean that in a bad way," she offered softly.

"I'm glad to hear that. Anyway, the reason I'm calling is to find out if you knew how I got home last night. Did someone call me a cab?"

There was a brief silence.

"You really don't remember?"

"Wisdom usually comes with age, but from time to time alcohol kind of wrecks that notion."

"I hope that's the case because usually when I go home with a guy he remembers me in the morning."

"You brought me home?"

"I didn't trust the cabbie who showed up and didn't think he would tuck you into bed like I could."

It was my turn to pause.

"I'm pretty sure we didn't," I finally said, "but we didn't . . ."

"What—get it on?" Dawn laughed. "I was lucky to get you through the front door and onto your bed. I'm not sure if you noticed or not but all your clothes were on when I left this morning."

I was understandably confused. "Don't you mean last night?"

"No, this morning. I had to work the day shift and figured I might as well crash at your place. I would have asked if it was okay but you were . . . well, not in a talkative mood, if you know what I mean."

"I regret being such lousy company," I said.

"That's all right," Dawn replied casually. "It was sort of fun playing mother hen for one night. Usually I'm the one passing out and being carried to bed. Unfortunately, I usually wake up naked."

"Well, I also apologize for all the creeps who have taken advantage of you in the past."

"You're not mad that I *didn't* take advantage of you, are you?"

"I'm furious," I said sarcastically.

"Because that was a one-time thing. Next time, I'll show you no mercy."

"I don't think there'll be a next time."

"Oh."

I believed I heard dejection in Dawn's voice. "What I meant was I don't plan on drinking so much in the future."

"Oh," she said more enthusiastically. "So were you calling to ask me out or to see if I still respected you?"

"Neither, actually," I said. "I'm trying to fill in a few blanks and apparently you're the one person who can help me out."

"You have to be quick. A bunch of businessmen are walking in for a late lunch."

"Okay, here goes. How did you get into my house last night?"

"The front door."

"Was it open?"

"No, it was locked. It took me five minutes to get the keys out of your pocket, because every time I tried you'd turn and say something funny like, 'Hey, I'm not that kind of guy,' or 'You better stop before my neighbours call the police.'"

"Sounds like something I might say while inebriated," I laughed. "So, when we stumbled into the house, do you remember if the lights were on or the TV was going?"

"No, everything was dark," Dawn said immediately. "I fumbled for the switch inside the door and went from there."

"But you're sure the TV wasn't on?"

"Positive. Now I've really got to go, Steve."

"One last thing. After you put me to bed, did you watch any TV or put on a video?"

"You're not asking me all these questions because you woke up and your TV was gone, are you? I didn't steal it—I left everything just the way I found it."

"The television is still here and I'm not accusing you of anything, I swear."

"Good, because after you passed out, I was so tired I crashed in the spare room. I left for work this morning at seven," she protested. "I even locked the front door when I left."

There was nothing in her voice that made me think she was lying. I looked into the guest room and saw the outline of a petite body on the comforter. On the nightstand, I saw a gold watch.

"Do you want me to drop your watch off at the pub or would you rather pick it up here?" I asked.

"I knew I left it there. I feel lost without it," Dawn admitted. "I get off at 3:30. Will you still be there?"

"I'm waiting for a long distance call from a high school friend I haven't talked to since graduation. He's supposed to call between 3:00 and 3:15, so drop by when you're finished."

"Are you sure? What if they call later and you start talking about your pimply-faced glory days? I wouldn't want to interrupt you or anything."

"This guy is very punctual and his present landlord is very strict about his phone privileges."

"Then I'll see you in a few hours."

"Great," I replied. "Before you go, Dawn, I'm sure you hear this all the time from your *boyfriends . . .* but thanks for last night. You were wonderful."

There was a brief moment of dead air before Dawn said, "To be truthful, Steve, you're the first one who actually sounded like he meant it. Thanks."

"You're welcome. Now get to table six and see what those loser businessmen want, but no souvenir coasters, okay?"

"Okay."

I put down the phone and stood in the middle of my living room, taking in my surroundings as if for the first time. My eyes took in the furniture, the entertainment unit, the prints on the wall, the lights on the end tables, the track lighting, the light switches, the smoke alarm—anything that could give me some clue as to what had taken place the previous evening. Someone had entered this space, taken the mysterious video, then shut off the lights and locked the front door behind them.

Who would do such a thing and why? Even more perplexing was how did they get in?

The video's contents were also very disturbing, as it proved Linda had been at the motel on that terrible night. I just couldn't quite figure out how this tantalizing fact could be used against me. The police and I both concluded Linda found out about the affair, had decided enough was enough, packed her things and left the house that evening. The end.

For me, the most troubling thing was the third party involved here—the guy with the camera. He had obviously been following us and passed the information on to Linda. I remembered how her head snapped around as she approached The Loser's Love Den. It was apparent the accomplice had honked his horn to alert her of the plumber's return.

My mind was slowly coming to terms with the fact that Linda and this other individual had been working together, when a more disturbing notion popped up: what if they knew the plumber and the three of them had plotted against Samantha and me? Was that possible?

I frantically tried to erase the idea from my head. There was no way Linda would knowingly be part of some twisted murder-for-hire plot. I've known several women in my disastrous romantic past who had possessed all of the traits needed for such a plan, yet I was certain Linda was not one of them.

"No way," I shouted at the empty room. She had been set up. There were no two ways about it.

That she hadn't returned my call was no surprise, but the fact Maria hadn't heard from her either was worrisome. Linda had confided in her about our problems in the past, so why not now? To be perfectly honest, during the past few weeks we'd had some nasty, dirty fights that were the beginning of the end of our engagement. We both knew it, yet couldn't bring ourselves to actually do anything about it.

I was now ambivalent about her so-called disappearance. On one hand, it was a fitting conclusion to our turbulent relationship; a dramatic statement, if she'd left voluntarily, as I believed she had. On the other hand, I began to feel queasy when I envisioned the person who'd shot the video taking her against her will for some unknown reason.

My mind tried to close down this avenue of thinking. *She'll call*, I kept telling myself. *Sooner or later, she'll have to return to work*, I tried to convince myself. *She is angry with life, with me and this city.*

She's fine. She has to be.

FIVE

At 3:01 p.m. my phone rang.

"Hello."

"Steven Cassidy?" a stern male voice asked.

"Yes, this is Steven Cassidy."

"Please hold."

After a couple of clicks, an automated female voice came on.

"Attention. This call is being recorded to ensure no criminal laws are broken."

There was another short pause followed by:

"This is the Farmington Penitentiary in San Dieppe. A request has been made by inmate Maxwell Feldberg to speak with you. At this time, you have two options: using your touch-tone telephone keypad, to accept this call press 1-1. To decline this call, press 2-2. Please be aware that by declining this call, your name and phone number will be permanently removed from this caller's contact list. If no response is registered, this call will be classified as declined. You have ten seconds to make your selection."

Maria hadn't told me of these options. I guess she assumed I would automatically press 1-1 to speak with Max but during my first few allotted seconds, my initial inclination was to decline the call. My life was screwed up enough and being tracked down by a convict didn't sound like a party I would want to attend. I was also briefly fascinated that by simply hitting the number "2" twice, Max would never be allowed to contact me again. How I wished this was a regular phone feature I could use for bill collectors or needy ex-girlfriends—Maria and Linda excluded, of course. Nevertheless, maybe Max was calling to tell me where he had stashed all the cash he'd presumably swindled from gullible patients.

As the seconds continued to tick away, from deep within my cranium my two favourite questions tormented me: *Why bother? Why not? Why bother? Why not?*

I pressed 1-1. *What the hell? It's always good to talk to old friends,* I thought.

The automated voice returned.

"You will now be connected to your party."

I smiled at the word *party.* Five seconds later, there was another click on the line.

"Hey, Steve—are you there?"

"I'm here, Max," I replied. "How's that golf swing of yours coming? Still a 12 handicap?"

"Are you kidding? I've got that sucker down to a 5 and was named Golfer of the Year by my peers in Cell Block D a few weeks ago."

"Well, I guess congratulations are in store. What do you guys play—Sega Genesis or Playstation?"

"Playstation all the way," Max laughed. "Their Pebble Beach game is so realistic you can almost smell the coconut sunscreen of the virtual babes in the spectator gallery."

"It's nice to hear they let you out every once in awhile," I quipped. "Aside from being the resident golf pro, are you still playing shrink? I'm sure there are a couple of people in there who could use a good doctor."

"You heard about that, huh?"

"Yeah, a few months ago that prick Francis McKillop gleefully updated me on the old gang's whereabouts."

"What's he doing now?"

"He's a lawyer."

"Get out!"

"For a day or so he was actually my lawyer, until I brought up Elaine Wakelin."

"Was she the girl in Grade 10 who thought she was pregnant?"

"The very one."

"What about Wayne Dugan? What's he up to?"

"Same old, same old. He raises livestock on his dad's farm and is married with three or four kids."

"Who did he marry?"

"Trudy Babich."

"Fruity Trudy—that mean old dog? She made homely girls look like Playmate Pets. What was he thinking?"

"Apparently alcohol and a shotgun heavily influenced his decision to get hitched."

Max began to laugh hard, to the point where he started to snort. Those sounds triggered long-suppressed memories from my youth. Prior to making this call, I wondered how Max might have changed over the years. One feature I knew would be the same—and could picture in my mind's eye now—was his dopey smile and the way he'd tilt his head to the left as he laughed and snorted. I had witnessed this particular mannerism hundreds of times at school, the arena, the ballpark, the beach—just about anywhere we'd ever gone together during our formative years.

"Max, I'm sure we could play catch-up for hours but I got the impression your handlers keep a pretty stringent schedule when it comes to outside calls."

Max's laughter slowly died down. "You're right, Steve, as usual."

"What's so important you tracked both Maria and me down?" I asked. "And by the way, how did you get her unlisted number?"

"I don't think you want to know," Max replied hesitantly.

"I understand. I know these calls are recorded."

"No, it's not that. I did nothing illegal."

"Then what? She asked me to ask you."

"It isn't something I'm really proud of but—"

"But what?"

"The simple answer is Maria gave me the number years ago and I never forgot it."

"Okay," I said. "Where does your pride come into play?"

"Well . . . she gave it to me after we went out on a date," Max said. "This was like a couple of years after high school. I briefly returned to Delta one summer before heading off to become rich and famous. Or should I say infamous?"

"So? What's the big deal?" I asked.

"You're not mad we went out?"

"Why would I be mad?"

"Because she was your girl and you were my best friend."

I reflected on this for a moment. "You said this was after high school? After I left town?"

"Yeah."

"Then why would I be mad at you?" I asked.

"I want you to know I didn't try anything with her," Max continued to stammer. "The whole time I felt guilty. It was almost like I was cheating on you—you know what I mean. Every time I looked into her face all I could think was, *Stevie Boy should be here, not me.* And at the end of the date, I didn't even try to kiss her good night."

"I'm sure that really boosted her confidence," I chided him.

"I felt so bad, I never called her again."

"You really had a way with women," I laughed. "And look where it got you—a place where you're surrounded by a group of guys for as far as the eye can see. That'll teach ya."

Our conversation was interrupted by an announcement:

"This call will be terminated in one minute."

"Time is of the essence. I'll stop talking, Max," I said. "Why did you call?"

"Because I need someone to look into my case."

"Don't you have a lawyer?"

"I fired him," came the startling response.

"Why?"

"Because he doesn't believe I was framed for manslaughter. I had nothing to do with that woman being killed. I swear."

"Look, Max, I know very little about your case," I said, getting a bit annoyed. "All I heard was you were playing a head doctor without a licence and conned some hard cash from your patients. Is that correct?"

"That's all true, but I was helping them figure out their problems. I'm not lying."

"Hey, trust me when I say I don't care," I stated. "The other part of your sorry tale was that a patient died and you were convicted of her death."

"I didn't kill her."

"Keep going—time's running out," I instructed. "Why should I believe you and not your jury? Are you saying she jumped to her death and that you weren't in your office when it happened? Did she slip on a banana peel or something? Tick, tick, tick, Max."

"I . . . ah . . . I . . ."

"Spit it out before it's too late, Max," I demanded.

"I was there."

"And?"

"I can't say any more over the phone."

"The word *can't* isn't in my vocabulary."

"This call will terminate in 30 seconds."

"You've got to help, Steve."

"Help you what?"

"Find him."

"Find who?"

"The man who killed her."

"Now you're saying this woman was murdered but not by you? Is that what I'm to understand?"

"Yes. You've got to find him before he kills again."

"This guy didn't have a scraggly beard and one arm, did he? Because Harrison Ford and David Janssen both had a heck of a time tracking him down in *The Fugitive*."

"I know it sounds nuts, I do."

"I guess you'd be qualified to make that judgment, right? What's that saying—Doctor, heal thyself?"

"Please take a look at my court file. Treat this like a cold case investigation. I swear this guy has got to be stopped."

At this stage in our conversation, I wished I had pressed 2-2, but I figured in less than a minute my dealings with Max would come to an end.

"Cold case files are for retired coppers or wet-behind-the-ears rookie detectives who've played too many games of Clue. That's not me," I said, as I followed the second hand on my watch continue to count down the final minute. "Just because you have twenty–four hours a day to go over your trial and conviction doesn't mean I do."

"This call will terminate in 15 seconds."

"Sure you do, Stevie," Max replied, his voice unexpectedly cold, almost menacing in tone. "With your licence suspended, it's not like your P.I. business is going anywhere these days."

"So I have the time, big deal," I countered. "Give me one good reason I should help, besides for old time's sake?"

Ten seconds to go, I thought.

10-9-8-7-

His delivery was slow and deliberate. "I'll give you two: Maria and Linda."

The line then went dead.

"This call has been terminated."

I had barely taken a breath when there was a rap at the front door. I slammed down the phone and made a beeline to the foyer, screaming at the top of my lungs, "You better start running, you sick bastard. I've had enough of this sh—"

I grabbed hold of the handle and almost ripped the door from its hinges. Instead of encountering one of Max's henchmen on the porch,

I was confronted by a terror-stricken Dawn. We stared at each other in stunned disbelief for several moments, before she broke eye contact to glance down at my hands.

"I was going to make a run for it," she said slowly, "but feared you might be armed with a kitchen knife or something." She paused, then continued, "And the last image I want my mom to have of me is of being attacked by a madman wielding a meat cleaver."

"You're a good daughter," I replied, trying to ease the tension. "I wasn't yelling at you, I swear."

"In the back of my mind I knew that," she said. "I've never been called a sick bastard before but there's a first for everything, right? I wondered if you had started drinking again and the alcohol mixed with your medication had an adverse effect on your mental state."

"I'm not on any medication."

"That could be your problem," she deadpanned. "Maybe you should be." Her facial muscles relaxed and a smile formed on her lips. "An anger management class or two wouldn't hurt either."

"I am so sorry, Dawn," I apologized again. "I received some disturbing news on the phone and believed the caller had sent someone over to further illustrate their point."

"You need some new friends," Dawn advised. "Forget about those high school losers you used to hang out with. Was the guy on the phone—Mr. Sick Bastard—looking for money?"

"How much does a pound of flesh cost these days?" A quizzical look came over Dawn's face. I couldn't tell if she was repulsed or confused. "Forget I said that. It's not about money—at least not yet."

With both our blood pressure rates restabilized, I asked Dawn inside.

"You're sure it's safe?"

"I promise nothing will happen that will give your mother nightmares."

I scanned the street before closing the door, expecting to see someone or something out of place, but found nothing amiss.

Too bad, I thought, internally still wanting to cause great physical pain to my unseen tormentor.

"Your watch is on the coffee table," I told Dawn.

"This place looks bigger in the daylight," she said as she walked into the living room. "And there's your precious TV, right where I left it. Safe and sound," she added as she put on her watch. "Without this, my shift seemed to go on and on and on."

"I know what you mean," I agreed, trying to keep the conversation casual. "I'm sorry about all the questions earlier. It's just that—"

"You don't have to explain," Dawn stopped me. "I once dated a guy who went ballistic when one of his prized hockey cards went missing. It turned out he had forgotten he'd lent it to his little brother for Show and Tell." She turned to face me. "I don't know why guys get so attached to inanimate objects. I've never been a big collector of anything."

"Except boyfriends," I interjected, which made Dawn laugh.

"The difference is they aren't inanimate—at least not in my presence."

"No doubt."

"Do you have anything to drink?"

"That depends," I said. "If you're looking for an alcoholic drink, the answer is no. If however, you'd like juice or bottled water, then yes."

"Juice sounds good."

As I poured her a glass of fruit punch, Dawn took a seat at the kitchen table. I grabbed a bottle of water and sat down across from her.

After taking a sip of her drink, Dawn asked, "Are you aware you have the same exact name as a P.I. they've been writing nasty things about in the newspaper?"

I gave her a knowing nod. "Let me guess—this morning your boss brought you up to speed about me?"

"You're pretty good. Keep going," she challenged me.

"Let me see . . . how about this: He told you if he'd been working last night, he would never have allowed you to take me home, regardless of how wasted I was."

"His exact words were, 'I'd have tossed that slimeball in the trash bin and he could have slept it off in the clean fresh air.'"

"To which you—my reluctant guardian angel—replied?"

"I told him how much you'd spent and what a big tipper you were," she chuckled at the memory. "And next thing you know, he was planning to keep the rear booth reserved for you 24/7."

"You may be the best new friend I've ever had."

"And I promise never to ask you for money."

"That's always nice to hear," I said. "Then again, I'm sure my drunken tips should keep you in fine wine and caviar for at least a couple of months."

"At least," she agreed with a grin. She took another swig of juice. "So, do you want to talk about your friend from high school?"

I looked into her innocent, honest and far-too-young face. She reminded me of Maria, which is a compliment of the highest order. However, unlike my former love, I did not intend to drag this beauty down to my seedy level.

"I appreciate your concern," I said. "For the time being though, I'm going to try and find my way through this mess alone. I might not come out unscathed but I will come out of it, I promise."

"Okay, no problem," Dawn stated nonchalantly. "If you do want to talk sometime, you've still got that souvenir coaster, right?"

"I do somewhere."

Dawn laughed. "You'll find it under your bedroom phone. I put it there for safe keeping."

I was amazed by this pretty stranger who had entered my broken life.

"Who are you and why are you being so nice to me?" I asked in a cheerful, yet serious tone. "You can spend time with any guy in town—why waste your youth with me?"

Dawn got up from the table and carried her empty glass to the sink. When she came back, she stood in front of me.

"To answer your first question, I'm just a girl who likes a boy."

"Isn't that a line from a Julia Roberts' movie?"

"Does it matter?" she replied with a toothy grin.

"Not at all."

"And as far as wasting my time, haven't you heard the saying that one person's trash is another person's treasure?"

"I don't think anyone has ever described me as a treasure," I said sincerely. "Thanks . . . again."

"You're welcome."

I walked her to the front door.

"I'm glad you came into the pub last night," she said, stepping out onto the porch.

I waited for the "but" which didn't materialize.

"So am I," I said.

As she made her way across the front lawn, she said she hoped maybe we could go for a walk down by the beach—once my life had returned to some semblance of normalcy. As I was about to make a smart-alecky remark about the planets aligning, the phone inside rang, rudely interrupting our light-hearted mood. By the time I had decided to let the machine pick up, Dawn had strolled out of my life as easily as she had strolled in.

I entered the house and checked my message. Once again I had to deal with the same heavily modulated voice that had directed me to my garbage can the previous day. This afternoon's message, however, would turn out to be much worse than the first.

"The box on your rear porch should get you started. If I were you, I would begin right now. Lives are depending on it."

I ran to the back door, as my heart rate accelerated into the stratosphere. I knew I wouldn't find anyone in the yard putting away his cell phone, yet the quick steps gave me a sense of *flying into action*— the first physical moves in this life-sized game of chess with Max.

It sat ominously on the steps: a large banker's box, with its cover secured tightly by packing tape. I looked briefly in all directions and found nothing of interest. Obviously, I had again been under surveillance. My mystery caller knew when I was in the house. As interested as I was in finding out how this was being accomplished, I set my sights on the box, which I carried into the kitchen and opened using a sharp knife from the butcher block. I then lifted off the cover, never once entertaining the idea it might be booby trapped somehow.

Inside I found dozens of file folders, with labels like Police

Reports, Witness Statements and Patient Information. It was the large manila envelope marked *STEVE*, though, which caught my eye.

I emptied the envelope's three items onto the table. The first was a very grainy black-and-white photocopy of a clean-shaven male with the name "Jarvis Larsh" written at the bottom of the page. The second item was a newspaper article from the Santana Hills Sentinel from December 1992 with the heading: CON MAN CONVICTED OF MANSLAUGHTER. The third item was a typed letter for me:

Dear Mr. Cassidy,

Please find enclosed all pertinent information regarding People vs. Feldberg. As you are aware, Mr. Feldberg was convicted of manslaughter resulting from the death of a female acquaintance. It is our belief this woman was killed by Jarvis Larsh, a former patient of Mr. Feldberg's, who stated during numerous therapy sessions he often had dreams of killing red-haired females. He also advised on many occasions, he would awake from these dreams covered in blood.

As you may have guessed, the female who fell to her death from Mr. Feldberg's office had red hair. This evidence was not allowed at trial due to doctor-patient privilege, as Mr. Larsh had no knowledge Mr. Feldberg was not a licensed psychiatrist.

Mr. Larsh's present whereabouts is unknown.

We are asking you to review the files provided and use any means at your disposal to locate Mr. Larsh. It is our goal to present new evidence to the court in order to reverse this injustice and to bring Mr. Larsh to trial.

Sincerely,
The Pro-Justice League

P.S. Your own sense of justice is well documented and it is our hope this has not changed, for the sake of the loved ones of all those involved in this case.

A low pulsing sensation began behind my left eye. *Not a good sign of things to come.* I stared blankly at the letter before me and tried to comprehend what I had read. I immediately dismissed the gobbledy-gook of the main body of the letter, condensing all the words down to *Locate - Jarvis - Larsh.* What exactly I was to do once this was accomplished was unclear, but I was sure my mystery caller would provide new details in the future.

Another missing person case. Great.

It was the cryptic postscript, however, that caused me the most concern. The part about my *well-documented sense of justice* could only be referring to my time on the police force, a dark period I've been trying to forget for some time. The second half's reference to *the loved ones of all involved*, was a direct reminder that somehow Linda and Maria's safety be kept in my thoughts at all times.

Do what we ask and no one gets hurt.

Of course, it's hard to trust a convicted con man currently rotting in a federal pen, who hides behind veiled threats and the so-called Pro-Justice League. I will admit this box and letter were clever devices to get me to start my investigation. The letter was unsigned and there was no address information provided. The contents were in the style of a form letter, no different from ones televangelists send out asking for cash to fight the good fight on behalf of Jesus and unborn babies everywhere.

If something did go sideways in the days and weeks ahead, Max could deny any knowledge of this box. He would claim The Pro-Justice League must be a group of concerned citizens who meet once a week in a church basement or a member's rec room to discuss legal cases where justice had not been fulfilled. Some of these groups deal with death penalty cases, he'd argue, while others look at smaller cases, such as his.

SIX

ALEXIS

Alexis Penney held the cashier's cheque in her hand, which she noticed was shaking slightly. Was this due to the giddy excitement she felt about her pending investment or a subconscious neurological tick warning her to stop this madness?

She tried to recall when in her past she had handed over her life savings to a person she barely knew and came up with two such events: the day she purchased her first car, when she was nineteen, and the day she bought her first house, at the age of twenty–six. Both of those investments had worked out nicely, she reasoned, as she folded the cheque in half and placed it in her purse. Those payments of $988 and $12,000 were a pittance, however, compared to the $150,000 cheque in her possession. She was thirty-five, recently divorced, coming out of a relationship which had ended very badly and wanted to—needed to—feel independent. This venture seemed like the right opportunity at the right time.

Besides, she thought, as she exited the bank, *Dr. Max was the man with the plan and could never lead me astray. What self-respecting therapist would set one of his patients up for failure?*

The past year and a half had been the worst of Alexis' life. During that period, she'd begun a torrid affair with a married man that, unfortunately, their spouses both soon discovered. When you live in the rural town of Ravenwood, if you didn't know your neighbour's business when you walked into the R.W. Café for your morning coffee, you would by the time you left. She and Randolph "Randy" Mayer had not been the most discreet adulterers and were exposed when they'd been seen together at the White Plains Shopping Mall, located an hour out of town. The grade school's sixth-grade teacher and local busybody, Lizzie Cantner, had witnessed them kissing in the parking lot prior to departing in their respective vehicles. The Alexis-Randy scandal took hold of the small community about thirty seconds later.

Upon their return home, the whispering and odd glances they received were bad enough, but it was Randy's wife's premature death the same evening that really put a kink in their relationship. Poor Patricia Mayer had been bludgeoned to death with a shovel as she sat in her back yard, drinking iced tea by the pool. An elderly eyewitness told police she had seen a Chevrolet Malibu—a car similar to Alexis'—being driven out of the subdivision around 9:15 p.m. She could not say, however, with absolute certainty that Alexis was behind the wheel. The coroner concluded Patricia had met her maker roughly between 9:00 p.m. and 9:45 p.m.

Alexis did not help matters by refusing to give a credible alibi, not wanting to lead police to the mall's surveillance videotape collection. When the tapes did surface, Alexis admitted to the affair but continued to deny her involvement in the murder. Unfortunately, Randy was a bit more forthcoming and Alexis was charged with being an Accessory to Murder. Randy would eventually take a plea bargain and was sentenced to twenty–five years in prison with a chance of parole in twelve years. In exchange for his light sentence (under the circumstances), he was required to testify at Alexis' trial, stating she had handed him the shovel and encouraged him to end his marriage in a most remarkable fashion. Alexis' defence lawyer was working on getting a similar deal when word came down Randy had been killed in the prison cafeteria during an argument over a pudding cup.

The newspaper headline the following day said it all:

FREE TO KILL AGAIN? MISTRESS WALKS
Prosecutor forced to drop all charges against Penney

It was a sad day for Lady Justice but a very good one for the soon-to-be ex-Mrs. Penney. Her husband—who just wanted Alexis out of his life as soon as possible—agreed to a swift divorce, settled her share of their vast real estate holdings and bid her a not-too-friendly fare-thee-well. Now loaded with cash, she headed west for a fresh start. Even the release of the quickie tell-all true crime book, *The Murdering Mistress*, written by a court reporter and her ex-husband, had not dampened her enthusiasm for a new life. She figured no one outside the three counties surrounding Raven-wood would even care or buy it. In case it did become a bestseller though, she made a few changes to her appearance, the first of which was dying her naturally strawberry-blonde hair—which figured prominently in the picture that adorned the book's front cover—to a darker shade of red.

Once on her own, Alexis found herself dealing with bouts of depression and realized she should seek professional help. One day she flipped open the Santana Hills yellow pages and began her search. Coming from a small town, the only experience she had with shrinks was gleaned from TV shows. She had no idea of the difference between a "psychiatrist" and a "psychologist"—both of whom sounded very official and a bit scary. The term "therapist" however, produced no such adverse reaction. Quickly 90% of the listings were irrelevant. She focused on the remaining few ads until she came across one featuring a picture of an appealing-looking gentleman named Max Feldberg. She immediately dialed his office number and an appointment was set for the following Tuesday at 9:00 a.m.

Their first few sessions went smoothly. Dr. Max, as he preferred to be called, seemed to possess a very worldly persona and they clicked immediately. She told him about her upbringing, her marriage and the affair with the local married butcher. The related topics of murder, prison deaths, and exploitative book publications were never raised. Those were areas she had shelved away in her mind under "P" for "past" and had no interest in resurrecting. As the weeks went by, Dr. Max had been instrumental in helping her deal with the loneliness that came with moving to a new city—even if it was her choice to do so.

Their get-togethers became less and less formal, until Alexis felt their doctor-patient relationship had transformed into a friendship. He even began giving her stock tips that one of his other patients had passed along. "If you invest in this stock today, by tomorrow afternoon you'll have recouped the money for today's session," he'd told her. Never having dabbled in money markets before, he convinced her he could buy the stock on her behalf and she could pick up the paperwork the following morning. She was at his office at 8:55 a.m., where he handed over her stock certificates and showed her an official looking printout indicating she had already made $106.

"I think my luck is about to change, Dr. Max," she said with a wide smile.

"I think so too, Alexis," Max had replied. "It's not a lot of money but it's a start. If you want, I could keep my ears open and pass along any other tips I think might appeal to you—and your bank account."

"Really? You would do that for me?"

"There's just one small catch."

"What's that?" she asked, thinking she might have to perform some sexual favour with the nice doctor in exchange for the tips—a requirement that she would not dismiss out of hand, mind you.

"Well, technically, getting tips from one patient and then giving them to you is a violation of the doctor-patient ethical code. A mild violation in my mind, as I could probably get the same information from a newspaper column or a financial channel. However, these kinds of tips," he pointed to the certificates in Alexis' hand, "are a bit more detailed. In legal terms, what we did here was a crime called insider trading. You've heard of that term, right?"

"People go to prison for that," Alexis replied, suddenly terrified of the consequences of making a whopping $106 profit overnight.

"Only those making millions, not us small potatoes. Our buys are too low to make a blip on the government's radar. We're safe, trust me."

"I do."

"Good," Max said. "I wanted to be completely up front with you. I am the only one taking the risk here anyway. You could have heard me talking in the hallway about this sure thing and decided to play along on your own."

"Like playing a hunch on a horse at the track."

"Exactly."

She glanced down at the printout and said, "Small potatoes, huh?"

"The smallest."

A month went by before Max started hinting that a major financial opportunity was on the horizon. He'd continued to give her sound advice on four more "small potato" stock buys, each one more profitable than the last. They were on a roll and she'd made it very clear she might consider a substantial investment if the right prospect presented itself. He advised her not to go too big too fast. "People lose their retirement savings that way. Remember, if it sounds too good to be true, it probably is." Nevertheless, three weeks after making this statement, he had shown her stock certificates made out in his name adding up to over $300,000.

"I would never recommend any stock I had not checked out myself," he told her, handing her five other certificates. "These are the same companies I advised you to buy. You can see from the dates that I purchased them prior to passing along the information to you."

She was amazed by Dr. Max's openness and confirmed these were the same stocks she had purchased. "I don't know what to say," she said, placing the stack of certificates on his desk. "But what happened to small potato stocks? Three hundred thousand dollars is only small potatoes to billionaires and sheiks."

Max had been ready for this question all week. "This didn't come from my patient. When I had lunch in the financial district a few weeks ago, I overheard two brokers arguing about these stocks in a booth at the Trader's House Grill."

"You overheard it? Really?" She remembered their earlier discussion about how an overheard conversation wasn't insider trading.

"I swear to you, Alexis," he said excitedly. "I checked them out and found this is a computer company jointly owned by Microsoft, Apple and IBM. They are about to launch a new system that will revolutionize the industry, if not the entire world."

"Why haven't I heard of this before?"

"It's top-secret. If any of the three boards found out their research departments were working with their rivals, they'd get scared and pull out immediately." She gave him a disbelieving look. "I know how far-fetched this sounds, but I verified everything. Do you think I would invest three hundred grand of my own money into some crackpot idea?" He paused and looked directly into her eyes. "I had hoped by now you would trust me about these things. If you don't, I'll understand."

"No, it's not that. You've completely gained my trust with your tips so far."

HOOK.

"Then what is it?" Max asked slowly. "Like all the other investments, you don't have to buy this one on my say-so."

"No, I want to buy it."

LINE.

"Okay, that's good to know. Now, if you want to start with a low amount—say $500—that's fine."

"Actually, I wasn't thinking about starting low at all," she said with a savvy smile. "I did pretty well in the divorce and was wondering how much I could invest all at once?"

AND SINKER.

SEVEN

The problem with giving your heart to someone is not knowing in what condition they'll give it back. Maria, followed closely by my ex-wife and now Linda, had all entrusted me with theirs and each had lived to regret it. Sadly for Samantha, she had paid the ultimate price for loving me.

Today I had the unenviable task of warning Maria I may have put her in a risky situation. I also needed to ask if she would help me track down the mysterious Jarvis Larsh and, in the process, Linda as well.

The call went as well as could be expected. Being told your life may be in danger would shock anyone. To then be advised this threat had nothing to do with you personally, aside from your association with someone evil—me—would be even harder to comprehend.

"So, you want me to drop everything and just run off out west with you to search for this Jarvis Larsh person?" There was a long pause. "I don't know, Steve," Maria finally said. "I'm still trying to make sense of what's happened lately."

I could hear the conflict and doubt in her voice.

"I know I'm asking a lot, Maria," I started, "but I honestly feel you are in some danger and the best way to protect you is to have you with me."

"Did you ever think maybe I don't need your protection? I have plenty of people here in Delta who will watch out for me," Maria stated, somewhat forcibly. "What if Max threw our names into the mix as motivation to start your investigation?"

"I'd rather be safe than sorry," I countered. "I don't like all the coincidences lately. First, Max tries to get hold of you, instead of finding me directly. Then a mysterious person videotapes Linda the night she vanished. Next, someone associated with Max begins stalking me and leaving packages at my back door." Simply recounting these details gave me the chills. "And finally, Max referenced you and Linda, implying something terrible would happen if I didn't take his case."

"But you are taking his case," Maria said, "so his threat is an empty one." As I pondered the logic of this, she added, "Do you really think Linda disappeared, Steve? Isn't it possible she decided you two were through and cut the cord? Is there any evidence she was taken against her will?"

"No, it's just a feeling I have."

"When you were a cop, did you ever get a feeling about someone you knew for certain was guilty, only to find out later they had nothing to do with the crime?"

"Yeah, sure, but—"

"Maybe all these interlocking coincidences are just that. Nothing more, nothing less."

"I know what you're trying to say, Maria. Still—"

"When you came home to find Linda gone, was your first thought that she had been kidnapped? Of course not."

"That was before all these other incidents occurred," I interrupted her. "At first glance every crime scene appears to be a random act, until you learn the culprit had a connection to the victim. In my heart I believe Linda left me of her own free will, but until I see her again my mind believes there's a connection to Max and, by extension, you."

"I get the whole Max-Linda connection. She was your fiancée. What I don't understand is how you think Max could get you to do anything because of me. Until six months ago, we hadn't spoken in years—a fact I seriously doubt Max even knew. What kind of leverage am I? Why not threaten some other girls from school like Shari Taylor or Lauren McCain? It really doesn't make sense."

I am losing her, I thought. "I think it's because of something I told Max the day before I left Delta. The day of my mother's funeral."

The silence on the phone line was deafening. Even though we had talked about our feelings for each other during the Barry Jones investigation, I wasn't sure how she'd respond to my confession to Max, so many years ago.

"Which was?" she asked slowly.

I took a deep breath and began to unburden myself.

"Prior to the start of the service, I had told Max of my plans to

70

leave town. When asked if you knew, I said you didn't and swore him to secrecy. He told me the idea was dumb and that I shouldn't do such a thing to you." I hesitated, hoping Maria would say something. Greeted by sustained silence, I continued. "We looked over at you crying in the front pew and at that moment you gave me one of your angelic smiles of encouragement. Even with this sign, I told Max I believed I was doing the right thing. Then I said if anything ever happened to you, I wouldn't be able to live with myself, because I would always love you, no matter where our paths would lead."

Maria's response was quick and brutal.

"I'm utterly stunned, Steve," she said coldly. "First, I think you're delusional to believe that little speech registered in Max's mind. And secondly, I'm having a hard time believing you made that statement."

"You think I'm lying?"

"I think you're trying to manipulate me into going on this human scavenger hunt." She let out an angry sigh and added, "My heart is telling me you did say that to Max, because you followed through with your escape plan. Still—"

"I swear it's true."

"—my head is screaming, It's a trick! That you're toying with my emotions due to our past. It's all very confusing."

I didn't reply immediately. I was guilty of her last charge and we both knew it.

"You asked me why I thought Max would use our relationship against me and I told you," I said. "But regardless of his motivations, the fact remains he brought up your name in a menacing manner and I think you're at risk."

"I can't do this right now. I have to think about it and talk it over with someone," Maria replied, her voice agitated.

"With Trudy?" I inquired, knowing Wayne's insufferable wife would certainly talk her out of coming with me.

"With someone," came the short retort. "It's complicated."

"Okay, I guess."

"When are you leaving?"

"I was thinking Tuesday."

"I'll call you Monday afternoon."

"Maria," I implored, "you might be in real—"

"I can take care of myself," Maria interrupted me. "Max isn't going to harm me or Linda before your investigation starts. Like most of the events of the last few days, that doesn't make any sense." Her tone softened a bit. "I promise I'll call Monday."

The line went dead.

I placed the phone in its base and realized I had lost Maria for good. The only thing we really shared was our idyllic few years of high school together. In the decade-and-a-half since, I had ignored her, frustrated her, angered her and confused her. Who was I to think I had any control over her? I knew she would call Monday but figured I should start making solo plans, as there was no way she would be accompanying me anywhere, anytime soon.

With only time to kill, I decided I might as well start looking through Max's box of investigative fun, hoping to uncover some buried clues I could use to shortcut this strange assignment.

I took the various folders out one at a time, carefully removing every piece of paper to make sure there were no hidden bugs, bombs, or surprises attached to them. After inspecting the box's inner walls, I replaced all the folders, except the one marked POLICE REPORTS, which I set on the kitchen table. Finally, I put the box in a corner, not wanting to be reminded of it—out of sight, out of mind.

The contents of the box formed the prosecution's case against Max, plus a few items he felt supported his case. I knew from experience the arrival of this cardboard container often meant the end of the line for a defendant. After seeing the evidence collected against them, many criminals swiftly embraced the plea-bargain route. Obviously, this did not happen with Max, who probably fought this charge tooth and nail using his ill-gotten funds to buy his own legal dream team.

I cracked open the POLICE REPORTS file, somewhat fascinated

to learn how the jury came to its Guilty verdict. Max was right when he suggested I look at this as a cold case. I was disgraced off the police force before I made Detective, a rank I knew I could have achieved in time. Maybe now I could use my skills from my bad old days as a copper to bring peace to my present convoluted life.

"Good luck with that, pal," I said to the kitchen appliances.

I began to read Officer David Morse's handwritten notes from Tuesday, June 23, 1992, at the Upstate Medical Building. After finishing his entries and subsequent formal report, the case against Max seemed solid. At approximately 10:38 p.m., an unidentified male called 911, reporting a woman had been thrown off a 23rd floor balcony. The caller stated he had witnessed this crime from his 24th floor office across the street. He further claimed he saw a male in his 30's, with bleached blonde hair and a medium build, arguing with the redheaded female on the balcony. During this fight, the male appeared to be very angry and was screaming at the woman. It was then he hauled off and hit her in the face, causing her to lose her balance and fall over the safety railing to her death. This male was wearing a black turtleneck shirt, black jeans and dark-coloured shoes which had a white stripe on the side.

I stopped reading and returned to the discovery box, where I quickly located a colour photo of Max taken at the police station. Sure enough, his physical appearance matched the 911 caller's description and he was wearing a black turtleneck.

"Doesn't look good for you there, buddy," I commented to Max's ugly mug.

Unfortunately for my former good friend, it was a very slow crime night in the big city and six cops in three cruisers were at the medical building within two minutes. A minute later, an ambulance arrived to attend to the gravity-assisted victim, now sprawled on the sidewalk. *Not enough time to get an elevator from the 23rd floor to the parking garage or main level, let alone take the stairs*, I thought. Officers quickly surrounded the building and then started their ascent of the floors via elevators and stairwells. Once on the 23rd floor, a search of offices was commenced, at which time, only one was unlocked—Suite 2309—the headquarters of Max Feldberg, Therapist.

The following lines from Officer Morse's report made me gravely doubt Max had been set up and why he had been sent to jail for the rest of his mortal life:

> *Upon entering Suite 2309 we found Max Feldberg lying on a couch with his eyes closed. Only after we identified ourselves as police officers did Mr. Feldberg move from his position on the couch and ask, "What is going on?" At this time, it was noted he appeared to be groggy and he was asked if he had taken any medication recently, to which he stated, "No." He again asked what was going on and stood up. Mr. Feldberg was asked if he had been in the office during the past thirty minute period, to which he replied he had. Mr. Feldberg then became agitated and began yelling, "What the hell is going on here? You can't barge into an office with your guns drawn, without clueing me in on what's happening here."*
>
> *At this time, we informed Mr. Feldberg we were placing him under arrest for suspicion of murder. Mr. Feldberg was read his rights, handcuffed and taken into custody.*

At first glance, this was a slam dunk case for the prosecution. I read the report again and saw only two contentious areas: that Max was unresponsive when the police stormed his office and the unknown identity of the 911 caller. I recalled seeing a MEDICAL INFORMATION file, which I guessed would contain test results showing Max had been drugged or was under the influence of some substance. I made a mental note to confirm this hypothesis at a later time.

I tackled the WITNESS STATEMENTS folder next. It established the identity of the dead woman and what office unit she was planning to visit that fatal night. A cab driver confirmed he'd dropped the victim off around 8:30 p.m. and she appeared to be in good spirits. "It's not often I get such a beautiful woman in my cab, whose smile makes me forget how crappy my life is," he'd stated. The next witness was the front desk security guard, who said the woman had signed in and then taken the elevator to the 23rd floor. The name in the visitor book read "Alexis Penney" and that her destination was Suite 2309.

Finally came the statement of a cleaning lady who was the last person to see Ms. Penney alive—at least outside Max's office. She said the victim passed her in the hallway and then entered "that shrink's office." As it was the end of her shift, the cleaner estimated the time to be 8:35 to 8:40 p.m. There were statements from people on the street below, near the victim's final sidewalk resting place, but none could shed any new light on the circumstances of her fall. Collectively they put Alexis' touchdown at around 10:35 p.m., thereby corroborating the 911 information.

So we knew when Ms. Penney arrived, where she was heading and when she left the building (so to speak). All solid timeline information needed at trial. Unfortunately, I did not have the 911 transcript. Had the authorities been able to locate the caller? Was he unco-operative and if so, why? I hoped his information was in the DEFENCE CASE folder.

I replaced both folders and slid the banker's box into the corner of the kitchen. I didn't want to overload my brain with too much information all at once—we all know how painful that can be, right? I just wanted to chew over the basics of the case a bit and try to picture the scene from everyone's point of view: Max's sleepy perspective; Alexis' happy-to-terrified standpoint; and the witnesses who had last observed her alive.

That I had not come across the name Jarvis Larsh in any of these documents did not cause me to panic—yet. When initially emptying my magic box of evidence, I'd seen a folder marked JARVIS LARSH and knew it would be the last one I'd read before heading out on Tuesday. Why waste time on a figment of Max's imagination any longer than I needed? Max was clearly guilty of Alexis Penney's death. I had no doubt about that. What worried me was why he wanted me to find Mr. Larsh and what he would do to him once I had. Maybe Larsh had nothing to do with the balcony fight but had everything to do with the stolen funds Max had siphoned from his patients.

I convinced myself I had plenty of time to go over the remaining files and the only thing I wanted to do right now was get a drink. The fact Dawn would be serving it would be my reward for working so hard this afternoon.

The Sunsetter Pub & Eatery was not crowded and I took my usual booth in the back corner. As I entered, Dawn acknowledged me with a smile and somehow I felt as if I was (metaphorically speaking) home. *A notion only a true blue alcoholic would have,* I mused to myself. I surveyed the gang of regulars and noted a few of them averted their eyes. I had become something of a celebrity, yet no one wanted to have their picture taken with me, undoubtedly fearful they too would vanish into thin air.

I vacantly perused the menu until Dawn arrived at the table, placing a large frosted mug of beer in front of me.

"Let me guess," I said with a smile. "Compliments of the hot blue-haired lady at the table near the front door?"

"Close," Dawn laughed. "It was her husband. He heard you were good at making loved ones disappear. This beer is a retainer for your services."

"Tell him my fee has gone up since I became infamous. It's now two beers and a pound of wings."

"I'll make sure to give him the message."

I took a longer look at the couple in their late 70's, and felt equal parts of envy and sadness. "If something happened to her tomorrow, he would die within six months—that's a fact."

"A medical fact or a convenient fun bar fact you made up?" Dawn asked skeptically.

"Medical. I think it was written up in Mortician Monthly," I laughed. "Front page story, I recall."

"I'm glad to see you're keeping busy during your time off. Have you considered reading something a bit less morbid though?" Dawn suggested.

"Like what—Tiger Beat?"

"What's Tiger Beat?"

"You know—it has fluff stories about today's hottest heartthrobs." She looked at me with an *I know you're serious but obviously mentally challenged* expression on her face.

"When was the last time you actually saw this magazine?" she asked. "Maybe this is a generational thing."

I recalled my bedroom walls covered in posters of Charlie's Angels, Marie Osmond, Kristy McNichol and Pamela Sue Martin. "I don't know, 1976, 1977?" I looked up into Dawn's face and saw a blank expression. She had no clue who these women were or how their weekly appearance on my tiny 13" black and white TV had helped me reach puberty. I began to laugh aloud. "Just what year were you born?"

"1978."

"Ah . . . I guess it is a generational thing."

"Yeah," Dawn said with a mischievous grin.

"Okay, how did we get on this subject?"

"You started talking about the high mortality rate of very old people."

"Right. Well scratch that," I said. "New topic: how's your shift going so far?"

"Pretty slow."

The front door opened and we both watched a male in his 30's, with a 70's porn star-style moustache, walk in and take a seat at a side table.

"Your boyfriend's here," I chuckled.

"With a 'stache like that, he's more apt to be yours." Dawn gave me a light, playful punch on the shoulder and said, "Duty calls. Your wings will be ready in about ten minutes."

As she walked away, I muttered, "Dawn, I've got nothing but time today."

A few moments later, the husband of old blue-hair approached the cash register to pay his bill. As he waited for Dawn, he casually looked in my direction and I raised my beer and gave him a wink. "I'll take care of your problem," I said in a low tone.

He clearly had no idea what I was talking about and a look of alarm came over his face. When Dawn appeared, she spoke with the man for a few seconds, which resulted in her glaring daggers at me. After she made a comment to the old man, he shook his head in disgust.

Upon the elderly couple's departure, Dawn came by with my wings. "What did you say to that nice man? You almost gave him a heart attack."

"The real question is this: What did you say to him?" I asked.

"Oh, only that you were a drunken degenerate with irreversible psychological problems," she deadpanned.

"Whew," I said as I took a sip of my beer. "For a minute there I was worried you said something bad about me. At least you told him the truth," I laughed. "It's one of your best qualities, I think."

"I'm a quality person," Dawn stated proudly.

"That you are," I replied. "So, what's the porn star's story? Did he try to recruit you?"

"If you must know, the two of you actually have a lot in common."

"We've both appeared on film having sex?"

"Yeah right," Dawn snorted. "At least in his case he was the payee and not the payer!"

"Are you generally this sharp or just around me?"

"Don't flatter yourself, stud. I'm this quick 365 days a year."

"Okay, I believe you. Anyway, what do I have in common with Buttons Graham over there?" Another quizzical look came over Dawn's features. "Buttons was an actual porn star in the 70's," I informed her.

"Of course. Silly me for not remembering him," she said waving her hand dismissively. "Your friend is actually a P.I. Says he's looking for someone."

After the initial shock wore off, I asked, "Not for me, I hope." Before she answered, I slid further into the booth, out of Buttons' eye line.

"He didn't say," Dawn replied.

"Could you find out for me?"

"Hmmm . . . for you . . ." she teased. "Anything—within reason," she added.

"I'll make it worth your while," I said as she wandered away from the table.

"If I had a quarter for every time a loser barfly told me that," she laughed, "I'd own this place."

She went into the kitchen and returned with the private dick's lunch. She hung around his table making small talk for a minute and returned to my table with an anxious expression. She placed my bill on the table and said, "Leave me $20 and then go out the exit by the washrooms."

"What's up?"

"He's looking for Linda," Dawn said bluntly.

I'm sure the blood drained from my face. "Anything else I should know?" I asked, throwing two tens on the table.

"He drives a black Dodge Caravan, which is parked out front." She looked at the P.I.'s table. "I'll call you if I get more information, but you have to go now."

I grabbed one of the drink coasters sticking out of Dawn's apron and wrote down my home and cell numbers.

"This is a commemorative coaster," I smiled as I handed it to her. "Don't lose it—use it."

Dawn looked down at the coaster. "Don't lose it, use it? Are we in Grade 6 again?" she laughed.

As I exited the booth I said, "When I was in Grade 6, Tiger Beat was the king of the magazine racks and you were still a dream in your mother's mind." As I stepped around her, I leaned into her and said, "Thanks for the info, Dawn. I owe you one."

"No problem," she said as our eyes met. "Now get out of here."

As I walked stealthily toward the rear exit, I was confident no one had seen me leave. A rush of adrenaline propelled me forward, through the alley and down the side street behind the pub. I didn't know why I was running, but Dawn's uneasiness was infectious. If this guy was looking for Linda, he would surely want to speak with me at some time.

I half-walked, half-ran to my place and entered via the back door, in case another P.I. had staked out the front. I went to the living room windows and discreetly peered out. No unknown vehicles were parked on the street. *An excellent sign,* I thought.

I hadn't heard from Dawn and decided to grab my gear to do some counter-surveillance of my own. Nearing the pub, I located the only black Caravan on the street and wrote down the licence plate number for future reference. I then set up a position on the opposite side of the road. While putting a new tape in my video camera, I saw my subject come into view. My cell phone immediately began to ring.

"What's going on, Dawn?" I asked, recognizing the pub's number on the caller display.

"He's heading to the library to interview Linda's co-workers and he's staying at Holiday Cove," Dawn replied without hesitation, although she did sound a bit out of breath.

"I'm impressed," I commented. "Does he have a name?"

"Casey Ellerby. He gave me his card."

"What agency?"

"F.Y.I. Services out of Kelsey Lake," Dawn said. "Where's Kelsey Lake?"

"Near Delta, our hometown," I said haltingly, trying to digest this news.

"Is that a good thing or a bad thing?"

"It depends on who hired him, I guess. I gotta go, Dawn, he's leaving now," I said as I put my van in gear. "Call me when you're done work. Or better yet, drop by if you want—but call first!"

"Okay. Be careful."

"I will."

Fifteen minutes later, P.I. Ellerby entered the Great West Library to continue his investigation. I established a position in the parking lot of a nearby plumbing supply store. The irony that I was doing surveillance on a fellow P.I. while at a plumber's place of business was not lost on me. I was fairly certain, however, the day's events would not end in a hail of police bullets and two deaths. Then again, the P.I. who had followed Samantha and me to the Tecumseh Motel had probably believed the same thing and, man, was he wrong!

Although Ellerby was in the library for about an hour, it seemed like five. As the great Tom Petty famously observed, the waiting really is the hardest part. When Ellerby did return to his van, I couldn't tell from his expression if things had gone well or not. He had the look of a juror walking into a courtroom to pronounce the verdict on the accused: cool and detached. I was about to follow Ellerby when I noticed Linda's co-worker, Amanda Masterson, slip out a side entrance and start toward the bus stop. I made a snap decision to let my new friend carry on his journey alone and walked to where Amanda was now standing.

I had only met Amanda briefly a few times, when I had dropped by the library to visit Linda or to pick her up at the end of her shift. Amanda was in her late 20's, with a slim build, naturally golden blonde hair and soulful, hazel-coloured eyes, which I'm sure had made more than a few men's hearts flutter, sputter and stop in mid-beat.

"Amanda—hi," I said when I came within a dozen feet of her.

When she turned to face me, I had no clue how she would react. In the split-second before full recognition hit her, she had a smile on her face, probably thinking I was one of her many adoring library patrons. When she figured out who I was, I was glad the smile didn't completely slip.

"Steve, I didn't expect to see you today," she said as she took a few steps toward me and gave me an awkward hug. As we stepped away from each other, we took in our surroundings to confirm our friendly embrace had gone unnoticed. "Have you heard from Linda yet?" she finally asked.

"No," I admitted. "I don't deserve a call and don't expect one. Still, I was hoping she'd made contact with someone at the library."

"Not yet. We're getting kind of worried. The administration is dealing with this as if she's on emergency stress leave, so when she does hopefully return, her job will still be here."

"How long can they do that?" I asked.

"I don't know," Amanda said with a sigh. "It's not a situation that comes up every day. You know, everyone really likes Linda and can't imagine what she's going through right now." Amanda looked me in the eye as she finished her sentence, yet somehow I didn't feel she was condemning me for my past actions. She was simply being straight-forward, which I appreciated immensely. I was the first one to break our connection, as I sheepishly looked at my shoes. "I bet your ears have been burning the last hour," Amanda said, thankfully changing the subject. "There was a P.I. here asking the same questions as you. Do you know him?"

"No. I just became aware of his presence in our fine city a short time ago. I'm sure we'll come face to face when he thinks the time is right."

"For what it's worth, he seemed like a pretty decent fellow," Amanda stated.

"Did he tell you who he was working for?"

"We asked but he said he couldn't tell us because of privacy issues."

"Which is true," I said. "So, what did he ask you—if you don't mind me asking? If you do, I'll understand. I'm not the most popular person these days and wouldn't want to get you into any trouble."

Amanda gave me a little smile and said, "I'm a big girl, Steve. I can handle the condemnation of my spinster colleagues, but there really isn't much to tell. He asked the date of her last shift and if she had called to take any time off. Then he wondered if we had heard from her since she had gone missing or knew some place she may have gone."

"All pretty standard stuff," I interjected.

"And then . . . he asked our opinions about you."

"I can only imagine what Dolores had to say."

"Under the circumstances, she was pretty supportive, saying you had your faults—"

"Obviously," I concurred.

"—but she couldn't imagine you harming Linda in any way."

"Was that the general consensus amongst you ladies?"

"Yeah, pretty much. We all knew you two were having a bit of a rough stretch. We've all been there at some point in our lives."

I was tempted to ask Amanda if Linda had ever brought up any concerns I was cheating, but let the idea fall away. *Of course she had*, I concluded, feeling like a fool all over again.

"Did Mr. Ellerby say where he was going next?"

"Not really. All he said was he had other people to talk to before returning to Kelsey Lake."

"I'm sure I'm on his wish list," I said, shaking my head in disgust. "I think I've talked to everyone else, except the one person I really want to speak with." The sentence drifted off as the city bus arrived.

"This is me," Amanda said, as the bus doors opened and several passengers brushed by us.

A young man in his mid–teens said, "Hi, Mrs. Masterson," as he walked toward the library.

"I hate when they do that," Amanda said with a smile.

"It's a sign of respect," I countered. "Be thankful they don't call you ma'am."

"They do sometimes, that's the scary part," she said, stepping up into the bus. "If Linda contacts any of us, I'll let you know."

"Thanks. I'll do the same."

I watched Amanda take her seat near an open window. "If you need to talk, give me a call. My number is listed in the staff directory."

"I'll do that," I lied, knowing Linda's staff directory was no longer at the house. "Take care," I said with a wave as the bus pulled away.

"You too, Steve."

WHEN ANGELS FAIL TO FLY

EIGHT

When I arrived home I found Private Investigator Casey Ellerby's business card sticking out of the mailbox. *At least it wasn't ticking*, I thought as I scrutinized his information. I had never heard of F.Y.I. Services but felt it must be legitimate. I was curious, however, to find out if it was a small operation run out of someone's kitchen or a large-scale business. I called the 1-800 number provided and was informed by the receptionist they were a fully operational agency associated with the highly respected law firm of Whatmore, Charron, Cabanaw, and I was now even more intrigued to find out who had paid some serious bucks to hire these people. I figured I would find out soon enough.

"Hi, Casey," I said, after P.I. Ellerby picked up his cell. "This is Steve Cassidy. I think we just missed each other."

"Oh . . . yes . . . hello, Mr. Cassidy," he stammered. "I dropped by your place about an hour ago."

"Yeah, sorry about that," I said, trying not to sound too insincere.

"I went to lunch at a great place around the corner called the Sunsetter Pub and then to the library to see an old friend."

The silence that followed brought a smile to my face, although I doubted Mr. Ellerby would have found any humour in the situation. I wanted to let him know, regardless of what that blow-hard Jeremy Atkins wrote in the newspaper, I was still at the top of my game.

"That is quite astonishing, as I also ate at the Sunsetter today and visited the library—but you already knew that, didn't you?"

"As I'm sure you've discovered, Casey, the city of Darrien is really a small town dressed up as a sprawling metropolis. Everyone knows everyone," I suggested, not believing it for a second and also wanting to shield Dawn's involvement. "If you still want to talk and possibly exchange information, I'm free for the next hour or so."

"I have one more stop to make, then I'll come by."

"Sounds like a plan."

With time to kill, I grudgingly tore the top off the banker's box again and withdrew two new file folders: MEDICAL EVIDENCE and BANK RECORDS.

As I had expected, Max's blood sample taken at the time of his booking, showed the presence of diphenhydramine citrate, the active ingredient in many over-the-counter sleeping pills. This would explain his apparent grogginess when the good guys with guns breached his office door. The problem with this stellar medical finding was that quite a bit of time had passed between the time Max was forcibly taken from his place of business to the moment a syringe pierced his skin in search of a vein. Sleeping pills are meant to dissolve quickly. Therefore, Max could have popped a few into his mouth when he heard the elevator doors on his floor open. A bigger problem, though, was that cocaine and two other illegal barbiturates had also made a starring appearance in his bloodstream.

"The hits keep on coming."

The next sheet I retrieved was a forensic report stating there were no traces of the victim's DNA found in samples taken from under Max's fingernails. A second report also concluded there was no evidence of Max's DNA under the victim's fingernails. Again, this proved nothing. Max could have worn gloves during the attack and the victim simply didn't or couldn't fight his advances. I'm sure if she knew what her fate would be, Alexis would have fought to overpower Max, at which time some of his flesh would have been transferred to her hands.

The final file enclosed for my reading enjoyment was the autopsy report and accompanying pictures. I set the photos face down on the table and read the findings of the coroner. Not surprisingly, he determined the victim had died of catastrophic internal injuries, sustained from her inability to fly through the air and land softly on the sidewalk below. The only other finding was bruising around her neck and upper arms, indicating someone had forcibly restrained and choked her prior to her fall from the 23rd floor. Still, there was nothing from a medical standpoint conclusively linking Max to the victim on that deadly evening.

I gingerly placed the report in its folder and hesitated to turn over the autopsy photos. Until now, this investigation had been almost hypothetical in nature and a bit surreal at times, but I knew the instant I laid eyes on Alexis Penney's corpse that would change in a hurry. I would be confronted with the seriousness of Max's crime and I didn't know how I would react in my present frazzled mental state.

While on the police force, I had viewed many lifeless bodies and attended several actual autopsies. The difference was the majority of the dead were bad guys—drug dealers, child molesters, rapists, thugs, armed robbers—the lowest of the low on the criminal food chain. They didn't deserve my sympathy for losing their lives and I didn't offer it. The same could not be said for the crime victims I encountered at the morgue. I always saw myself as a hardened, seasoned professional who didn't get emotionally attached to someone I did not know in life. Don't get me wrong—I do feel for them and their families—just not too much. I have seen many quality officers destroyed by their emotions when they took a case too personally. Somewhere along the line, they forget policing is like a well-paid factory job, which needs to be worked day after day after day.

I recall only one time when I slipped across this line of sanity. I had to take several days off to collect my thoughts and get my head on straight. It was early in my career—I was probably two years into the job. I was dispatched to a call in a two-block area affectionately known as High Times Headquarters, which consisted of several mammoth high-rise apartment buildings, each infested with rats, cockroaches and addicts. Veteran officers actually refused to attend minor calls there. They only reluctantly ventured into this seedy, soulless, war zone when a shooting occurred, knowing that turning down such a high priority call would get them into trouble with the Mayor—a man who grew up in these once-proud projects, before the dealers took them over.

I was sent to investigate a suspicious package found near one of the more notorious buildings, the Dutton Towers, known simply as "The Dutton." A group of kids had made the discovery while playing near a dumpster and one of their mothers had phoned it into the station. As it was not a 911 call and there was no mention the package was an explosive device, I didn't exactly rush to the scene. When I did arrive in the area, I saw a group of four teenagers, two males and two females, milling about the tenant parking lot.

"Hey, did one of your mothers call about a suspicious package?" I asked out my cruiser's side window. I noted these kids already had that hardened look associated with strung-out users and abusers. The four of them looked at each other, a knowing in-joke smirk rapidly appearing on each of their lips. "Do you know what I'm talking about or not?" I asked with more of an edge in my voice this time.

"I don't know anything about someone's mama calling the fuzz," the taller male mouthpiece proclaimed, trying to act tough in front of his friends. "But I think what you're looking for is over there." He pointed across the boulevard to a group of battered industrial-sized metal dumpsters. "Maybe behind that blue one," he added.

I followed his outstretched hand and asked, "Do you know how long this package has been over there?" The four of them again began to snicker, finding my question highly amusing or maybe they were simply high and found life amusing all of a sudden.

"Ah . . . maybe a day or two," the rail-thin older girl with long greasy hair replied.

"A day or two?" I said, my gaze drifting to the distant dumpsters. "Anything I should know before I go over there? Do you know what this package looks like? Is it a box, a bag—what?"

"Hey, man," the other male wiseass spoke up. "Why don't you stop harassing us and go do your job? You'll know it when you see it, trust me."

I looked at the second girl in the group, who appeared to be thirteen years old and who kept tugging absentmindedly at the ends of her ratty t-shirt. "Do you have anything to offer?" I asked, singling her out.

She seemed caught off guard but then in a voice devoid of emotion said, "It smells real bad."

Her tone, coupled with the abrupt slackening of expressions on her friends' faces, made me very nervous. As the group walked away toward the building's entrance, I contemplated calling for back-up. Something wasn't right here, but until I checked out those dumpsters there was no use getting anyone else involved. If it looked like a bomb, I'd call in the explosive experts. If it looked like a package of drugs, I'd call in the street crime team and so on.

First, I had to find out what I was dealing with here.

I drove the cruiser up over the sidewalk and proceeded slowly across the vacant lot, paying no attention to the number of broken beer bottles and crack vials being crushed under the weight of my wheels. *A flat tire is the least of my concerns*, I concluded. As I approached the area that smart guy #1 had indicated, adrenaline—along with a dose of raw fear—coursed through me. I felt like a kid approaching the darkened doorway of a haunted house, scared out of my mind, unable to turn and run.

I got out of the cruiser and looked at The Dutton, expecting to see my four new partners in crime; they were nowhere to be found. I glanced up at the hundreds of balconies surrounding me on all sides and noted something odd: no one, not a soul, was watching me as I made my way over to the blue dumpster. *All the tenants know what I'm about to find and can't bear to be a witness to it*, I thought to myself. The idea sent a shiver through me. As a precaution, I unsnapped the clasp on my holster and placed my right hand on the butt end of my 9mm gun.

As I stepped around to the rear of the suspect dumpster, I really believed this was simply a big set-up—some druggie's idea of a practical joke. Get the rookie copper all paranoid out here in the centre of hell and see him freak out. When I learned the only item resting on the ground was a child's car seat with a doll strapped into it, a smile began to form at the corners of my mouth. A wave of relief came over me, as I realized this had been a hoax and that I had been had.

"Unreal," I said aloud, as I turned to walk to the cruiser.

Then the wind changed direction, causing dust and garbage to begin swirling around my legs. That was when the unmistakable odour of rotting human flesh filled my nostrils and made me gag.

It smells real bad, the girl had said and she was right.

I staggered over to the car seat and set it upright, getting a good look at the doll for the first time.

You'll know it when you see it.

To this day, I don't remember exactly what happened after finding Josephine Grogan's tiny, lifeless one–year–old body. She had not simply been placed in the seat, she had been strapped in for her own protection, with no possible way to escape her deadly destiny.

And they had all known. Every one of those teenagers, along with their friends and family, knew that just outside their front door there was a helpless baby strapped in a car seat, set beside a dumpster and left to face the ravages of Mother Nature alone. Yet no one breathed a word to anyone in the real world, outside the invisible walls of High Times Headquarters. They feared retribution from a powerful drug lord who had gotten arrested two days earlier, but never informed the arresting officer his daughter was in his car twenty feet away. After being denied bail, Mr. Big's associates dutifully took care of his small problem the only way they knew how.

I was later told that before my call for back-up went out across the air, a 911 call had been received. The caller stated an officer was screaming at the top of his lungs near a dumpster where her children often played.

"And where do you live, ma'am?" the dispatcher asked.

"At the Dutton Towers," came the woman's curt reply.

"I need the exact address."

"I don't know the exact address. It's the Dutton Towers apartment building. D-U-T-T-O-N. You cops are out here all the time—just not yelling your fool heads off, like this moron is doing."

"So you don't know your own address? I need it to direct other officers out there."

"I don't have time for this!" the caller screamed. "Stop harassing me and come out here and do your damn job." Before the phone line was disconnected, the caller could be heard yelling at her kids, "Get out of here and go play outside! Just not near that crazy man. He's bound to shoot ya."

I replaced the autopsy report in the file and stared at the back of the coroner's photos before me. *Not yet*, I decided, picking up the BANK RECORDS folder. I had expected much more documentation. The first two sheets were basic garden-variety account records, which come in the mail once a month. They showed that on the day of his arrest, Max had the following funds available to him: Chequing: $6,893; and Savings: $3,579. A little over ten grand. As with the findings in the medical file, these numbers meant nothing. They showed week in, week out bank activity, typical of many people in their 30's. Max's true wealth, I was sure, was awaiting his release in untraceable offshore accounts. As I leafed through the remaining sheets, I didn't find evidence to support such a theory, although the government must have presented it at trial. *A curious omission*, I thought.

More intriguing, however, was the inclusion of Jarvis Larsh's bank statement for the same month as Max's arrest. For the first twenty–three days, his account was on life-support, bouncing between a high of $376 to a low of $198. From the look of things, it seemed Larsh did not have a steady job. He'd make small deposits every few days, but when his nest egg had a couple of hundred dollars built up, he'd pay a bill or take out a substantial amount by his standards, which would again put him on the verge of personal bankruptcy. Having not read the dossier on him, I wondered if Larsh was a starving student or maybe a drifter.

Neither scenario explained how he could pay Max for his therapy sessions. I made a mental note to pursue this path later.

Then on the 23rd of the month, something transpired that must have altered his universe and which could play a big role in my investigation: the amount of $9,999 was deposited into his savings account. I looked at the transaction code and noted the letters "ABD"—Automated Banking Deposit. I was puzzled by the odd used-car-sticker amount. "Why not throw the poor guy an even ten thousand?" I mused aloud. Then the tiny part of my brain I used to access when I was a cop awoke from its sleep. It kindly reminded me that cash deposits higher than ten thousand dollars required a separate bank form to be filled out, something Larsh's benefactor probably didn't feel the urge to do. It was something I would have to ask Mr. Larsh about, provided I ever had the chance to sit down with him. As you might expect, like a drunken sailor on leave with a pocket full of cash, in the days following this inexplicable windfall, Larsh withdrew and withdrew and withdrew, until on the 30th his new balance was a paltry $256.

"Unbelievable," I said to the four walls.

I didn't quite know what to make of the contents of this folder. They shed no light on Max's true financial dealings and very little light on Jarvis Larsh's. I replaced everything in the folder and put it on top of the medical file. Taking a deep breath, I reached for the autopsy report, knowing this would be my final task of the day in regard to these discovery papers. It would also be the first time I could put a face to the victim.

Thankfully, the first picture was a medium close-up shot of Alexis Penney at rest. It was easy to determine she had been a very striking woman, with an oval face, clear complexion and straight collar-to-shoulder length auburn hair. As I stared at her dead expression, a wave of nausea came over me as I unexpectedly remembered the red wig Samantha had worn for the Plymouth plumber. I envisioned her face in place of Alexis', lying still on a cold metal table, as a coroner took one final photo of her for posterity's sake. I suddenly felt sick to my stomach and violently shoved all the autopsy pictures into the banker's box, which I kicked across the floor.

I had the idea of running out to grab a bottle of whiskey and hiding in my house for the remainder of the afternoon, evening, night and beyond. I chastised myself for looking at Alexis' picture. During the course of my investigation, I would surely see personal photos or newspaper clippings showing Alexis alive and well. I felt the inclusion of these pictures was for the sole purpose of upsetting me.

Dying for a stiff drink but with only non-alcoholic ones at hand, I grabbed a juice bottle from the fridge and sat in my recliner chair, attempting to settle my nerves. However, solace would not come. I couldn't shake the images of Alexis' or Samantha's lifeless faces. To compound the problem, I looked up at the fireplace mantle and again saw an empty space where a framed picture of Linda and me had once been.

Not knowing her present whereabouts or if she was happy and healthy, I fought the urge to think of her in any type of peril. *She had simply walked away from a bad relationship*, I kept repeating to myself, like some kind of soul-cleansing mantra.

The ringing of the front door bell, followed by three short knocks, shook me out of my malaise. It was too early for Ellerby's visit, unless his last appointment had fallen through.

"Hey, Steve, are you home?" came Dawn's perky voice down the hall.

"Yeah, I'm here," I said, as I exited my living room of gloom.

When she saw me, there was a slight change in her happy demeanour. "And how are you doing this afternoon?" she asked very slowly.

"I'm fine."

"Is that the story you're going to stick with?"

"For right now."

"Okay . . ." she replied, not pleased with my answer, but smart enough to let it go for the time being. "You should really keep your doors locked," she continued, as she closed and bolted the front door. "You never know who'll walk in off the street," she said in a mocking tone. Turning to me, she was again semi-serious and asked, "Can you at least fill me in on what happened after you left the pub or is that also off-limits today? Because if it is, I could go straight into my boy-friend problems—a topic that always seems to bring a smile to your old face."

"So, I now look bad and old?"

"Pretty much," she answered without hesitation.

"Do you want something to drink?" I offered, moving into the kitchen.

"Sure, whatever you have is fine," she said as she took a seat at the table. "How did your counter-surveillance go—that's what you guys call it, right?"

Over the next twenty minutes I brought her up to date, leaving out the trauma the autopsy photos had caused. For the first time, I also gave her a bare-bones account of my missing person case, saying I was about to track down an old high school buddy. At the conclusion of my tale, I asked, "Any questions, comments, suggestions?"

"Just one thing—which in the overall scheme of things is probably insignificant," she started. "Do you think this Amanda chick has the hots for you, now that Linda is out of the picture, so to speak?"

I stared blankly at her. "After all my details about this investigation, the only item that caught your interest was whether Linda's co-worker wants to sleep with me?"

"Not at all," she said, waving her hand dismissively. "Do you really think I'm that shallow?" She didn't wait for my smart-ass response. "Because I'm not. I'm always interested in how relationships start. I have plenty of other questions about your investigation, but I didn't think you were in the mood to discuss anything heavy."

"So you went with the lighter topic of women who date their friend's ex-boyfriends?" I laughed at the simplicity of her thinking. "I appreciate that, honestly I do. I was just expecting something else."

"I'm very unpredictable," Dawn said proudly. "You'll see."

"I bet."

"Well?"

"Oh, yeah—Amanda, right?" I replied, trying to form a proper answer. "On a scale of 1 to 10, with 10 being the highest probability she wants to jump my bones . . . I would say she is a . . . I don't know . . . let's say, a solid 7."

"Interesting. That high, huh?"

"That's just a gut reaction. I'm not entertaining the idea, if you must know."

"I've found in relationships first impressions are always the truest. She was obviously sending a signal with her 'call me to talk' comment. I've seen that one used a lot. The fact she didn't overly sell it, I must admit is an admirable trait. I give her full marks for that. She's willing to wait . . . at least for a little longer."

"She may have to wait quite a while," I said.

"Why? You don't find her attractive?" Dawn inquired.

"No, she's very attractive."

"Not your type then?"

I had to think about that. "Well, if I'm going to be completely truthful here, I guess an attractive woman who works in a library is my current default type."

"Interesting," Dawn said again without elaborating.

"I guess it is, isn't it? Anyway . . . let's change the subject to something more important. What are your thoughts on what I told you about the P.I. looking for Linda?"

"Well, with this big law firm involved, it's apparent someone has some major scratch to hire their investigator," she began. "You have no clue who it might be?" I shook my head side to side. "Did you ever meet her parents?"

"No."

"Why not?"

"Because Linda had a falling-out with them, after she eloped with her loser ex-husband."

"Aren't you just the pot calling the kettle black," Dawn said with a smirk.

Another direct hit, I thought.

"Maybe they had a change of heart and want to find their little girl."

"Anything is possible."

"As for the P.I., it doesn't sound like he learned anything new from the ladies at the library."

"What is there to learn?" I said. "A few of them, including Amanda, may have known we were having our differences, but there really is nothing else to tell."

Dawn took a final sip of her juice and put the bottle on the table.

"Are you worried something may have happened to Linda, Steve?" she asked point blank. "And I don't mean a car accident or something like that." She studied my face and must have observed some small change in my expression. "You're not telling me every-thing, are you?"

"No, I'm not," I confessed. "What I'm holding onto, though, doesn't change the situation that when I returned from the police station, all of Linda's belongings had been cleared out and she'd left me a *Dear Steve* letter. I swear I had nothing to do with moving her stuff or her apparent disappearance."

Dawn continued to scrutinize my features. "I've never told you that I have three older brothers, have I? Growing up, I got pretty good at telling if they were lying—to me, to my parents, or when playing cards—and I want you to know I believe you. Would I bet the family farm on it? Ah . . . no. But if push comes to shove, I'll back you up if I can."

I could also tell, from my years of interviewing, she too was telling the truth and genuinely meant what she said. "I appreciate your honesty, Dawn, and will try not to let you down."

"That's what friends are for, right?" she asked, echoing Wayne's sentiments.

"So, now we're officially friends?" I asked, lightening the mood.

Dawn laughed. "We've been friends ever since I dragged your sorry, drunken butt home and stayed the night. You wouldn't let a stranger do that, would you?"

It was my turn to laugh aloud. "You have a point there."

Dawn got up to put her empty bottle in the garbage. "What's next on your sleuthing schedule?"

"Talk to Ellerby. Hopefully, he'll spill some of his findings," I said. "I'll be his most co-operative interview yet."

"It's good to know you can play nice with a fellow P.I."

"We dicks have to stick together."

Dawn gave me a dismayed look. "Thanks for putting that porno-graphic image in my mind."

"Hey—what are friends for?"

Dawn came around the table to where I was now standing and stopped in front of me.

"Steve Cassidy, you're a very interesting person and I'm glad you came into the Sunsetter to drink your face off." She looked directly into my eyes and remained silent.

I gave her a quizzical look, not knowing where she was going with this compliment and a bit apprehensive about what she was expecting from me in return.

"Okay—your turn," she finally said. "And don't screw this up either."

I hesitated for a moment as if carefully considering my response before saying, "Me too."

"That's it?"

"For now . . . I guess," I answered slowly. "Too wordy?"

"I expected a few more syllables to come out of your mouth but I guess it's the quality of the words, not the quantity that's important."

"They were definitely quality words and I meant every one of them," I stated with a sly smile.

"That's all a girl can ask for I suppose."

Even though this topic of conversation was technically over, our connection to each other remained intact. There was something about Dawn that went deeper than her youthful attractiveness, yet I hadn't been able to pinpoint exactly what it was.

"Okay, on a scale of 1 to 10, how would you rate the probability that you want to kiss me right now?" Before I could answer, she gave me a quick kiss—a peck really—as she balanced on the tips of her toes. "Too slow," she said, as she stepped away and started toward the door, leaving me a bit bewildered by the entire incident.

"A solid nine," I finally said, after finding my tongue.

Dawn opened the front door and gave me a warm, beguiling smile. "Me too," she said before closing the door behind her.

I went out onto the porch and yelled after her, "I'll give you a call later tonight."

She turned and smiled at me again. "Yeah, yeah, sure, sure. That's what all my boyfriends say," she proclaimed, as she began to cross the street. "But they're not as trustworthy as you, Stevie-boy. Talk to you soon."

I was about to respond when I noticed Ellerby sitting in his parked van. He rolled up the driver's side window and got out. He first looked in my direction, then over to Dawn.

"Damn it," I whispered under my breath, as he started up the walkway.

"I know that girl from somewhere," he stated, as he glanced toward the street. "Did she call you her boyfriend?" Ellerby stopped in front of me and offered his right hand. "We can get into that later, Mr. Cassidy." I shook his hand and found he had a strong grip. "I'm glad we've finally met face-to-face."

"Me too."

Recalling I had used the same phrase with Dawn only moments earlier and in a completely different context, I half-snorted a laugh at the stupidity that had become my life. Believing I was being disingenuous, Ellerby took his hand back, as an expression of revulsion formed across his face. Even that unshaven, unhip, caterpillar-like moustache that resided under his nose appeared to be angry with me.

"Oh, no, please don't be offended, Casey. A tragically funny thought—which has nothing to do with you or your investigation—popped into my mind. I'm sorry, really," I continued to apologize. "Please come in. There is a lot we have to discuss."

As with Dawn's assessment of Amanda, I had to give Casey props for taking me at my word that he was not the cause of my outburst. Ellerby took a seat in the kitchen, where he retrieved a leather portfolio from his briefcase, which he placed on the tabletop. He did not, however, open it immediately, which I recognized as a tactic many interrogators use. The portfolio's mere appearance was to indicate to the interviewee valuable information was contained within it, which had already been reviewed by the interviewer. For police purposes, in the right circumstances, this non-verbal threat of *Tell me one lie and I'll nail you to the wall with what's inside this folder*, was extremely effective. I obtained several confessions using this method, but most of these would-be criminals were young and naïve—two traits not applicable to me here in my kitchen.

After Ellerby declined a beverage, I sat across from him, reached for the portfolio and opened it up. Much to my surprise, Ellerby didn't flinch. "So, what do you know and how can I help?" I asked brazenly, as I began to peruse his handwritten notes. I soon learned his investigation was in the very early stages and consisted of talking with Linda's co-workers—no bombshells there—and a meeting with someone named Tamra Collins.

"The girl who left here," Ellerby said suddenly, "works at the pub. She was my waitress—Dawn."

"If I had a prize to offer, Casey, I would gladly give it to you," I said, closing the portfolio and sliding it across the table. "Like I said on the phone, in Darrien everyone knows everyone."

"Did Linda know Dawn?" Ellerby countered, opening the portfolio and grabbing a pen from his suit jacket.

Game on, I thought, still admiring Ellerby's composure and professionalism. From what I had seen so far, he did appear to be a decent chap, who wasn't going to be intimidated by the likes of crusty old me. I decided to play nice, as I had promised Dawn earlier.

"Not that I know of," I replied calmly. I had nothing to hide. "We—Dawn and I—met a short time ago."

"Before or after Linda's . . . departure?" Ellerby asked, trying to be delicate, which I took as another sign he wasn't here to railroad me.

"After," I stated.

Ellerby seemed shocked by my answer and put his pen down. "We're talking within the week, right?" I nodded. "I've heard of speed dating, Steve, but in your present circumstances—one girlfriend dead, one fiancée missing, your licence suspended—I would have to say your prowess with women or your insatiable appetite for sex while under extreme stress is, in a sick sort of way, quite impressive. I think," he added, as he shook his head in disbelief.

"I don't know if that was meant as a back-handed compliment or an indictment," I replied. "Regardless, I know exactly what this looks like, especially with Dawn implying I was her boyfriend outside but that isn't the case, I assure you."

"Hey, I'm not here to judge you. I just—"

"Have you ever been married?" I asked, cutting him off.

"A couple of times."

"Ever cheat on your wife?"

"Sure did."

"Ever get caught?"

"A time or two."

"Then you know what I am going through."

Ellerby leaned forward and placed both hands on the table. "The difference is no one died because of it and no one disappeared off the face of the planet. Honestly, I couldn't care less if you were banging that pretty young waitress on the front steps as you watched Linda's moving truck pull away. My only concern is finding out where Linda is now and if she's safe and sound. From what I've gathered so far, I don't think you had anything to do with her *disappearance,* as you were being interrogated by the police all night."

"Moving truck?" I asked curious about this little detail, which Ellerby didn't seem to think was very important. "Do you know where she rented it from?" Until now, I hadn't thought much about Linda's getaway vehicle. I had assumed she called someone else from work to come by to pack a few things. She hadn't taken any furniture—only clothing and other personal items she'd brought along from Delta.

Ellerby looked into the living room and the idea Linda had not taken any large items with her appeared to trouble him temporarily. "The cops said she had cleared all of her stuff out, so I figured she must have rented a van or truck."

"She grabbed her clothes and other knick-knacks, nothing else. Everything she had fit in her car when she moved in here and I presume it all fit when she moved out."

"I'm sorry if I got your hopes up, Steve. I don't have any information about a rental, I swear."

"I believe you. It just got me thinking." I liked Ellerby but didn't trust him enough to divulge the information about the cameraman at the motel, who may have helped Linda move. This mystery person had gained her trust; otherwise, she wouldn't have gone with him to witness my infidelity. A theory I had desperately tried to suppress was there were two separate individuals playing head games with me:

Max's henchman—the one who dropped packages off at my house— and the video camera operator helping Linda.

If that were the case, I knew she was in trouble.

"Do you have any information that might help me find Linda?" Ellerby asked. "My budget isn't unlimited and if you could point me in the right direction I'd appreciate it."

His tone was serious but also sincere. "Who is paying for this investigation?" I asked, changing the subject slightly. "Her parents? Her brother? The library?"

"You know the rules, Steve. I can't reveal that."

"Privacy and confidentiality, yada, yada, yada," I said. "I also know some rules are made to be broken. How long have you been in this business?"

"Twelve years."

"From past experience, I'm sure you've investigated many cases, from suspicious deaths to questionable store fires to bankruptcies, correct?"

"Correct."

"And what is the first question a good investigator asks before starting any problematic file?" I could sense he knew what I was fishing for, although he remained silent. "The question is: Who benefits? Who gets the insurance company's cash when all is said and done? The first avenue you investigate is the money trail. Follow the money—that's what Deep Throat told Woodward and Bernstein and they ultimately brought down the President of the United States."

"I don't know what this has to do with me—" Ellerby started to say.

"Because I'm not only curious about who is paying your wages, but why? I'm pretty sure Linda's estranged parents don't have the funds to hire a P.I. The same goes for her employer and brother. If there was foul play, the most likely suspect would be me, yet the authorities don't believe that to be the case. Which begs the question: Who benefits from Linda being located—dead or alive?"

"I can see your point, Steve, I really can," Ellerby said hesitantly.

"If it's her parents or some rich do-gooder who wants to live out his dream of playing Columbo or Matlock, fine," I continued. "The problem is no one outside her immediate circle of friends feels she's been harmed or abducted. We all think she is simply clearing her head, somewhere outside the city of Darrien. This again brings into question your client's motives."

In Ellerby's eyes, I could see the effect my words were having.

"Let's play a game," I suggested. "I ask you a question and you answer yes or no—no names."

"Isn't that a bit childish?"

I ignored his question and asked, "Her parents?"

Ellerby shook his head, as if clearing the cobwebs between his ears. "No."

"The library administration or her co-workers?"

"No."

"A relative?"

"No."

"Her ex-husband?"

"No."

"A friend from Delta?"

"No."

I let out a sigh and said, "I really want to believe you, Casey, but there is nobody left."

"Give it one more shot."

I looked at him expecting some kind of smirk but his features were hard as granite and his eyes were begging me to continue our little charade. *Just tell me, you little creep*, I wanted to scream.

"There's no one left," I said. "If it's not her family or friends, who is left—someone off the street, who doesn't even know her? That's insane."

"What if my client knew you?" Casey asked.

I shook my head and glared at him. "Knew me? From where?" He remained close-lipped. "Are you telling me your client is a friend of mine? Because I have no family left and work alone." Still no reaction. "Am I getting close? Is it a friend of mine—yes or no?"

"Yes, sort of."

102

I'd had enough of this nonsense and blew my top. "What the hell does that even mean? I don't have any sort of friends, Casey!" I yelled, leaning forward to get in his face. I grabbed the side of the table and pushed it out of our way, eliminating his comfort zone. This was mano-a-mano and I was not about to back down. I could tell Ellerby was not a fighter—probably never had been—and didn't possess that killer instinct which was drilled into all young police recruits at the academy. Now, inches away from him, I saw the fear in his eyes and then recognized my own reflection in them. That's when true terror took hold of me. In recent years, I had attempted to eliminate the savage animal that resided deep within my psyche and knew the dire consequences if it were set free.

I stood up quickly, scaring the wits out of Ellerby, who probably believed I was about to strike him. As he closed his eyes anticipating the impact of my fist, I grabbed his briefcase, which I opened and emptied onto the table.

"You can't look in there," Casey shouted, as he opened one, then both eyes. "That's private property."

I lifted my left foot off the floor and firmly placed it on his crotch, which momentarily stopped him from standing up. "My house, my rules," I informed him, as I separated the reams of paper that covered the tabletop. "Here we are," I said, seizing upon one of Ellerby's assignment forms, which had the words Client Information printed on it. "And the winner is . . ."

When I finally found the right box and read the client's name, Ellerby could have taken me out simply by exhaling in my direction. "This can't be," I said, dropping the form to the floor. "He's no friend of mine," I protested in a voice that was barely audible. I stumbled backward until I encountered the wall, where I remained standing unable to move. I watched as Casey came to his senses and began to shove the strewn papers into his case while screaming obscenities at me. He ran out of the kitchen and slammed the front door behind him.

I made no effort to stop him; the damage had already been done and there was no way my mind could function properly. I bent my knees and slowly slid down the wall to the floor.

"This isn't possible," I remember saying aloud, as I looked at the information form that now lay on the cold ceramic tile beside me. At the time it didn't make any sense, but everything I needed to know about Linda's disappearance and Max's reappearance in my life was typed in two small boxes:

Client / Contact: Mr. J. L.

There was no better motivator for finding Jarvis Larsh than this, and as soon I was able to stand again that was exactly what I intended to do.

NINE

MAX

Max was in a foul mood when he reached his Santana Hills office. The previous day's blow-up with Jarvis Larsh, a classic sociopath, had troubled him all night, but he could do nothing about the situation until their next session.

Tuesday mornings used to be fun, he thought, remembering of how much he enjoyed his meetings with Alexis Penney before he had to reschedule her appointments to later in the week due to a scheduling conflict.

This Tuesday had started poorly when he had checked his messages and discovered his 10:00 a.m. client had cancelled. This meant he now had to find something to do for an hour until the formerly vivacious Melissa Wilkinson, a.k.a. Destiny Rose, a.k.a. West Coast Stripper of the Year 1987, was to arrive.

Like many exotic dancers who dabbled in porn to cover their cocaine expenses, Melissa/Destiny had *daddy issues,* as in "Why don't you love me, Daddy?" Unfortunately, as she blossomed from a flat-chested girl into a 34DD Cup teenager, her daddy had loved her, but in a very unacceptable way by any standards.

Max had heard this story many times, and with each new telling he was able to help these women better understand their feelings. He even felt he cured a few of them. As he did not have a degree in psychology, however, he could never be completely certain. When they thanked him at the conclusion of their last session, never to book another appointment, Max took it as a sign of success. He knew Melissa/Destiny would never get to that point, no matter who was treating her. She just wanted someone to talk to and was willing to pay $100 per hour to do so.

Once behind his desk, Max opened his day planner to refresh

his memory of who would be stopping by next: after Melissa/Destiny, came the neurotic thirty–seven–year–old housewife who heard creepy voices in her head; followed by a man looking to come to terms with an embezzlement plan which had caused his business partner to commit suicide; and finally, there was Kelvin Crabble, who thought he was Jesus and was distressed that the ability to walk on water had failed him while visiting a public pool. "All the kids laughed at me when I stepped off the side and immediately sank into the deep end. I need to find out what I've done to anger my Father so," he'd stated, pointing his finger in a heavenly direction. Even without formal training, Max knew Kelvin's *daddy issues,* although similar in nature, would be harder to cure than Melissa/Destiny's. Regardless, on any given day he felt he always gave his best effort no matter who was sitting across from him.

Max went to his filing cabinet and pulled each of his patients' folders to review his notes. Although the medical profession didn't officially recognize him as one of their own, he took great pride in his work, from the way he conducted his interviews—the questions he asked and the answers he gave—to the handwritten notes he jotted during each session. There was nothing about his operation that could be deemed shoddy. He possessed the one character trait all people in need of comfort and counsel required: he was a terrific listener—always had been, even in high school. The difference these days was he was paid in one form or another for this skill.

In his youth he was known as The Big Ear, which all his pretty female friends loved to bend; talking about the problems they had with their dickhead boyfriends. After dumping their loser lesser-halfs, these same girls would tell everyone what a nice guy he'd been, effectively neutering him to half the school population. It was worse than falling into the dreaded "friend zone."

After graduation he recognized his talent for talk and attended a small university a few hundred miles away from Delta to study psychology. Unfortunately, from a scholastic standpoint, he found the classes at once challenging yet also mind-numbingly boring at the same time. He dropped out during his second year due to middling marks and financial reasons. Unlike other students with cash flow issues though, Max's problem was not a shortage of funds but an abundance of incoming money—all of which was ill-gotten through one confidence scheme or another. His career as a con man actually began innocently enough one evening with the help of his roommate, Ray. Unable to scrounge up enough cash for a good night of drinking, Max devised a simple plan to make a quick twenty bucks—or at least nineteen.

"It's really easy, Ray. Trust me," Max said as they made their way to a nearby convenience store. "You walk in and buy a pack of gum, paying for it using this twenty." Ray took the bill from Max's outstretched hand.

"I don't get it—" Ray began, before being cut off.

"Stop talking because this is the important part," Max instructed. "You hand the old lady this bill and she'll give you $19 in change. Follow me so far?"

"I buy a pack of gum. What's not to understand?"

"Anyway . . . you leave and I walk in. I also buy a pack of gum but as I'm about to pay, you walk in again and say in a loud voice, 'I forgot to buy my lotto tickets,' which will temporarily distract the cashier. During your big entrance I'll hand her my money, which she'll put in the register. You then keep talking directly to her—say something stupid like, 'If I win a million dollars, I'm going to buy this store for you!'—and keep walking toward the counter. Then, getting back to my transaction, she will give me my change."

"I'm still confused. How are we making money buying two packages of gum?" Ray asked.

"I'm getting to that," Max insisted. "You see, the old lady will correctly hand me twenty-five cents change from the dollar I gave her."

"And?"

"And—here's the genius part—I say, 'Hey, lady, I gave you a twenty. You owe me $19.25, not twenty-five cents.' She will be temporarily confused and say that I gave her a dollar. I will get a little irate and yell, 'You're not gonna rip me off! I can prove I gave you a twenty—it's sitting right there in your drawer.' She'll then demand, 'Prove it.'"

Ray, who had heard a great number of Max's other outlandish ideas, stood fascinated waiting for the punch line he knew must be coming. "Lay it on me, brother," he said with a laugh.

"I'll prove it to her," Max replied nonchalantly. "She will have no choice but to hand over the other $19 and I'll walk out of the store."

"But you handed her a single," Ray noted, clearly baffled by his friend's logic. "How can you prove you gave her a twenty when you didn't? Did you learn how to hypnotize people in one of your 'I Want To Be A Shrink When I Grow Up' classes?"

"So close and yet so far, Ray," Max said, shaking his head as if disappointed. "I thought you had it there for a second. The answer lies in the fact that, yes, I didn't give her a twenty-dollar bill—you did."

"I'm not stupid, I got that part of the plan," Ray protested.

"Well, that's the key to the whole thing, buddy. Proving that the twenty you gave her was actually mine."

"How?"

"By identifying something unique on the bill."

Ray, now thoroughly confused and getting hungry, studied the bill in his hand and said, "This looks like every bill out there. How can you prove it's your special magic bill?"

"Look on the other side, Einstein."

Ray turned the bill over and saw the inscription written on the back.

"I tell the cashier I got a call from a girl last night and wrote her number on this bill," Max said, pointing proudly to the inscription he'd placed on it earlier.

"She asks what the girl's name is and you say Jenny," Ray said.

"And then I go one further and recite her phone number."

"867-5309." A huge smile crossed Ray's face. "That's freakin' genius, Max."

"Oh yes, it is," Max acknowledged. "So as long as the cashier never hears that song on the radio and puts two and two together, we're up $19—which should buy a pitcher or two tonight."

Later that night, when the pub DJ put Tommy Tutone's current hit single "867-5309/Jenny" on the turntable, Max and Ray raised their beer mugs and yelled, "To Jenny," much to the amused bewilderment of their fellow drunken classmates.

Over time, Max's cons got bigger and better, more elaborate and much more profitable. "From small acorns, large oaks grow," his grandmother often said. The line became his philosophy in life. He even had a plaque of the saying hanging on the wall opposite his desk, visible just above the heads of the patients who sat in front of him.

With ten minutes left before she arrived, Max, although thoroughly bored, was looking forward to seeing Melissa/Destiny. Life as a career stripper and porn star had taken its toll on her beauty, yet at thirty-four, or so she claimed, there were times during their sessions when Max caught wonderful glimpses of her former, youthful self. Had she not fallen into a trap of hazy peeler bars, lustful men, and an ample supply of drugs and booze, she could have been very successful in any career she chose to pursue.

Recently, Max had noticed she was going through a mid-life crisis. She began showing up wearing short jean skirts, leggings, ridiculous-looking open-toed high heels, and topped everything off with t-shirts so tight you could almost make out the scar on her chest where her fake boobs had been inserted. This fashion statement reminded Max of his wasted youth, when Pat Benatar wore similar outfits in her endless 80's music videos—which wasn't entirely a bad thing. However, a decade later this particular retro-look was more suited to impressionable girls between twelve and sixteen who had no fashion sense whatsoever. On Melissa/Destiny, however, these same clothes made her look whorish. There was no doubt when she ventured downtown she would receive plenty of attention from men, but it wasn't the kind of admiration Max knew she craved or deserved.

Max grabbed a pad of paper and jotted down a topic for Melissa/Destiny's appointment:

> *Discuss clothing and the image she*
> *really wants to convey to the public.*

When the phone rang, Max was afraid Melissa/Destiny was also calling to reschedule.

"Dr. Feldberg's office."

"Hi, Max. It's me, Alexis. Do you have a patient right now? I trust I'm not interrupting anything important."

"Not at all," Max replied, as he put both feet up on the desk. Hearing Alexis Penney's sexy voice was always a pleasure. The fact she was about to finance his latest get-rich scheme made her call that much more enjoyable. "You know I always turn off the ringer during sessions."

"Of course," she said sweetly. "Well, I wanted you to know I talked with my financial adviser and he thinks your investment is pretty sound."

"I'm really glad to hear that," Max said, as a wide grin formed on his lips. "You know, if your adviser was smart he'd invest right along with you," he laughed, knowing such an advisor only existed in Alexis' mind. He did, however, like that she was playing the game, giving the impression she had researched this project thoroughly and made a smart decision on her own—just as he had counseled her to do during their many sessions. "Recent divorcées are the best," Max once confided to a fellow grifter. "They are usually rich, angry and ready to prove to everyone how independent they've become, now there is no man around to screw things up." Thanks to Max's helpful advice and tutoring, Alexis Penney was now all of those things and more.

She had originally made an appointment to deal with the collapse of her marriage and her feelings of unimportance. She was emotionally battered and bruised, but after a few feel-good one-on-ones, Max had led her down the path of healthy self-worth and self-sufficiency to the point where she trusted him implicitly. After giving her a couple of hot stock market tips, which appeared to pay off the following day, he had hooked her. He did not explain to her the difference between paper wealth and actual wealth. On paper, it looked like she had made money almost instantaneously. In reality, her stocks were essentially worthless; part of the bigger con Max was about to pull off before high-tailing it out of town.

"I have the cashier's cheque with me now."

Come to Papa, Max thought.

"Do you want me to drop by and give it to you today?" Alexis asked.

"I have several appointments set up this afternoon. The last one will be done around 7:25. We could get together later, if you want."

"I have to visit a friend uptown for dinner. So . . . how does 8:30 sound?"

"The sooner, the better, Alexis," Max replied. "I'll see you then."

TEN

Even after apologizing for my temper and lack of decorum, Ellerby was not pleased to be hearing from me again. I also discovered during our very brief conversation that he was not a forgiving man.

"I can't wait until the Board of Ethics crucifies you!"

"Look, I said I'm sorry," I reiterated. "This never would have happened if you had told me your client's name as a professional courtesy."

"If I thought for a second I was dealing with a professional, I might have offered it up," Ellerby countered. "As it is, you're the main suspect in Linda's disappearance. Why would I give you any information?"

"You can't honestly believe that."

"I don't have time for this conversation. You answered my questions, which I'll dutifully put in my final report. What my client decides to do with this information is up to him."

"And that's what scares me," I said. "Have you ever met Mr. Larsh, Casey?"

"I don't know where you got that name. Cassidy, this conversation is—"

"Have you met him or not?" I broke in, incensed at his continued stonewalling. "Has anyone at F.Y.I. ever sat down with him face-to-face or did this file come in over the phone, followed closely by a money order? Answer this one question and I'll stop harassing you."

"I doubt that," Ellerby stated, "but just for fun I believe the file was received over the phone. How that helps you I don't know and don't care."

He hung up before I could genuinely wish him luck locating Linda, hopefully in the very near future. I was dismayed his response did not help me to come to any solid conclusions about Jarvis Larsh. Had he personally hired Ellerby or had someone pretending to be Larsh set the investigation in motion? In either case, their interest in Linda's whereabouts was disturbing. I grabbed the assignment form off the kitchen floor and looked at it again. Conspicuously absent from the client's information were an address and phone number. I suspected the retainer cheque probably had false information on it as well.

I threw the assignment form into the banker's box, wanting to file it under "U" for useless. Ellerby had not provided any new information, which was also disappointing. He had left me with what I hoped was a new lead: Tamra Collins of 347 White Avenue. The name was not familiar, but I recognized the street name and knew it was only a few blocks away. I grabbed my coat and decided a walk would do me good. Even if this person turned out to be no lead at all, at least I would get some badly-needed exercise and fresh air.

Several minutes later, I found myself standing in front of a new one-storey residence where weeds and various thistles made up the greenery of the front lawn. Small pieces of wood, siding and bricks littered the area around the porch, indicating the builder would be doing touch-ups for a little longer. As I approached the front door, a woman spoke to me from the sidewalk.

"Are you looking for Tamra?" she asked.

I turned to face a very pregnant woman who kept her distance from me, remaining near the curb. I guessed she was in her late 20's and in her final trimester.

"Actually, I am not sure she lives here," I replied, remaining on the front porch. "The telephone book has a listing for a T. Collins," I lied, "and I thought I might get lucky. Are you a friend of Tamra's?"

"Why do you want to see her?" she asked, ignoring my question. "Do you know her? Because she only recently moved here and I'm pretty sure she hasn't met many people yet—especially men. I'm also certain there is no phone book listing for her."

There was something in her voice that betrayed her apparent self-confidence. I didn't get the feeling she was the confrontational type, although she was trying hard to act like it now. Her eyes, however, were the biggest giveaway that something was not right. They stared at me with a hatred only women who truly knew me could muster, but it wasn't me she despised, it was my kind: male.

"My name is Steve Cassidy," I said, still not making any sudden moves, so as not to frighten her. "I live in the neighbourhood." Getting no response, I decided to continue. "I'm a P.I. looking into the possible disappearance of a young woman named Linda Brooks."

"What does this have to do with . . . Tamra?" she asked, stopping just short of saying 'me.'

"Well, I was speaking with another investigator who is also tracking down some leads, when Tamra's name came up," I replied with a smile.

"Why isn't he here?"

"I think he was earlier, but no one was home."

"If you're working together, why don't you know Tamra's connection to this Linda person? Doesn't the other investigator trust you?"

I laughed. "That's putting it mildly. We may be working the same case but that doesn't mean we're working on the same team."

"So, do you want to find this woman or make sure she stays out of sight?"

It was more of a statement than a question.

"Trust me, I want to see Linda alive more than anyone. As for Tamra, I was hoping she could help me in some small way. Maybe she saw something she doesn't know is important to the case. The other investigator was tight-lipped, so I figured I'd drop by Tamra's place to ask a few questions. That's all. I have no hidden agenda."

"How can you say that, Mr. Cassidy, when Linda was your girl-friend?" came the blunt reply. "You screwed around and embarrassed her in front of the whole world. Then when she leaves, you feel the need to track her down like an animal? No hidden agenda? I read the papers. I know who you are and what you did."

"I'm guilty of all charges, Tamra," I replied. At the mention of her name the expression on her face turned from anger to fear. "I want you to know I have no idea who you are, where you came from or what your story is. I'm here because an investigator named Casey Ellerby wrote your name on a piece of paper that I saw earlier today. That's it. Whatever or whoever you're running from is not my business. I was hoping we could talk about Linda for a minute and then I'll leave."

"I want to believe you, I really do," Tamra said, now fighting back tears. "I just wanted to start over with my baby and next thing I know two investigators are at my door."

I took a tentative step off the porch. "I used to be a police officer and know exactly what you're going through. You probably got married too young to the wrong guy, then decided enough was enough and walked away, right?" Her facial features softened and she nodded her head. "I'm not here about your past. Neither is Mr. Ellerby. We're looking for Linda, hoping to find her happy and healthy."

"But I've never met her, Mr. Cassidy." She wiped a tear from her cheek and I wanted to depart, yet knew I couldn't.

"Ellerby thinks you have and he's not as dumb as his porn star moustache looks—you'll see." This brought a smile to Tamra's face and for the first time, I felt we had made a sincere bond. I turned and looked at the house. "This is a very nice place. Nice neighbourhood too."

"I moved in last week. Everything is a mess right now."

"When last week?"

"Monday. Why?"

"Because that's the day Linda left me," I said.

"I still don't see a connection," Tamra stated.

An idea popped into my mind. "What company did you use to move here?"

"It was Get Out of Town Movers."

"I've never heard of them," I admitted. "Now, I know I said your personal life wasn't of any interest earlier but could you tell me where they're located?"

She eyed me warily for a moment. "Out of Timlinville," she said cautiously, "although they have quite a few other locations as well."

"What time did the movers leave here?" I asked excitedly.

"I don't know—maybe around five, five–thirty."

"Do you have their number?"

"I think I have their card here," she said opening her purse. Moments later she handed me a business card.

"How long in advance did you book your move?" I asked, trying to figure out some time when Linda may have called this company.

"It was very short notice—like a day. That is their specialty. They apparently got their name after helping deadbeats or criminals move everything overnight."

"Get Out of Town Movers, of course," I said. "Pretty clever." I thought back to when I came home to find Linda's possessions gone. Maybe she'd had help moving her stuff after all. I had just never considered professionals doing it.

"I still don't know how the other P.I. got my name," Tamra said.

"Maybe he figured Linda hired a company and in the course of his inquiries your name came up as someone who also moved that day. He might have hoped you and Linda had bumped into each other at the office or the movers mentioned they had another job that night." I noticed Tamra's eyebrows furrow. "Did they say anything about another move that night?"

"Nothing specific," she said. "Only that they were happy no furniture would have to be moved at their next job."

"Did they say where they were moving this person?"

"Not that I recall."

"Doesn't matter," I said, not wanting to pressure her more.

"I wish I could help you, Mr. Cassidy."

"It's Steve and you already have."

Before leaving, Tamra asked what she should tell Ellerby when he came by.

"Everything you told me. He may have contacts I don't who could lead us to Linda."

"And what if she doesn't want to be found?"

"Like you?"

"Yeah—like me."

"When you hastily left your former home, did you tell anyone your plans? A family member, a co-worker or friend?"

"Of course."

"Then you really haven't disappeared, have you? The information is out there with people you trust. The important thing is one particular person has no clue where you are, right?"

"That's what I'm hoping," she said as she gave her belly a circular rub with both hands.

"In Linda's case she hasn't contacted anyone she trusts, which is very worrisome. As for you, Tamra, your secret is safe with me." I took a pen out of my coat pocket and wrote my telephone number on the mover's business card, which I handed to her. "I don't know if you know anyone in Darrien but if you ever need help, give me a call."

She took the card and said, "Thanks, I will."

All the way home my thoughts were of Linda and how I hoped her disappearing act was one she'd planned alone. So far the execution of her great escape had been perfect. Evidently, no one—not even Ellerby's mysterious client—knew her whereabouts.

"Just call someone, Linda," I said aloud, as I climbed my front steps.

I entered the house and did a quick tour of the rooms, confirming I'd had no unwanted visitors while away. A check of my answering machine revealed I had two messages.

"Hi, Steve. It's Maria," the first message started. "Can you give me a call at home when you get this?"

Short and to the point. This was not a good sign she would be accompanying me on my road trip. The second message was equally discouraging.

"Hey, Steve. Remember that creepy P.I.?" Dawn asked. "Well, he came by again and asked me a whole pile of questions about our relationship. What did you tell him? You didn't take that kiss too seriously, did you? It was a joke . . . kinda . . . I guess. I don't know—anyway, give me a call."

I called neither.

"Hello. Is this Get Out of Town Movers?"

"Yeah. How can I help you?"

"I'm hoping you can find an item that was somehow misplaced during my sister's move last week—last Monday, to be exact."

"What's her last name and where does she live?"

"The name is Collins. She moved to 347 White Avenue in Darrien."

"Hold on."

I could hear papers being rustled on the other end, as well as a few choice curse words spoken in a low tone.

"Yeah—we moved her. What's the problem?"

"Well, she's missing a small box containing some family heir-looms and—"

"And she thinks one of my guys stole it?"

"No—not at all. She was very happy with their work. She said they were very professional."

"That I'm glad to hear. Now, why does she think we have this box? At the end of each move, our truck's cargo hold is completely empty. We sweep it out as soon as they return to the garage."

"She thought it might have been hidden under the moving blankets. I guess they were bunched up on the floor and she swears she packed the box that morning."

"Like I said, we sweep the truck out and also fold up the blankets. So there's no way—"

"But she said your movers were heading to another job. She thinks that maybe this small box was mixed up with the next person's possessions. Do you see what I mean? Your guys didn't go back to the garage, they went to another job. Probably, at the end of that move they swept everything out and folded up the blankets."

"Hmmm . . . give me a sec." I could hear him walk away from the counter and then yell, "Kenny, did you find any small boxes in the truck last Monday?" I couldn't hear Kenny's response, only the manager's. "I dunno how small it was. Small—that's all I know. There's a guy on the phone says you clowns buried it in the blankets or something." Again, Kenny's response was unintelligible. "Is it possible you threw it in with the next move?"

For the first time, I clearly heard Kenny's response. "That guy's crazy. There was no box. Period."

The manager came back on the line. "My head guy doesn't remember any box. I'm sure your wife or sister—whoever—put it away in a safe place and just hasn't unpacked it yet. We see that all the time."

"Well . . . I suppose that's a possibility," I said, as I finally got around to the real reason for this call. "My sister is pregnant and under a lot of stress with the move and baby and all. I wanted to make sure."

"Hey, no problem."

"An idea just occurred to me though. I know you're a busy man and I believe your guys didn't cause any mix-ups, but could you give me the address they went to after my sister's? Maybe the box got missed and ended up at the other house. I want to cover all the bases before calling her."

In the background, I heard Kenny yell, "We could use your help, Murray."

"I really don't think that is the case, mister."

"Neither do I . . . still . . . I would like to check it out for myself. If the box is found, great. If not, my sister isn't going after your company for compensation or anything like that. I promise."

"Murray!"

"Under normal circumstances, I don't give out this information."

"I completely understand."

There was more shuffling of papers. "Got a pen? The address is 3795 Adelaide Crescent."

"Do you have the address you moved these people from and their name?"

"Holy cow, I didn't think this was going to be twenty questions. Hold on. Okay, here it is. The name was J.L. Brooks and the address was 199 Graham Street. Now I gotta go."

Murray hung up, leaving me on the line dumbfounded. I put the phone down and stared at a water bill on the counter. The address in the small plastic window read: 199 Graham Street, Darrien.

J. L.

Yet another Jarvis Larsh reference. Great.

I'm in over my head, I thought to myself. *Way over.*

"Maria, it's me. I got your message." I was so pumped I didn't wait for her to reply. "A couple of those coincidences are no longer coincidental and hope you've decided to come with me."

"Hello to you too, Steve," Maria said with a sarcastic edge in her voice. "What new developments have occurred since we last talked? Can they wait until I get down there?"

"Yes, they can wait," I said slowly, realizing Maria was planning to help me find Larsh. "Actually, they can't." I proceeded to update her about the initials on Ellerby's client contact and the mover's customer information.

"So, all this danger stuff you've been preaching is for real?" Maria asked.

"Yes . . . well, maybe . . . I don't really know," I stammered. "Someone is either trying to scare me and the threat against you is genuine, or this is all some type of cruel practical joke. One thing I now know for sure is there appears to be a definite connection between Linda and Jarvis Larsh."

"Or someone impersonating him."

"Maybe," I admitted. "However, imagine if someone was copying a serial killer's crimes. Would they be any less dangerous than the original? The answer is no."

"If you're trying to scare me, you're doing a good job."

"I promise I'm not. It's just that I can't rest until I know what is really going on and who is behind all this turmoil. That's why I want you on this trip—so you're close to me."

"As friends, right?"

"Yeah, friends."

"A knight in shining armour protecting a damsel in distress—how medieval," Maria laughed. "I will go on one condition."

"Anything."

"That we won't get bogged down in our romantic past, when we were young and stupid."

"When I was young and stupid," I corrected her.

"Yeah—that's what I really meant," she chuckled.

"I'll do my best to keep things on the up and up, how's that?"

"Sounds wishy-washy."

"I'm hoping we can work as a team to solve this thing and get you back to your pleasant stress-free life in Delta in no time," I said. "With Trudy and Wayne and their clan."

"And others," she said, her voice trailing off as if teasing me.

"Is there something you want to tell me?"

"Not on the phone. There will be plenty of time over the next few days to get caught up."

"Sounds ominous."

"You can handle ominous, can't you?"

"I can handle anything you throw my way—I think."

We talked about her schedule and decided I would pick her up at the train station in two days. We would then fully plan the trip and leave Darrien by nightfall.

"The goal is to take care of this stupidity as soon as possible. I think Max's search for Larsh and Linda's disappearance are related somehow. I believe once we solve one mystery, the dominoes in the other will start to fall."

"And we'll live happily ever—" A loud clicking sound interrupted her sentence. "Steve, I have to go. There's another call I need to take."

"Okay," I said tentatively, not accustomed to Maria blowing me off so casually. "It must be important."

"He is," she replied. "See you Tuesday morning. Goodbye, Steve"

"Yeah, sure. See you then."

With a flick of her finger she disconnected our call to talk with some new man in her life. I began to worry our cross-country trip might not be the nostalgia-filled journey I had hoped. Even after setting down the phone, fragments of my conversation with Maria would not be silenced.

As friends, right?
Not on the phone.
And others.

He is.

Goodbye, Steve.

Two's company, three's a crowd, I thought. Of all people, I should know. I had been doing this pathetic arithmetic with women all my life and still hadn't managed to get it right. With Linda gone and Maria going fast, I wondered where my love life was heading.

Just then the phone rang.

Without pleasantries Dawn's insistent voice greeted me with, "I have to talk to you."

"I'm walking out the door this minute," I said, thinking I would take a tour by Linda's supposed new address.

"I'll be there in ten minutes."

"I honestly have somewhere I need to go," I protested mildly.

"This is important and I'm hoping you can clear this up right now."

"Clear what up?"

The line unexpectedly went silent. I could picture Dawn grabbing her coat and running out of the pub. From the tone in her voice, my concern was she was running from someone or something and not simply running to me.

I placed the phone back in its charger and vowed not to pick it up again until morning. It was causing far too much chaos in my life.

I was sitting nervously in the living room when I heard the front door open. Then it was slammed closed and Dawn came stomping across the hall toward me, waving a piece of paper in her hand.

"I thought I could trust you, so I'm only going to ask this once, Steve. What is this?" Dawn demanded, stopping in front of my chair, hovering over me like a hungry vulture.

For a moment, I was transported back to my old bedroom where I was listening to Pink Floyd's *The Wall* through headphones. I remember the door flying open, scaring the crap out of me. Thinking we were under attack and this was a home invasion, my body instinctively lifted off the bed like a rocket, with my arms flailing in all directions and my ears almost ripped off as the headphones were thrown across the room. During those first few frightening seconds, I don't know what came out of my mouth but I do recall my mother was not very pleased with my language. The fact she was already in a heightened state of irritation also did not bode well for the celebration of my upcoming sixteenth birthday.

"What did I do wrong?" my mom screamed at me, her face red with anger and frustration. I had no idea what she meant until she threw a condom package at my chest. "What is this?"

"Well . . . it's a . . ." I stammered.

"I know what it is! I'm not stupid, Steven!" she declared for the entire neighbourhood to hear. "I want to know how this got into your jeans and I want to know now!"

By the age of fifteen-and-a-half you're either no longer intimidated by your parents or they still control you night and day. I was in the latter category, still trying to get through puberty in one piece. So, instead of telling her the truth—that out of curiosity, I had borrowed it from a jar my friend Korner had under his bed—I lied and said, "They were handing them out in health class, Mom."

"They were not!" she stated categorically.

"Well . . . Mr. Snyder was talking about them and showed us what they looked like in class," I offered up, trying to think of an explanation that would satisfy my mother. "At the end of class I noticed one of the packages on the floor and picked it up." I foolishly believed I saw a slight fading of colour on my mother's cheeks. To top off my far-fetched explanation, I said something that makes me laugh even today.

"I wasn't going to use it or anything!"

"It's worth a million dollars, Steve."

How a condom could be worth that much was beyond me, until I realized it was Dawn—not my mother—making the statement.

"I'm confused," I said truthfully, as I snapped my thoughts back to the present.

"Read it," Dawn demanded, throwing the piece of paper at me.

I had never seen her like this and could not imagine how I had upset her. However, as I skimmed the contents of the life insurance policy she'd brought, it began to make sense.

"Where did you get this?" I asked, waving the photocopy in front of her. "Because it's bogus, Dawn. This doesn't exist."

"It sure looks real," she said, not backing down.

"Someone fabricated this to make me look bad, which seems like a complete waste of time when you think about it. The press hasn't exactly been complimentary to me."

"Is that your signature?" she asked, pointing to the bottom of the policy.

I looked at the penmanship again and it certainly did resemble my handiwork. "My signature is all over the place. On contracts, bank paperwork for the house or my investigator's licence application. This proves nothing."

"It's dated two weeks before Linda disappeared."

"It's dated two weeks before Linda left," I corrected her as I got out of the recliner, causing her to step back as if fearing repercussions. "It's not true, Dawn," I said in a soft voice. "It's a smear campaign."

"I . . . I just . . ."

"I know what this looks like, I do." I let out a long sigh and started toward the kitchen. "Do you want a juice while you're here?" I stopped and turned to face her. She was staring at the pages in her hand with a lost expression on her face. "Can I assume you're going to stick around awhile? And yes, I know you should never assume anything, because it usually makes an ass out of you and me."

Dawn looked up at me. "My dad used to tell me that all the time," she said with a slight smile. "I guess I'm guilty of that tonight, aren't I?"

"Maybe, maybe not," I replied. "If you contact that insurance company tomorrow and they have an agent who can identify me as the person who signed that policy, then your assumption will be correct. No harm, no foul." I walked to the refrigerator and opened it. "On the other hand, I seriously doubt the company or salesman exists and if it does, there is no record of that particular policy."

"Then why would Ellerby leave this for me if he knows it isn't real?"

I popped my head out of the fridge. "Ellerby did this?"

"After leaving here he came to talk to me at the pub. I told him you and I had only known one another a short time and that we were definitely not romantically involved."

"Good," I replied, still a bit puzzled. "When did he show you the policy?"

"He didn't exactly show me. After he left, I found it between the ketchup and mustard bottles at his table. It was in an envelope with my name on it."

He's got to be in on this, I thought to myself. I began to ponder how many other people he had shown this fake to during his investigation. I worried what Tamra would think when he returned to speak with her. Reluctantly, I decided there was nothing I could do. I would simply have to find out how Ellerby was connected to Larsh and Linda's *departure*. First, I had to get Dawn onside again.

"If that policy were real, don't you think Ellerby would have given it to the police on a silver platter? It practically proves I had something to do with Linda's . . ."

"Disappearance?" Dawn suggested.

"Yeah—whatever," I said, shaking my head and rolling my eyes.

She folded the paper and put it in her pocket. "I'm going to check this out, you know that, right?"

I ignored her. "Apple or fruit punch?"

"You're changing the subject. Isn't that an indication you are avoiding this conversation?"

"No. I've dealt with it and the new subject is about beverages that live in my fridge," I said. "Apple or fruit punch—and don't even think of changing the subject again."

This brought a full smile to Dawn's thin lips for the first time. "Apple. How's that for an answer?"

I walked into the living room and handed her one of the bottles in my hand. "It's a good answer but I may have to interrogate you later to learn what you have against fruit punch."

As I stood before Dawn our eyes locked and for the second time today a current of electricity ran through me.

"I have to follow up a new lead on the case," I said slowly.

Dawn's gaze did not move from mine. "You're changing the subject again," she said.

"Weren't we finished with the topic of our favourite beverages?" I said.

"We were."

"Then?"

"Are you ever going to make the first move?"

Ironically, it was Dawn who moved first, taking a small step toward me.

"I'm a bit perplexed—again. Didn't you come storming through the front door five minutes ago ready to rip me apart limb by limb, accusing me of kidnapping or murder or something of the kind?"

She ignored the question and changed the subject, almost losing me along the way. "I watch a lot of television," she said, still not allowing me to break her stare. "I especially like old shows like Cheers and Moonlighting. They play them all day long on the Rerun Channel."

"I personally don't consider those two shows to be particularly old—"

"And what I really like about them," Dawn said cutting me off, "is when the male and female leads get into heated arguments, even when everyone knows they are really attracted to one another. All we want is for them to shut up and get it on, but do they? No. Week after week the writers dance around the issue, writing foreplay dressed up as smart dialogue, until the poor sex-starved viewer at home is about to explode all over the couch cushions." She briefly paused to gauge my reaction to her foreplay dressed up in smart dialogue, before continuing her dissertation on famous television couples. "Then, after three or four seasons they finally do it. The ratings skyrocket and the entire country rejoices in unison from sea to shining sea. But do you recall what usually occurs moments before their first embrace?"

I thought I did—at least in the case of Sam Malone and Diane

Chambers on Cheers. "They were screaming at each other about something stupid, like the number of cardboard coasters they needed to order."

"Are you sure it wasn't about a shady insurance policy taken out on the bar?"

"Yeah, pretty sure."

Unlike earlier, I now succumbed to temptation and leaned slightly forward to kiss Dawn. I confess the idea of her standing sexily on the tip of her toes to reach my lips had popped into my wretched mind on a few occasions throughout the day. The first real kiss is almost always magical, even if the mechanics are sometimes off. After a few moments, we collapsed on the couch where we found a happy balance between lust and romance.

"You're not going to run away like you did this morning?" I asked.

"Only if you do something wrong," she said with a warm smile.

"Are we still going to be friends?"

"Not if you keep talking."

I willingly obeyed and let Dawn take control of me for the next hour. I had no idea where this would lead and didn't care. I didn't feel I was taking advantage of Dawn and honestly thought we had something, which could not be defined currently. In my last two ill-fated relationships, I had made snap judgments which had real emotional consequences for both Linda and Samantha. With Dawn, though, I didn't get that same vibe. She was completely independent and making up her own rules as she went along. I couldn't hurt her if I tried. Would it have been better if we'd met a few months down the line? Probably. Would our attraction and compatibility be diminished? Probably not.

Then why not live in the now, now?

At one point during our lovemaking, I felt a pang of guilt and saw myself at a Dumbass Anonymous meeting saying, "Hi. My name is Steve and I need help. I am my own worst enemy and constantly screw up my life for no apparent reason."

Still . . . as Dawn fell asleep in my arms I was at peace, even though I knew this calm could not last. Regardless whether Dawn had used me like her other boyfriends-on-the-side, I wasn't worried. If this was the one and only time we spent together, I would be fine with it because you only live once.

As I turned off the night table lamp, I was fairly certain Dawn was also living her life by this same motto. If she wasn't, things were about to get a lot more problematic for the both of us.

ELEVEN

JARVIS

From the moment he'd laid eyes on Alexis Penney he was smitten. With her long red hair cascading past her shoulders, he really had no choice in the matter. They once had shared an elevator at the Upstate Medical Building. Well, they hadn't actually been on the elevator at the same time—he was stepping off, as she was getting on—but in his mind they had been linked forever as they brushed by one another on the 23rd floor. He'd been too overwhelmed by her beauty to say anything and for days afterward he chastised himself for not being able to utter a simple, "Hello."

After his new love began her lonely descent to the lobby, Jarvis realized she had left something behind for him. He stood in the hallway a yard from the elevator doors, just as she had done moments earlier, and inhaled the lingering scent of her perfume. It was a breathtaking mixture of fruit with a hint of lavender, which made his head spin in ecstasy. As his mind swam in her intoxicating bouquet of raw sexuality, his hands instinctively reached forward as if to pull her phantom body toward his.

"Are you okay?" a female voice asked him.

As a woman walked into view, the spell was broken and he immediately put his hands at his sides.

"Yes, of course," he said, giving her a brief smile as she pushed the elevator button on the wall. She continued to gaze at him with a concerned expression. "I get a bit disoriented at these heights. I've never been this high up in a building," he lied.

"Oh," she said. "You get used to it." Seeing as this peculiar man wasn't moving from his spot, she asked, "What office are you looking for? I might be able to help."

"2309."

"Dr. Feldberg. His office is down the hall to the right."

"Okay, thanks." Jarvis took a few steps in the direction she had indicated and stopped. "I know this is going to sound strange," he said, facing the woman again. "Would you know what brand of perfume is currently in the hallway here? A moment ago a woman got on the elevator and she wears the same fragrance as my girl-friend. I wanted to buy a new bottle as a gift—a surprise—and can't remember its name." He gave her an awkward sincere smile, which she returned.

"Well, I don't know . . ." she said as she turned up her nose and tried to locate the aroma in the air. After a few sniffs, her face lit up. "You know, I think it's called Majestic or Magical—something along those lines. I'm pretty sure it starts with M."

"Can I buy it in stores or is it a special order?"

The woman thought the question was odd but knew Max Feldberg dealt with some strange people. "You can buy it at any department store or drug store. I don't think it's too expensive."

At this news Jarvis lit up; a wide appreciative grin beamed across his face. "Thank you. Thank you very much," he said, before walking down the hallway.

"Glad I could help," the woman said, pleased the elevator had arrived. As she pressed her floor number all she could think was how it took all kinds to make the world go around.

Jarvis caught his reflection in the windowpane of an invest-ment office and assessed his appearance. At 6'2", with a gangly 179-pound build, short-cropped brown hair and a three-day growth of scruffy beard, he knew when he entered a room he didn't turn heads or set women's hearts aflutter. He wasn't unattractive; just not movie star attractive. During his twenty-nine years on the planet, he had gained the interest of several females—"Are you ready to ride the Jarvo train?"—and felt he had satisfied them, whether they'd known each other a few hours, a few days or a few months. Yet lately he was enduring quite a lengthy dry spell. He'd brought up his dilemma with Dr. Feldberg at the end of their previous session and hoped they could continue their discussion today.

He took a seat in the reception area, knowing the doctor would call him in shortly. He liked Dr. Feldberg, who was less formal than all the other court-ordered stuffed shirts he usually saw. It was as if the doctor was a regular Joe, not some highly trained windbag, which appealed to Jarvis immensely.

He's normal, just like me.

The reception door opened and Max greeted Jarvis with a warm smile. "How are things going today, Jarvis?" he asked as they entered the inner office.

"I just met a girl and think she might be the one," Jarvis said excitedly.

Max took his place in a leather chair across from Jarvis Larsh. "Let me guess—she's a redhead, right?"

Over the next several weeks, Jarvis and his dream girl continued to pass one another in the hallway, each encounter an answer to his nightly prayers. It wasn't until he caught a whiff of her perfume in Max's office that his world began falling apart.

"Are you seeing my girlfriend behind my back?" Jarvis asked at the start of his session.

"What are you talking about?" Max asked. His patient had brought up many off-the-wall topics but this one was new. "I don't know your girlfriend, Jarvis. Where did you get such an idea?"

"Because I see her in this building all the time."

"Does she work here? I might have run into her on occasion."

"She wears Mystical perfume," came the blunt response. "I bought her three bottles at the drug store."

Still puzzled, Max asked, "Did you give them to her?"

"Not yet. I'm saving them for a special occasion."

"Like her birthday or Christmas?"

"Stop asking questions and answer mine!" Jarvis demanded, looking every bit a wild animal preparing to pounce.

"Slow down. Take it easy. It's me, Dr. Max. I'm your friend and friends don't fool around with other friend's girlfriends, right?" The answer briefly pacified Jarvis. "So . . . to answer your question, no,

I am not seeing your girl. I wouldn't do that to you."

Jarvis stood and anxiously began pacing the small office. "I can smell her in here," he said. "She's been here!"

Oh, crap, Max thought, as he slowly got out of his chair and made his way behind his large mahogany desk, creating a barrier between them. He was also now within reach of the telephone, where he tried to recall which speed dial number would bring security running. "Why do you say that? Help me to understand what's going on here."

Jarvis walked out into the reception area and began inhaling deeply through his flared nostrils. He then ventured into the hallway and started toward the elevators. Max had to decide quickly if he should run to the hall door, close it softly and lock it, or investigate what Jarvis was doing. Against his better judgment, he stuck his head around the corner of his office door and peered down the hall.

"This is where we met," Jarvis proclaimed. "Right here at these elevators."

"This is news to me. You've never said where you two lovebirds first hooked up."

Jarvis started toward the office and Max again made a beeline behind his desk. He grabbed the cordless phone, ready to alert the building's guards of a crisis in Suite 2309.

"You two must think I'm pretty dumb," Jarvis said as he entered the office. "What's the deal—she comes here an hour before my appointment, so you can do her on the desk? Or does she ride you in the chair I sit in week in and week out? Do you know how sick that is?"

I certainly do, freak, Max thought to himself. "Why exactly do you think she was here?"

"Her perfume. It's all over this place. So don't keep lying to me, Dr. Max, I know what she smells like."

"Lavender," Max said under his breath, finally clueing in to what Jarvis was trying to say. "Red hair," he muttered, shaking his head in disbelief. "Your girlfriend is Alexis Penney?"

Jarvis stared blankly at him. "Penny?" he asked, hearing for the first time the names of his beloved. "Alexis?"

Max had treated Jarvis long enough to know exactly what was going on and he feared not only for his life but for Alexis' as well. From day one, Jarvis had indicated his absolute loathing for all women with red hair. Yet, in the same session he would profess his desire to be around redheads. From court papers, Max had learned Jarvis' abusive mother was a natural redhead, as was his girlfriend—the one he had beaten to within an inch of her life. His prison sentence was six years but with good behaviour, and presumably, no interaction with auburn-haired female staff, he'd been paroled after three-and-a-half years of incarceration. However, a condition of his release was he had to see a shrink once a week for one year. After three court-appointed psychiatrists deemed Jarvis uncooperative, someone offered up Max's good name and he now found himself in a pickle.

"She is also a patient of mine," Max said enthusiastically, attempting to defuse the human bomb standing across from him. "What are the odds of that? At your wedding you two better give me credit as a bona fide matchmaker." For a fleeting moment, Max felt he had dodged a bullet; Jarvis remained in place with a dazed expression on his face. Believing his patient had entered some type of self-induced trance, in a stern authoritative voice Max said, "I now want you to relax and take a seat in your chair, Jarvis. Let all the stress in your body float away."

Jarvis made no effort to sit or allow anything to float from his body.

"I trusted you, Dr. Feldberg."

"And you still can. Nothing is going on between Alexis and me, I swear. She's my patient and talks about her new boyfriend all the time," Max lied, desperately seeking a way out of this situation with all his limbs intact. "I just didn't know the lucky guy was you."

"Stop it!" Jarvis cried out. "I know you're not telling me the truth. There is something going on between you and . . . ah . . . Alexis."

Jarvis stormed out of the office, slamming the door behind

him. Max grabbed his phone and called the security desk. "I want to give you a heads-up. One of my patients is a bit upset and may show it when he leaves the building. His name is Jarvis Larsh—a very tall, gawky male with short dark hair. He's wearing a blue shirt, jeans and running shoes. Please ignore his rants and let him leave peacefully. He's letting off some steam and isn't a threat to anyone."

"If you say so, Dr. Feldberg. We'll keep an eye out for him."

"Thanks."

The next issue Max had to deal with concerned Alexis. Should he inform her that a crazed ex-con believed they were a romantic item? *Things are too complicated with her as it is*, he thought. She'd promised to call him in a couple of days about a stock investment he'd been touting the past few sessions. He definitely didn't want to spook her in any way with matters not related to money. To eliminate the possibility of Jarvis and Alexis seeing each other again, he would simply schedule them at opposite ends of the week. There was no way Jarvis was smart enough to track her down. If by some miracle he did locate her in the coming weeks, it wouldn't really matter to Max. He figured he'd be long gone from the scene and setting up his palatial estate in the Bahamas.

As expected, Jarvis stomped out of the elevator cursing and screaming. The security guard stood up from his chair and carefully watched the man head toward the main doors. Upon Jarvis' exit from the building, the guard sat behind his desk, thankful he didn't have to subdue Dr. Feldberg's patient.

The guard had been so focused on Larsh's departure, he'd paid no attention to a man in his late 30's who was also intrigued by the crazy man's actions. As soon as Jarvis hit the sidewalk, the man was on his tail, walking several yards behind him. This wasn't the first time he had followed Larsh, but he hoped it would be the last. A short time later, just as he had done after the previous four Dr. Feldberg appointments, Jarvis walked into the Shakin'

Pussycat Bar and took a seat in a booth beside the stage. By now the man knew what to expect next: Jarvis would order a double shot of whiskey with a splash of cola and then wait anxiously for his favourite dancer—a red-haired peeler named Destiny Rose—to perform.

That he had even become aware of this person still amazed the man. He'd been tracking Alexis' movements for weeks when he noticed this poor sap following her as well, hanging around the edges, out of view. Due to his amateur investigative techniques however, Jarvis would lose sight of Alexis as she entered a mall or taxi, and still had no idea where she actually lived. This would play nicely into the man's overall plans for the woman.

From Jarvis' haggard appearance, something extraordinary must have happened during today's session. Believing there is no one better with whom to discuss your problems than a stranger in a sleazy strip club, the man hastily formulated a strategy.

Before making his move, he allowed the hard-working stripper to perform on stage without interruption. After she departed, he brought two glasses of whiskey to Jarvis' booth and placed them on the table. "Mind if I sit here, friend?"

Already half in the bag from his own drinks, Jarvis said, "Sure, why not?" He eyed the glasses. "Is one of those for me?"

"You betcha," the stranger said. "Have both if you like. I have to get to work soon anyway."

"Where do you work?" Jarvis asked, as he snatched up a glass and brought it to his lips.

"The Indelible Corporation building. You know—across from the Upstate Medical Centre." His building name-dropping had its desired effect.

Jarvis let out a loud, long belch. "I know the place. Full of liars and cheaters."

"Really? Anyone in particular I should avoid there?" the man asked, feigning interest as he took a quick sip of the remaining drink.

"Max Feldberg! Suite 2309! He fools around with his patients' girlfriends." Jarvis' words were becoming heavily slurred.

It is now or never.

"Is that what he did to you—sleep with your girlfriend?"

"Yes," Jarvis stammered.

"Sorry to hear that. I should be asking what your former girlfriend's name is as well, so I can avoid her too. I wouldn't want you to be upset with me."

Jarvis looked at the man and tried to figure out how they knew each other. The most likely place they might have met was in prison, but this man was clean-cut and wearing a nice suit. Still, somewhere in Jarvis' increasingly disordered mind he felt a kinship, as if they were old army buddies—even though he had never enlisted. Or fraternity brothers—even though he never graduated from high school.

"Do I know you?"

"Not yet," came the reply. "First, what's your girlfriend's name?"

"Penny," Jarvis blurted out.

"And she cheated on you with this doctor?" the man asked, believing Jarvis was simply too drunk to differentiate between his prey's first and last names.

"No!" Jarvis bellowed. "He cheated on me—the doctor. He seduced her or something."

"Don't kid yourself, it takes two to tango. While your doctor was doing her, she was screwing you, pal. I'd seriously think about killing my girlfriend if that ever happened to me."

Their conversation took an unexpected break as they watched Destiny Rose take to the stage with her six-inch high heels, thong bikini bottom and mesh tank top.

"Redheads are the worst," the man stated, turning his attention to Larsh. "I once went with a woman who did every guy in my office without my knowledge. When I found out, she disappeared."

"Did you kill her?" Jarvis asked with a sloppy grin. "I would have," he added.

"I didn't have the opportunity. She just left." The man stirred his drink with a finger and said, "You and I have a lot in common, friend." He lifted his glass in a toast. "To Alexis Penney—may she rot in Hell!" he declared. "Cheating little tramp."

Jarvis stared flabbergasted across the tabletop, realizing he had mixed up her names earlier. "I . . . I know her," he spat out. "She's the one who—"

"Slept with the doc? Get outta here. You've got to be kidding." Jarvis, now in a complete state of shock, shook his head. "That bitch screwed both of us over and you say you know where she is today?"

"I do."

"I think you and I are about to become very good friends. I didn't catch your name."

"It's Jarvis Larsh."

The man put down his now-empty glass and stretched his right hand across the table.

"Nice to meet you, Jarvis. My name is Derek McDonald."

TWELVE

Watching someone sleep can be very relaxing and thought-provoking. My ex-wife used to tell me how she'd sit in a chair at the side of our bed and simply watch me. She'd monitor the rise and fall of my chest and the rapid eye movement under my lids as I dreamt, making sure I was okay after a long police shift. I asked why she would do such a thing, to which she replied, "Because I want to get to know all of you. Not just the Steve Cassidy who eats, drinks, goes to work and sits in front of the television set every day."

Hearing this, I inquired if she liked this year's Steve Asleep or Steve Awake model.

"I guess the Steve Asleep one. He's less complicated," she said with a beguiling smile.

Upon waking up alone, I wondered if Dawn shared the same sentiment as she had awakened to go to work. I'm sure she glanced down at me for at least a moment or two to assess her latest conquest and decide if she had made a sound decision or a huge mistake. When I checked my reflection in the mirror I was certain the first thought that screamed through her pretty head was, "What have I done?" I could almost picture her throwing on her clothes and running out the front door.

For a thirty–two–year–old, my body is still in reasonably good condition. On the force, you stayed in shape so you could keep up with all those fleeing criminals. It was much more fun tackling them a few blocks away and beating the bejeezes out of them for resisting arrest than getting winded after forty steps because your meals were ordered at a drive-thru window. Dawn never mentioned the three-inch scar that ran down my left cheek from the base of my eye to the jawbone. I am sure the topic will come up once we have come to know each other a bit better. That scar, however, was not as troubling as the one on my stomach, which I hoped Dawn hadn't noticed as we played in the dark recesses of my bedroom. Even after three years of healing it looks nasty, running horizontally across my abdomen for ten long inches. The most hideous aspect was that the cut had not been clean. The crazed gang member I was fighting made sure of that, as he twisted and moved his mini-machete side to side, leaving a mangled, jagged flesh wound across my skin. Had he applied a tad more pressure, he would have succeeded in gutting me like a fish and I surely would have died with my intestines bursting outward as if escaping a chamber of horrors. Luckily, my partner arrived in the nick of time and blew the vicious attacker away with a shot to his forehead.

"She's probably repulsed by you," I said to my mirrored twin. "You look like a botched Frankenstein experiment. It's too bad because I think we really like her."

My lookalike remained silent—never a good sign in these circumstances.

I found a handwritten note on the kitchen table.

We're a pretty good undercover team. Call me.
- Me

Evidently not all the townsfolk were scared of Frankenstein's creature, I thought.

I had a shower and made a quick call to the pub. "I wanted to make sure you got to work okay."

"I did," Dawn said, "Although I wish I'd had the day off."

"If you had, you'd be stuck in my van for a couple of hours on a mini-road trip to Sussex this morning."

"That's not exactly what I had in mind."

"I'm sure," I laughed. "I have to follow up that lead I was telling you about last night."

"Checking out your girlfriend's new love pad?"

"Ex-girlfriend."

"Whatever," she replied nonchalantly. "When will you be back?"

"Hopefully this afternoon. Did you want to get together for dinner?"

"I can't. Remember that guy from the beach?"

"The one who only likes techno-music?" I asked, surprising myself with this nugget of trivia.

"Wow—you should try out for a game show today." Dawn said. "But yeah, him. We're going to see a band at Oranges tonight."

"What band?"

"Sex At Seven"

"Is the opening act called Foreplay At Six Forty-Five?" I chuckled. "Needless to say, Dawn, I am not familiar with their body of work."

"That's too bad. You don't know what you're missing," Dawn said.

"I do like the name. I'm sure they have a big following of horny college students."

"And hot pub waitresses," she added. There was a pause before she asked, "So, you're cool with me going out with Kyle?"

"Is this a trick question?" I responded. "Because if I say no, I look like I'm the possessive kind. And if I say yes, I'll either be very open-minded in your eyes or a loser for not being jealous."

"Hmmm . . . I see your point," she said slowly. "Let's forget I asked that question and for the time being, I will only think of you as a possessive open-minded loser? How does that sound?"

"Perfect."

"I have orders up, so have a good trip and call me . . . sometime."

"I will. Have fun tonight."

I was relieved Dawn had a date because it proved she was here for a good time, not necessarily a long time. No matter what her motives, or views were on casual sexual encounters, she had brought a breath of fresh air into my joyless life, for which I was grateful.

I have always believed in Fate. Unlike most, I wholeheartedly embrace both aspects of this belief—the good and the bad. When something goes surprisingly right many say, "Well, it must be fate I saw that one-day job ad and could make the interview—which I aced!" But when they don't get the job, they fail to understand that fate had something to do with that also.

What I am trying to say is this: if there is some Master Plan that includes women leaving me, surely it has provisions for women entering my life as well. Therefore, Dawn's appearance must be part of The Plan. Otherwise, I am simply an oversexed, immoral degenerate—a label I refuse to accept entirely.

Flawed human being? I can live with that.

After breakfast, I hopped in my van feeling more alive than I had for days. Today was one of action. In a few hours, I'd be at Linda's new place to tell her how sorry I was, and what a moron I'd been. I doubt there was another person on the planet so excited about the prospect of having to apologize.

The City of Sussex has a posted population of 8,974 and is located half-way between Darrien and . . . well . . . nowhere. It kind of just exists as a self-supporting community which has all the same restaurant chains, department stores and movie theatres as the big bad city, without the crime, smog, traffic or headaches. I had worked a few files there and never encountered any negatives. I could see why it would appeal to Linda. It was larger than Delta, yet small enough to have that homey feeling she craved—an attribute she could not coax out of Darrien. I drove non-stop down the four-lane highway and got off at the first exit, landing me in the city's east end, which was unfamiliar territory.

I soon found that Adelaide Crescent was a narrow street, consisting of tiny brick bungalows without garages. As I drove toward 3795 all I could think about was that Linda had far too much class to be stuck in this bland, depression-era subdivision.

If this is where her new life is beginning, I clearly owe her more than an apology, I thought.

I parked on the street and noted a *For Rent* sign on Linda's front lawn, which seemed odd, considering she had moved in several days earlier. I couldn't imagine her having to find a roommate to cover the rent in one of these dumps. I walked up the two front steps and peered in the window of the front room, which appeared to be empty. At this point, I was ready to call Get Out of Town Movers and have them ship all my furniture here—pronto! I pressed the doorbell but didn't hear it ring inside. I then knocked on the unlocked front door, which slowly opened on the second rap.

"Hello?" I called out. "Linda? Are you home?" No response. I looked at the neighbouring properties and saw no activity. "It's me, Steve," I said as I took a step inside. "I want to talk for a minute and then I'll leave, I promise." Still only silence. I quickly closed the front door, locked it and took in my surroundings. There really was no furniture in the front room. No pictures on the walls. An old-fashioned rotary phone lay in the corner, attached to a phone line which snaked out of the floorboards. Propped against the phone was a standard-sized flashlight. I walked into the kitchen where an old wooden table and two chairs, beaten and abused during decades of daily use, sat in the middle of the room. The green stove appeared to be at least fifteen years old, the yellow refrigerator maybe a year or two newer. I opened the fridge, only to find it was empty; the same with the freezer compartment. The large bedroom off the kitchen was also without furniture, as were the two small rooms on the roof-sloped second floor.

This is crazy.

I opened the basement door and felt for a light switch. I flicked it on and off a couple times, but the basement remained dark. I recalled the flashlight in the front room, which I retrieved. As I made my way down the unsteady stairs, I unconsciously reached toward my right hip for the gun holster that used to accompany me on calls like this. Finding only the side of my jeans, I began to shine the flashlight beam wildly around the basement, not certain of what deep, dark secret I might illuminate. The basement was empty except for one small box in a far corner. At that moment the only images that ran through my mind were of the final scenes of the movie "Seven," when Brad Pitt opens a similar-sized box containing his girlfriend's severed head.

"It's an old house with many tenants. It's probably a forgotten box of toys," I said aloud, as I walked across the basement floor. "It has nothing to do with Linda."

I was wrong.

I gingerly opened the cardboard box and found a picture that used to adorn our fireplace mantle. The small portrait of Linda had been marked with an "X" across her smiling face. I stared at the image, trying to make sense of the situation but came up with no reasonable explanation for any of it. I flipped the picture over.

To my sexy book babe,
Love, always
Steve

I dropped the flashlight on the basement floor and charged out of the house. I looked around the neighbourhood; I was still all alone. I jumped into the van and quickly left the area, not sure where I was headed or exactly what was expected of me. It would appear either Max or Jarvis Larsh had set me up and for the life of me, I didn't know why. If this was Max's doing it didn't make any sense, as I was taking the case. If, however, this was Larsh's dirty work, I couldn't understand how he would know about my investigation and he certainly wouldn't be aware of Linda.

Or would he?

I drove to a convenience store several blocks away to use a payphone, not wanting to use my cell phone. I dialed the number from the For Rent sign, which was answered by a man who sounded as if I had interrupted his late morning nap.

"I'm calling about the house you have for rent on Adelaide Crescent," I said.

"What about it?"

"Could tell me how long the place has been empty?"

"What's it to you?" came an abrupt reply. "It's clean and ready to be moved into at the first of next month."

"A neighbour said a woman named Linda Brooks recently moved in and then out a few days later."

"Are you a cop or something? You seem to know all the right answers to your own questions, which makes me kind of suspicious of you and that Brooks lady."

"So, you actually saw her when she moved in?" I asked, desperately

146

wanting verification that Linda had recently been seen alive.

"Not exactly."

"What does that mean?"

"Well, I faxed the tenant agreement, which she signed and returned by courier the next day."

"But she did move her stuff in last Monday, right?"

"I couldn't tell ya. I never went over there until yesterday. I was talking with one of my other tenants in the neighbourhood and he said a man with a truck had arrived late at night and started packing stuff up. Maybe an hour later, the truck was gone and the house was empty."

"Did he say if he had ever seen the female tenant? Could you give me his name?"

"Look here, I don't know what this is all about. Maybe new furniture will arrive tomorrow," he said cynically. "I have a signed sub-lease agreement, which runs out in 26 days. If this Brooks woman doesn't re-sign, I'll rent it to someone else. That's all there is to it."

"Why is the sign up now then? And why did you tell me it would be available at the first of the month?"

"I'm making a list of potential tenants. Nothing illegal about that," he countered. "I've been a landlord for a very long time and know in my heart your friend is gone. I've had tenants move in one day, only to move out the following evening. In that neighbourhood, a lot of people are running from their past and need a breather for a few weeks, to regroup before moving on. No big deal to me, as long as the cheque clears."

"She paid you by cheque?"

"No, it's just a figure of speech. Most of my tenants don't have bank accounts. There was $600 cash in the courier package along with the lease."

I asked a few more questions, none of which produced new leads. I would have to return to Adelaide Crescent and canvas the area.

An hour later, I was again on the highway. None of the area tenants I spoke with had even seen a woman at Linda's house. Even the supposed "eyewitness" turned out to be a bust, as he didn't recall the pickup's make and couldn't describe the man loading boxes.

I pulled the small picture I'd found out of my pocket and placed it on the dashboard.

"Where are you, Linda?" I asked. "Please call somebody."

The trip to Darrien was painfully slow, after a transport truck roll-over shut down the highway for two hours. When I finally did arrive home, I found a Sex At Seven disc stuck in my mailbox and a message on my answering machine.

"Hi, Steve. It's Maria. I came up tonight instead of tomorrow morning and checked into a nice hotel downtown called The Beacon Shores Inn. Do you know it? Anyway . . . I'm going to hit the pool and turn in early. Give me a call in the morning so I can get instructions to your place. I am in room 580. Talk to you tomorrow."

Her voice was much softer than our last conversation and I played it a second time, to confirm my troubled mind hadn't been playing tricks on me. No, it was true; Maria was in town and sounded positive about our fact-finding excursion. After what I had experienced in Sussex, I took this as a sign the future was about to become more productive and life-affirming for all of us.

I awoke in the morning feeling spent. I'd had a restless sleep thinking about the three women in my life: Linda and her mysterious living arrangements; Dawn and her date with Kyle; and Maria, and how she would react to seeing me again.

The last time I saw Maria was at the conclusion of the Barry Jones case. At the time, Linda and I had unexpectedly hit it off and I think Maria wanted to give me her blessing, of sorts, to pursue a long-distance relationship with the town's librarian. I had even suggested she come and visit me in Darrien.

"I'll show you the sights and we'll have a good time."

"What would Linda think of that plan?"

"I was hoping you'd come up on the train together. That way when you got bored with my Neanderthal-man act, you could talk to one another."

"Hmmm . . . sounds interesting, I think," she'd replied slowly. "So, I guess this is goodbye."

"Goodbye sounds so final. I prefer until we meet again."

She'd given me one last, warm smile and said, "I like that—a lot."

"Take care of yourself and keep in touch."

"I will. I promise."

Now six months—one tell-all true crime book, one dead mistress, one vanished fiancée, one felon's request and a few threats on my well-being—later, I found myself walking nervously into the lobby of The Beacon Shores Inn to meet Maria. She was sitting on a couch reading a magazine and didn't noticed my arrival.

"Miss Antonio, your limo has arrived."

Maria looked up from her magazine and gave me a very friendly grin. Glancing at her watch she said, "I'm impressed. You're two minutes early."

"I have no intention of making you wait for me again. Been there, done that, with terrible results."

"I'm glad you've learned one lesson along the way," she said kidding as she stood to give me a hug. "It's good to see you again, Steven."

"It's good to see you too, Maria," I replied, as we found ourselves in an embrace that lasted a few moments longer than necessary. "Look at you," I said as I took a step backwards. "I don't know what you've been up to lately but whatever it is agrees with you."

"You don't look too shabby yourself," Maria said, paying me an obligatory return compliment.

"You're not a good liar," I laughed. "You never were. I guess it's good to know some things in life don't change, because I look and feel like a weathered old doctor's bag."

It was now Maria's turn to give me a good once-over. "You may be right there. But don't forget, it's what's inside the doctor's bag that is important, not how it looks on the outside."

"You really know how to make a guy feel good. I'm glad I didn't use the old 'ridden hard and put away wet' analogy."

Maria let out a small laugh. "I think it would have taken me awhile to find the silver lining in that one."

After a few minutes of awkward small talk, I carried Maria's suitcase to the van and placed it on the back seat.

"You know, I could have taken a taxi to your place this morning."

"And what fun would that be?" I replied. "This way we can grab some breakfast and get caught up a bit. I'm sure your life has been much more interesting than mine these past few months."

"Ha! I doubt that," she interjected.

"Then we can get down to the business of this trip. How does that sound?"

"Exhausting," Maria laughed, "but I'm your guest and will follow your lead."

"I'll try to make this experience as painless as possible."

"Is that a guarantee?"

"Not quite. This may be a wild goose chase and I'm sure we're going to encounter a few bumps along the way, because that's part of Max's grand plan."

Unfortunately, the first bump we encountered had nothing to do with Max, Jarvis Larsh or the box of evidence in my kitchen. Our first obstacle was simply trying to relate to each other in light of recent events. As we ate, our conversation touched on a number of different topics—Wayne, Trudy, Delta, her flower shop, the book, gossip—but we both danced around the subjects we really wanted to discuss. To the couple at the table beside us, Maria and I must have sounded like two lovelorn strangers on a blind date. We were being polite and gracious, listening intently and speaking in slow measured sentences, making sure nothing objectionable escaped our lips.

Truth be told, it was the worst meal I'd ever had.

"Our place isn't too far from here," I said as I drove out of the diner's parking lot. I realized I had said 'our' instead of 'my' and was about to correct myself, but the always-classy Maria ignored my slip and saved me any embarrassment.

"Is it in a newer part of the city or in one of those old, established neighbourhoods with huge trees lining the street?"

"Somewhere in the middle, I guess. It's about twenty years old."

"I remember Linda saying it was like a cottage surrounded by an asphalt lake."

I chuckled at the description. "Sounds about right and like something Linda would have said." As I stopped at a red light, I felt the unofficial *No Personal Stuff* barrier had been breached, and decided to go with it. "So . . . what's his name?"

The question visibly startled Maria, but she recovered quickly. "It's Daniel, if you must know—and you must or you wouldn't have asked."

"Tell me as much or as little as you want. I'm just interested in what's happening in your life, that's all. No ulterior motives."

"Somehow I doubt that."

"Have you been seeing him long?"

"A couple of weeks," she answered easily. "It's not serious. He's on the road a lot. He calls me every other night though."

"A traveling salesman, huh? Aren't you afraid he has a different woman in every town he services?" I asked as we stopped at another traffic light.

"Not really," Maria replied, looking straight ahead. "I don't think he's cut from the same cloth as you."

At this point we had been together for two hours without incident, however with that one rehearsed line Maria's true feelings were exposed.

"I was out of line with that comment. I'm sure Daniel is a very nice guy. That he makes you happy is the important thing."

"Steve, I didn't mean—"

I cut her off in mid-sentence. "Never apologize for stating the truth. I deserved that and we both know it. In a way, I'm glad you got it out in the open. My only question is, if you really feel that way why agree to come on this trip?"

"Because you said I was in danger and *that* I believed," she replied, her voice a touch softer. "When I spoke to Daniel about this Max stuff and what had happened to you subsequently, he thought it was a good idea I come as he couldn't be around to protect me right now."

I am not certain I would have agreed to such a plan. Then again, she probably made it very clear what a scumbag I was and that she did not intend to get caught up in my web of chaos again.

"Daniel sounds like an okay fellow. Maybe one day we'll meet and compare notes."

"Compare notes on what?"

"You, of course."

"That would be a fairly short discussion. Neither of you knows the real me. You have vague high school recollections of when I was young and naive, and his impressions consist of a few phone calls, dinners and a show or two."

"Guys can always find something to compare. That's why we're guys."

Maria looked at me and squinted her eyes in a disapproving manner, only to shake her head and laugh. "If you meet, I'll be on the other side of town, so you can gossip about me freely—just like old women at a sewing bee."

"Sounds like a plan."

We reached my house and I gave her the grand tour. I sensed she felt a bit ill at ease due to Linda's absence, yet she said all the right things about how the place was nice and the neighbourhood seemed quiet, etc. etc. etc. In the kitchen, I began to make a pot of tea as Maria took a seat on the couch.

"Sex At Seven?"

"Excuse me?"

"Is this a group or a seduction disc you left out for me to find?" Maria asked. She paused and added, "Please tell me it's a band."

"It's a band," I called to her.

"Are they any good?"

"A friend of mine swears they're the next big thing. I haven't listened to it yet."

I waited for a follow-up question about my friend, which never materialized. I would have told Maria about Dawn—omitting the one-night stand aspect of our friendship so as not to completely alienate her.

She already had major misgivings about me, so why pile on?

I entered the living room carrying the infamous box of evidence and placed it on the coffee table. Over breakfast and during the ride to the house, I had filled Maria in on the basics of Alexis Penney's swan dive off Max's balcony. She too had serious doubts about Max's innocence, but the key to uncovering the truth was to find Jarvis Larsh.

"Before heading out, I wanted to go over Larsh's file with you."

"You haven't read it?" Maria asked.

"No. I didn't want to fill my head with more junk until I absolutely needed to. I have enough crap swimming around in there as it is."

"I bet."

I opened the Larsh folder and separated the sheets into two piles: Dr. Max-related papers in one pile and everything else in the other. I gave Maria the Max stuff, figuring she might get a better feel for our former classmate and also Larsh. I would tackle the police reports and other helpful information provided. We read in silence for several minutes. When Maria put her final piece of paper down, I asked, "So, who's loonier—Max or Jarvis?"

"Well, if we believe everything in these documents, Jarvis is pretty screwed up. We have to keep in mind, though, the person writing the reports was a pathological liar, living a double life. So . . . it's kind of a toss-up."

"I agree. However, I think Max really was trying to help people by being their therapist," I said. "Double life or not, I believe he tried to be the best shrink out there. He just didn't have a degree on the wall." I laughed at my last comment. "Let me correct that. I'm sure he had several degrees on his office walls—all fake."

"From the best programs in the country, no doubt," Maria joined in. "It's unbelievable there are people who think taking a short cut will help them in the long run. It's depressing."

"Then there are people like me, who do all the hard work and actually achieve their goals, only to throw them all away. Now that's sad."

"More pathetic than sad."

"There's a difference?"

"Sure. You're pathetic because you knew exactly what you were doing when you made the decisions that led you down the wrong path, or at least an alternative path. Same with Max," she said. "Now Jarvis Larsh is just sad because the decisions he makes are not based in reality. If we believe Max's session notes, Jarvis was constantly delusional about the people around him—especially red-haired women."

"What's the deal with that anyway?"

"Well . . . it seems he was quite the mama's boy, although she apparently treated him very poorly during his upbringing."

"Let me guess: she never won the red-headed Mother of the Year award, right?"

"She was never even in the running."

"Anything else? Max seems to think Jarvis had something to do with Alexis Penney's death and possibly other red-haired women in the area. Aside from the fact they were both patients, is there any connection between the two?"

"Funny you ask," Maria smiled. "Jarvis seemed to believe Alexis was his girlfriend and that Max had slept with her."

Dubious about this revelation, I asked, "Is there any proof either claim is rooted in truth?"

Maria picked up Max's session notes. "Max writes, 'The mere idea Alexis Penney is Jarvis' girlfriend is ridiculous. It is another example of his need to psychologically attach himself to a woman who reminds him of his mother. His accusation that I have a sexual relationship with Alexis is clearly an opportunity to display his Alpha male tendencies and to prove his dedication to the woman he loves.'"

"Anything about Jarvis' violent tendencies?"

"After spending a few years in jail for beating up his girlfriend, he was ordered to see Max as a condition of his parole. There isn't anything in here that says he had slipped back into his old boxing routine but you never know."

"Yeah, that's what Jarvis told the police too," I said, examining a statement he'd given a few days after Max's arrest. "He had paid his debt to society and wanted to live a simple life. He said he'd seen Alexis coming and going from Max's office but never spoke to her."

"Does he have an alibi?"

"Alone at home watching TV."

"That's convenient."

"He claims there was no altercation with Max during his session the previous day. He also said he would never have guessed Max was capable of such a violent act, as he was always very kind and courteous. He believed Max simply must have snapped."

Maria gave me a quizzical look. "So, why are we trying to find this Larsh character again? What does Max think we'll find when we talk to this nut?"

"Your guess is as good as mine. Maybe with our combined powers of persuasion we can coax Jarvis into a full confession, like I did in the Barry Jones case."

"Do you really think lightning will strike twice?" Maria asked.

"I guess we're about to find out."

We continued to compare notes. The address and phone number Max had for Jarvis were the same as the ones Jarvis had given the police. Maria called the operator and discovered a current Desmarais County telephone listing for a "J Larsh."

"It seems Max's friend is alive. He is just living at a new address," Maria said, as she handed me the information. "That's a good sign, right?" She turned to hand me the sheet but my mind was elsewhere. "What's wrong?" she asked.

As I watched Maria speaking on the phone, I vividly recalled Samantha at the office the day she'd learned the name of her fiancé's mistress and how proud she was of her investigative skills. The image unsettled me. I'd never really mourned her death, but standing behind Maria now I felt a rush of guilt and remorse sweep over me. Maria didn't need to see me grieving over Linda's archrival, regardless of the tragic circumstances surrounding her demise.

"Nothing," I lied unconvincingly. "Something unexpectedly popped into my head. Everything's okay, trust me."

She gave me one of her concerned looks. "If you want to talk about anything, I'm a pretty good listener."

"I know."

I took the telephone data and grabbed one last folder from the box. "We'd better get going if we want to catch that plane. I've made notes of all the pertinent information on the case so we don't have to lug this box around. With any luck we'll talk to Jarvis tonight, do a couple of other follow-up inquiries and have you home in no time."

"You really think the case is that straightforward?" Maria asked.

"It certainly seems like it is," I said as I handed her the folder. "Have a look over this Alexis Penney profile that Max also sent along. I can't imagine the relevance of the victim's background to this particular case. It's not like we can interview her or anything now." I shook my head and added, "Probably just another path that will lead us nowhere."

"If you say so," Maria said slowly, glancing at the file's contents.

With bravado and an air of superiority, I made a statement I will always regret.

"It's an open and shut case," I declared. "What could go wrong?"

The flight took less than two hours, not even long enough to get lost in a new paperback thriller. Maria and I bounced some ideas off each other about how best to approach Jarvis. While I advocated a standard question-and-answer script, Maria was more interested in the *good cop, bad cop* routine, with her playing the bad cop role.

"I usually play that part," I quipped. "Females are the good cops because they can create feelings of comfort and warmth, settling the suspect down before the hard questions have to be answered."

"So, I soften the guy up, then you come in and pummel him into submission?"

"Something like that," I responded, feeling quite confident.

"That won't work with Jarvis," Maria shot back. "He may have been a mama's boy but he responded to her domineering side as well. I think what he really needs is to be told what to do by a female—any female. That's where I come in. He'll obey my orders before yours."

"You may have a point there," I admitted. "Let's play it by ear. Maybe everything we've read about him is a complete fabrication. If, however, Max was on the money, we can always switch gears and go with your plan. How does that sound?"

"Like we're partners."

"Just as long as you don't expect to be paid for this little excursion."

"I'll consider this my on-the-job training."

"Sounds good to me and to my withering bank account," I said with a grin.

We landed at the Greater Desmarais County Airport mid-afternoon and were soon touring around in a rented Ford Windstar van, much to Maria's dismay.

"You drive a green van everyday. Why not get a sporty two-door or a big comfortable sedan?"

"Because you can't do surveillance in a sporty coupe or luxury sedan," I replied.

"Who said anything about doing surveillance? I thought we were only conducting interviews."

"That's the plan, but I'd rather be prepared for the unexpected. By renting a Windstar I already know where all the controls are and won't run the risk of turning on the headlights at an inopportune time, possibly alerting our subject to our presence."

"Yeah, whatever."

I bought a map and learned Jarvis' place was about thirty-five miles away. After eating a small lunch on the plane neither of us was hungry, but I thought we should have some down time before jumping right into work. "Why don't we check into one of those hotels and freshen up? It's been kind of a crazy day and I don't want us to be overwhelmed in any way when we interview Jarvis."

Maria looked in the direction of my outstretched hand and saw the row of hotels beside the freeway. "Sure, I guess," she said apprehensively.

"Don't worry, we'll still see Jarvis today. Business is business and the only reason we're out here," I said, trying to reassure her. "Let's catch our breath for an hour or two."

We checked into a nice hotel that had a pool and restaurant, which I hoped would be ideal for both business and personal purposes.

"Here you are," I said as I gave Maria the key to her room. "I'm right next door in 209. Let's meet in the lobby at quarter to five. By the time we get to Jarvis' house it'll be dinner time, which is always a great time to bug people," I laughed.

"What if he thinks we're door-to-door salespeople or religious freaks and ignores us?"

"If that happens we retreat to our surveillance vehicle and wait him out."

"And you're certain we couldn't do that in a Lincoln Town Car?"

"Pretty sure. See you in a bit."

Maria entered her room and I entered my mine.

"Hey, Steve, I think we're joined here," I heard her yell through the walls.

I heard a deadbolt being unlocked and a knock on the narrow door beside my dresser. I opened the door and found Maria standing inside her room. "I swear to you, I had no idea these were adjoining rooms."

"Are you saying I should keep it locked at all times then?" she asked with a smirk.

"Absolutely. I think Daniel would feel better if you did "

"You're probably right," she said as she closed her door.

Maria turned on her television but didn't secure her door's deadbolt. I closed my door and also left it unlocked. I tried to understand her thinking and concluded she might actually feel safer knowing that in case of an emergency I was only a few steps away. I decided to put all my faith in that idea, because if I started to think of ulterior motives I felt my head would surely explode.

And what use would I be to anyone then?

Neither one of us realized how tired we were until we met in the lobby.

"What would you think about just staying around here tonight?" Maria asked.

"Grab a late dinner and check out the local sights?"

"Exactly. I know you were rushing to do this interview on my account, but I think we'd both be better off doing it in the morning."

"Your wish is my command, Maria."

After a relaxing dinner at a nearby steak and burger joint, we cruised the area, however, nothing caught our attention and we returned to the hotel.

"So . . . I guess tomorrow is the big day," Maria said with a warm smile as she unlocked her door.

"Let's hope so. I want this investigation done as quickly as you probably do," I said. "Right now, I feel like I am a dog chasing his tail." This statement made Maria laugh. "Don't say it—yes, I know I am a dog in real life."

"I wasn't going to say a thing," Maria replied as she stepped into her room. "Good night, Steven."

"Good night, Maria."

THIRTEEN

JARVIS AND ALEXIS

When the Shakin' Pussycat Bar closed at four in the morning, and after exchanging phone numbers on paper napkins, Jarvis and his new friend went their separate ways. Once home, however, Jarvis discovered the napkin Derek had given him had no writing on it whatsoever.

No big deal, he thought. *I'll get it when he calls this afternoon.*

"Jarvis, it's Derek. How's your head? You can really throw back those whiskeys. I think I may have exceeded my credit card limit."

"I'm not feeling too bad, actually," Jarvis replied. "You know what they say—practice makes perfect. Instead of playing the piano, I play with alcohol. Over time, I've become very good at it!"

Both men laughed over the phone line a few moments, until Derek said he was calling about Alexis. Suddenly the jovial mood turned bitter.

"She's going to see the good doctor tonight at 8:30 for a very special one-on-one session," Derek said in a low conspiratorial tone, knowing this would incense Jarvis.

"In his office?" Jarvis asked with disbelief. "Tonight?"

"That's what I've heard."

"From who?"

"My sources at the medical office are very reliable."

"I can't believe they're still doing this to me!"

"To us," Derek responded. "You're my friend, Jarvis, and I hate the fact that she's putting you through this like she did to me. I just want to kill her."

"Me too. I want to catch them in the act and get rid of their cheating asses at the same time."

Derek didn't speak immediately, allowing the words to hang in the air. The previous night he felt his guardian angel had sent Jarvis to him—a man who also hated Alexis Penney and wouldn't be afraid of confronting her or, if need be, harming her. After a few free drinks, Jarvis was very open about his criminal past and how he had learned from his mistakes. "My last girlfriend got off lucky," he had stated.

"I have a plan," Derek finally said. "Tonight we can kill two birds with one stone. You take care of my problem and I'll take care of yours."

Since learning of his therapist's and girlfriend's affair, Jarvis had wondered how best to deal with Alexis' infidelity. He didn't think he'd have a problem with her. Dr. Max was another issue altogether, as he would definitely fight for his survival. With Derek's offer to take care of Dr. Max, however, Jarvis could concentrate on Alexis alone—a much more appealing plan.

"Tell me the plan and then I'll tell you if I'm interested."

"Very well," Derek said.

It was a simple bait-and-switch plan. Fortunately, Alexis had inadvertently taken care of the bait aspect by planning to arrive at Max's office at half past eight. The switch would take place when she found a note on the doctor's door, telling her to wait in the next office - Suite 2311. Once inside she would find Jarvis, who would punish her whatever way he saw fit. During this time, Derek had told Jarvis he would be in Dr. Max's office pretending to be a client. That way if Alexis made any noise, he could subdue the doctor immediately. Then when both cheats were dead, they would leave the building separately from a rear door which had no surveillance cameras.

"Two birds with one stone," Derek reiterated to Jarvis, who had remained silent during his five-minute speech.

"What about the security guard at the front desk and the cameras in the lobby?" Jarvis asked, knowing how the medical building operated.

"We're going in when it's still busy. No one will notice us."

"And then what—hang out in the stairwells? No way. Too risky."

"Relax, I've already taken care of it," Derek said in a soothing voice. "You will wait in Suite 2311, which is without a tenant right now. There are, however, still chairs in the waiting area. It's set up exactly like Dr. Feldberg's office."

"Won't the door be locked? How do I get in?"

"The door will be unlocked after 4:05 this afternoon. I signed a bogus tenant agreement a few hours ago and I can pick up the office keys at 4:00. After you get inside, lock the door until around 8:15."

It took Jarvis' still whiskey-soaked brain some time to comprehend everything Derek was telling him. It was all happening so fast.

"What about the note?"

"I'll leave it for you to put on Dr. Feldberg's door before Alexis arrives. I'll make sure he doesn't leave the office." There was a long pause on the line. "Are you up to this or not?" Derek asked, breaking the silence. "Because if you can't do this, I'll find someone else. Even on short notice, I'm positive someone could use a quick $10,000."

"What was that?"

"The money I'm willing to pay to have that bitch snuffed out. We talked about it at the strip club. Don't tell me you've forgotten."

Jarvis had no recollection of such a discussion but wasn't going to admit to it. He'd been so hopped up on the idea of revenge, finding cash was now involved was icing on the cake. "I remember," he stammered. "And yeah, I'm in. All the way."

"That's good to hear, because this opportunity is once in a lifetime."

"I agree."

"There's one more thing."

"Now what?"

"To make Alexis feel comfortable, I'll leave you some clothes like ones Dr. Max would normally wear. That way when you enter the reception area, for a split second, she'll think it's the doc. Then you pounce on her when she least expects it. Capitalize on that moment of surprise and make her pay for all our suffering. Do you understand me, Jarvis?"

Jarvis recalled the look on his previous girlfriend's face as she stepped into the kitchen and was greeted with a smashing left hook. "I know exactly what you're talking about and I can't wait to do this."

Derek told him they would meet at the strip club at 10:00 p.m. to celebrate. As Jarvis asked Derek for his phone number again, the line went dead.

No problem, Jarvis thought. *I'll get it from him tonight.*

Deviating slightly from Derek's plan, Jarvis entered the medical building through a street level clinic, and took the stairs to the 23rd floor. He looked at his watch: 4:20 p.m. He peered out of the stairwell, and seeing no activity in the hallway, moved quickly to Suite 2311 which, as promised, was unlocked. He ducked inside and immediately bolted the door. Looking up he saw the note.

Group Session In Progress. Please wait in Suite 2311
- Dr. Feldberg

The reception area was almost identical to the one next door, which helped calm his nerves a little. Alexis would be just as fooled, he mused. On the receptionist's desk he found a duffle bag that contained a small hand mirror, a black turtleneck, black pants and dark shoes with a white stripe. To top off the disguise, there was also a man's blond wig that matched the colour of Dr. Max's hair. "Very thorough, Derek," he said as he placed the wig on his head and admired himself in the mirror. "Hello, Alexis. You can come in now," he laughed. He took off the wig and examined the other contents of the bag: a ham sandwich, two cans of cola and a small bottle of whiskey. He also found an unsigned note.

Eat, drink and be merry.

"You can bet on that."

To pass the time, Jarvis had brought along a book he'd purchased titled *Absolute Complications* by Susie Christopher, who seemed to address all the trauma in his life and how to fix it in seven days. The book was divided into seven relevant chapters and so far he had accomplished the goals set out in Chapter One: *Identify Your Problems – Admit You Have A Problem.* With the discovery of Alexis' and Dr. Max's affair, he'd been forced to admit his relationship was doomed. Chapter One, done. Having accomplished that objective, he turned to Chapter Two: *Deal With Your Problem – Banish It Forever.* With Derek's brilliant plan, by 8:35 this evening Jarvis felt this goal would also have been easily reached.

At the appropriate time, Jarvis placed the "group session" sign on Dr. Max's door and slid back into the office area of 2311. His heart was racing and the anticipation of Alexis' arrival was almost unbearable. He had decided to let Alexis sweat it out awhile in the outer office, and even left his new book out so she would have something to read before she died. It was the least he could do for her.

With every ding of the elevator doors, he would spring into position behind the door off the reception area, only to be disappointed time and time again.

At 8:25 the hair on Jarvis' neck stood on end and he knew Alexis had arrived. He imagined her walking down the hallway, stopping briefly to check her hair and outfit in one of the glass doorways along the way. He knew she would look stunning. Only now he knew the truth: she got dolled up not for him, but for Dr. Max. She'd been playing with his emotions all along and he'd fallen for it. *What a sucker*, he thought. *But not anymore. Not tonight.*

When Jarvis heard the hallway door open and Alexis call,

165

"Hello," his carefully planned actions completely vanished from his head. He found himself rushing out into the main office and attacking Alexis with all the rage of a lion on a gazelle. She had barely closed the door when she sensed someone coming toward her. Hoping it was Dr. Max, she turned with a sly, sexy smile on her ruby red lips and said, "This is quite the surprise, Doctor," a second before Jarvis' right fist connected with her face, unhinging her jaw. The force of the blow sent her sailing backwards against the door and downward, as her knees gave out. The right side of her head then connected with the polished chrome armrest of a chair, and she collapsed like a sack of potatoes.

Jarvis stood over her motionless frame waiting for a verbal or physical response. "Come on, whore, get up!" he growled in a low tone, aware someone might hear him in the hallway. "My last girlfriend had a helluva lot more fight in her than you, Alexis," he stated, kicking her hard in the torso. "You're pathetic." He bent down and turned her over. Her head flopped from side to side with no resistance; her mouth remained open, unable to close properly ever again. When he saw her lifeless eyes, he knew she was dead. Killing her didn't bother him. He had achieved the goal he and author Susie Christopher had set out: to banish his problem forever. The only thing that scared him now was how to deal with the aftermath. He and Derek hadn't discussed how they were going to dispose of the bodies. He really needed to talk to Derek, but was afraid to interrupt his time with Dr. Max next door.

Even with all this internal instability, the criminal side of Jarvis' brain kicked in and he remembered to take the "group session" sign off his therapist's door. With that taken care of, he locked himself away in Suite 2311 awaiting Derek's instructions.

FOURTEEN

DEREK, DESTINY ROSE AND DR. MAX

"You're a wonderful dancer," Derek said to Destiny Rose, as she repositioned her halter top across her ample bosom and pulled up her skimpy, faux leather skirt. "This will go down as one of my top five nights of all-time."

"Either you're drunk or your previous top five all-time great nights were pretty lousy in the first place," Destiny Rose said with a smirk. "I'm a good dancer but I'm not that good," she proclaimed. "That'll be sixty bucks."

Derek laughed at her sarcasm and peeled off five twenty-dollar bills. "Keep the change."

Destiny Rose took the money and placed it in a little purse she carried with her at all times. "You know, for another hundred you can spend the next hour with me. Maybe I could actually top your list, if you know what I mean."

"Tempting, my dear, very tempting. Unfortunately I have to meet a friend in a few minutes to talk over some business."

"For another two hundred, I think I could top both of your lists." Destiny Rose took a seat across from him, pulled up her skirt a few inches and gave him another unobstructed view between her thighs, free of charge. She ran her hand up her left leg until it disappeared from view. "I'm not a great dancer but I am really good at this," she said, letting out a soft, whimpering moan.

"We're going to be here for a while. I'll see what my friend thinks about your offer," Derek barely managed to say, his eyes fixed on the stripper's crotch. "I know he really likes you."

The expression on Destiny Rose's face swiftly went from one of pleasure to bewilderment. "Your friend isn't that tall guy who's always hanging around here?"

"Yeah, Jarvis. That's him. Why?"

Destiny Rose abruptly headed toward the curtain that divided the V.I.P. section from the general bar area. "That guy gives me the creeps. I ain't doing nothin' with him."

"Sorry to hear that," Derek said as Destiny Rose walked away. "I was thinking of giving Jarvis a bonus for doing my dirty work." He continued to sit in the sweat-covered chair and looked at his watch: 9:49. "In eleven minutes this will be all over," he said to his reflection in the mirror on the ceiling. He raised his glass of whiskey in the air and made a toast. "To Jarvis." He took the last swig of alcohol and walked out into the stage area to watch and wait.

Derek was plenty concerned when his accomplice was a no-show and was not answering his home phone. After following Jarvis for the past few weeks, Derek knew he could always be found at one of three places: the Shakin' Pussycat Bar, his small apartment in the east end or stalking Alexis. As he wasn't celebrating with strippers or at home, there was only one option left.

Until this moment, the plan had seemingly gone off without a hitch. After the cleaning lady unlocked the door to Suite 2311 for him, he had paid her $500 for her silence. He was positive she knew he didn't want the room for a late-night business meeting. Maybe she envisioned him shooting a porno movie which needed an authentic office setting. Who knows? She barely spoke English, yet somehow completely understood the language of the mighty dollar—what a shock.

After leaving the duffle bag for Jarvis, Derek took the stairwell to the 16th floor, where he caught the elevator. There, he took up position in his rented office space across the street and watched for Jarvis to arrive, which he did—right on time.

The only thing left to do was wait.

A short time before Max's final session ended, Derek again

found himself lurking in the shadows outside of Max's office. When the day's last patient departed, Derek entered Suite 2309 and quietly locked the hallway door. "Dr. Feldberg, are you in?"

Max was startled by the strange voice in the outer office. "Yes, come on in."

Max didn't quite know what to make of the man who walked in a few moments later. He was in his late 30's, well-dressed and carrying two take-out cups from a nearby bistro where he usually lunched. "I don't believe we've met."

"Danny Murphy," Derek said with a wide, lying smile. He put one of the cups on the desk and offered his hand, which Max shook cautiously.

"What have I done to deserve a late-night visit from a stranger with good taste in beverages? In my line of work, I'm good with faces and names but Danny Murphy doesn't ring any bells. Should it?"

"Probably not," Derek said as he took a seat. "We actually have a mutual friend. You know Alexis Penney, don't you?"

"Yes, of course," Max said uneasily. Was this the advisor she'd spoken about over the phone? If so, he was in deep trouble. "I've only known her a short time. Are you two old friends?"

"Old enough, I guess. I know her from her days in Ravenwood—a small farming community. She moved from there about a year-and-a-half ago and we've kept in touch on and off. I guess she's never mentioned me," Derek said, as he deliberately took a sip from his coffee and let out an appreciative sigh of pleasure. "Best coffee around. Drink up before it gets cold."

Max eyed the cup suspiciously. "No, she's never brought you up, sorry to say."

"I guess in the greater scheme of things, I'm not that important in her life." He took another mouthful of coffee and said, "I'm intrigued that you didn't know I was coming to this meeting with her tonight. Alexis said I might be able to invest some of my money with you. It was set for 7:30, right?"

Derek had been rehearsing that "gotcha" line for days, after hearing Alexis talking to a friend on her cell phone about a great financial opportunity she had stumbled across. He hadn't been in town for more than three hours before he found someone who cloned cell phones and offered other useful services such as clandestine recording of conversations. Derek was more than happy to buy this entrepreneur's package plan for thirty days. The more he learned about his prey, the better prepared he was when it came time to kill them. Due to legal loopholes and outright trial failures, these criminals had escaped justice once, but they would not escape him, especially after their true crime book hit the bestsellers list.

Max's reservations about this stranger and the cup of steaming coffee in front of him began to dissipate. "You're an investor? Alexis never said she'd be bringing a friend along. A friend of hers is obviously a friend of mine." Max removed the lid of his cup and inhaled the rich aroma of the Brazilian Blend, also known as "B.B." when ordering at the counter, and took a long drink of the coffee. "This stuff really is the best around. Thanks," he said, taking a second gulp, emptying half the cup's contents. "I have no problem telling you about the investment. I don't know what Alexis has told you already. Our meeting was actually scheduled for 8:30, so while we're waiting for her I can go over the specifics with you."

"I'm sorry for the intrusion. I must have the times mixed up. You didn't have any more patients coming tonight, did you?"

"Even if I did," Max began, as he pulled out his fake financial prospectus from the top desk drawer, "I would reschedule for the opportunity to show you the benefits of investing in this terrific company that's about to go global."

Derek listened to Max's impressive pitch and realized how good a con man Alexis was dealing with here. He loved the idea that even without his intervention, in a few days Alexis would have found herself penniless with no one to turn to for help. Being broke and homeless, however, was not a just punishment for getting away with murder, which was why he had hunted her down in the first place.

No, this investment speech by "therapist" Dr. Max Feldberg was simply an amusing aside to the real task at hand, taking place next door. He'd grown tired of imagining scenarios where Alexis would appear to die accidentally, only to see his plans fail for one reason or another. Meeting Jarvis allowed him to cut through all that and get this business over with once and for all.

He watched Max begin to shake his head and slur his words, trying to fight the effects of the sleeping pills he had unwittingly drunk.

"I don't know what's come over me, Danny."

"No problem, Max. It's probably been a long day listening to other people's troubles. That alone must tire you out." He glanced down at his watch: 8:21. "Look," he said as he stood up, "Alexis is going to be here in a few minutes. Why don't you rest your eyes? I'll run across the street and get us all something to drink. What do you think of that idea?"

Max could barely stand on his own and started toward his couch. "That would be perfect," he managed to say, as he collapsed onto the leather cushions.

"I'll be back shortly."

Derek waited in the reception area a few minutes, making sure Max was unconscious. He walked into the hallway and noted that Jarvis had attached the "group session" note as instructed. As he made his way into the stairwell, he heard the elevator doors open behind him. He quietly opened the hall door and peered down the corridor.

"Good evening, Alexis. For a murderer you look particularly striking tonight," he said under his breath. He continued to watch as she read the note on Max's door and made her way into Suite 2311. "Sweet dreams, Alexis. This one is for Patricia, rest her soul."

He turned and closed the stairwell door again, never hearing the loud thud of Alexis' body colliding against the door twenty feet away. He then walked down to street level and escaped into the night through a nondescript service exit. Five minutes later, he was getting a very vigorous lap dance while he waited for Destiny Rose to finish her performance on stage.

Undetected and unscathed once again, he thought. He grabbed his whiskey off the table and made a toast to the young, half-naked woman gyrating in front of him. "To my dear Alicia. I'll love you always."

"My name is Soreena," the dancer laughed, as she climbed on Derek's chest, "but you can call me Alicia any time you want."

This late at night, getting into the medical building would have been much harder had Derek not placed a piece of duct tape over the service door latch earlier. Buzzing from too many shots of whiskey, smelling of sweat and sexy whores and with his ears still ringing with the refrain of a Bon Jovi song, he pulled on the outside handle, praying his handiwork had not been uncovered. When the door opened he thanked the heavens for lazy security guards. Although he was in no shape to climb to the 23rd floor, he did so anyway, not wanting to alert anyone to an elevator run. This was too important.

He cracked the stairwell door open and listened. Hearing nothing, he made his way to Suite 2311 and knocked lightly on the door. His main objective was to confirm Alexis was dead. How Jarvis and Max were managing was much lower on his priority list.

"Jarvis? It's Derek. Are you in there?" He tried the handle and found it locked. As he was about to let go of it, however, it turned from the inside and he came face-to-face with his partner in crime. "Why are you still here?" he asked, pushing his way into the office. "We have to get out of here." Derek saw Alexis' body on the floor. The look on her face was one he had imagined since he finished reading *The Murdering Mistress* months earlier. "You did it. She's dead," he praised Jarvis. "So, why are you still here?"

"Were we going to leave her like that?" Jarvis asked, pointing to the floor. "In a few days her body will begin to rot and there'll be cops everywhere. The last thing I need is to be linked to this. How are we going to get her out of here, Derek?"

Dealing with emotionally challenged people is always . . . well . . . a challenge, but the best method Derek had found in the past was to be direct and forceful. This dolt had forgotten their discussion about throwing her body to the street to cover up any bruises on her skin from the attack.

"Here's the new plan. Follow me," Derek instructed, walking from the main office to the balcony. "See that office with the computer on across the street? That's my office. That's where I work." He turned and watched as Jarvis tried to focus on the task at hand.

"One floor up from here—on the left?"

"Exactly."

"How are we going to get Alexis over there?" Jarvis asked, confused, peering over the railing, then across the busy intersection below and finally up to Derek's office. "There's no way."

Derek bit his lower lip to halt the string of expletives about to escape. "We're not going over there, only I am. I'm going to be a witness to a murder."

"Alexis is already dead," Jarvis replied slowly. "What murder are you going to witness?"

"Alexis' murder at the hands of Dr. Max."

"Is he still alive? You said you were going to—"

"I was," Derek responded coolly, "but then thought it would be more fun if we framed him for Alexis' murder. Don't you want him to suffer—rot in jail—for the rest of his life?"

"I do . . . but I still don't see how—"

"Listen to me, Jarvis! We don't have much time!" Derek barked.

"Anything you say," Jarvis replied, his face registering shock, "but I'm not returning to prison."

Derek placed his hand on Jarvis' shoulder. "Do as I say and we'll be out of here in ten minutes."

After giving Jarvis some final instructions, Derek made his way down the stairwell one last time, congratulating himself for coming up with such a creative solution on such short notice. Setting up the con man for the murder of one of his cons was sweet irony. Both Alexis and Dr. Max had caused others unspeakable pain and now he'd bring them to justice. It was brilliant. The only loose end was Jarvis, but he could be bought off. He was never going to squeal to the cops. Even if he did have a pang of conscience in later years, Derek McDonald did not exist. He was a ghost. A figment of Jarvis' overactive imagination.

He entered the Indelible Corporation Building and took the elevator to the 24th floor, where he entered Suite 2418, his current base of operations. He'd picked this building after realizing Alexis and Jarvis spent time across the street visiting the good doctor and he could keep an eye on them from above. With the way things were working out, his belief that a higher power was looking out for him was reinforced.

It was a small one-room office, which he had leased using an assumed name. It reminded him of his former life right out of university, when he found himself working in a number of small, windowless cubicles. Although he enjoyed the solitude, he had yearned to see the sun rise and fall each day. After Alicia's death and at the start of his crusade, he found himself longing for the comfort an office provided and began renting rooms with large windows facing the street in every town his targets lived. In these offices, he felt at home.

"Good evening, Alicia, my love. Did you miss me?" he asked the framed picture set on his otherwise empty desk. "You are the most gorgeous bride in the whole wide world. Have I told you that today?" He leaned forward and gave the photograph of his wife in her wedding dress a quick kiss. "This will only take a second, honey. Please bear with me."

Derek walked to the window and peered out to the medical building. There was still no sign of life in Dr. Feldberg's office, but that was not the case in the office next door. Jarvis was standing in the balcony shadows looking upward. Seeing Derek, Jarvis gave a quick wave. Derek flicked the light switch up, then down rapidly, briefly illuminating himself. As he surveyed the other medical offices and the sidewalks, he was certain only he and Jarvis had witnessed their preordained signal.

Almost immediately Jarvis reappeared, struggling to keep the body of his dead girlfriend upright. As planned, in case there were other witnesses in the area, he tried to make it look as though they were fighting. With both hands he finally grabbed hold of Alexis' tiny waist and shoved her body hard against the balcony railing.

"Just a little more, Jarvis. You can do it," Derek said, as if cheering an athlete on from the stands. "Now!"

In the night air, Alexis' body twisted sideways several times before making a spectacular landing next to a parked car. The fact she touched down face first was particularly gratifying, as her previously broken jaw would now be tiny fragments of her pulverized skull. "Good job, Jarvis," Derek said, as he watched by-standers below react to the red-haired angel who'd had her wings unceremoniously clipped in mid-flight. He turned his attention to the south end of the medical building where, a short time later, he saw Jarvis walk through an alley into the street. After looking at the results of his night's work, Derek saw a wide grin come over Jarvis' face as he headed to their rendezvous at a nearby convenience store.

"We're done here, my sweet," Derek said, gently picking up his wife's bridal portrait and slipping it under his arm. "After I pay Jarvis his richly deserved reward, we can start packing. Right now though, I have one last thing to do."

He took his cell phone out of his pocket and punched in 911. "Hello, police. I would like to report a murder at the Upstate Medical Building."

FIFTEEN

After a quick breakfast at the hotel, Maria and I began our adventure. We missed most of the rush hour traffic and arrived outside Jarvis' house around 9:30.

"For a psychopath, Jarvis seems to have done okay for himself," I said, looking at the two-storey, three-car garage, mini-mansion in front of us. The neighbourhood reflected the wealth of its inhabitants. Manicured lawns, long winding laneways, tall majestic trees and an abundance of high-priced luxury vehicles parked in the driveways.

"Aren't you glad you rented this van now?" Maria asked sarcastically, closing the passenger door. "It fits right into the surroundings, don't you think? We couldn't be more conspicuous if we drove up in a clown car."

"I'm here to investigate, not socialize," I said as we made our way up the cobblestone walkway. "As long as we get from Point A to Point B and back again, I'm happy."

"That makes one of us."

I rang the doorbell not knowing what to expect next. I couldn't imagine the person Max had written about in his patient reports had managed to turn himself around in such dramatic fashion. "Maybe he married into money," I suggested, as we waited outside the oversized front doors.

"Maybe," Maria agreed half-heartedly. "Or more plausibly, he married some unsuspecting girl and then killed her for the insurance money."

I was about to reply when the door opened. We were greeted by an arresting-looking woman in her mid-thirties whose hair colour confirmed we were at the right household.

"Hello, Mrs. Larsh?" I inquired, trying not to display any signs of the shock I was experiencing. I glanced quickly over to Maria, who was also having a tough time containing her disbelief.

"Yes. How can I help you?"

"My name is Steve Cassidy. I'm a private investigator. This is my associate, Maria Antonio. We were hoping to speak with your husband. Would he be in?"

"Well . . . no. Not right now. Is there a problem?"

"Not at all . . ."

"Chantal. My name is Chantal."

"It's very nice to meet you, Chantal," Maria piped up, sensing our host's nervousness. "We're looking into an old insurance case—a car accident from several years ago—which we believe your husband may have witnessed."

"Was he involved in the accident?" she asked Maria, ignoring me completely.

"No. He witnessed one," Maria reassured her. "This might have taken place before the two of you met." Maria glanced at Chantal's left hand. "That's a lovely wedding ring. How long have you been married?"

"In October we'll celebrate two years," came the reply.

Having no choice but to play along with Maria's accident premise, I said, "This fender bender occurred six years ago and was so minor I doubt your husband has mentioned it to you."

"Right now we're just hoping he recalls the accident," Maria said with a laugh. "We haven't had much luck so far have we, Steven?"

"No, we haven't," I replied slowly.

Very few people call me by my full first name. It was usually shortened by family, friends and co-workers to, "Hey, Steve," or "Yo, Cassidy." Maria was the exception. Although she used the shortened version most of the time, when dating in high school and in a romantic mood, she would almost always call me Steven. I was never sure if this small change was intentional as a way to convey her true feelings for me, or an unconscious act she wasn't aware of. I didn't care either way. I just loved the way those two syllables sounded together when she spoke them.

I studied Maria's face and decided this "Steven" was only part of the playful banter we'd adopted to put Jarvis' wife at ease.

"Do you expect him back later this afternoon—tonight, perhaps?"

I asked. "Or would it be possible to drop by his place of work? This will only take a few minutes, I assure you." I wanted to meet Jarvis away from his house because I had no idea how we could get into his true relationship with Max in his wife's presence.

"Well . . . he doesn't actually work these days. He kind of putters around the city shopping during the week, to keep his mind active." Chantal must have noticed our quizzical looks and added, "You see, Jarvis has been through a rough few years and hasn't really held a job for some time."

"Sorry to hear that," Maria chimed in with her best sympathetic voice. "It must be very hard for the two of you, especially living in such a beautiful community." She turned to appraise our lovely surroundings and then came back at Chantal.

Again, I had to hand it to Maria for her cunning investigative technique. In one breath she exuded empathy for the couple's state of affairs, which was still a complete mystery to us, and in the next breath tactfully asked the question on both our minds: How can you afford to live in this palace with no money is coming in?

Mrs. Larsh looked past us. "Fortunately my husband came into an unexpected family inheritance and we live off those proceeds. In this community we are referred to as *new money* behind our backs. That is not meant as flattery but if that's the way it is, then that's the way it is," she said, letting out a little sigh.

After that bombshell I had a lot of follow-up questions, none of which would be appropriate. "We're going to be in the area until tomorrow afternoon speaking with other witnesses," I said, handing Mrs. Larsh my business card. "My cell phone number is listed at the bottom and I can be reached twenty–four hours a day."

"Although we might have given you the impression your husband's involvement is minimal, it really is important we speak to him—at his convenience, of course," Maria said gently. "Our client is willing to cover any expenses Mr. Larsh may incur to meet with us."

"As you might imagine, his social schedule is pretty flexible," Chantal said with a laugh, "and I'm certain he'll talk to you."

"That's terrific," I said. "I think our luck is beginning to change."

Maria gave me a knowing smile and reached out her hand to Mrs. Larsh. "It was a pleasure to meet you, Chantal. Thank you for all your help."

"It was nice meeting you too."

Reversing the van out of the driveway, we gave Jarvis' wife a fast wave and a smile as she closed the front doors of her luxurious home.

"I'm sure you've been told by better men than me, Maria, but you were really good back there," I said. "I'm very impressed."

"Thank you, Steve," she replied with a grin. "And yes, better men have told me that before. What can I say? I'm a woman of many talents."

Our eyes locked and we began to laugh.

"You seem a natural at interrogating people without them knowing it."

"Probably comes from working in the floral business for so many years," Maria said. "Customers come in with an arrangement idea in their heads but have no clue what types of flowers or extras they want. It's my job to ask questions about the occasion, the recipient's preferences and their price range. Before I can finalize the sale, I might ask fifteen questions of someone who walks in with a simple request like, 'I want to send my Aunt Selma a bouquet of flowers.'"

"Being able to read people—their words, their body language, their emotions—is a very tricky process. I've known veteran cops who could never manage that skill. But I've known wet-behind-the-ears rookies who can accurately assess suspects and witnesses after talking with them for two minutes."

"Are you saying I'm a wet-behind-the-ears rookie?" Maria asked.

"I'll tell you after you give me your assessment of Chantal. Think of this as a pop quiz."

"Okay . . ." Maria said, as her eyes closed slightly and a more studied expression came over her features. "I think Mrs. Larsh is generally a happily married woman who feels isolated in her big house and snooty neighbourhood. I got the impression she was content with her husband's aimless roaming, but there did seem to be a bit of sorrow for his circumstances. Maybe he hasn't changed all that much since his sessions with Max, regardless of his living arrangements."

"You may be right," I concurred. "Anything else?"

"I think she's an honest person. She didn't appear to be hiding anything from us even though we are total strangers. She definitely wasn't alarmed that we wanted to meet with Jarvis. I believe as soon as he comes home she'll hand over your card and tell him to call us, just for curiosity's sake. It's not every day two private investigators come knocking at the door seeking your help."

"It's a good thing you used that car accident excuse. When tracking people down in the past, I'd tell their relatives I was working on an inheritance matter. I don't know how that would have played today."

"Do you really think there was an inheritance?" Maria asked. "It certainly would explain how Jarvis could afford that mansion."

"I don't know what to think," I said cautiously. "We'll have to do some more investigating on that front. He might have told his future bride it was an inheritance from a long-lost uncle but as you stated when we arrived, the money could also be from a large insurance payout from the untimely death of a previous wife."

"How can we find that out?"

"If we go with the lost uncle's large estate theory, I can't imagine other family members letting a psycho like Jarvis get all the cash without a fight. I'm sure the will was contested and, if so, there'll be a record of it in the court system."

"And if we go with the dead wife theory?"

"We check for a marriage licence, then death notices." I replied. "If government taxes are involved, there is a record some place. Fortunately, it'll be one-stop shopping at the courthouse. We'll also search for any news stories or obituaries at the library."

Maria gave me a dirty look at the word 'library' but any comment went unsaid.

I located the downtown county courthouse/municipal building/

library a short time later and decided we should split up to save time. I asked Maria to search at the library for any mentions of Jarvis or Chantal, as I sifted through court papers. "My stuff shouldn't take too long," I said. "Why don't we meet here in an hour?"

"Fine with me. With any luck, Jarvis will contact you in the meantime."

"Yeah, hopefully."

We went our separate ways. I trusted Maria didn't think I was giving her the easier task or that I now had fears of entering libraries because of the *Linda situation*. The real reason was that I knew my way around the court system better. This part of the investigation was also a make-work project of sorts, as we had technically already found Jarvis. This trip, however, was also a game—Max's game—and I figured the best defense is always a good offense. Therefore, before we met Mr. Larsh I wanted to know as much about my opponent as possible.

Against my better judgment, I actually believed Max's notes on Jarvis were on the up-and-up. The problem was they did not jive with the opulent lifestyle he now lived and I needed to explain such a turnaround. As well, I couldn't understand why Max wanted me to speak with Jarvis at all. I had no proof he was responsible for Alexis Penney's death or had somehow framed Max. Of course, my client was a convicted liar and like most inmates had claimed his innocence from the very beginning. In truth, I was more interested in talking to Max than Jarvis, who might be a red herring in this convoluted mess.

My records search was fruitful in two areas: that Jarvis had purchased his house in 1994 for $459,000 and that he and Chantal were married on October 22, 1996. There was no indication he had taken out a mortgage, meaning he'd paid the whole amount in cash—a very interesting and fortunate situation to be in at any time. In the intervening years, he'd evidently banked much more than the $9,999 he'd received the night of Max's arrest, but I could find no official record of how he'd come upon his new-found wealth. On their marriage certificate application, I also noted neither of our lovebirds had checked off "divorced" or "widowed."

"So much for the dead first wife theory," I said to myself, as I made my way out of the courthouse. On the front steps I grabbed two cold drinks from a hot dog vendor and went to the van to wait for Maria. When she hadn't returned at the agreed upon time, I began to worry that my divide-and-conquer plan was a mistake. I scribbled a note and left it on the windshield, telling Maria I would be right back. I jogged into the library, frightened that something terrible was taking place just out of view.

I should never have let her out of my sight, I chastised myself.

The library was a large, modern, two-storey structure that was warm and inviting. The tables inside the front doors were filled with young and old, men, women and children. I began to scan each face trying to locate Maria among them, with no luck. Not wanting to miss her, I went to the front counter and asked if they could page her, which they did without question. Several excruciating minutes passed and still no Maria. "Where are your newspaper archives?" I asked the checkout clerk.

"Upstairs. Turn left when you step out of the elevator."

I couldn't wait for the elevator and took the nearby stairs two at a time. There weren't the high stacks of books on this floor and I could see all the tables at once. Still no sign of Maria.

Don't panic, she's here, I thought, trying to calm the storm brewing in my head.

"May I help you?" a female voice asked from behind me.

I turned to face a girl in her late 20's who was pushing a cart full of books.

"I'm looking for a friend of mine—female, in her early 30's. She's wearing a green top and black pants. She was going to check out some old newspaper articles for me."

"When did she come in?"

"About an hour ago, I guess."

"Come with me."

I followed her to an information desk, where she looked at two log-in books. "Maria?"

"Yes," I stammered.

My helper pointed to a booth in the far corner. "She hasn't checked out yet, so you should find her in number 3. That's where our archive machines are located."

After thanking the girl, I made my way across the second floor at a very quick pace, causing some patrons to look up from their books in case there might be an emergency in the area.

I haven't been so relieved in all my life as when I saw Maria seated at a desk in front of a large computer screen. Over her ears was a set of headphones. I tapped lightly on the door before entering and tried to act blasé. "I paged you," I said, as Maria took off her headphones.

"I was listening to some music," she said looking at her watch, "and completely lost track of time. I'm sorry. You didn't think something had happened to me, did you?"

"Actually . . . the thought did briefly come up but I decided I was being paranoid and erased it from my mind."

Maria took a few seconds to examine my face and said, "Liar."

"Hey, libraries and I do not have a good history. Cut me some slack."

"I know."

"Anyway, here's a semi-cold drink." I handed her the can of pop I'd purchased several stress-filled minutes earlier.

"I guess the sweat on your brow is from running around trying to find a pop machine, huh?" Maria laughed, as she opened the can and took a sip.

"Something like that." I looked away from Maria's amused face to the computer screen. "While playing Nancy Drew did you find anything of interest? The only things I could confirm were that Jarvis and Chantal are legally married and he is rolling in some serious dough from unknown sources."

Maria turned to the screen. "I kind of struck out too. I didn't find any listings for them in the newspaper archives. However, the girl helping me earlier said the neat thing about this library is some computer company bigwig gives them the latest technology to use for free. I guess as a kind of thank you for all the time he spent in libraries in his youth."

"And how does this cutting edge stuff help us?" I asked.

"Because one of the services they have is an archive of old television news clips, which apparently you can also view on your home computer as well. Isn't that cool?"

"The coolest," I said with a smile.

"I came across two reports dealing with Max and Alexis Penney's death," Maria replied, ignoring my sarcasm. "Do you want to see them?"

"Sure," I replied, knowing how useful old TV reports had been in cracking the Barry Jones file.

Maria typed some commands on the keyboard while I continued to hover behind her. When both playbacks were ready, Maria said she needed to stretch her legs a bit and walked out of the booth. "I'll watch them later, if you think I need to."

"Okay, no problem," I said as I sat in front of the computer and pressed the play button. A second later the screen was filled with an image of anchorman Dan Wilson sitting behind the Action 11 news desk.

"Murder or suicide? Police are asking that question today after a woman plunged to her death off a downtown medical building. For more on the story, let's go live to Action 11's Denise Walker."

A photogenic female reporter came on screen, standing on a sidewalk and dwarfed by two large office buildings. Several members of the public could also be seen in the background.

"Thanks, Dan. Witnesses say around ten-thirty last night a woman was seen falling from a balcony here at the Upstate Medical Building and landing on Bismarck Street, narrowly missing a couple walking to their car."

The screen switched to a night shot of the same street, where ambulance and police lights lit up the area. In the foreground you could see a bright yellow blanket covering the body of Alexis Penney and another small crowd gathered on the sidewalk. A couple gave their account of what they had seen.

"It was horrible," the woman said, looking to her boyfriend for confirmation. "One second you're walking down a quiet street and then you hear something coming from above you, which lands a few feet away from where you're standing. To realize it was a person . . . well . . . I couldn't believe it."

As the reporter's voice-over continued, the camera panned up to show the side of the building and began to zoom in on balconies high above.

"Others say they saw the woman leap from a balcony between the 20th and 25th floors. All the witnesses also confirm they did not hear the woman screaming as she fell to her death." The screen switched to a live two-shot of Dan and Denise. "Due to the woman's silent free fall, the early speculation was this was a suicide. However, we have now learned police took a man into custody late last evening, but we do not know if his arrest is related to this sad incident. I will have more on this story during the Noontime Report at twelve."

The screen went black as the segment ended.

Intriguing, I thought, as the second report began to play.

Once again it showed Dan the anchorman behind the oversized news desk, looking very much like William Shatner as he captained the U.S.S. Enterprise across the galaxy.

"Now for some breaking news. Con man Max Feldberg, once known in the community as a respected therapist, has been found guilty of second-degree manslaughter in the death of Alexis Penney. As you may recall, last year witnesses saw Ms. Penney fall to her death from the Upstate Medical Building. Initially thought to be a suicide, police discovered she had been involved in an argument inside Feldberg's office prior to her fall. Feldberg, a career confidence operator, was also convicted of defrauding some of his trusting patients of several hundred thousand dollars. He is to be sentenced next month."

The screen went black as Maria returned to our booth.

"What did I miss?" Maria asked. "Anything new?"

"Not really. Just a rehash of the facts," I replied.

"So, what's next?" Maria inquired. "Just wait for Jarvis to call?"

"We don't really have a choice, but I hate wasting time for the sake of wasting time."

"What about going to the scene of the crime? It can't be too far from here. Maybe we'll get some inspiration."

"Or a bite to eat," I laughed. "Yeah, might as well. We've got nothing better to do."

Ten minutes later, we were circling the Upstate Medical Building. I found a parking space and grabbed my camera. "Might as well take a few pictures while we're here. You never know, they might come in handy later," I said.

The building and street looked unchanged since the news report we'd viewed at the library. We actually walked to the spot where the reporter had been standing and took in the whole area with our own eyes. There was nothing remarkable about the surroundings. It was a typical bustling city intersection with buildings on every corner and a steady flow of traffic.

"At night, with all this concrete and offices, I bet this area resembles a ghost town," Maria observed. "After business hours, I don't see many clubs or restaurants that would keep people coming down here."

"I agree. Right now it's the heartbeat of the city but at five o'clock everyone wants to get as far away from here as they can."

"I don't consider myself to be a small town bumpkin," Maria laughed, "but it astounds me more people work in just one of these office towers than reside in all of Delta. What is the appeal?"

"Beats me. I've never had a problem living in big cities, but that small-town boy in me still exists, trust me."

"That's good to hear," Maria said with a grin. She then lifted her eyes and focused on the upper floors of the Upstate Medical Building. "I can't imagine falling from that height to the pavement below. It would be absolutely terrifying."

I also scanned the floors downward, until my gaze came to the point of impact. "We can only hope Alexis was dead or unconscious before her descent. Remember how the witnesses said she wasn't yelling or anything? If I were falling to my death I would be screaming bloody murder all the way down, regardless whether my words were going to be heard or not."

The sounds of the busy street temporarily filled our silence, as we contemplated the horrible scene that had played out years earlier. In my life as a cop, I had been to many suicide scenes, none of which were pleasant to attend. After the fourth or fifth, neither your compassion nor your shock kicks in as hard as they once did. You're not without feelings, it's just they are now muted. You feel sorry for the those left behind more than the victim.

As these thoughts came to mind, I realized just how little we knew of Alexis Penney's background. Max had supplied me with a very thin patient folder, listing her personal information and noting she was trying to cope with her divorce. There was no mention of her mental state. Obviously, the police had discarded the suicide angle after learning about an argument on Max's balcony.

What if Alexis was suicidal? Could that change the outcome of my investigation?

I turned my attention to the Indelible Corporation Building, located on the southeast corner of the street. It was almost a mirror image of the medical building, except the offices had no balconies. I recalled one report in the witness statements folder stating the 911 call came from a building across the street. Again, I was struck by how little information I had on this caller's identity and testimony. The jury had clearly believed him when he described the physical appearance and clothing worn by Alexis' attacker, but who was he? My guess was Max hadn't included this information because it did not bolster his contention that the police had arrested the wrong man.

"We have to go back to the courthouse, Maria."

"Why?"

"I have a serious problem with loose ends and coming down here highlighted a couple for me. They may turn out to be nothing, but as we still have some free time we might as well use it wisely, right?"

"Does that mean you aren't springing for lunch?"

"Not at all," I scoffed. "I'm sure the hotdog vendor is still outside the court building."

"You really know how to treat a woman right, Steve."

"I try my best," I laughed.

In no time we were at the courthouse, where we devoured two Polish sausages loaded with all the trimmings. I updated Maria on my thought process and reluctantly we decided to split up once again. I would attempt to get the transcript from Max's trial, while Maria did more research at the library, this time concentrating on the mysterious Alexis Penney.

"Do not leave the second floor," I instructed her, as we walked in different directions. "I will meet you there as soon as I get the transcript and we can go over it together."

"What about taking candy from strangers? Is that permissible?" Maria asked with a sly smile.

"Only if it's sealed," I replied with a chuckle. "I'll see you in awhile."

At the court archives desk, a very helpful clerk named Brad located Max's trial number in the computer system.

"It'll take about sixty minutes. There are over 700 pages to print off."

"You do bind them somehow, right?" I asked, a bit discouraged by the time delay.

"For an extra $25."

"Of course."

I paid the $125 service charge on my credit card and took a seat in a waiting area. I grabbed an old magazine and started to read reviews for films released two years earlier. Occasionally, I would look over to the clerk's counter hoping to see my order, with no luck. Twenty minutes into my wait, I noticed a police officer stop to have a few laughs with Brad before walking down the hall out of sight. This officer was in full police dress with bars on his shoulders. A Sergeant? A Staff Sergeant? I guessed he was in his late 50's. He also had an air of superiority, which made me curious.

"Does the officer you were speaking with work in the courthouse?"

"Garelick? He runs the courthouse. Sergeant of the Courts. A real nice guy. Why?"

"Has he held that position long?" I asked. "I mean, would he have been around at the time of Max Feldberg's trial?"

"Sure," Brad said. "He's been walking these halls for fifteen years, maybe twenty."

"Where can I find his office?"

"Go to the third floor. You can't miss it."

"Thanks," I said, making my way to the row of elevators.

I soon found myself standing in front of the Sergeant of the Court's gatekeeper, a civilian secretary named Eileen. "I would like to speak with Sergeant Garelick. Would he be in?"

"He is in," came the curt, professional response, "but he's very busy this morning. Would you like to make an appointment?"

He didn't look busy when he was talking with the clerk a few minutes ago, I wanted to say. "What time is it now?"

Eileen consulted her watch. "11:14."

"I'll get back to you on that appointment," I said, walking out of the office. I went around the corner and took a seat on a bench near the elevators. *He's got to get some lunch sometime,* I thought to myself. I picked up another outdated magazine and began to read how light yellow and green were this season's hottest decorating colours.

Luckily, I didn't have to wait long.

"Sergeant Garelick?" I asked the man as he walked into view. I got off the bench and strode confidently toward him, my hand outstretched. "Brad from downstairs said you were the one and only man who could help me today."

Garelick gave me a somewhat suspicious smile but didn't hesitate to shake my hand. He had a firm grip, which telegraphed the message, *I'm an important man. Don't even think of wasting my time.*

"My name is Steve Cassidy. I'm a private investigator working on the Max Feldberg case," I said cutting right to the chase.

"Con artist, right? Threw a woman off the Upstate Medical Building as I recall. Open and shut case. What's at issue?"

The elevator doors opened and Garelick stepped inside, assuming I would follow, which I did.

"He's under the impression he was framed."

"Feldberg is your client?"

"In a matter of speaking, I guess," I confessed. "It's complicated."

"I bet. Defence work always is, especially when you know your guy's guilty," Garelick said without emotion. "Who does he think framed him and how does this concern me? I had nothing to do with his case."

"I was hoping you might have some insight from the trial or remember something that would not show up in the official transcript, that's all. As we speak, I'm waiting for a call from Max's theoretical framer to set up a meeting."

Garelick gave me a quizzical look. "Do you have any tangible evidence Feldberg was set up?"

"Only his word."

The elevator doors opened and we stepped out into the basement level. I noted a cafeteria sign and we started down the hallway in the direction of the arrow.

"Interesting."

"Max and I were friends in high school but we lost touch when he headed out west. I only became aware of his circumstances in the past few weeks."

"He contacted you then?" Garelick said, coming to a halt. "Why would he do that after all these years?"

"At present, your guess is as good as mine," I lied, never breaking eye contact.

We stood in complete silence for several moments, sizing one another up.

"I don't believe that for a minute, Cassidy. However, I'm not in the mood to get into a pissing contest with an ex-copper who clearly knows how to lie. You must have had a lot of experience in your former career to pull off such a display of insubordination." He paused and added, "Or you're a damn good poker player."

"Yes, to both observations."

We were on the march again.

"I'm getting a ham and cheese sandwich, a bowl of soup and a coffee, which I will then eat in my office. When I'm finished my lunch,

I will be finished with you. How does that sound?"

"Lunch it is," I said, although not hungry after eating that huge sausage. "I'm buying."

"You got that right."

As we went through the line Garelick gave me a brief overview of his career. He loved the courts because nothing exciting ever happened aside from the occasional distraught mother causing a disturbance after one of her beloved kids was unjustly found guilty.

We returned to the third floor and as we walked past Eileen she gave me a dirty look.

"I will be in a meeting with Mr. Cassidy for about ten minutes and I don't want to be interrupted, Eileen," Garelick said without slowing down. "Close the door behind you, Cassidy," he instructed after we entered his spacious office.

Behind his desk he unwrapped his sandwich, took the lid off his container of soup and took a sip from his coffee cup. "After years of grabbing something on the road between calls, I'm a pretty quick eater. So, you should start your interrogation now."

He was old school and I knew not to toy with him.

"Does the name Jarvis Larsh ring any bells with you?"

"None."

"Did the police or prosecution do any type of investigation into Alexis Penney's background or mental state at the time of her death?"

"You'll have to talk with Detective Remy about that. He's now in Internal Affairs and was the lead on that case."

"But you don't recall anything off hand?"

"About Penney?" He put down his sandwich and leaned back in his chair. "What do you know about her so far?"

"That she can't fly."

That brought a smile to the Sergeant's face. "I recall that being clearly established during the trial as well," he said. "Other than that, the prosecution only had to show a link between her and Feldberg, which his lawyer fully acknowledged. Once that relationship was confirmed, she became kind of a non-issue—aside from her falling twenty-odd stories from his balcony."

"About that . . . were the police able to determine definitively she fell from Max's balcony? And what about the eyewitness—the 911 caller? Did he check out?"

"As I understand it, his testimony was rock solid. A business-man working late across the street. Saw the whole thing in 3-D. He described the fight in detail and what Feldberg was wearing. The whole nine yards. He even named a few objects on the balcony—you know, a chair and a potted plant. Feldberg did this, no doubt about it."

I watched as Garelick began on his small bowl of soup and knew that with each slurp from his plastic spoon my time was running out.

"From what you're telling me, this really was open and shut."

"Pretty much."

"What about all the money Max duped out of his clients? What happened to it? Were his patients paid back somehow?" This was another very foggy issue Max never addressed in his box of goodies.

"Very few people came forward, probably fearful of being ridi-culed by their family and friends," Garelick said, taking another drink of coffee and crumpling up the now-empty sandwich wrap. "People who fall for scams carry a huge amount of guilt with them, whether they lose twenty bucks at a three-card monte game on a street corner or their life savings to a door-to-door salesman."

"And with the added press exposure due to Alexis' death, I'm sure no one would want to be associated with Max or his practice."

"Exactly." The lid for the foam soup bowl was fastened over the rim and the whole container found its way into a garbage can at the side of the desk. "Before you leave, do you have one last question, Cassidy?"

I watched as the Sergeant drank the last few drops of his coffee. "If you were a betting man, what percentage of the farm would you gamble that Max was correctly convicted and I'm wasting my time trying to prove otherwise?"

The Sergeant stood from his chair, leaned forward, placed both hands on his desk and said, "My farm. My neighbours' farm. And their neighbours' farm."

I got up and shook his hand. "Thank you for your time. It was a pleasure meeting you today, Sergeant."

"I'm sure it was, Mr. Cassidy. You know your way out, don't you?"

"That I do, sir."

"And thanks for lunch."

As I stepped out of the office, Eileen gave me another evil look. "Have a great day," I said as I walked toward the elevators. I then noticed the stairwell and decided to get some exercise. Three floors later, I found myself in the lobby being summoned by my friend Brad.

"Your transcript is finished, Mr. Cassidy," he said, as he put his hand on a large binder on the counter.

I picked up the massive tome and shook my head. "You don't have the Reader's Digest condensed version back there somewhere? I'd pay another $25 for it."

"Sorry. You get the unabridged version or nothing."

I thanked Brad for his help, grabbed my heavy purchase and headed to the library to see how Maria was making out. Even with my unexpected lunch appointment it had only been about an hour since we'd parted ways. I found her in booth number 3 once again with a map filling the computer screen. I placed the transcript in front of her and said, "Please tell me one of your hidden talents is speed reading."

She examined the binder's label that read *People vs. Feldberg* and laughed. "Even if I did possess such a gift, do you really think I would tell you? This thing is huge."

"Tell me about it. It's going to take all day and night to read it."

"And what exactly are you looking for?"

"Answers to some nagging questions about this investigation and the original crime," I said. "Finding Jarvis was too easy. In fact, after all these years he's still out in the open, ready to be found by any Tom, Dick or Harry investigator out there. From my lunch with the Sergeant, it doesn't appear Jarvis Larsh has any bearing on Max's case."

"Lunch with the Sergeant?" Maria asked.

"Not really lunch," I replied with a grin. "More of a quick question-and-answer session in his office." I dug into my coat and produced a blueberry muffin. "Before you get all bent out of shape, here." I placed the muffin on the desk. "This was the lunch that I didn't have time to eat."

Maria looked at the semi-squished baked good and then up at me and my smirky smile. "A warm pop, a sausage on a stale bun and now this morsel of nutrition. You really shouldn't have, Steven. You're placing me on a very high pedestal which I don't know I really deserve to occupy."

"I promise I'll make this up to you," I said seriously. "I thought you'd be happy I remembered blueberry was your favourite."

"That's not the point and you know it."

"Yeah, yeah. I know it. Anyway . . . how did your research turn out the second time around?"

She gave me an Eileen-worthy nasty look, before returning to the computer. "A bit better, I guess. There wasn't much information from old newspapers about Alexis Penney, aside from the fact that she'd moved here only a short time before her death."

"From where?"

"I couldn't find an exact location listed anywhere, but there aren't many Alexis Penneys in the country. One of them, however, was charged with murder around the time our girl moved to town."

"Are they one and the same?" I asked, intrigued at this new wrinkle, not knowing how this could have involved Max or what effect it had on Alexis' death.

"I was about to find out when you dropped War and Peace on the desk."

I put the trial binder under my arm. "Please, don't let me stop you from super-sleuthing. I'm going to start reading this thing out there. If you find anything of interest, just whistle."

"In a library?"

"You know what I mean. Stop being difficult." As I closed the door behind me, I couldn't resist saying, "Enjoy that muffin."

I didn't wait to hear Maria's reaction and took a seat at a nearby table. *This really is going to take me forever*, I thought. As I opened the transcript, I was relieved to see an index listing each day of the trial and the corresponding page number. Unfortunately, individual witnesses were not similarly catalogued.

I turned to Day One of the trial and read the prosecution's opening argument. I soon learned it was a rehash of the material I had at home. In the end, opening arguments are generally useless, whether they are by the crown or the defence. What really matters is the overall substance of their case; the evidence that will prove a person's guilt or innocence. Of course, circumstantial cases can go either way. In some instances, the jury still doesn't convict or acquit based on the evidence presented. Once you find yourself on trial, the outcome is never a sure thing. As I continued to read, I realized that on another day, before another judge and jury, Max could have very well been set free to fleece and con again.

The high-pitched electronic ring of my cell phone scared not only me, but many of the second-floor patrons. I saw Maria spin in her chair to give me a look my mother used when I did something unthinkable in front of her church friends. I quickly found the phone in my jacket and jammed my finger on the Send button. "Give me a second," I said to the caller, walking into Maria's booth.

"Is it Jarvis?" she whispered.

I looked at the display window: Dawn. Maybe taking this call in Maria's company was not a great idea.

"Hey, Dawn. This really isn't a good time to talk."

"Oh," she said slowly. "Are you working on the case?"

"I'm in a library and they are about to take away my lending privileges. Can I call you in a few minutes?"

"Dawn who?" Maria inquired in a low whisper.

"A waitress friend from Darrien," I said, before putting my index finger to my lips trying to silence her.

"I'm leaving work right now. I called to let you know they aired a news report saying a life insurance policy on Linda has surfaced and the police are now looking for you."

"What are you talking about? That's insane," I said quite loudly.

It was then I saw one of the librarians get up from her desk and begin making her way to our cramped room.

"It's got to be Ellerby. Unless . . ." Dawn's voice trailed off.

"There's no other policy out there, Dawn. Please believe me," I said emphatically. "And you already know Ellerby's policy is a load of crap."

There was a knock on the door, which Maria opened.

"Sir, I am going to have to ask you to leave. You are disturbing the other patrons."

"No problem," I stammered. "I'll get right back to you, Dawn. Don't leave work." I terminated the call and turned to Maria. "I'll meet you in the lobby."

"What's going on?" Maria asked as a concerned expression formed on her face.

"I don't know. Try finding something on the web about a warrant for my arrest in Darrien or a life insurance policy on Linda."

"Sir, I must—"

"I'm going. I'm going." I picked up the mammoth trial transcript and jogged to the stairwell.

I called Dawn back and asked, "Was this on the radio or TV?"

"Both."

"Great. Maybe I'll have to stay out here a little longer than expected."

"I don't think being a fugitive is going to open many doors for you, Steve."

"I'm not a fugitive. At this point I'm a person of interest."

"That's not the way my customers see you. To them you're a very interesting fugitive on the run."

"So far it's only a local story, right?"

"I guess."

"Then it shouldn't immediately affect my investigation. No one even knows who I am. I'm one of hundreds of private eyes around here."

"There was also a brief mention of the Barry Jones case and that became national news, right?"

"Damn it!" I cried out, again bringing unwanted attention from other visitors of the municipal building. "This is outrageous! I'm going to beat the living daylights out of Ellerby when I find him."

"So, you're coming back?"

"Not yet. We still have to talk to the guy at the centre of this whole mystery."

"When will that be?"

"To be honest, Dawn, when my phone rang I thought it was him."

"Well, I'll let you go so you don't miss his call."

"Thanks for the update. I really appreciate it."

"If anything else comes up, I'll call you. Until then, keep a low profile."

"I'll try."

The line went dead. Dejected, I slumped my tired carcass onto a hallway bench.

"What else could go wrong?" I asked aloud. Out of the corner of my eye I noticed Sergeant Garelick appear to my left and make a beeline to Brad's counter. *I spoke too soon*, I thought, as I began to walk in the opposite direction toward the main front doors.

"Steve, wait up."

I looked to see Maria rushing down the stairwell to my right, waving her hands clutching several pieces of paper. I gave her a searing look, kept my head down and walked silently out of the building.

I was halfway down the front steps and heading toward the parking garage when Maria emerged from the building. "Steve, slow down. What's wrong?"

I tentatively glanced over my shoulder and yelled, "Meet me at the van in five minutes. No more questions and do not follow me."

I ran across the street into an alleyway, where I stopped to see what was happening in my wake. Maria was staring blankly in my direction and then at the building behind her. She had no clue what was going on but was smart enough to trust me for the moment.

What she didn't notice was Sergeant Garelick and another uniformed officer fly out the front doors and begin to survey the area. I could only presume that after I left his office, Garelick ran my name through a police database and stumbled across the latest news. A few moments later, they re-entered the building, no doubt to alert their comrades a potential scoundrel was within their midst. It wouldn't be the first time an All Points Bulletin had been issued in my name but I feared it would be the last.

In the time it took me to get to the van, Maria had worked herself into a state of near hysteria. I found her crouched at the front fender of the van, looking over the railing to the street below, surveying everyone and everything. When she finally saw me walking toward her, I was stunned by her appearance. Her hair was disheveled, tears were running down her cheeks and her skin was a sickening shade of white.

"Everything is fine, Maria. I promise. I am so sorry I ran away from you like that. It will never happen again."

She stood and instantaneously the expression of sheer terror on her face was replaced by a look of disgust and fury, all of which was aimed directly at me.

"You got that right, Steven! It won't because I'm not sticking around long enough for you to do this to me again. I'm going home."

She crushed the pieces of paper into my chest and let them go. I was able to grab a few before they fell to the parking garage floor. "What are these?" I asked gently.

"Just please open the door and get me to the airport as soon as possible." Maria glared at me and my legs nearly buckled. "Do you think you can do that?"

Without a word, I unlocked the passenger door and then picked the papers off the floor. Maria got into the van and slammed her door closed.

LIFE INSURANCE POLICY FOUND
Missing librarian's fiancé sought by police

I cringed at the writer's byline: Jeremy Atkins, my old foe at the Darrien Free Press.

I placed the papers on the floor between the front seats and started the engine. "It's all lies, Maria. I had nothing to do with Linda's leaving."

"Are you kidding me? You and your female co-workers and waitress friends had everything to do with Linda's leaving. The difference now is I don't know if you had a hand in her actual *disappearance*."

"Linda did not disappear," I said firmly. "She is alive and well somewhere."

"Do you have proof of that?" Maria countered.

"No, but there is also no proof something terrible happened to her either."

"You're saying she's on an extended vacation?"

"Maybe, who knows? I don't know. The last time I saw her, she was alive. If something has happened to her since, I did not have any involvement in it."

"And the insurance policy? Why didn't you tell anyone about that detail?"

"Because it's phony, Maria. It was planted by a private investigator looking into her case. I never took out any life insurance policies on Linda and in time I'll prove it to everyone. Trust me on this one. I know what it looks like."

"And looks can be deceiving, right?"

"Exactly."

"Well, when you get back to Darrien, I will look forward to being proved wrong. Until then, I want to go home and get on with my life."

The final words carried a slight tremor and Maria could no longer look me in the eyes.

"I'm sorry I got you involved in this thing, Maria."

"So am I, Steven. So am I."

The ride to the hotel was silent. With every corner I turned and every mile we traveled, there was the added stress of not knowing if Garelick was hot on my trail. When I pulled into the parking lot, I was glad to see no police officers waiting for us. We went to our rooms and packed—Maria for the flight home and me for safety's sake. The rooms had been prepaid for the next two days, so I decided not to check either one of us out. This way, when the police verified my credit card activity, they would come directly to this hotel and stake it out, believing we would return shortly. This would give me time to find new digs. My only fear was Maria might be stopped at the airport, as her ticket had been purchased on my card.

"You don't have to wait around here alone for five hours, Maria," I said as we arrived at the airport's departure terminal. "Let's go for that lunch or something."

"I can't. I want to get home and away from all of this."

She had already expressed these sentiments several times and I didn't want to provoke her anger again. "If you have any problems getting on the plane, call my cell and I'll be back here as soon as I can." This was another area of great concern to me, that Maria would be treated like an accomplice because of her involvement with me. "I'm glad you came out here. You've helped me tremendously with your research and how you handled Jarvis' wife. You are amazing."

Maria inhaled deeply before saying, "I wish I could help you more but I just can't. There are too many unanswered questions about you and Linda. I am emotionally out of my league here and know I would be a hindrance to you from this point on."

"I understand. I put you in an impossible position and I'm sorry."

Maria got out of the van and grabbed her suitcase from the backseat. "I'll call you when I get home."

"Thanks," I replied, resigned to the idea we might not see one another for a very, very long time. "Have a good flight," was all I could say as she closed the sliding side door.

I watched her enter the terminal and felt as though I had lost my best friend. When I had left her behind after high school to forge a new path alone, I knew that what I was doing was wrong. I honestly felt she'd be better off without me. When I returned to look into Barry Jones' disappearance thirteen years later, I realized how my selfish actions had adversely affected Maria's life, and vowed never to cause her that type of pain again. Yet today, without even trying, I had hurt her more than I cared to know or she would ever admit, and this time, I knew the scars would be permanent.

For the next five hours, I aimlessly watched planes take off and land, come and go from the safety of a nearby parking lot.

At the top of each hour I turned on the local radio station, wondering if there were any news items about me. There never were though. At the end of each newscast, I turned the radio off and stared out the front window enveloped in a self-imposed silence, broken only by the roar of jumbo jets as they flew overhead. As the time of Maria's flight approached, I looked through my trusty binoculars to determine each departing aircraft's call numbers. Fifteen minutes after its scheduled departure time, Maria's plane soared overhead, taking her a safe distance away from all the chaos that surrounded me.

"Take care, Maria," I said, watching the plane slowly disappear into the horizon.

I was grateful I had not received a call from her from inside the airport. As I drove away—destination unknown—I wondered if she would have called me if there'd been trouble. As disheartening as that idea was, more depressing was the prospect she wouldn't call when she landed. If I were in her in position, I would keep moving forward and never look back, not even to make a promised ten-second telephone call.

SIXTEEN

After paying cash for a room in a less prominent hotel, I called Dawn.

"Nothing new to report," she said. "The stations ran the same story all afternoon, only now they say your whereabouts are unknown."

"That's comforting, I guess. My house is most likely under surveillance. Officer Anderton wanted to throw me in jail when he had no cause, so I can imagine his giddiness over this development."

"About an hour ago, there was a blacked-out van parked on your street."

"And how would you know that, Dawn?" I asked in a very light-hearted way.

"Well . . . I might have taken an evening stroll through your neighbourhood. You know—for the fresh air and exercise."

"Two things in this life I do not get enough of, it seems."

"You're hanging around with the wrong women, that's all."

"You may be right. Unfortunately, I could use another good female investigator."

"What happened to Maria?" There was a pause before she added, "What did you do to drive her away, Steve? I hope she at least told you goodbye to your face."

"I dropped her off at the airport, where she had the courage to kick me to the curb in person."

"This is becoming a habit of yours. Am I next?"

I let out a belly laugh at the absurdity of the comment. "Only if you're lucky," I joked.

"You're going to miss me when I'm gone. You know that, don't you?"

"That sounds like another one of your movie quotes."

"Does that make a difference?"

"Not at all," I said quickly. "And yes, I would miss you if you mysteriously disappeared from my life. With my recent track record though, I can't imagine the feeling would be mutual."

"I have no intention of vanishing anytime soon. At least not while you're on the lam from the fuzz," she said with a laugh.

"For you, I'll be on my best behaviour. Then when I get back to Darrien, you can decide if our association is worth the hassle or not."

"Deal."

"When you go to work tomorrow, could you do another round of counter-surveillance?"

"Sure."

"Just don't get caught, okay? I've had my fill of worrying my friends will be grilled by the police because of my actions."

"You don't have to fret about little old me. By the time I got through with my interrogators, they would be telling me all their secrets. You know—like how they used to put on their sister's panties when they were home alone."

"I'm sure they would be putty in your hands," I replied.

"You better believe it." There was another short silence. "Are you going to be okay, Steve?" Dawn asked in a tender voice. "Aside from periodically spying on the cops, is there anything else I can do?"

"Not really," I said with a bit of sadness. "This is my screwed-up case—and life—and the faster I deal with everything out here, the sooner stuff back there will calm down and I can return to a normal life, whatever that is."

"I thought I'd offer. I wasn't angling for a plane ticket or anything," she laughed. "Still . . . I could really use a vacation right about now."

"Me too, Dawn, but trust me, I'm not having much fun so far on this trip."

As she began to respond, her words cut in and out. Thinking we had a bad connection, I glanced at the display window: Incoming Call.

"Dawn, I have another call coming in. I'll get back to you later."

"No problem. Call me tomorrow."

I pressed the Send button and said, "Hello."

"Hi, I'd like to speak to a Mr. Steven Cassidy."

"I'm Steve Cassidy. How can I help you?"

"You were by my house this morning and spoke to my wife. My name is Jarvis Larsh. Apparently you wanted to talk to me about a car accident. The problem is I don't recall witnessing any accidents. So, I don't know how I could be of assistance to you."

"First, I appreciate you calling me, Mr. Larsh," I said in a slightly stilted manner, before recovering my self-confidence. "This accident happened in 1992 when you lived on Stinson Drive."

"Stinson Drive. Wow, that was a long time ago," Jarvis replied.

"You apparently gave your name to one of the drivers. However, there was no follow-up investigation, so no one contacted you about giving a statement. Circumstances have changed and I was hoping you might be able to assist me. Even if you only remember a few vague details, it might help my client."

"I don't know."

"As we told your wife earlier, this will only take a few minutes." I let that sink in a few seconds and then added, "Between you and me, Mr. Larsh, the insurance company is just trying to cover all its bases in this matter. They aren't really expecting any new evidence from you or others."

"When you put it that way I guess I have nothing to lose if I meet with you. Could you drop by the house tomorrow around 10:00?"

I desperately needed to talk with Jarvis at a neutral location. Speaking to him at his residence was far too risky.

"Unfortunately, I have to check out another promising lead around that time. Your wife mentioned you often come into the city. Would it be possible to meet somewhere downtown, maybe around 11:00?" I held my breath waiting for his answer.

"I suppose I could do that," he finally said. "Do you know where The Denby Eatery is located?"

"I'm sure I'll be able to find it. If I can't, you'll know I'm not that good a private investigator, right?" I said with a laugh.

Thankfully, Jarvis laughed along with me. "You were able to track me down from Stinson Drive, so I'm guessing a restaurant won't be too difficult for you to find."

"Just in case I get disoriented in the downtown core, is there some landmark that might help me out?"

It was Jarvis' turn to chuckle. "Well, I don't know if the city council would designate it a landmark, but for many of us the Shakin' Pussycat Bar is a shrine of sorts, if you know what I mean. The Denby Eatery is a few doors down."

"I like the way you give directions, Mr. Larsh. You're like the hip tour guide who takes his customers to the places they really want to visit and not just the ones listed in the brochure." This produced another small laugh from Jarvis. "The Denby Eatery it is then. Tomorrow at 11:00. I'll see you there."

As soon as I was off the phone, I opened the yellow pages and located an ad in the entertainment section for the Shakin' Pussycat Bar. I wrote down the address and found a listing for the restaurant Jarvis had mentioned. On my city map, I estimated the locations of both businesses and noted they were within walking distance of the Upstate Medical Building. I wondered if this was simply coincidental or had some significance. I remembered a police college instructor once telling us, "There is no such thing as a coincidence. Everything happens for a reason. Call it luck. Call it providence. Call it Shirley if you want, but everything is connected when it comes to a criminal investigation. Everything."

As I was heading into the city, I was also thinking of how humans are such creatures of habit. We take the same route to work every day. Stop at the same donut shop or convenience store on the way. Park in the same spot every morning. The fact Jarvis mentioned this strip club at all conveyed he was more interested in checking out the peelers than meeting me about some forgotten accident. My guess was that after our meeting he would stroll up the street for a bit of midday eye candy. If I was right, I doubted the lovely Chantal would be coming along for the ride tomorrow.

In my ever-changing quest to understand my target, I decided a visit to Jarvis' favourite bar might be beneficial—for research purposes only, of course.

While forking over a steep $15 cover charge at the front door, my cell phone began to vibrate.

"Hi, Steve."

"Hey, Maria," I said, stepping out into the quiet street. "No problems getting home?" I asked, trying to sound casual.

"No. Everything went smoothly. Daniel came to pick me up at the airport."

"Good. Glad to hear that."

"Well . . . I hope the rest of your investigation goes as planned."

"I'm meeting with Jarvis tomorrow morning."

"That's great."

"Yeah. He sounds normal on the phone but you never know, right?"

"Be careful."

"I will."

"All right then . . . I wanted to let you know I got back safely."

"I appreciate that, Maria. And thanks again for your help."

"I really have to go."

"Maybe we can talk when I get back?"

"Maybe," she said without conviction. She then concluded our conversation with a phrase I felt might haunt me for a long time. "Goodbye, Steven."

I felt hollow. I knew making this call would have been hard for Maria on many levels. As much as I wanted to call her to apologize again, I knew it would accomplish nothing. My only hope was that at the conclusion of this file, I could repair the damage I had caused.

I stepped into the bar area where a large bouncer with a huge grin welcomed me to the club. I took in the ambiance and realized I had frequented much worse strip clubs in my time. I could also understand how this place would appeal to someone like Jarvis. It was dark enough to have a seductive feel, yet bright enough that you didn't feel like the pervert you feared you were. Only a quarter of the tables were occupied, with all of the usual suspects in attendance: slackers, gruff-looking blue-collar labourers, a few men not afraid to wear their wedding rings in public and a group of smartly dressed businessmen celebrating the closing of a big deal.

I bought a beer and took a seat in the far corner of the room so I could see the entire club at once. The girl performing on stage couldn't have been more than a day over the legal limit. I watched her gyrate and kick her legs above her head. Chances are if she had found her way here, her upbringing wasn't filled with sunshine and roses. On the other hand, when I was down on my luck I had met several exotic dancers and discovered they were only slightly more screwed up than everyone else. They claimed taking off their clothes was only a job and they took pride in their work, like every other hard working person out there. To be honest, I never completely bought this view. There really is no comparison between a custodian waxing a gym floor and a woman pushing her private parts in your face at twenty bucks per three-minute song. Now if a school principal regularly stuffed a handful of bills down the front of that same janitor's pants for a vacuuming job well done, I admit the lines might begin to blur.

Every few minutes a dancer would stop by to ask me how my night was going and if I would like a lap dance. When I declined the offer, they'd usually look around to the other potential takers to see if there was another fish willing to bite. As I was in the back corner, by the time they got to me they had already waded through the aisles, making contact with all the other men. This actually worked well for both of us, as the dancer, seeing no hope of making a few bucks until some new blood walked in, would take a seat in the shadows and we would start talking like long lost friends. With each performer, I tried to envision who might be Jarvis' favourite. They were all young and surprisingly very attractive.

To attract such talent, this must be the high-end strip club in the city, I thought.

Sixty minutes later, having behaved myself with every offer that came wandering seductively my way, I decided I'd had enough excitement for one day. Tomorrow would be pivotal to my investigation and I wanted to be physically and mentally prepared for my big meeting. Getting loaded and being entertained by one of these lovelies at the hotel could not be on my agenda, though the idea had crossed my mind. Maybe it was Maria's sudden departure coupled with Dawn's sweetness over the phone which made me conclude chasing every available woman with a skirt—or in this evening's case, a tiny thong— might not be in my best interests.

My getaway plan, however, was compromised when I approached the main entrance. Much like the reaction Maria and I had at the sight of Chantal Larsh, a surge of electricity rushed through me when I saw a red-haired woman walk into the club.

My night was definitely not over yet.

"Any problems with customers, Dillon?" she asked the bouncer.

"Nothing I couldn't handle, Melissa," he replied with a laugh. "Now that you're here, I doubt anyone will be stirring up trouble."

She looked across the room to evaluate the evening's clientele. "How have the girls been doing tonight?"

"A few have done okay but I get the sense these guys are waiting for you."

"Then I better put on a good show," she replied, as she walked toward a back room.

Trying not to be too conspicuous, I went to a payphone where I briefly pretended to place a call. On the way back to my table, I stopped and asked the bouncer, "Who's the redhead?"

"Destiny Rose," came the reply. "The most popular dancer in town."

"I bet."

SEVENTEEN

In every area of the entertainment industry, there are professionals and there are amateurs. Any actor can read a script but there is a real difference if the performer is Tom Hanks and not Joe Schmoe, the star of the local community players group. Or a singer like Bruce Springsteen, compared to the lead vocalist for an up-and-coming band called Unfinished Tattoos. It all comes down to *presence*, something Destiny Rose oozed from every exposed pore on her tight body. Compared to the other dancers, her physical movements were more polished. Unlike the earlier performers who tried valiantly to grab your attention, Destiny Rose commanded the stage and, through sheer seductive determination, demanded you pay attention to her and only her.

I glanced around the room and noticed no lap dances were being offered during Destiny's three-song set. When that happens, you know you're a superstar. The DJ mentioned in his introduction that she had been Stripper of the Year, so obviously she was a known commodity.

At the conclusion of her routine, wild applause, whistling and hollering filled the air. The DJ told the crowd Destiny Rose would be performing twice more and that they should stick around to see what she had in store for them. He then announced that Kendra—a smart, beautiful girl who'd told me she was working her way through medical school the hard way—was up next. When she hit the stage, the other girls began to revisit the tables, enticing the flesh connoisseurs Destiny Rose had sufficiently aroused.

As I watched Destiny Rose leave the room, I involuntarily made eye contact with the bouncer, who gave me an *I told you she was the best* smile, to which I nodded silently in agreement. I debated how best to approach her. I knew it was entirely possible there was another red-haired dancer employed here, but my sixth sense kept telling me that simply wasn't the case. This was Jarvis' girl. I had no doubt.

"Is Destiny Rose a featured dancer in town for the week?" I asked my waitress Maryann, after she placed another drink on my table.

"Nope, she's 100% home grown. Been working here a long time. She's a legend around these parts."

"Interesting," I replied, as I tipped her five bucks, which brought a smile to her face.

"Thanks. Since they raised the cover charge, we don't get many big tippers anymore. That money used to be spent on the dancers and wait staff. Now, everyone figures they can stiff us."

"Sorry to hear that," I said sympathetically, believing this girl might also be a gold mine of information. "Even the regulars?"

"Especially them. They think their loyalty should be rewarded."

"Why wouldn't they just go somewhere else?"

"Because for all their grumbling about the cover charge, they know they get more bang for their buck here than the clubs in the area."

"So, their own high standards keep them returning again and again."

"Yep. Crack addicts have their favourite dealers and these guys have the Shakin' Pussycat," she laughed.

"When Destiny Rose came in I overheard her ask the bouncer if he'd had to deal with any customers. Is that a problem here?"

Maryann thought a moment and shrugged her shoulders.

"Not really. Every once in awhile some guys have a few too many—usually during a bachelor party—and get carried away. None of the dancers have been assaulted or stalked, if that's what you mean." She glanced over at the front door and said, "Besides, would you like to mess with Dillon over there?"

"No thanks. My life is difficult enough," I replied.

"Exactly."

As Maryann was about to leave, I asked, "Does Destiny Rose do private shows?"

"Do you mean for parties or in our V.I.P. area?"

"V.I.P."

"Sure. She charges more than the other girls, but I haven't heard anyone complain yet," she said with a smile. "She'll probably be out in a few minutes. Do you want me to arrange a private dance? I tell

Dillon and he tells Destiny Rose."

"Yeah, why not?" I said.

"Okey-dokey."

She walked over to Dillon and I headed to a V.I.P. room. Once seated in a very large, comfortable chair, I counted the cash in my wallet to make sure I didn't have to use the bank machine again. I had withdrawn the bank's daily limit, afraid the authorities might be monitoring my accounts to find me. I'm sure Garelick had informed the Darrien cops I was in his jurisdiction. By taking out that much money, my hope was everyone would think I really was on the run and had left the area. That I had not used my airline ticket at the same time as Maria would hopefully also fuel such speculation. What idiot would stick around a few more days knowing he was wanted by the police?

"Steve. Steve Cassidy," I told Destiny Rose when she asked my name a few minutes later.

"That's a very nice name," she said, as she closed the curtain of our spacious enclave. "Most of my gentleman friends don't like to use their last names. What makes you so special, honey?"

"Maybe it's my stage name," I replied with a smile, "like Destiny Rose is yours."

She took a seat on the edge of a small couch across from me. "So, you're into role playing? I can be anyone you want but I draw the line at being some animal or space alien. I had one college customer want me to play a wizard or a magical gargoyle from Dungeon and Dragons. I had to refuse him because I had no idea what he was talking about."

"Well, college wasn't my thing, although now that you mention it I do have a hazy recollection of fantasizing about being a magical wizard when I was going through puberty."

This asinine comment made her laugh and temporarily broke her whole serious Sex Goddess persona. As I watched her lean into the cushions, I was briefly allowed to glimpse Destiny's true self— Melissa—the hard-working, semi-famous, exotic dancer with a heart of gold I desperately wanted to connect with tonight. As Destiny tried to compose herself, I placed a $100 bill on the couch beside her.

"I heard you might be a big spender," she said, although she didn't touch the bill just yet. At this point her mannerisms and attitude were half-Destiny, half-Melissa, a combination that suited her well; a little softer around the edges but still nobody's fool.

"There's more where that came from," I said, trying to keep her interested.

"I could see that," she replied, pointing to the pocket where I had put my wallet. "So . . . I guess the only thing left to negotiate is what services you require to make your business trip a bit more pleasurable." She finally picked up the bill and placed it into a small purse she had with her. She then got off the couch, walked over to my chair and opened her flimsy blouse, exposing her firm, mature body.

"For a hundred bucks, you can pretty much call the shots for fifteen minutes. Remember though, I don't do any kinky stuff. If you just want lap dances, you get me for thirty minutes."

"What if I only want to talk?"

With the money part of our transaction now complete, my girl Melissa had vanished from the room. Destiny Rose, however, leaned forward and in her most seductive voice whispered in my ear, "While I'm performing you can talk as dirty as you like—free of charge." She then flicked her tongue across my earlobe which, I'll admit, sent a tingle up and down my spine and directly into the front of my jeans. "So what will it be, Mr. Steve Cassidy?" she asked, as she continued to linger over me.

This is a test! This is only a test!

Keep the penis in the pants!

I stared up into her face, which appeared much older than viewed from the back row. Don't get me wrong, she was still a very attractive and sensual woman, but there was a hardness in her eyes which I had seen too many times in my former career. She was now in full robotic stripper mode and I had to muster every ounce of willpower to say, "I need to speak with Melissa. That's all."

It took her a few confused seconds to comprehend my request and to turn off the Destiny Rose persona. Ever the consummate professional, she coolly stood and walked to the couch to retrieve her purse. She pulled out a $50 bill and said, "Like I said earlier, I don't do kinky shit. Here's your change." She threw the bill on my lap and took a step toward the curtain.

Knowing Dillon was only ten feet away and ready to pummel any customer who showed disrespect to the dancers, I put my life and investigation on the line as I gently reached out to grab Destiny Rose's free hand.

"Let go of me now," she said very slowly.

Still tempting fate, I held on as I pled my case. "I'm a P.I. and I think you might be able to help me." I let go of her hand. "One of your regular customers may have killed a woman and I was hoping you could give me some background on him. Honest—that's it." I pulled out my wallet and held out another hundred, plus the fifty she'd thrown at me. "Trust me, this *No Touch All Talk* policy is also completely foreign to me."

I had stopped her forward momentum (a good sign) and she hadn't interrupted me or cried, "Rape!" She was also looking at my outstretched hand (the best sign of all). At her core she was a businesswoman who always listened when the mighty dollar came her way. However, she could still decline my offer.

"Toss in another fifty and you get Melissa for twenty minutes," she countered. "Then it's fifty more for each additional ten minutes. Take it or leave it."

"Done," I said.

She put the money away in her trusty purse and stretched out on the couch. Her body and features relaxed immediately. Melissa had returned. "I hope your client will reimburse you for this. I would love to see how you describe this meeting on your expense sheet."

It was my turn to smile. "You've heard of creative accounting, right? This would be an example of creative writing for a creative accountant. I used to be a cop, so making stuff up to make me look good has never been a problem."

"Used to be? I would think officers have better pension and health plans. What happened?"

"I'll tell you after my twenty minutes are up. If we got into my life

215

story, I would have to take a large cash advance on my credit card—something I'd rather not do tonight."

"Fine with me. The clock is always ticking and time is money, Mr. Cassidy—if that really is your name. You've got about nineteen minutes left, not that I believe I can help you in the least. So, which of my so-called regulars do you think killed someone?"

I couldn't tell if Melissa had been born this bold or if she had learned it over the years working at various nightclubs. In her position, cultivating a thick skin and tough exterior was a necessity for staying alive.

"I know this will sound like a really dumb first question," I began, "but have you always been a redhead—at least during the time you've been performing?"

"I've had a full head of red hair from the second I was conceived in the backseat of a Buick. Why? Do you have something against us?"

"Not at all."

"You'd be shocked at how many men used to pass me over so they could get a dance from some dumb-as-a-piece-of-driftwood bleach blonde." She looked at the mirror above us and ran her fingers through her hair. "You can't get this from a bottle," she said seriously. "In a world filled with brunettes and blondes, I always figured because there were so few of us on the market we'd be seen as special. You know—more exotic somehow."

"Oh, believe me, there are plenty of men out there, including myself, who appreciate you and your fellow sorority girls. Those bozos who go for the fake blondes don't know what they're missing."

"Their loss."

"Exactly," I agreed, attempting to keep the conversation light and upbeat. "Okay, next question. How long have you worked at this club?"

"Nine years, give or take, I guess. I started as a waitress and saved all my tips until I could afford my girls here," she laughed, cupping her huge fake breasts in her hands.

"And the owner suddenly thought you were wasting your time as a waitress, right?" I asked.

"Something like that," she smiled as she folded her hands across her stomach. "I started dancing in my late 20's, which is much later than most girls. Now, every year they get younger and younger—not just looking but age-wise. When an eighteen–year–old baby comes in for a job, I want to take her hand and lead her to the community college down the street."

"Like a den mother."

"Right. The funny thing is even if I did that, most of these girls would produce their student I.D. anyway. It's unreal. I remember when I was coming up in the biz the majority of the dancers were single moms who needed the cash to feed their kids."

"Or their habits," I added. "I used to work in Vice. I've seen and heard everything."

"I am one of the few who didn't get involved in any of the hard stuff. By the time I graduated from being a waitress, I had seen too many friends lose everything because they were strung out on some stupid drug. Plus, I'm deathly afraid of needles," she said, a winning smile forming across her lips. "When are you going to tell me about this killer you're trying to find? It isn't drug-related, is it?"

"Not that I'm aware of."

"Does this guy have a name? Because like I said earlier, most of my customers give me their first names, which may or may not be real. When did this happen anyway?"

"About five years ago."

"That's an awful lot of lap dances under the bridge."

There was still a glint of excitement in Melissa's eyes about this unnamed regular, but when I divulged his name her whole attitude changed. Radically. The enthusiasm that had graced her face disappeared instantly and a noticeable tremor shook her as she sat upright on the couch. I could tell she was genuinely scared by this revelation.

"Jarvis Larsh?" she stuttered. "Tall, gangly guy, in his 30's?"

"I've never met the man. We're supposed to have lunch tomorrow at the Denby Eatery."

"Wait—I don't understand. To discuss what?"

217

"Hopefully the death of a woman thrown off the medical building."

"Alexis?"

This time I was the one rendered speechless. "How do you know her?" I finally stammered. "If you tell me she was your roommate at the time, I will fork over another hundred bucks right now to extend this meeting."

Melissa actually looked as shocked at this offer as she had at the mention of Jarvis' name. "Forget the money. Tell me about Alexis and Jarvis," she insisted.

"You first," I shot back. "Up until now I didn't know there was a connection between the two of them. Your reaction makes me believe there was. So let's start over. How do you know Alexis? Was she a dancer here at one time? Or a waitress?"

"No," she replied a bit flustered. "At least not that I know of. Anything is possible, I guess."

"Were you friends outside the club?"

"We never met."

"But when I mentioned her name—"

"This is getting confusing," she said as she began to pace nervously around the room.

"Take your time," I suggested.

She sat down on the corner of the couch and leaned toward me.

"I remember the name because there was a dancer here whose stage name was Alexis. Then when that woman's death hit the news, I just kind of associated her with my friend."

"But you're sure they weren't the same person, right?"

"Completely different women," she answered quickly.

"Okay, sorry, that was dumb question number two," I said. "So, we have unrelated women—one alive and one splattered on the sidewalk. Got it. I don't understand where Jarvis fits into all of this though." I could have told her about Max's killer theory, but as I was still on the clock I thought we'd flesh out Melissa's story first.

This is why my clients pay me the big bucks; to make the hard decisions when required. The fact that Max is technically not my client, let alone a paying one, was irrelevant at this point of my conversation with Melissa.

Onward.

"I saw them together."

"Where?"

"Downtown, around here."

"She knew him?"

Melissa hesitated. "I don't think so. I mean . . . I never saw them together-together, you know."

"No, I don't," I said, as my head began to hurt. "Let's try another avenue. Did Alexis Penney—the dead girl—actually know Jarvis? And if not, explain to me how and when you saw them together."

"Okay," she said, taking a deep breath. "I came to work one day and noticed him on the other side of the street."

"And Alexis? Where was she?"

"Well, I didn't know who she was then but I watched Jarvis staring at her when she passed by me on the sidewalk. At first I thought he was looking at me, until he started to walk away. I followed his gaze and concluded he was following this red-haired woman. At the time it was kind of funny to know I wasn't his only auburn-haired obsession."

"Then what?"

"I came into the club."

"That's it?"

"Pretty much. When I saw Alexis' picture in the paper, I realized it was Jarvis' friend."

"Did you tell the police?"

"And say what? I saw a law-abiding citizen admiring a woman?"

"Yeah, I guess." I considered this new development and how I could use it to my advantage. "Is your friend Alexis—stripper girl—still in town?"

"I think so. She doesn't dance anymore, I know that. She married some corporate executive and moved to the suburbs."

"Could you get me her number?"

"I guess. I'll see if they have it in the office."

"Did she stop dancing to become a respectable soccer mom?"

"I don't like your implication that dancing is not a respectable profession but no, she quit about a week after your Alexis' death hit the airwaves."

I was stunned. "Did she ever tell you why?"

"When I tried to find out she clammed up. I haven't really talked to her since."

"When Jarvis used to come in, did he get any dances or socialize with your friend?"

"He might have, but never when I was working."

"Lucky you," I said with a sarcastic smile. "Did he ever come into the club with a buddy?"

"Not that I recall. I always dread when he shows up because I know I'm his only choice and I'll have to entertain him."

"So, he still comes in? How often?"

"Not as much as before, thank goodness. Usually on the weekends. Maybe two or three times a month."

I silently congratulated myself on being smart for recognizing that Jarvis had mentioned the club for a reason. Getting back to the point though, I remembered Jarvis' large bank account. "Did he flash a lot of cash around or spend time in the V.I.P. area with you?"

"I refuse to do private dances for him," came Melissa's abrupt response. "He's too disturbing. I tell everyone that."

"What about the other girls? Do they entertain him here in the V.I.P. area?"

"Nope. Like I said, he only has eyes for me."

"But outside the club, he had eyes for Alexis Penney."

"At least for that one day."

I was running out of ideas. The link to Max's dead patient and another woman with the same name was an amazing lead which I needed to follow up before my meeting with Jarvis. "Could you get that number for me now?"

Melissa gave me a curious look. "That's it? We're done?"

"For the moment," I said. "You look disappointed."

"I guess I am. I'm usually the one ending the session, not the customer." Melissa stood and adjusted her top. "When you said we were done for the moment, what did you mean by that?"

"Well, I was hoping we might talk again tomorrow, after my lunch date with our mutual weirdo."

"I'm not in until 8:00 p.m." There was a dash of hopefulness in her voice that I couldn't quite understand. "Do you really think Jarvis had something to do with that woman's death?" Melissa asked. "Cause I believe he's capable of doing it. They may have convicted that fake doctor but I wouldn't be surprised if they were in cahoots with each other somehow."

"Max? Did you know Max as well?"

"No, I remember the case, that's all." She eyed me suspiciously and said, "You called that doctor Max. You knew him?"

"A long time ago," I said without explanation.

"Figures," she sniffed indignantly.

"What do you mean by that?" I asked, aware I was once again speaking with the tough-talking Destiny Rose.

"Cops, private dicks and con artists—you're all the same. Some of my girlfriends lost their life savings to that bastard and now I find out you're one of his friends."

"Melissa—I mean Destiny Rose, I had nothing to do with Max's con out here, I swear. I knew him in high school."

"But you know him now, right?"

"In a way," I said slowly, which only seemed to infuriated her.

"What's next? Is Jarvis your brother or something."

I shook my head and remained silent for a moment. "I'm looking into a murder case—Alexis Penney's murder. I have never met Jarvis and I never crossed paths with Alexis in my life." She gave me another scathing look.

"I'm leaving now," she said as she grabbed her small purse. "I'll get you that number and then I'm done with you."

There was nothing left to say except, "Fine."

A few excruciatingly long minutes ticked by with no sign of Destiny Rose. Finally she reappeared and stuck out her hand for me to shake. I was puzzled until she said, "You didn't get this from me," and palmed a small piece of paper into my hand.

"Thanks. I really appreciate this," I said.

Without warning she lifted her right hand and smacked me across the face with the force of a heavyweight. "I told you I'm not into kinky shit!" she screamed, before walking away in a huff, heading straight for the comfort of the back room.

I felt a large hand on my shoulder. "Time for you to go," Dillon said in a cool, yet menacing tone.

I turned and gave him a smile. "I guess it is," I said and walked out of the club.

I checked my watch: 9:52. Did I dare call the former dancer this late? Figuring time was of the essence, I punched her number into my cell phone hoping we could meet early the next morning.

"Hello," a woman whispered.

"I'm sorry to call this late. Would Alexis be in?"

There was a long pause, followed by an even longer pause. "Who is this?"

"I'm a friend of Melissa's," I replied. "She gave me this number tonight at the club where you used to work."

She didn't reply immediately and I thought I heard the closing of a door. "I haven't talked to Melissa in years. Who are you?"

"My name is Steve Cassidy. I'm a private investigator looking into the murder of a woman named Alexis Penney." I heard a quick intake of air. "I understand you're no longer in the club business but was wondering if we could talk at a more convenient time tomorrow morning? I don't want to cause you any problems at home."

"That you called here in the first place is already causing me troubles."

"This will only take a few minutes, trust me."

"Hold on," Alexis said. I heard her yell, "It's my sister. I'll be right up." She then came back on the line. "Call me between 9:15 and 9:30 tomorrow morning. I'll talk to you then."

"I'll do that," I said appreciatively. "Again, sorry to bother you so late, Alexis."

"Please stop using that name. That was my stage name in another life."

"Got it."

She abruptly terminated our connection. I wondered if she might contact the club to check on my story. If Melissa came to the phone, I thought I would be fine. However, if Destiny Rose took the call I'd be in real trouble.

I returned to the van and headed to the hotel. It had been a whirl-wind day: meeting Chantal Larsh; the release of the fake life insurance policy; Maria's exit from my life; interviewing Destiny Rose; and finally, uncovering a connection between Jarvis and Alexis Penney—something Max had contended all along.

As I hit the freeway, I recalled Destiny Rose's claim that cops, private dicks and con artists were cut from the same cloth. She was right, of course. I am living proof of that. In my 30+ years I have been all three in one form or another—not that I'm bragging. In many ways, I am most comfortable doing P.I. work, a profession I never envisioned myself in until I single-handedly sabotaged my promising police career.

I suppose that last statement isn't entirely true. I had plenty of help along the way.

After my mother's funeral, (my father had passed away a short time earlier), at the age of eighteen, I walked away from everything I knew and loved—the town of Delta and Maria—to try to find myself. This rash decision was the beginning of the end, although I didn't know it for many years. I moved to a big city on the east coast to disappear for a while. Money really wasn't an issue, as I had cashed in my savings and knew my parents' life insurance would be settled shortly. Like most angry young men, I drifted aimlessly for a couple of months, taking odd jobs here and there to keep busy. I assembled bicycles for a department store, delivered pizza and chicken, and even had a stint delivering newspapers and flyers.

It was during this period one of my customers asked if I had ever thought of applying to the local police force. Figuring I had nothing to lose, I gave it a shot and soon found myself attending Cop College, learning all about the criminal code, martial arts and most important, how to shoot to kill. The pay and health benefits were also a step up from the usual $1.25 tips I was making at The Chicken 'n Pizza Snack 'n Shack. Most of my classmates were like me: young, single, eager to find a purpose in their lives and take on more responsibility.

There were a few commando types whose sole reason for joining the force was to smash heads and kneecaps. I tried not to associate with them very much. This choice would factor into my later demise, as these type of rogue officers were the ones I would expose in exchange for saving my skin.

When I first hit the road as a rookie, I portrayed myself as a hard-working, honest, small-town boy, trying to make the city a better place to live. That thinking might have lasted a month, maybe two. Having come to understand you can't stop crime, only manage it, I threw my hands in the air, shrugged my shoulders and went out each day praying to make it home alive. During this time of enlightenment I met Carissa, a pretty brunette who worked at the courthouse. I would see her in the hallways and we'd make small talk but nothing more. Then out of the blue, she asked if I would like to be her date for an upcoming wedding.

"When is it?"

"This Saturday," she answered sheepishly. "I know it's kind of late notice. My date decided he didn't want to be exclusive anymore."

"What loser would dump you?" I asked with a laugh.

"Sergeant Mallan."

"Oh."

"Not many people knew we were seeing one another."

"I thought he was married."

"He is."

"Double oh."

The fact two officers got together or that one was married did not shock me. I wasn't that innocent. I'd learned early on many cops felt certain laws didn't apply to them. My training officer used to have me sit in the cruiser for a half hour every other shift, as he "interrogated" one of his street snitches in her apartment. Although she was a known hooker and he'd return perspiring after each visit, he would never admit the truth. "What you don't know now, you'll never have to testify about in divorce court later. I'm watching out for you, kid."

"The wedding is out of town, so you wouldn't have to worry about bumping into anyone you know."

"Whose is it? A friend's?"

"An old college roommate. We weren't that close, especially after she stole my boyfriend."

"I take it he's not the groom, because that would be really awkward."

"Thankfully, no," she said with a smile.

"Why me? Not that I don't appreciate the offer."

"Well, it's not because you're tall, dark or handsome. That's for sure."

"Ouch."

"It's because I know your shift doesn't work this weekend and figured I'd give you a shot."

"How important is it you show up to this thing with a date?"

Without hesitation she said, "Very. Plus, I hoped we could get to know each other a bit better." She paused. "Unless our two-minute hallway conversations are all you're interested in."

As if to evaluate her, I took a step backward and cocked my head to one side. She was a few inches shorter than me, had a well-shaped body, though her uniform hid most of her womanly features, a very cute face and a killer smile. "I don't know. I might be just a little interested in getting to know you outside the job," I kidded. "Would I have to wear a suit?"

"Of course."

"I have a black one that's a couple of years old. I doubt it would clash with your outfit."

"Basic black is good," she said.

"And what will you be wearing?" I ventured, imagining her in a slinky, tight-fitting dress.

"Let me put it this way, Steve. If the groom sees me before Angela, there's going to be trouble."

"Payback's a bitch, right?"

"You got it, Cassidy."

The wedding and overnight stay were perfect. Not only did Carissa blow the bride away in the hotness department, she and I discovered we had wasted an awful lot of time only talking in the court's corridors. I was tempted to send Sergeant Mallan a bottle of scotch when we returned. The following few months became a blur for both of us, as our fling blossomed into something more meaningful. Although my ideal woman had always been Maria, I knew that relationship fell into the category of High School Romance. With a new hometown and profession, I felt my relationship with Carissa fell more under the heading of Adult Love. We were both career-oriented, but still young enough to take time to have fun. During a week-long vacation in Mexico that summer, I proposed on the beach, and when she said, "Yes," I believed my world was complete.

"I'm looking forward to aging gracefully with you and only you," she said, sealing her promise with a kiss.

"As long as we grow old together, not just grow old, together."

"Never," she pledged to me.

During our tumultuous two years of marriage, it was one of the few promises she wasn't able to keep—although she tried.

Oh, how she tried.

The problems began when I was transferred to the Street Crimes Unit to fill in for another officer on short-term stress leave. While the official line was his departure wasn't work-related, by the end of my first week in the unit I highly doubted that. Every day was a fresh and dangerous challenge, as we dealt with the lowest of the low. There were drug arrests, high-risk takedowns, undercover assignments, interrogations, and too often, using threats or outright physical violence to coerce suspects into giving us information.

"When you work the streets you play by their rules, not the police commissioner's," a superior told me after horribly beating on a suspected drug dealer. "They understand that," he stated, pointing down to the wounded man. "So should you."

I have always prided myself on being a fast study, no matter the task. Show me how it's done once and I can duplicate it the next time out. Unfortunately, with this group of officers I learned too quickly and too well. The adrenaline rush from chasing some suspect down was only exceeded by the additional rush I attained from beating the living daylights out of him. In a few weeks I had a new nickname: Killer Cassidy. I hadn't actually killed anyone—yet—but my unit buddies believed it would only be a matter of time.

I was now a member of a very elite group of city-sanctioned thugs. In some neighbourhoods we were more feared than the gangs we were hired to shut down. When the officer I had replaced was ready to return, my superior lobbied to have me stay on and the request was granted. It was only then I was let in on a dirty little secret: the unit was actually being run like a team of mobsters. My co-workers had shielded me from their numerous off-duty projects, which included charging store owners protection premiums, ignoring illegal business activities, loan sharking, bootlegging, ticket scalping, extortion, bribery, and last but not least, murder for hire—although to my knowledge, this service had never been carried out.

Along with their hard work ethic, my colleagues played hard as well, which translated into lots of alcohol and drugs, on and off duty. As we could set our own hours, many night shifts were spent in strip clubs or each other's houses while we claimed to be out doing surveillance. It was this new wrinkle that had the most devastating effect on my marriage. Carissa bided her time, but was counting the days until I returned to my regular platoon, so we could get back to our happy life together. When that didn't happen she could read the writing on the wall, even though I couldn't.

The end came when I returned home at 4:30 in the morning, after being away for three days with no contact. No phone calls. No messages at the courthouse. I learned later my superior had assured Carissa that I was on official police business and could not be reached. The first and last clue this was not the case was when I stumbled into bed reeking of booze, perfume and sex. That I was higher than a kite from some pill a hooker had slipped me completed the betrayal.

When I awoke from my stupor a day-and-a-half later, Carissa was gone for good. I went to the courthouse, only to be stopped at the door and advised she did not want to talk to me. I was also warned if I insisted on seeing her, a restraining order had already been drafted and needed only her signature to become law.

In the ensuing months, my house became P-A-R-T-Y Central, not only for the unit but anyone else who wanted to let off some steam for a day or two or three . . .

This lifestyle would have killed me eventually, had it not been for the intervention of an irate gang leader and his trusty mini-machete. A concerned Carissa briefly re-entered my world, not for reconciliation but to make sure I returned to work clean and sober. The fact I was taking handfuls of wonderfully effective painkillers for weeks didn't deter her enthusiasm for "Project Save Steve From Himself."

When my wounds had healed and I'd passed the psychological evaluations, I returned to work as an ex-member of the Street Crimes Unit. The Chief proclaimed my incident had been so high-profile, I could no longer effectively perform undercover assignments. Instead, they stuck me in the Vice Unit's surveillance truck to watch the same criminals who used to masquerade as my friends. Now operating with a refocused mind and uncontaminated body, I was even happier to leave my former uniformed partners in crime behind. Unfortunately, my brief involvement with them would come back to bite me.

Hard.

We had been waiting for a pimp to return to his apartment building, to be picked up for questioning. On this day, my new superior was hanging out in my surveillance truck when our target arrived on the scene. Before Vice could pounce on him, however, Larry Dumar, one of my old Street Crimes cohorts, jumped out of a parked car and slammed the pimp against the side of the truck. While a camera from another Vice vehicle caught the action on tape, an exterior microphone picked up the audio.

"Hey, motherfucker," Larry screamed. "It seems you're a few weeks behind in your payments."

"I don't know what you're talkin' 'bout."

"Oh, is that right?" Larry swiftly reached his right hand down between the pimp's legs and grabbed his crotch. The pimp let out a howl of pain. "Yep, you certainly do have a large set down there, Romeo, but I can take care of that. By the time I'm done not only will the ladies no longer be interested in you, neither will any guys." He gave Romeo another violent squeeze. "Now, where's the money you owe me?"

"I don't owe you nothin'," Romeo said in a raspy whisper. "I only deal with Steve Cassidy. I've got *his* money and he ain't been around to collect. If you have a problem with that go talk to him, 'cause I'm not payin' you a dime."

"Don't you read the papers?" Larry asked sarcastically. "Stevie was put out of order by one of your low-life buddies. Therefore, I'm your new best friend. If you still have a problem with that, I can always have Coogan stop by to straighten things out."

"Hey—I don't want no trouble," Romeo squealed. "Not Coogan. Not after what he did to Tania."

"Yeah," Larry responded menacingly. "And don't forget, she was a girl. Imagine the damage he'd do to a scumbag like you."

I can't recall Romeo's comeback as I had zoned out at the mention of my name, then of Captain Coogan's—the highly decorated head of the Street Crimes Unit. I was only brought back to reality when my superior turned to me and asked, "So, Steve, who is this Tania woman and what can you tell me about Coogan, Dumar and the rest of the boys in Street Crimes?"

Our corruption trial began six months later, with me as the reluctant star witness. As I said earlier, if I had befriended those head crackers at college I probably wouldn't have turned on my fellow officers the way I did. The whole "honour amongst thieves" motto might have persuaded me to deny, deny, deny. If this had happened prior to my machete incident, I'm sure that's exactly what I would have done.

However, like many decisions in life, some are made for you. There is no such thing as a coincidence, remember? I had survived that attack so Carissa could help me get clean which, in turn, placed me in that surveillance truck on that fateful evening when Larry confronted Romeo. Of course, the real irony of the situation was that I was filling in for a sick officer and hadn't reviewed the file. If I had known my street pal Romeo was our evening's target, I'm positive I would not have volunteered for the overtime.

I also might not have taken the plea deal had the Chief not personally "advised" me that if I didn't, Carissa's promising police career would come to a standstill, as she would never be promoted within the service. The other defendants and I were suspended with pay until the end of the trial, when five of my former colleagues were sent away for two years. I was fired for discreditable conduct and subsequently harassed by other officers every time I ventured outside my house.

At this low point in my life, I needed a fresh start. It was then I moved to the lovely lakeside metropolis known as Darrien to begin my exciting new career as a private eye.

And we all know how well that's working out, don't we?

EIGHTEEN

I was wide awake by the time sunlight began to creep across my bed. I had a quick shower, shaved, put on fresh clothes and drove out of the area in search of breakfast.

Not far down the road, I saw a restaurant sign outside a large hotel. After the night I'd had, just walking through the finely decorated lobby gave me a psychological boost. As I passed the front desk the clerk wished me a hearty, "Good morning," which I returned in kind. I grabbed a complimentary newspaper and was soon seated in a booth, trying to determine if my presence had been picked up on the newspaper wires. Examining each page, I learned I was not news, which allowed me to fully appreciate my Meat Lover's Ultra-Omelette and peanut butter-smothered toast.

When finished, I paid the bill in cash and started through the lobby, heading to the parking lot.

"Will you be checking out today, sir?" the clerk asked, thinking I was a guest.

"Not today. Maybe tomorrow," I replied with a smile and a laugh.

"Well, have a nice day."

"I'm going to do my best, believe me," I said with a grin. As I pushed the front door open something caught my eye. Somehow I had missed it during my initial walk-through. "Do I need a password to use the visitor's computer over there?" I asked.

"No. It's free to all our guests," the clerk stated proudly.

"I can get on the internet?"

"Of course."

Linda and Samantha had been my internet navigators in the past as I have always delayed embracing new technologies. I only bought a computer after Linda moved in, as she needed it for library projects. She soon persuaded me to buy a second one for my P.I. work.

"You can't use a typewriter for your surveillance reports forever," she'd chided me.

"Wanna bet?" I countered, even though I knew she was right. When Samantha came on board, I was thankful I had purchased one for the office. If she wasn't on the road, she was at the keyboard doing up my handwritten notes, printing invoices and videotape labels—all chores I used to do on a pawned electronic typewriter. As Samantha and I began to spend more time together, a few of her helpful computer suggestions sank into my dinosaur mind.

I typed my name in the search window and in 0.23 seconds my eyes were greeted with several hundred articles, many of them dealing with other Steve Cassidys on the planet. I narrowed the results by adding "investigator", "insurance" and "Linda Brooks". In the span of another nano-second, ten listings appeared. The first was Jeremy Atkins' article in the Darrien Free Press. Only the opening two paragraphs dealt with new issues, while the remaining three-quarters simply rehashed my past misdeeds.

LIFE INSURANCE POLICY FOUND
Missing librarian's fiancé sought by police
Foul play not ruled out

By Jeremy Atkins

Private Investigator Steve Cassidy's personal world continues to mesmerize and trouble the good citizens of Darrien. The days of fascination will no doubt come to an abrupt end today with the news that a life insurance policy in the name of local librarian Linda Brooks has surfaced.

"This is a very troubling development," Officer Kenneth Anderton stated at a hastily-organized news conference. "Linda Brooks has not been seen for almost two weeks. Today, the department received a copy of a life insurance policy in Ms. Brooks' name, signed by Steven Cassidy whose whereabouts is also unknown. In

232

light of this new matter, we cannot eliminate the possibility foul play may have been a factor in Ms. Brooks' disappearance. Anyone with information regarding the location of either Ms. Brooks or Mr. Cassidy should contact the police immediately."

No wonder Maria wigged out, I thought.

Most disturbing about this report was it appeared the police believed the policy was legit, even though I knew it was fake. I scanned the other search listings, which revealed the same article printed in other newspapers. I tried to reassure myself the story was still local and wouldn't jeopardize my interviews with Jarvis and the lap dancer turned housewife.

I was preparing to log off the computer when I heard Maria's voice in my head.

"There aren't many Alexis Penneys in the country. One of them, however, was charged with murder around the time our girl moved to town."

I cleared the search window and typed "Alexis", "Penney", "trial" and "murder." At first I figured I'd made a mistake as hundreds of listings instantly appeared. I read a few newspaper accounts from a town called Ravenwood, and sure enough, a woman named Alexis Penney had got away with murder. I surfed a couple of articles, not believing this woman was *our girl.* I was about to disregard this avenue of investigation when I was transferred to the True Crime Book Fan Club website. Listed was *The Murdering Mistress,* written by Wendi Gibbons and Joe Penney. The book's cover showed a smiling, strawberry-blonde female in a fashionable business outfit.

I stared at the image for several moments. In the autopsy photos I had reviewed, the corpse was not smiling and her facial features were badly altered by the unforgiving pavement . . . yet . . . I immediately recognized my freefall girl. This cover girl was without a doubt *our girl.*

"Is there a bookstore around here?" I asked the startled clerk, as I bolted from my chair and walked briskly to the reception counter.

"There is but it doesn't open until 9:00."

"How far?"

"Two blocks that way," he said, pointing to the street and then to the right. "You can't miss it. It's outside the mall."

"Thank you very much."

"No problem," I heard him say. "Have a nice day!" he added, as I ran out the doors.

If I could only elude the authorities, lunch with Jarvis, talk privately with Destiny Rose's former colleague and purchase a copy of *The Murdering Mistress*, I felt it would be a very nice day indeed.

I had to commend the owners of the BOOKS! BOOKS! BOOKS! store for having the foresight and ingenuity to point out the obvious to the buying public. I debated whether this store name was above or below my previous favourite—Finger Turnin' Books—and came to the conclusion it was the winner. If you were looking for a new book to read, the best place to find one would be at BOOKS! BOOKS! BOOKS!

Unlike the name of the establishment, my search was not so simple. I soon learned they did not stock the book book book I was look look looking for, as it had been out of print for several years.

"They are the hardest to keep in the store, because it seems a hundred new titles are released each month. Six months from now, about 90% of the titles here today will be gone and replaced by other sordid tales," the saleswoman stated, after helping me to search in the True Crime shelves. "Let's check the computer. Maybe we can find it there."

A short time later, she found several used copies available through online stores and auction sites.

"Are there any used bookstores around here?" I asked, dismayed by our findings and not wanting to wait for a copy to be shipped.

"A couple. Would you like me to call them for you?"

"That would be great," I replied as my 'call Alexis' watch alarm alert began to beep. "I want to check out some other stores in the mall. Can I get your results later this morning?"

"Sure thing."

I went to the van and dialed the former Alexis' phone number. She picked up on the first ring.

"Hello?" she said in a questioning, frightened tone.

"Hi, this is Steve Cassidy again. How are you this morning?"

"Under the circumstances, as well as could be expected."

"I can understand your apprehension."

"My husband doesn't know I paid my way through school as a dancer," she replied.

"I promise never to let that secret out," I said in a soothing voice. "Trust me, I'm not interested in your former career, but in a person you came into contact with back then."

"Another dancer?"

"No, a customer," I said. "Now, I want to advise you that when I mentioned this man's name to your friend Melissa, she became quite upset."

"It's Jarvis Larsh, isn't it?" she blurted out. "Isn't it?" she demanded again.

I tried unsuccessfully to reconcile the image of a happy, smiling Chantal Larsh with the look and sound of terror coming from two women who also knew Jarvis.

"It is," I said very slowly, "but I want to assure you that you are in no danger whatsoever today. None." I honestly couldn't imagine what was running through her head at this moment, aside from the fight-or-flight instinct which kicks in every time we feel cornered. "As I've said, I am investigating the death of Alexis Penney. At the club, Melissa thought you might have some information about a possible relationship between Jarvis and this woman, of which I was unaware until last evening. So, I have no idea what—if any—relationship you had with him. From your reaction, I'm pretty sure you no longer have any contact with him."

"He's the reason I quit dancing."

"Did he threaten you in some way?"

"He asked me to marry him because his fiancée had just died. Would you consider that a threat?"

"Apparently you did," I replied, trying not to convey my disbelief that Jarvis had been engaged to yet another woman.

"How could I not? He said his girlfriend had recently died and thought the best way to preserve her memory was to marry another woman named Alexis."

I had to be completely certain what I had heard was correct. "He told you Alexis Penney—the woman who fell to her death from the Upstate Medical Building—was his fiancée?"

"Yes."

"And believing your real name was Alexis, he asked you to marry him instead?"

"I swear he did, Mr. Cassidy. I was terrified. We all knew he was disturbed, but this was too much. The last straw was when he bragged about all the money he'd come into."

"Money? Melissa said he never flashed cash around. Are you sure his claim was legitimate?"

"He gave me a bank statement and it showed a balance of over $150,000."

"Could that money have come from an inheritance?" I asked absently.

"How should I know?" she snapped. "All I could think about was how this weirdo's girlfriend recently died a horrible death and he was now loaded. At the time, I assumed the money was from a life insurance policy or something. It freaked me out and I wanted nothing to do with him. I even told him my real name, hoping that would back him off."

"And did it?"

"What do you think?"

I let the question go unanswered. "What happened next?"

"He just kept coming around, talking about a big house he had his eye on and how we would live happily ever after."

"I'm sorry to ask you to relive this part of your life. This information is a real eye-opener. I had no idea about any of this. I wish Melissa had brought it up last night."

"She had her own problems going on. You know—drugs, her kid. When that doctor was convicted, most of her life savings vanished with him. My problems with her best customer didn't really concern her."

"She was a patient of Dr. Feldberg?" I exclaimed.

"She didn't tell you?"

"No," I admitted bitterly. "I think I may have to revisit her tonight."

I heard a doorbell ring on the other end of the line.

"I have to go, Mr. Cassidy. I hope I helped you in some way but please do not call me again."

"You've been a big help—" I managed to get out before the line went dead. "And have a nice day," I said to my phone's display window.

I sat in the front seat livid with Max. I couldn't believe that when he conned me into this trip he knew I would uncover all these related clues. If he had, he was a much smarter individual than I had given him credit for. Ultimately, his goal was to have me uncover any type of evidence which would help him appeal his manslaughter conviction.

While I wasn't at that stage yet, I was starting to believe his proclamation of innocence might have some validity. Some. He hadn't landed in jail for stealing hubcaps. He'd lied to vulnerable, trusting people looking for help and then callously destroyed their lives. If it were up to me, he would be put away forever for his deeds as a con artist. Unfortunately, not even I could agree with keeping someone locked away for a crime they did not commit.

How do I get involved in these types of situations? I asked myself as I returned to BOOKS! BOOKS! BOOKS!

"You are a very fortunate young man," a kindly old female clerk advised me as I re-entered the store. "Stuart has a used copy."

"Stuart? We like Stuart, right?" I kidded my happy salesperson.

"Very much."

"I take it Stuart lives around here?"

"Take Addingham Place, go over the bridge and follow the river for about two miles. You can't miss it. His store is on the right side, between an occult shop and a coffee house."

"I can't miss it because it's between those businesses or because Stuart's store is named Used Books! Used Books! Used Books!" I asked with a smile.

"Close," she smiled. "It's called Stuart's Used Books."

"Not as original as your store's name but still very precise."

"He used to work here years ago and wanted to use the name you mentioned. My husband and I told him we'd sue if he did."

"And he bought that?"

"He was young and inexperienced at the time. He's a nice kid though, and you should get along with him just fine."

I glanced out the door. "I'm looking at five or ten minutes?"

"Only if you get lost."

I thanked her for the help and followed her directions. She was right—it is hard to miss a store outlined in tacky neon lights and with a red STUART'S USED BOOKS! sign the size of a school bus on the roof. Even in broad daylight the place gave me a headache. I could only envision what it looked like after dark.

"Let me guess," the clerk said after I walked in. "You're the true crime fan, right?"

"That's me," I said, walking up to the counter and noting my newest friend's name tag read Stuart. "You can't imagine how glad I am to finally get my hands on this book."

"You got lucky, no doubt about it. I found it in the 2-4-1 Bargain Bin."

"I didn't know used bookstores had bargain bins," I said. "I just believed the whole place was one big . . . ah . . . bin, so to speak."

Stuart laughed at my comparison. "It is in a way. I never thought of it like that before. Like every store though, we have to get rid of some of the old before putting out the new. Luckily, the same people who bring me new books usually buy one or two of my old ones at the same time."

"Then everything balances out."

"Pretty much. Sometimes even my cheap customers need to feel like they're getting a real bargain."

"Hence, the 2-4-1 Bargain Bin." I glanced around the store. It was nothing like the crammed used bookstores I had frequented in the past. It was very reminiscent in feel and layout to Stuart's former employer's premises. He couldn't copy the name, but he could duplicate everything else that made them successful. Smart man.

Stuart reached under the counter and presented *The Murdering Mistress*, as if handing me an antique handwritten bible. "It sounds like a real interesting case. Then again, they all do from the back cover description." He pointed to Alexis' picture and said, "That's not even the best shot of her. There's one in the middle section with her in a bikini on the beach. I don't know if her husband or her boyfriend took it. She looks hot, though."

The autopsy photos briefly flashed through my mind. Not wanting to scare my good-natured host, I replied, "You can be sure it wasn't her boyfriend's wife," which brought another chuckle from Stuart.

"You seem to know a lot about this case."

"Fortunately—or unfortunately—depending on your viewpoint, I'm learning more and more about it each day." I checked the inside cover of the book and found the pencil-marked price. I pulled out a five from my wallet and handed it to Stuart.

"You can pick another book out of the bin. It's free."

"Do you have any self-help or relationship books in there?"

For a moment Stuart mentally tried to take inventory of the container's contents. "I don't think so. That genre sells pretty well. Most of the books in there are murder mysteries or true crime stories."

"That's too bad. After I read this one I'm hoping to swear off all mysteries—fiction and non-fiction—for some time."

"I know what you mean," Stuart offered. "It's good to mix things up a bit."

"I've been involved in so many of them lately, I feel as if my whole life revolves around them now."

"Wow—that must be very time-consuming."

"And tiring," I added. "Don't forget tiring."

I wished Stuart well and said I would send all my friends to his store for future book purchases. Possibly as a parting jab at his former employers, as I walked out of the store he yelled, "Tell them used books are as good as new—and cheaper!"

In the van, I leafed through my purchase and had to agree with Stuart about that bikini shot. Alexis Penney was a stunning woman. I looked at a few less flattering pictures and felt I could see Alexis' evil side subliminally shining through. *Beautiful and dangerous*, I thought. *Not a good combination, no matter how horny you get when she stops by for a lunchtime drink or an afternoon roll in the hay.* I wanted to believe the French guy who came up with the term *femme fatale* survived his encounter with a villainous woman, but I doubted it. For all I know, it was one of his surviving buddies who coined the term in his honour, as a way to warn other men who might entertain crossing paths with the same sexy vixen.

As I drove over the bridge en route to my lunch date with Jarvis, I wondered if I was making a huge mistake. My theory that Jarvis was stalking Alexis might be entirely off and the reverse might be true. She had manipulated men in the past and Jarvis may have fallen for her, just as Randy Mayer had in Ravenwood. Even when a clue supplied by Max looked straightforward, with a little digging it turned out to be a distorted half-truth which would then lead me to yet another half-truth and so on.

As I found a parking spot near The Denby Eatery, I remembered a saying my friend Wayne's father often quoted when we'd get into trouble on the farm: "There's your side, there's my side and then there's the truth," he'd say in a patient tone, knowing one or both of us would ultimately confess. I think he secretly enjoyed the game of mentally breaking us; countering our lies with logic and then watching us squirm. I used this same technique years later when I interviewed suspects, which usually produced the same results: Good Guys 1 - Bad Guys 0. I was hopeful I could duplicate that score today.

At 10:57, Jarvis Larsh suddenly walked in front of my van,

startling me. He was exactly as Destiny Rose had described. As I watched him, I got the bizarre feeling I had seen him before, then concluded my mind was playing tricks. I had been thinking about this idiot for weeks and felt I already had some relationship with him, that's all. Before entering the restaurant, he hadn't paused to look around to see if he was being followed. He was like every other person entering this popular establishment; uninterested in his surroundings and with a look of hunger.

I almost envied him, as I stopped on the sidewalk to make sure I was not being watched. My only consolation was I knew I was on the run, while Jarvis was still oblivious his hunter had him cornered and was not about to show any mercy. My world had been turned upside down by the unwelcome addition of Jarvis into my life and I was about to return the favour, whether he liked it or not.

Let the mind games begin.

"When I was a little boy, do you know what my grandmother liked to tell me, Mr. Larsh?" I asked, sounding like a pushy car salesman, as I took my seat across the booth from him.

"Well . . . I . . ."

I cut him off. "She used to say, 'Stevie, strangers are just friends you haven't met yet.' I trust you believe that, because by the end of this lunch I really hope you and I are still friends."

My goal today was to catch Jarvis off guard and distract him from his own game plan, if only for a moment or two.

"You didn't sound this upbeat on the phone," he said, taken aback by my approach. "You are Steve Cassidy, the private investigator, right?"

"That I am," I replied, toning down my over-the-top persona. I extended my hand across the table, which Jarvis shook without hesitation. "I didn't scare you, did I? I was just trying to lighten the mood."

"No, not at all," Jarvis lied. With things settled down between us,

I sensed his original apprehension of this meeting was beginning to resurface. There was a *What's next?* look on his face. "Were you planning on ordering food or only drinks? Like I've said before, I don't think I can help with your accident investigation. In fact, I tried to recall ever witnessing an accident, let alone giving someone my phone number and came up empty."

How to delicately raise this next subject? *Honesty is always the best policy,* was another of granny's favourite sayings. "Well, that's probably due to the fact there was no accident and there is no insurance investigation."

"I don't understand. Why are—"

"We here at The Denby Eatery, instead of drinking in the gloominess of the Shakin' Pussycat?"

I quite enjoyed the expression of confusion that temporarily clouded Jarvis' eyes. He kept his cool, however, for which I gave him credit.

Our waitress dropped off glasses of water and asked if we needed more time, to which I replied, "At least a few minutes, probably more." We did order a couple of non-alcoholic beverages and once our server was gone, Jarvis spoke up.

"What do you want from me? Are you a cop or something? Cause if you are I have nothing to say to you," he stated.

"Once upon a time," I admitted. "Today, I'm a lowly P.I. And you—what type of work do you do these days? Your wife Chantal was a bit fuzzy on that."

Jarvis leaned forward and said, "Keep her out of this—whatever this is—or you'll be sorry. You're not the only one with connections around here, Mr. Cassidy."

I considered this threat to be credible—his tone and body language were about right—although I didn't completely buy the whole *I know people* threat. Figuring I might be wrong, I agreed to his one condition. "No problem," I replied. "I'm fairly certain she wasn't around during the time I need to talk to you about anyway."

He leaned back in the booth. "And what time period are you looking into?"

His cocky attitude was that of a criminal who was amused he was only now being asked to discuss one of his many perfect crimes. I decided to throw him a curve ball, and leapt ahead one topic.

"Alexis Penney and Dr. Max Feldberg. Remember them?" That knocked the grin off his face. "Oh, I'm sorry. That wasn't the question was it? You were looking for five years ago, weren't you? I do that sometimes—annoys the heck out of my friends. And speaking of friends—"

"Who sent you?" Jarvis asked, his face a pasty white.

To be honest, I thought he would be more of a challenge. However, just as leopards can't change their spots, losers like Jarvis also can't change who they are, no matter how many inheritance cheques they cash.

"I think the who is less important than the why." Fearing he was about to bolt, I put my left foot firmly on the edge of the booth, resting it against his right outer thigh. "I'm here looking for answers to some very troubling questions."

"What's your point? I already said I can't help you."

"Can't or won't?"

Jarvis was about to reply, but stopped himself in mid-thought, pursing his lips instead. "Max was my therapist. I didn't know the woman he killed."

"That can't be right. At least not the Alexis part."

"I didn't know her."

I gave him a dirty look and then relaxed back in my seat.

"Did I ever tell you the story about being engaged for twelve hours?" At the word *engaged*, Jarvis took another solid emotional blow. He would have made a terrible poker player. "There were two problems with my plan. First, I was already married, and second, I barely knew the girl. That she was unconscious at the time also played a role in her breaking it off the next morning. My point is, regardless of how dumb it was or how drunk and stoned I was that night, I will always remember getting engaged." Jarvis was staring at me, as if I had recited the emergency escape procedures in the event the Mothership crashed into the ocean. "So, when you say you don't remember

243

asking the lovely Alexis Penney for her hand in marriage, I don't believe it."

Not only had I rendered Mr. Jarvis Larsh speechless, his breathing was so shallow I contemplated jamming a straw down his throat, to transfer fresh air into his oxygen-starved lungs.

"Are you okay, Jarvis?"

"I . . . I . . . don't . . . know . . . what . . . you . . . are talking about," he finally managed to spit out.

"Really, because that's not what I've heard," I said, as if crestfallen by this news. "Like I said earlier, I want us to be friends but if telling me bold-faced lies is your idea of friendship, I may have to go elsewhere for manly companionship. Do you know where the cop shop is located? I'm sure I could talk to some of those boys. When I was an officer, I loved to listen to some crazy man's story about a crime he may or may not have committed in the past. No matter how delusional these crackpots were, by law we had to do some type of investigation." I waved my hand in the air and added, "Sure, 99% of the time the story was pure fantasy, but sometimes that other 1% paid off and we solved a cold case."

"Goody for you. That's a great story, but it doesn't change the fact I was never engaged before Chantal and there is no cold case here either," Jarvis responded coolly but still cautiously. "Max threw that woman over his balcony and he was convicted."

"If I thought I could believe you, I would order lunch in a heart beat. I'm starving."

"Then order."

"I would if it wasn't for this darn upset stomach brought on by the knowledge you're still lying to me." I leaned across the table, picked up my fork and absently began to play with it. "Have you ever gone to a greasy hamburger stand and found the only eating utensil is a spork—you know, those plastic things that look like a spoon but when you pick them up you realize they have three fork-shaped prongs? Talking with you is kind of the same thing."

"You think I'm a spork?" Jarvis asked, bewildered at my statement.

"Ah . . . no. It's because you appear to be one thing, yet as we talk parts of your true self begin to come out. In my eyes, you started out as a spoon but then revealed your fork tendencies. This now leaves me dazed and confused about what exactly I'm sitting across from here. So, yeah—I guess in a way you are a human spork."

Overhearing the end of this brilliant analogy, our waitress gave me an odd look as she placed our beverages on the table. "A couple more minutes, gentleman?"

I looked at Jarvis, who glared at me. "At least," he said, never breaking our stare as our server walked away again. "I don't have time to waste all day with you, so what is it you want?"

"Fair enough," I said. "Why did you tell people you were engaged to Alexis Penney if you weren't?"

Although visibly irritated by this line of questioning, Jarvis eventually gave me what I believed was an honest answer. "Not that it matters but I told one person. A ditzy stripper who was also named Alexis. I said it as a joke to make her jealous."

"And did it?"

"I don't remember."

Although he believed he'd pulled the wool over my eyes, what he didn't realize was he had just confirmed he'd known Alexis Penney prior to her death. As they were both patients of Max, the idea they could have met at his office immediately occurred to me. It was a legitimate possibility, yet after hearing Destiny Rose's account of Jarvis following Alexis down the street, I felt something more sinister was at work. My poker face remained firmly in place.

"Do you think Max actually killed her?" I asked, not wanting to dwell on this disclosure.

"Why not?" came the reply. "Derek . . ." He abruptly stopped himself as a panicked look crossed his features.

"Who's Derek?"

"He's . . . ah . . . a friend of mine," he managed to cough up. As he took a long swig of his drink, he looked guilty as hell (for what I wasn't certain). "Used to be."

"Derek used to be a friend? He's no longer one?" I asked, trying to keep my composure in check. "What does he have to do with Max?"

"Nothing," Jarvis stated decisively. "What I meant was Derek believed Max had done it. That's all."

I waited a few more seconds, hoping Jarvis would expand upon his answer. When he didn't, I asked, "And why was that?"

"Around here everyone thought Max had done it."

Silence is often the best tool an interrogator has in his bag of tricks. Nobody likes silence, at least not for long periods of time. In a small confined area with another person, silence begs to be filled. It becomes uncomfortable for all concerned, regardless of where it occurs at a dinner table, a social function, a first date or worst of all, in bed. The need to keep the conversation alive becomes paramount, even if you have nothing interesting to say. Jarvis was already on edge. I had made certain of that. I hoped his thoughts consisted of the phrase *He knows! He knows! He knows!*—even though I knew nothing and could prove even less. Fortunately, I didn't believe my lunch guest was smart enough to realize that.

I continued to turn the fork over in my hand several times. "I hear you came into a lot of money," I said, breaking our awkwardness.

"I got an inheritance from an uncle."

"You've been pretty lucky with money simply falling into your lap—like that $150,000 five years ago. No wonder Chantal loves you. Every time you turn around, and without lifting a finger, it seems you find another pile of cash. If that is really the case."

Had we not been sitting in a booth, I'm sure Jarvis would have fallen out of his chair onto the floor. I pictured him giving me one of those bad guy double-takes you see in the movies and running out the door with his arms flailing in every direction.

Silence.

Sweet uncomfortable silence.

"I don't know what you're talking about."

"I have bank records that say otherwise.

Tick.

Tick.

Tick.

Talk.

"I won it."

"Congratulations. Where?"

"At the track."

"Really? Are you sure about that?"

[Note: *si `lence* (noun): a refusal, failure or inability to speak (see Jarvis Larsh)]

"That must have been quite the celebration," I continued. "Too bad your fiancée wasn't around to share in the wealth."

To regain any colour in his face, Jarvis would have had to swallow an industrial-sized bottle of suicide hot sauce in one gulp. Even then, he was so pale a second bottle may have been required to put a little rose in his cheeks.

"We're done here," he said, as he stood on wobbly legs.

"Oh, come on, one more question," I said. "Where were you the night Alexis plunged off that building?"

He stopped in his tracks as a number of other patrons looked up from their plates and conversation ceased. Jarvis gave an amused fake smile to a table of women to his right before facing me one final time. With the seriousness of an undertaker he stated in a loud, clear voice, "I was out of the country on business that week," and turned and made a grand exit, stage left.

Some of the lunchtime crowd returned to their meals, but many did not. They had watched our exchange, followed Jarvis' exit and returned their attention to my booth, where I now sat alone. The waitress came to my rescue.

"Who was your friend? And who are you?"

I glanced behind her and saw a table of women begin to pick at their food, speaking in low, whispering tones. "When I leave here, they aren't going to jump me, are they?" I asked.

"Maybe, maybe not," she replied. "Are you a trouble maker? Because you just opened up an old wound and I know several people who would like to know why."

"If by troublemaker, you mean truth finder—then yeah, I guess

247

I'm a troublemaker."

"What about your friend? He didn't seem like the truth-finder type."

"He's not my friend."

"Excuse me," said a man now standing beside us.

"Here's one of those people I was talking about," the waitress said to me. "Want your pie transferred over here, Paul?"

"Would you mind if I joined you?" he asked me.

"Not at all. My guest left to attend to his sick mother or some such emergency. Please sit down."

After I ordered a roast beef sandwich with curly fries, the waitress left Paul and I to get acquainted.

"What line of business are you in?"

"I own a small book publishing company. And what about you?"

"It seems that here at Denby's my job title is Troublemaker. Normally though, I make my living as an investigator."

"The guy who walked out of here, is he another investigator?"

"Who, Biff—my hot-tempered buddy? No, I don't think he could hold onto such a prestigious position as a private dick. To be truthful, from our brief conversation I think he's the real troublemaker around here, though I can't prove it."

"You mentioned the name Alexis and used the term *plunged* a minute ago," Paul began cautiously. "I don't know how to ask this, but are you looking into Alexis Penney's death?"

I smiled as I glanced around the room and noticed there was still very little conversing going on. "This scene reminds me of that old television commercial where everyone in a crowded room stops to eavesdrop on the conversation between a high profile stock broker and his friend."

"E. F. Hutton, right? I think the line was, 'When E.F. Hutton talks, people listen.'"

"That's the one. I remember each commercial had a bigger crowd in it, going from a small office to a huge sports stadium." I scoped out the dining area again. "You're not Paul Hutton or some relation of Mr. Hutton's?"

"I wish. My last name is Rumleski."

"Why all the interest in Biff and little old me?"

"Well, you and Biff brought the attention on yourselves. Five minutes earlier, no one cared who you were or what you were talking about over here."

"As a kid, my mother always told me to share," I quipped.

"Sharing's good. Maybe just not here in the downtown core."

"Alexis' death was a long time ago. The guy who did it was convicted and sent away for life, so why the sustained interest?" I asked.

"Because it was so shocking," Paul stated in a low tone. "Many people could not imagine what it must have been like for her to die in that manner. We rarely think twice about someone who commits suicide by jumping off a bridge or building, but to picture an innocent woman being forced to die that way was an insult to our sense of dignity."

"And she was hot." My attempt at dry humour, especially after such an honest and heartfelt statement, could have had disastrous consequences.

Paul gave me a quick disapproving look and said, "And she was hot."

To prove this, I reached into my jacket and tossed him my copy of *The Murdering Mistress*. I had planned to spring it on Jarvis, but his sudden departure kiboshed that idea. "Check out page four in the picture section and stop feeling guilty about your wildly inappropriate comment."

"Where did you get this?"

"Stuart's Used Books," I replied. "You're a book guy—Stuart might have a few of your titles in his 2-4-1 Bargain Bin."

"I'm sure he does," Paul admitted, as he began reading the back cover. Next, he looked at the copyright page and said, "This came out two years before she moved here."

"Nobody in the media broke this story? That's kind of hard to believe."

Paul pushed the book over to me. "You should put that away

before Harriett comes with our food."

"Okay. . ." I replied and did as I was told. "You've never seen that book before?"

"Nope, but I want to read it more than the pile of new manuscripts currently cluttering my desk."

"Why? Do you think it will change your perception of her death?"

"Reading the back cover did that."

"I'll ask you again. Why are so many people still fascinated by her? I only recently started to uncover details of her past, but for my investigation she is still just the victim. Her criminal history won't change that."

"What if it did, though?" Paul offered. "I'm playing devil's advocate here—not really knowing what your investigation actually entails—but what if something in her past had a direct effect on how and when she died?"

"Max would have told me."

"As in Dr. Max Feldberg, fake therapist?"

"If you tell me he swindled you or your sister or aunt out of money, I believe I'll have to leave and find another place to have lunch."

"You can stay. My relatives and friends are very well-adjusted."

"And you?"

"My wife may have a different opinion, but I think I'm pretty normal."

"That's nice to hear," I stated. "As for the good doctor, I used to know him in my teen years. These days, we have a loose arrangement where I look into the circumstances of his manslaughter conviction."

"And what do you get out of it?"

I wasn't going to trouble my new book buddy with the sketchy details of Linda's disappearance. "That's being negotiated on a daily basis," I said weakly.

Harriet arrived with our food in the nick of time. Wanting off the subject of my personal life, I asked Paul about his work. He told me he'd started his publishing business by releasing two short inspirational stories he'd written. With the success of those titles, he was able to expand his gift-book empire by helping other writers get their stories on the local store shelves as well. After years in the television industry writing for others, he was now writing novels full-time, while acting as editor to other up-and-comers.

"It's the perfect lifestyle for someone like me who can barely operate his TV remote, let alone work in an office cubicle or on an assembly line," he concluded. "What about you? How long have you been spying on people?"

"I'm still a newbie. Actually, your job sounds like a blast."

"Maybe we can team up to write our own true crime book. You do the legwork and I type up your findings. How does that grab you?"

"The possibilities are endless, I guess," I said with a laugh. "If only we had a crime to investigate . . ."

"Have you talked with Sabrina Howell at The Standard?"

"Should I?"

"That depends. What exactly are you looking for?"

"I'm not entirely sure," I admitted. "Do you think she could assist me with that?"

This brought another smile to Paul's lips. "She's a pretty good reporter. She covered the trial and wrote several articles for the paper."

"She can't be that good if she never looked into Alexis' past."

"That is kind of shocking, isn't it?"

"Is she discreet? Because right now I don't need any publicity."

"Why—are you on the run from the cops?" Paul asked with a chuckle.

"I refuse to respond to that question as it might incriminate me and implicate you. How's that for an answer?"

He gave me a suspicious look and reached for his cell phone to retrieve Sabrina's number. "Tell her you know me. I'll take my chances with the authorities."

Having finished lunch, I paid the bill and Paul escorted me from the restaurant.

"In your profession, you must have to be a quick reader, right?"

"Quick enough to decide if a story is worth publishing. Why?"

"Because I'm a lousy reader and I need a book report on *The Murdering Mistress* by tomorrow morning. Do you think you could help me out?"

"Those type of knock-off books are the quickest reads out there because they have no real substance to them. They give you a snapshot of the victim and the accused's background, and then condense the trial transcript into easy-to-digest terms. If I blow off my workload this afternoon, I could give you my review by dinner time."

"You would do that?"

"Sure, why not?" Paul replied. "It's like an exclusive sneak peek of a new John Irving novel. I will be the first in town to read it. Trust me, I'm excited about this."

"I can see that. What I'm interested in is a list of the individuals involved in the crime or mentioned in the book—from family and friends and law enforcement personnel. People I might be able to track down, if need be."

"No problem."

"As for the trust part, I wasn't kidding earlier. For the moment, this book and our conversation have to remain secret. If you don't think you can promise me that—"

"I can."

"Good." I handed him the book, which he put inside his jacket. He then asked for my cell phone number. "Again, Paul, not the greatest idea. Give me your number instead and I'll call around 7:00. How's that?"

"You realize I don't even know your name," he stated, as he gave me his business card. "Is all this cloak-and-dagger stuff necessary, or are you just trying to scare me?"

"Yes, to both."

NINETEEN

I left the downtown core, quite certain Paul the publisher was a man of his word and that his dog would not eat his homework. I called his reporter friend's number but only got voice mail. I left a short message and my cell number.

I know, I know—why give that information to her and not to Paul? Well, because she is directly related to the case. Paul, on the other hand, is a good guy who likes to read and stick his nose into other people's lunchtime conversations. Happy, now?

My next call was to the Sunsetter Pub. "Hey, got a minute?" I asked Dawn, who sounded happy to hear from me again.

"Yeah. It's died down a little in the last ten minutes. How's your investigation going?"

"I need your help."

"My bag is packed and I have the next two days off. What time does my flight leave?"

I laughed. "I haven't confirmed that quite yet."

"You are such a travel tease, Mr. Cassidy," she replied. I could envision the wide grin on her lips. "Does this mean Maria has returned to the fold?"

"Not in this lifetime," I said. "I don't think I'm going to be hanging around here much longer anyway."

"You've solved the case?"

"Not quite. It has taken on a life of its own. I was hoping you could sneak into my house to get a statement. I need the information to cross-reference it with something my subject told me today."

"What kind of statement?"

"A financial one. I looked at it briefly several days ago but can't remember the bank's name. I was also hoping the location of an ATM used for a transaction on June 23, 1992 would be listed on it."

"When you say sneak, do you mean break and enter?"

"Are the cops still on the street in their surveillance van?"

"They were this morning," she replied. "I would rather not have to talk to those guys during this operation."

"You won't have to," I assured her. "Avoid the front of the house and go through the rear laneway. Near the back porch steps you'll see three half-broken ceramic Chinese lanterns strewn across the ground, covered in dirt and weeds. Inside the middle one I've hidden a key."

"That's kind of ingenious. The lanterns look like trash, which means no crook would think to look in them for a hide-away key. Huh—you're too smart by half, Steve."

"Thank you. I think."

"The last thing you should be doing is more thinking," Dawn chuckled. "So, I get this hidden key and enter the house. What's the alarm code?"

"There's no alarm."

"But I've seen the security sticker on the back door window."

"To let you in on another little secret, the sticker is the extent of my security system. It's a visual deterrent and nothing more. I can't afford an actual security system on my income. Are you kidding me?"

I heard Dawn say something in a muffled voice, as if she'd covered the receiver with her hand. "I have to get back to work. I'll try to find that statement for you after I'm done."

"When is that?"

"In an hour. Is that fast enough for you?"

"That would be perfect."

"One more thing. Where will I find this mystery document?"

"In that box in the kitchen. It's inside a folder marked Bank Records."

"Of course. Silly me."

"Be careful and give me a call when you get to your place, okay? Don't call from my house, as they might have the line bugged."

"No problem."

"Now get to work."

"You owe me."

"I'll make it up to you when I return."

"No doubt," she replied mischievously. "Talk to you soon."

With an hour or two to kill, I walked up the street to the scene of the crime. As the Shakin' Pussycat Bar came into view, I debated whether I should confirm Jarvis' presence. I concluded I would not gain any new information from him or the on-duty staff. I was also planning a return visit to speak with Destiny Rose about her doctor-patient relationship with Max.

In a few minutes I was standing at the spot where Maria and I had been the previous day. This time I took the next logical step and entered the Upstate Medical Building, where I soon found myself stepping off the elevator on the 23rd floor.

It was somewhat eerie knowing Alexis had done the same thing, unaware that she would be bypassing the building's elevator system when she returned to ground level later on. I checked a sign that indicated where various suites were located and headed down the hall where Suite 2309 should be.

I didn't know what I expected but I have always felt better looking into all areas of an investigation. If something was missed and the file went south because of it, I would have only myself to blame. I passed Suite 2311, then a large open waiting area before coming upon the entrance of Suite 2307. Bewildered, I stopped and looked up and down the narrow hallway. For a moment I believed I had been mistaken about Max's office number. The more I thought about it, the more I knew I was right: 2309. I looked at the waiting area to my immediate right and felt the hairs on my neck rise.

They tore his office down, I realized excitedly as I became transfixed on the large window overlooking the street. *Or at least they did the next best thing.*

Hear no evil. Speak no evil. See no evil.

I walked to the window and noted it was just that—a window. There was no entryway leading to the balcony, which I could see was devoid of objects. The building management must have taken the entire front wall down and rebuilt the space with only this large window to bring light in. I peered out to the street below and felt another chill run up my spine. If Alexis was alive when Max launched her, it surely would have been a terrifying end to a productive life. My gaze next ran up the side of the building across from Max's old office and was greeted by fifty office windows, none of which could be penetrated due to the sun's bright glare. At night, that would not be the case. In the likelihood lights were turned on in one of those offices, Max very well could have observed the person who called 911. Lights on, lights off—it didn't really matter. The buildings were so close, even a one-eyed man with 50% vision could have identified Max and Alexis as they fought on the balcony.

I left the Upstate Medical Building and walked over to the Indelible Corporation Building, taking the elevator to the 23rd floor. There was no similar waiting area carved out of the hallway, only a row of closed wooden doors. I tried to estimate how far down I had to walk to be directly across from Max's former fraud headquarters. I found myself standing at a doorway marked The Morris Collection. I entered this office and was met by two casually-dressed men. I also noted the walls were decorated with several large advertisements for products and companies, which I assumed they had created.

"Good day," the older of the two men said, as he got up from his desk. "I'm Lawrence Morris. How can we help you today?"

"I'm not quite sure," I said truthfully, as I peered past the man to the window facing the street. From this vantage point, all the balconies in view looked the same.

Lawrence turned to see what was holding my interest and thought I was staring at a gigantic poster of a gorgeous female tennis player in mid-swing. The ad's tagline read *Beautiful Returns Are Our Business.* "After we plastered that poster all over the city, that income tax company's client base went up 60%. With the right campaign, we might be able to do the same for your business."

"Somehow I doubt that," I replied. "Unless you're Tom Selleck, the P.I. business isn't that glitzy, no matter how many stunning young women you have surrounding a Ferrari."

"A real-life P.I.?" Lawrence turned to his partner. "Marty, it seems your wife finally smartened up. Instead of buying new clothes and jewellery with the mad money you give her, she's checking up on you." He faced me again with a smile. "Please tell me Sandy hired you. It would make my day."

"Sorry to disappoint you, but I have never had the pleasure of meeting Sandy."

"Darn, he's telling the truth, Marty, because if he had met Sandy, I doubt the word *pleasure* would have popped into his mind." Lawrence let out a high-pitched infectious laugh, which also cracked Marty up. "If you're not here for Marty and I'm certain no one is looking into my affairs—numerous as they are—how is it we can assist you?"

"I know this will sound a bit odd . . . I would like to look out your window for a moment."

"Are you spying on someone on the street?"

"More like across the street."

"Oh." Lawrence walked to the window and past Marty's desk. "Sure. Come on over."

I followed him to the back wall to look at the balconies and office windows before us. "How long have you and Marty been tenants here?"

"In the building?"

"No, this office."

Lawrence and Marty exchanged a glance before Marty spoke up. "It'll be six years this November. Why?"

"Have either of you ever testified at a murder trial?"

"No," Lawrence replied, with a slightly worried expression on his face.

Marty stood and looked across the street. "This is about that woman being thrown to her death, isn't it?"

"Unfortunately, yes. I was hoping one of you had been the 911 caller, who later gave evidence at the trial."

"That wasn't us."

"I have yet to go through the trial transcript and don't know the witnesses' identity. You wouldn't be able to help me with that, would you?"

"He was a bit of a ghost—at least that's what we heard at the time. No one really knew him or ever saw him much," Lawrence offered.

"They didn't even know what type of business he was conducting here," Marty added.

"But he did lease an office here, correct?"

"That's open to interpretation. From what I remember, he kind of subleased the office above us—2418—but there was something wrong with the paperwork and he disappeared."

Fabulous. Another disappearance, I thought gloomily. "But he was still around at the time of the trial."

"Maybe disappeared wasn't the best word," Lawrence backtracked. "He didn't skip out or anything like that. I'm pretty sure he paid his rent. What I meant was he apparently vacated the space right after that poor woman's death."

"That's interesting."

"I don't know," Marty said, taking his seat again. "I might think of moving to another office too, if I saw a woman killed right outside my window."

"I guess so," I agreed. Inwardly, my thoughts were whirling like a carnival ride. "Who would I talk to about 2418's lease? Is there a manager or rental agent here?"

Marty began to rifle through a rolodex and pulled out a card. He wrote down the information and handed it to me. "Thomas or Betty should be able to help you."

I took the slip of paper and noted they were in the building. "This is great. I'll try to catch them now."

As I neared the door, Lawrence asked, "Are you working for her family? The dead woman's?"

"I'm not really working for one side or the other. I'm looking at the case as a whole. Double-checking the details."

"But that doctor was convicted. What is there to investigate?"

"Like I said, I'm merely making sure the facts presented at trial were correct, that's all. Trust me, the last thing I want is to find a reason to release that con artist."

"What if you do find something?" Lawrence appeared to have taken Alexis' death personally, as Paul said many residents had.

I smiled reassuringly. "I'll cross that bridge when I come to it. Between us, I've found nothing that would indicate the trial's outcome was a miscarriage of justice."

I thanked both men again and proceeded to the lobby, where I got directions to the rental office. Unfortunately, it was closed. I tried to call the emergency number listed on the door and got voice mail. *Thank goodness this wasn't a real crisis,* I mused. I left my first name and cell number but didn't go into detail.

When my phone rang and I saw a Darrien area code in the display window, I expected it to be Dawn, who would have executed my plan and be calling with the bank statement information.

I was half-right.

"Hey, Dawn. That was quick."

"Steve, there's a problem."

"What kind of problem? Are you okay?" I asked cautiously.

The next line was not from Dawn's lovely lips but my sworn enemy's foul mouth.

"Oh, she's doing all right under the circumstances. I made sure the handcuffs weren't too tight."

"What's going on, Anderton? Let her go!" I demanded. "She isn't part of your investigation."

"No, she's part of a new one I recently started. There are a lot of break-and-enters happening in your once-quiet neighbourhood—no doubt a byproduct of your moving into the area—and we happened to catch your sexy waitress pal in the act."

"Of what—breaking into my house?" I yelled.

"Exactly."

I was fuming at Anderton's arrogance and the idea Dawn was in handcuffs because of me. "You can't charge someone with break and enter if they have the permission of the owner and a key!"

I doubted the ensuing silence was caused by Anderton second-guessing his decision, and guessed it was more of a stalling tactic to annoy me. "You're right, I can't. Due to the odd circumstances surrounding this event, we're going to require the homeowner to vouch for Dawn's claim of privileged entry into the residence."

"I'm vouching for her now, you moron."

"In person," he replied dryly.

"You're an asshole, Anderton," I countered. "And I'm going to have your job for this."

"I'm so scared."

"What you seem to forget is, I've done it to smarter officers in the past and I'm not going to rest until you're working the nightshift at the Red Hot Wiener Shack. *That* I will definitely vouch for."

This time the silence recalled our first contact on my front porch.

"I'm keeping your new girlfriend in custody until you make an appearance at the station, dickhead. There's a flight leaving there at 2:45 your time. I expect to see you walking through my doors later today to surrender." He paused again. "Did I say surrender? I meant to vouch for your partner here."

"Let me talk to Dawn."

"That's against the rules, Cassidy."

"So is beating you to a pulp in a dark alley, but I'm willing to bend if you are. Now, let me talk to her!"

"You've got ten seconds, starting now."

"I'm sorry, Steve."

"Don't apologize. Everything will be fine. I'll be leaving in a few hours."

"The Merchant Credit Trust. 489," Dawn desperately blurted out.

I heard Anderton yell, "That's enough!" just before the line went dead.

"Enough is enough!" I yelled at my phone, which I wanted to throw against the nearest wall. "Damn it, Max. I'm going to kill you when you're paroled, even if we're both 130 years old at the time."

I checked my watch: 12:56. I had less than two hours to get myself organized and to the airport on time. I walked back into the Indelible Corporation Building and stopped the first businessman I encountered. "Could you tell me where Merchant Credit Trust is located? It's downtown here, right?"

"Two blocks. Go out the doors and turn left," my snooty travel guide stated without missing a stride.

"Thanks," I said, as I ran outside. Two blocks turned into four, until I finally found it. Walking up to the service desk, I said, "I need to see someone about an account. Is there a manager on duty?"

The receptionist probably thought I was some crackpot, as my hair was mussed and I was huffing and puffing like a marathon runner. "Do you have an appointment?"

Knowing that flashing my private investigator licence would only complicate matters, I replied, "No, but I need to speak to someone in charge. It's kind of important." As she reached for the phone, I knew she had two options: security or manager. I prayed for the latter.

"If you can wait a minute, Mr. Orchard will be right with you."

"Thank you." As I headed to the waiting area, I was relieved to see the security guard at the entrance was not paying any attention to me. A few minutes later, a sharply dressed man in his 30's walked across the lobby and introduced himself.

"Hello, my name is Conrad Orchard."

I shook his hand as he led me to a small office. The sign on the wall read Accounts Manager.

"I've been informed you have a problem with an account and that you're in a rush. If I can get your name, I think I can help you. You'll be on your way in no time."

"It's Steve Cassidy, but I'm not in your system," I said, as he began to type my name on his desktop computer. "I really have a question about a friend's recent transaction. He asked me to come down, as he's sick with the flu."

"Unless you have power of attorney over your friend's financial affairs, I'm not able to give you any specific information."

"Okay, I understand. Bank rules. No problem."

"I might be able to help you out if it's just a general inquiry," Orchard offered graciously. "What exactly is the problem?"

"It's no big deal, really," I replied. "It's sort of stupid when you think about it. He forgot that he withdrew cash from a bank machine and now he's freaking out that someone stole his client card or hacked into his account."

A concerned look came over Orchard's face. "Why does he think that? Has he had security issues in the past?"

"No, just memory issues," I said with a small laugh. "There was a number on his statement—489—which he thinks is significant. Like it's the thief's calling card or something."

"I can only guess that 489 refers to machine 489. You see, each of our ATMs is numbered."

"I knew it was something simple like that," I said, trying to look relieved. "Could you tell me where 489 is located? Maybe it will jog my friend's memory if he knew where the withdrawal took place."

Orchard's attention returned to his computer and several keystrokes later he looked up and said proudly, "It's one of our few full-service machines. It's located around the corner, inside the Quickie Shop & Go convenience store. Does your friend ever shop in that store?"

"All the time," I replied, shaking my head and rising from my chair. "I really appreciate your help, Mr. Orchard."

Orchard stood and shook my hand again. "Tell him to always keep his receipts, so he can double-check his account when he updates his bankbook."

"I'll definitely do that."

I was soon out on the street, asking directions one more time. Five minutes later, I entered the Quickie Shop & Go store and began to look for surveillance cameras. I saw three: one over the cash register, one facing the freezer compartments and one aimed at the ATM in the corner.

"How long has that bank machine been over there?" I asked the young clerk on duty.

"Since I've been working here," she said in a wary tone.

"How long has that been?"

"About a year."

"Is there someone here who might have worked here longer—say, five years or more?"

"There is," a man replied from behind me. "What seems to be the problem?"

I turned to face a middle-aged man wearing a red jacket with the name Mankin embroidered on the left pocket. "I'm a private investigator looking into a fraud case and believe your bank machine may have been used in the commission of a crime."

"This is the first I've heard of this," Mankin replied, very concerned. "My family has run this store for almost fifteen years and we've never had any problems with the law."

"Don't get me wrong, Mankin," I said, adding his name to put him at ease. "The police aren't involved in this case yet and I honestly don't believe it will come to that. I have two quick questions and I'll be out of here."

"Okay."

"How long has that machine been in the store?"

"I don't know exact dates. Maybe ten years."

"In that same spot?"

"Yes. It's too hard to relocate. We actually have to make renovations around it. Because of its spot in the back aisle, it hasn't caused any problems. Is that all?"

"One more," I said, pointing to the camera mounted on the wall near the ATM. "Have you always had a camera up there?"

"Not always," Mankin said. "We installed them about six years ago."

I had to catch my breath at this admission, even though I knew I was going to be disappointed by the answer to my next question.

"How long do you keep the surveillance tapes?"

"When the cameras were first installed we used to keep them for a week. Back then if there had been no trouble in the store, we didn't see the purpose of keeping all these big videotapes in the office. With today's time-lapsed recorders and mini-tapes, we keep them for about a month now—before taping over them." He stopped and looked at me. "I can tell by your expression that doesn't help you. How long ago did this crime take place?"

"About five years ago."

"Unfortunately, those tapes are long gone."

"It was worth a shot."

I exited the store only slightly depressed, as I would have loved to watch the tape showing Jarvis depositing $9,999 into his account. This exercise wasn't a total loss, as I now knew he was not at home watching TV or out of the country, as he had claimed to the good folks at the Denby Eatery. This was another piece of circumstantial evidence which could form the basis of a future case against Jarvis. Yet it was still too weak to amount to anything except wild, irresponsible speculation by an equally wild and irresponsible private eye.

I returned to the van and headed to the airport. For the time being, my work here was finished. Once in Darrien, if Anderton had his way, I would probably have to continue the investigation from a jail cell. After paying for the van at the rental counter, I took a seat in the waiting area and began to reflect on all the new information I had uncovered. Several minutes into this examination, I became very agitated with the entire case and wanted to end everything. It didn't really matter if Max had killed Alexis alone or with Jarvis' help. And why was I so involved in establishing Jarvis' source of personal wealth or his fascination with beautiful strippers? Regardless of my investigation, it appeared the local authorities had done a good job the first time around. I also came to realize that Max's subtle threats to Linda and Maria's well-being were as hollow as two-foot chocolate Easter bunnies.

When my flight's boarding call was announced I grabbed my small carry-on bag and said, "Homeward bound," for the benefit of no one.

The vibration of my cell phone momentarily stopped my march toward the gate. I expected to see a Darrien area code and to hear Anderton warning me not to miss my flight. Instead, it was Maria's number.

"Maria. Is everything all right?"

"They found Linda, Steve."

"What do you mean?" I asked, barely able to stand. "Who found her? And is she okay?"

"I don't know," she replied, sounding exasperated and strangely excited at the same time. "An officer from the Darrien Police called wanting to know what we were investigating together and why I had returned alone."

"What did you tell him?"

"I told him about the investigation, that's all."

"And?"

"And nothing. He didn't seem all that interested."

"What about Linda? What did he say about finding her?"

"He wasn't specific. He said he might have to speak with me again, as they had located Linda, or at least knew of her whereabouts."

"What does that mean, Maria? Did they find her or not?"

"I don't know. He wouldn't say."

I could tell Maria was getting upset with this new development.

"Okay, Maria, you did good. Everything will be fine."

"I want to believe you. I really do, Steve."

"I swear that Linda is alive and she has been all along." I heard the final boarding call. "I'm about to fly out for Darrien. I'll call you tonight with anything I find out about Linda, okay?"

"The officer told me not to have any contact with you."

"But here we are talking on the phone. That tells me everything I need to know about you, Maria, and how much you still care." There was silence on the line for a moment, before I added, "I have to get on this plane right now. Don't worry about Officer Anderton's threat. I'll be doing all the talking with that idiot in a few hours. He won't be bothering anyone again."

"I never told you who called me."

"You didn't have to. We cops have a sixth sense. Unfortunately, today it's a curse, not a blessing. I'll call you later."

"Be careful," she advised in her soft sweet voice.

"I will."

TWENTY

POLICE QUESTION CASSIDY
New clues to fiancée's disappearance
Revealed for the first time

By Jeremy Atkins

It is not clear whether P.I. Steve Cassidy was sporting a suntan when he was detained at Darrien Airport yesterday. Police did, however, reveal that Mr. Cassidy was not co-operative during an intense interrogation that took place at headquarters. As a former police officer, Cassidy is well aware of his rights as a citizen, but did not ask for legal counsel and apparently waived his right to remain silent. Both issues raise more questions than answers, as police continue to confirm the whereabouts of local librarian Linda Brooks, Cassidy's missing fiancée.

Officer Kenneth Anderton, who is heading up this investigation, stated, "Mr. Cassidy continues to deny any involvement in Ms. Brooks' disappearance. When asked about a life insurance policy in her name, he claimed it was a forgery."

It was also disclosed Cassidy has recently been conducting an investigation unrelated to his fiancée's current situation. As Cassidy's private investigator's licence is suspended, police and the regulatory board overseeing investigators may charge him with a number of offences, including operating a business without a licence and impersonating an investigator. "We are looking at all areas of misconduct," Anderton told reporters late last night. "We believe Mr. Cassidy has knowledge regarding his fiancée's disappearance and we plan to pursue that avenue until her whereabouts can be established."

When asked if there were any new developments, Anderton revealed that a "very promising" lead had been uncovered and the police were following up on the information.

Cassidy was released from police custody with no charges laid.

"What lead do you think this Anderton cop is talking about?" Dawn asked, minutes after I returned to my house.

"Beats me," I said, collapsing beside her on the couch. "It's all smoke and mirrors. During my interrogation, he kept saying they had information on Linda, only he'd clam up when I asked for details."

"But didn't he tell Maria they knew Linda's whereabouts?"

"He *inferred* he knew, to scare her. Anderton has turned out to be a sick, twisted, little man who has it in for me. Facts are not going to stand in the way of railroading me."

It was a little after one in the morning, and Dawn and I were still coming to terms with our respective time at police headquarters. She had been treated relatively well and placed in a holding room until I was in custody. When released, she was told to go home. As a matter of defiance, or simply because she didn't want to go to her apartment, she returned to my place to await my arrival. When I stumbled through the door around midnight, she gave me a comforting hug and a welcoming smile, both of which were much appreciated. She told me how entering the house and finding the bank statement had went smoothly, but after replacing the key in its hiding spot, Anderton came out of nowhere to arrest her. This would explain why he had implied she didn't have a house key on her at the time.

Either way, Anderton was a bastard.

"Are you in trouble for investigating your friend's case?"

"First, I don't really consider Max to be my friend anymore. Second, everyone I talked to did so freely. You or Maria or my buddy Wayne could have conducted the same inquiries, with the same results," I argued. "Anderton's other problem, which he failed to tell the press, was that the P.I. board does not have jurisdiction outside this area."

"But they're still going to try and pin something on you, right?"

"Without a doubt. I'm Enemy #1."

My interrogation lasted for three hours, during which I was forced to endure Anderton go over the same ground dozens of times: Where was Linda? Was she alive? How did I dispose of her body? And on and on and on. When I thought we were finished, Anderton was called from the room for several minutes. When he returned, something had changed. He was cockier than before, which I didn't think was possible.

"We just got a tip," he proclaimed proudly.

"I hope it was less than the customary 15% because the service around here is lousy," I said.

"That's pretty funny stuff, Cassidy. Did you ever contemplate a career as a comedian?"

"No. Did you ever consider one in law enforcement?"

"You should get all those zingers out of your system now, because if this tip pans out, I doubt you'll be cracking jokes in prison."

"If you're in charge of tracking this big lead down, I have nothing to worry about, Anderton. Plus, the day you charge me with any crime—petty or otherwise—the only one of us looking at the inside of a cell will be you."

With that, the interrogation ended and I was released into the loving arms of several newspaper and television reporters. For the record, I was tempted to apologize to Linda and make a direct plea for her to come out of the woodwork, as things were getting seriously out of hand. Fortunately, my corruption case lawyer's voice penetrated these foolish ideas as I heard him declare, "Don't say a word without a lawyer present to advise you to keep your trap shut!"

It was good advice then and better advice now, I thought. I ended up issuing the standard, highly incriminating, "No comment," to the swarming media.

In the morning as I slept in, Dawn went to work at the pub, leaving a note behind for me to find.

> *As predicted, the sun once again came up.*
> *It's a new day. Live life to the fullest!*
> *Our days of freedom may be numbered!*
> *Hahahahahahahaha!*
> *- Me*

I couldn't agree with her more. I had a shower to clean off Anderton's egotistical stench and made myself some breakfast.

Prior to leaving on my road trip, I had turned off the answering machine. When she returned from her incarceration, Dawn went one step further and silenced the ringer because of the number of calls. I turned the machine and ringer back on, figuring I could screen my calls. I then tracked down my cell phone in my jacket pocket. It had been turned off by one of the officers at the police station. If I had been in charge of this investigation, I would have confiscated it and checked all the incoming and outgoing numbers in the memory for possible follow-up. Anderton, of course, was not that bright. As soon as it powered up, the message light flashed and the phone began to beep a happy tune. I had one new message from Sabrina Howell of The Standard newspaper.

"Let's stop playing phone tag and give me a call."

She sounded nice enough. I sat at the kitchen table with my box of evidence within reach and called her back. After a minute of small talk, we got down to business.

"Our mutual friend Paul Rumleski told me you covered the Max Feldberg manslaughter trial. I was hoping you might shed some light on the proceedings. You know—some juicy behind-the-scenes stuff that didn't make it into print or air on TV."

"Why the interest?" she asked.

"I'll be straight with you, Sabrina. I'm looking into the case for Max. We used to be friends in high school."

"He did it. You know that, don't you?"

"Everything seems to point in that direction."

"That's because there were no other directions to point," she said, sounding peeved. "Friendship only goes so far, Mr. Cassidy. He's guilty and no investigation half a decade down the road is going to change that."

I didn't respond immediately, likely giving Sabrina the impression I was either mad at her or there really was something down that road.

"Forget about my past friendship with Max. I hadn't heard from him in years and had no idea he was up to no good," I said slowly. "I haven't read your articles or even the trial transcript yet but in your opinion, what was the deciding factor in the jury's guilty verdict?"

"Two words: Derek McDonald."

If Satan himself magically appeared in the room holding Santa Claus' severed head, I don't believe I would have noticed. "Did you say Derek?"

"Yes, Derek McDonald. He called the police that night. Saw the whole thing."

He's a friend of mine. Used to be.

"Impossible," I muttered to myself, remembering Jarvis' slip at the Denby Eatery. There was no way this was a coincidence.

"What's impossible?" I now had Sabrina's full attention. "If you had read the court transcript, you would have known this. So, what exactly is impossible here?"

"I don't know yet," I replied, stumbling over my words as I frantically tried to jam this new square peg into one of this file's many round holes. "Did you ever interview him—Derek McDonald?"

"I wish," she replied, sounding a lot more conciliatory. "He was the star witness and no one could find him—let alone talk to him—

prior to the trial."

"What about after his testimony?"

"He vanished like a tumbleweed in the night."

"Are there any pictures of him anywhere?"

"Not that I know of," Sabrina replied. "Cameras were not allowed in courtrooms. They are today but that doesn't help you now."

"No, it doesn't," I said with a sigh. "A star witness in such a widely publicized trial and your photographers at the paper didn't snap one picture of him?"

"Why is this guy so important to you? He witnessed the murder, called 911 and testified at the trial. He was a model citizen doing his civic and moral duty. I get the feeling you don't see it in quite the same light and would really like to know why. After all, you called me. I answered your questions, so you could at least answer mine."

I glanced down at Dawn's note, which brought home the ugly truth that if Anderton's trumped-up tip came to fruition, my days of freedom could very well be numbered. It was time to act, the consequences be damned.

"What would you say if I stated I was beginning to believe there were other people involved in Alexis Penney's murder?"

"What every good reporter would in that situation: who, what, when, where and why?"

"I was afraid that's what you'd say."

I spent the next half hour going over what I knew, when I knew it and how I came about the information that now formed my fragile hypothesis about Max's possible innocence. Sabrina listened to my theories, asking relevant questions while making notations in a reporter's pad. At the end of my narrative I couldn't tell if she pegged me as a moron or an investigative genius.

"There are an awful lot of loose ends here, Steve," she said. "With most of them seemingly unrelated to the actual crime. You can't put this Jarvis character at the scene or confirm he knew Alexis Penney. Your half-naked club friends tell a good tale but neither would pass my sniff test—which I mean in a figurative way, not a literal one."

"Personally," I countered, "I do believe their stories—my sniff test may be a bit different from the one you use—but I think there's a thread of truth to Jarvis' involvement with Alexis."

"Even if they did have a relationship, why would he suddenly want to kill her? From what you've told me, Jarvis isn't the sharpest knife in the drawer. So for him to frame Max is too far-fetched for me. Furthermore, I don't believe for a second the two of them were somehow in cahoots."

"I know how unrealistic this seems," I conceded.

"You need to talk with Max again."

"I thought about that but I don't think I'll be making a return trip to your region in the near future."

"Why not? You don't have an order against you saying you can't travel, have you?"

"I'm certain it's being drawn up as we speak."

"Then you should get out here before it's too late."

"You're the second woman to give me that advice today."

"Well, from personal experience I know it's hard conducting an investigation from inside a cell."

"What did they get you on?"

"Obstruction of justice. I wouldn't give up my source at a bribery trial involving the mayor's son."

"How long were you inside?"

"Eight days."

"With a track record like that, I feel comfortable our conversation today will remain confidential—not that anyone is going to be asking you about it in the future."

"Just because I said there were a lot of loose ends in your theory doesn't mean I can't see the merits of your argument. To be frank, I am quite intrigued about a few of your points."

"Such as?"

"For instance, you spoke about Derek McDonald's actions at his office building—before and after Alexis' fall. Then there is my own frustration at not being able to interview him. This gives me a reason to put a feeler out for him. Maybe there really is more than meets the eye with our good citizen."

"You might want to start by tracking down the rental managers at the Indelible Corporation Building. Their names are Thomas and Betty. They could shed some light on the paperwork problem for Suite 2418."

I gave Sabrina their phone number and suggested she call before going downtown, as their office hours were arbitrary.

"Done," she said. "Anything else?"

"You might want to read *The Murdering Mistress* yourself or get the book review from Paul. I have to call him next. He's probably wondering why I didn't contact him last night."

"I'm sure he'll understand. After leaving television and before writing novels full-time, he wrote a crime column for the paper. That's how we met."

"He didn't tell me that."

"He only did it for a few months. He got bored writing about the same people and the same crimes all the time."

"Imagine how the front-line cops feel every shift."

"Every job has its burnout point, I guess."

"But you haven't reached yours yet?"

"Oh, on the contrary," she laughed. "I hit that wall about four years ago, only to decide to keep running regardless. I'm like those sharks that die if they stop swimming for too long. Not that it really matters. I don't know how to do anything else and am too old to pick a new trade."

"That's what I used to think, but look at me now on my second career."

"If you don't stay out of trouble, you might find yourself seeking a third one."

"At this stage in my life, I could think of worse things, believe me."

Sabrina said she would interview Thomas and Betty within the next few days and keep me updated. I promised I would keep her apprised of any new developments as well.

I hung up the phone and walked to the front window, expecting to see Anderton and his goon squad standing on the sidewalk ready to attack as soon as a judge signed my arrest warrant. Fortunately, everything seemed calm. I checked the front door lock and then the back. No one was getting in here without my permission or a battering ram. After locking the back door, I remembered what Dawn had said about Anderton appearing out of nowhere. He hadn't materialized like a magician in a puff of smoke. She'd said she had returned the spare key to the lantern when Anderton appeared. It was apparent he had not actually observed her finding or replacing the key. He had been so obsessed about finding a way to get me downtown, he never thought about how she'd actually entered the house in the first place.

With this peculiar notion rambling around in my head, I walked into the kitchen where I saw Max's evidence box. A sharp, sickening pain shot through my chest, as I realized that for the past two weeks I had been wearing the same blinders as Anderton had the previous afternoon.

Whoever took the Tecumseh Motel surveillance tape from the VCR had entered the house without breaking a window or jimmying a lock, my brain began to scream. *The evidence box, however, was left on the back porch. Why come in once with a key, but not a second time? It doesn't make sense.*

I ran out the back door, jumped off the porch and stared at the three overturned lanterns. Next, I looked at the spot where I had found the box and then to the open back door. As my head began to hurt and toxic acids continued to eat away at my stomach, I came to the alarming conclusion I had been dealing with two separate individuals all along—not just one.

One was Max's messenger, whose job was to drop off packages.

The other was also a messenger, but with one difference: he had access to a house key—either Linda's or the one hidden inside a forgotten Chinese lantern. The fact it had been Linda's hide-it-in-plain-sight idea left me with a very disturbing question: Was it possible she was involved in trying to frame me for her disappearance?

Like a ghost from the past, I could see my pint-sized, recently divorced English teacher, Miss Styler, standing in front of our Grade 11 class reading a line from one of her favourite plays: *Heaven has no rage like love to hatred turned, nor Hell hath no fury like a woman scorned.*

"Let that be a valuable lesson to all you young men here today," she advised. "If it's the only one you take from this class all year, I've done my job."

I had no idea where that line was taken from but as I fell into my recliner I had the sinking feeling I was in bigger trouble than I had imagined. When I turned on the television to video of Linda's empty house in Sussex, my suspicions were confirmed.

"This is a live shot of a police raid in progress. It has been reported this Sussex residence may be linked to local librarian Linda Brooks' disappearance."

I turned off the TV, grabbed my still-unpacked suitcase and was on the road in less than two minutes, trying to simultaneously outrun my past, present and future.

Have fun with that, my rear view mirror twin seemed to say as I drove out of the neighbourhood, possibly for the last time. I only began to breathe normally again after passing the Darrien city limits. Wanting to clear my head, I turned the radio to a modern rock station, where I caught the start of a song I vaguely knew.

Couldn't say goodbye, without slamming the door.
Couldn't say I love you anymore.
Started questioning the answers that you always gave.
You became the master, I became the slave.

The lyrics could have been written for Linda and me. The true connection to my sorry life came at the end of the song, when the announcer identified the group.

"That was Sex at Seven's new one, The Unexpected Kiss."

It was like a cosmic prompt to call the band's biggest fan before it was too late.

"It's all over the news," Dawn said after picking up on the first ring. "Are you okay?"

"I will be. I'm going to take a vacation for a few days."

"That's the house you went to when you were searching for Linda, isn't it?"

"It is."

"You didn't . . . you know?" her voice trailed off.

"No, Dawn. I didn't. Please believe me."

"For some reason, I do."

"That's good to hear. I wanted you to know I was fine and everything will work out. I just have to go. I'm sure the police are going to be monitoring my cell calls, if they haven't started already. So when they come by the pub, say I called to say goodbye and you don't know where I'm heading. Can you do that?"

"I didn't crack under the pressure yesterday."

"That you didn't."

"And I honestly don't know where you're going."

"I wish I could tell you, Dawn, I really do. This time around I would have loved for you to accompany me, because if anyone needs a vacation from Darrien right now, it's the two of us."

I could hear some type of commotion in the pub and then a man's voice calling out Dawn's name.

"They're here, Steve. I have to go. Be safe."

The line went dead and my heart almost gave out. Was running really the best option? It was for me, but what about everyone else I had entangled in this mess?

I stepped on the gas, wanting to get as far away as quickly as possible. As I overtook a pick-up truck in the passing lane, I noticed a bumper sticker on the tailgate which read *Where Does The Road To Nowhere Lead?*

I didn't have the foggiest idea, but knew I was about to find out.

TWENTY ONE

ARREST WARRANT ISSUED
Hunt on for Cassidy

By Jeremy Atkins

After a dramatic raid on a Sussex residence yesterday morning, Darrien Police issued an arrest warrant for troubled P.I. Steve Cassidy, alleging the kidnapping and forcible confinement of his fiancée. Following up on a tip, Officer Kenneth Anderton had earlier described as a significant lead, evidence was found that indicated local librarian Linda Brooks had been held captive in a house located at 3795 Adelaide Crescent in Sussex.

"We recovered articles of clothing and other personal items belonging to Linda Brooks, as well as fingerprints on a flashlight and throughout the residence which match Steve Cassidy's," Officer Anderton stated. "Ms. Brooks and her whereabouts are still unconfirmed." Witnesses have also confirmed Mr. Cassidy had recently been at the residence and had been inquiring about Ms. Brooks.

"With regard to speaking with neighbours and the property manager of this residence, we believe Mr. Cassidy's actions were meant to feign concern for Ms. Brooks' well-being. When you think about it, it's simply a ploy for sympathy by an individual incapable of taking responsibility for his actions and now on the run from the authorities."

Twenty miles outside of Darrien, I purchased an untraceable payphone calling card at a service centre and immediately put it to use.

"Hey, Paul. Steve Cassidy here—the mystery man from the Denby Eatery. Sorry I didn't get back to you sooner. I was tied up on another matter yesterday. I'm on the road right now and wanted to call before I forgot."

"No problem. It gave me a few more hours to digest the book."

"Was it worth the five bucks I paid for it?"

"I'm sure it didn't win any literary prizes, but it wasn't too bad," he replied. "It would be a real eye-opener for the locals. As I said at the restaurant, Alexis' death really affected a lot of people. She was young and beautiful, and bad things shouldn't have happened to her."

"Are you implying old, ugly people like myself, should have bad things happen to them?" I kidded him.

"Not at all," Paul laughed. "It's just that when people attain celebrity status, sometimes it's hard for the public to fathom them having a bad day."

"But no one knew Alexis was famous—or infamous—at the time of her death."

"Didn't matter. Remember, she was hot and very little was known about her actual past, likely helped create her legend."

"So, if everyone knew she was the murdering mistress, she wouldn't have been such a tragic figure?"

"I wouldn't go that far," Paul said. "We're still a pretty big hearted community, although I'm sure a small number of people would have thought she got what she deserved. You know—delayed justice."

"Can you give me the condensed version of her crime and the trial?"

Paul proceeded to chronicle an affair Alexis had with a married man and how the guy's wife turned up dead. The case against Alexis seemed to be airtight until the star witness also stopped breathing.

"She never did go to trial. The victim's husband agreed to testify against her and then died unexpectedly in prison."

I was surprised at this news. "Any way she could have played a role in his death?"

"None. It's the old story of two prisoners getting into a fight in the cafeteria. A death match ensues with only one man standing when the final lunch bell rings."

"She got off on a technicality then?"

"The entire case rested on her lover's testimony."

"Did the book say how she ended up in Santana Hills?"

"Not specifically. It ended with her getting a divorce, a big payout from the hubby and then skipping town."

"How big a payout?"

"When the market was soft, she and her husband bought a lot of real estate. They made a bundle when a car plant opened on the outskirts of Ravenwood and there was a housing boom."

I wondered if any of this blood money had made its way into Jarvis' account. Although still troubled by that mysterious $9,999 ATM deposit, what bothered me more was the former stripper's claim he had $150,000 in the bank, only days after Alexis' fall.

"Did Alexis have any brothers or sisters?"

"A sister named Lauren Rush."

"Does she live in Ravenwood?"

"She did at the time of Alexis' arrest," Paul answered. "She thinks Alexis was set up by the boyfriend."

"I wonder if she followed her sister's lead and bid the town good riddance."

"I do know a local bar held a going-away party to celebrate Alexis' departure. From what I gather, she wasn't that popular prior to the murder charges. If I were Lauren, I think I would have a hard time staying in the area if that happened to one of my siblings."

"I guess," I said, thinking again how my own actions had left Maria, Linda, Samantha and Dawn all hanging out to dry, or worse.

"I'm at my computer now. I could run a telephone search if you'd like."

"Sure, why not."

Lauren had not skipped town and had a current telephone number. Paul also gave me a list of other people from the book to talk to if I was planning a trip to Ravenwood in the future.

"I don't think a personal visit will be necessary," I lied. "But I appreciate your help."

"Do you want me to mail the book to you?"

"Could you pass it along to your reporter friend Sabrina Howell? When we spoke this morning she was interested in reading it."

"I can do that. I haven't seen her in awhile. Was she able to help you?"

"I have her doing some legwork for me, as I don't know when I'll return to your fine city."

"You're always welcome and maybe next time we can have a full meal together."

"For sure," I said earnestly. "Thanks again for your help, Paul."

I've always loved the saying *When the rubber hits the road.* Or is that *Where the rubber hits the road?* Either way, the idea of speed and forward motion has always given me a rush, regardless whether the rubber was attached to my tricycle wheels, my mountain bike or my first car— a black 1975 Chevy Monte Carlo. That feeling had returned as I made my way to Ravenwood for what could be my final destination on this tour of intrigue and utter stupidity. It was also the last place Anderton would be looking for me.

I arrived in Alexis Penney's hometown at dinnertime and cruised the short main street drag along with a few side streets to orientate myself. It was pretty much divided into two distinct sections: the original small town, and a large new subdivision close to an auto parts plant. Overall, it still had a nice Delta-like ambiance and I felt right at home, especially upon entering the Bud-E Hall-E Bar and Banquet Centre. It was like stepping back in time to a more innocent age, when Buddy Holly and Elvis were both considered kings. Record album jackets and 45's were pinned to the walls alongside row after row of classic black-and-white portraits of the biggest stars of the 50's and 60's. This was an era when you didn't mention the term "sex" on TV or in polite conversation, let alone have it as part of your rock band's name.

The place was half-full, with several families eating in the dining area. Most of the patrons, however, were seated at the bar drinking cold beer and noshing on pretzels and peanuts. My entrance caused the usual *Who's that?* stir amongst the regulars before they returned to minding their own business. I sat on a stool at the end of the bar and ordered a beer. Knowing how precious my time had become and recalling the reaction Alexis' name had generated at the Denby Eatery, I decided to launch a heat-seeking missile into the crowd and hope to survive the fallout.

"Would anyone here know where I could find a copy of *The Murdering Mistress?*"

"Tramp."

"Whore."

"Bitch."

Not exactly the response I had expected.

"Now is everyone referring to Alexis Penney or is there another trampy, whoring bitch I need to speak with about getting this book?"

If my first question hadn't grabbed their attention, my second one surely did.

"Who's asking?" someone called out.

"Who cares?" another chimed in.

Slowly the group's gaze drifted to a table in the middle of the room, where a man in his early 40's was dining with an elderly couple. "How many copies do you need?" he asked me, as he neatly folded his napkin and placed it beside his plate. "One? A hundred and one? Five hundred and one? I've got boxes and boxes of them stored in my basement's unfinished bathroom."

I adjusted my position on the stool and gave my full attention to this eccentric book collector. As I studied his face I knew I had seen him before, but there was something missing that threw off my identification of him. When I realized he no longer sported a moustache and goatee, I introduced myself to him and the interested throng.

"Mr. Penney," I said. "My name is Steve Cassidy. I'm a P.I. looking into your wife's death."

A low murmur began at all the tables.

"Former wife."

"Yes, of course. Sorry about that."

"Who hired you and why?" the woman next to me piped up.

"Unfortunately, I can't legally tell you the name of my client. I hope you understand. However, the 'why' part deals with the crime and whether the right person is sitting in jail for Alexis' murder."

Murmur. Murmur. Murmur.

"Well, she wasn't killed in Ravenwood," an elderly woman, I thought might be Alexis' former mother-in-law, said. "So why come sniffing around here? There was a trial, a man was convicted and that's that. A few of us would have liked to share the credit for her demise but we all have alibis. Isn't that right, everybody?"

The crowd was now animated. They were laughing, snickering and shouting out their whereabouts for that June night so long ago.

"I was at the gym."

"I was doing laundry."

"I was mowing the lawn."

I enjoyed the camaraderie of these friends and barflies. They had all lived through the Alexis Penney scandal and survived.

"And what about you, Joe? Where were you that night?" I asked in a casual tone.

Joe took a swig of his beer and said with a wide grin, "At home, doing what I've been doing since Alexis left town."

"Which was?" I asked, anticipating a great punchline.

"Counting my money and my blessings that that trampin' whorin' bitch was out of my life forever!" Waves of laughter filled the bar and any tension vanished. "And about that book—I'll autograph one and give it to you for free. I'll write it off as a promotional item," Joe said, still grinning from ear to ear.

"I might take you up on that offer."

I did a fast scan of the faces around me, looking for someone not quite as enthusiastic as the others. She wasn't hard to find: a middle-of-the-road beauty in her mid-40's with long brown hair who was sitting alone and pretending to be more interested in her chicken dinner than the banter of the other diners. I kept my eye on her as I tried to fade into the wallpaper. This was not entirely taxing, as no one talked to me except the bartender, who asked if I would like another beer. I declined and paid my tab. As I walked out of the bar, I heard someone yell, "Good luck finding the real killer, Magnum," which was greeted by more uproarious laughter.

Typical small town yahoos, I thought affectionately. Had I stayed put in Delta with Maria, I'm sure I too would be a small town yahoo and proud of it. As it turned out, to the townsfolk of both Delta and Ravenwood I was just another unwanted visitor.

"Mr. Cassidy—got a minute?"

I turned to find my dinner-for-one brunette coming toward me. "I have several of them," I replied. "Call me Steve."

"Hi, Steve," she said, reaching out her hand, which I shook. "My name is Robin Hannigan."

"Very nice to meet you, Robin," I said. "I was hoping we'd be able to talk. In fact, if you hadn't come out now, I was planning on waiting for you."

"Why am I so special? It's Joe you came to see, right?"

"To answer the first question, you're special because you didn't laugh at those lame remarks, like the others. This could mean one of two things: either you have a lousy sense of humour, or you didn't find their comments all that funny." These observations brought a smile to her sour face. "I'm hoping you do have a sense of humour and that we can talk about whatever is bothering you."

"You're pretty good at pegging people."

"It's one of my very few admirable qualities."

Robin looked toward the bar. "I'm interested in your investigation, which would probably shock the people inside."

"Why's that?"

"Because my sister was Patricia Mayer. She was the woman Alexis Penney killed."

TWENTY TWO

I followed Robin to her house, a small brick bungalow in the older section of town, far away from the new subdivision in the west end. As we entered the front door I noted the phrase on her doormat: You Have Arrived.

"I like your mat," I said.

"It gives my guests the impression they're going to be treated well and that it's about time they darkened my doorway," Robin laughed. "Make yourself comfortable while I let the dog out."

I heard the excited pitter-patter of a dog's long nails dancing on the hardwood and the back door opening. Before taking a seat on the couch, I perused the fireplace mantle and a large cabinet, checking the various pictures on display. I recognized the now-deceased Patricia and her husband Randy from similar shots in *The Murdering Mistress*. Compared to Alexis Penney, Patricia did not have the same glamorous physical features. She did, however, possess something far more important: the visible warmth of a good soul. As I studied her numerous smiling poses, I couldn't imagine her with a fiery temper or an evil nature—at least not in the same way Alexis appeared to exude in a few of those non-bikini photographs at the courthouse.

"She was an amazing person," Robin said when she came into the living room. "Everyone loved her."

"What type of work did she do?"

"She worked in a daycare in Huxley—that's a small city about 15 miles from here."

"I remember passing the sign on the highway. Is that what she was doing at the time of her death?"

"Yes and no." Robin rearranged a couple of the pictures on the mantle. "She was actually contemplating quitting. There were two old hippies who moved into the small apartment above the centre and turned it into a terrible drug haven of sorts. Each morning before the children arrived, the staff had to check the playground for dropped capsules, drug baggies or even worse, used syringes."

"Crackheads above the daycare. Sounds like the name of a punk rock group from the late 70's," I said, trying to lighten the mood with limited success. I watched as Robin's thoughts and eyes drifted over to the mantle photos.

"At the time of her death she had been off work, after one of the kids jumped on her, dislocating her shoulder." She paused as she stared longingly at one of her sister's pictures. "I often wonder if things would have turned out differently had that child not been so rambunctious—not that I'm blaming the little guy or anything. Still, it makes you think."

"A good friend of mine once told me, 'You can't live your whole life based on the past—the what ifs—because what if you're wrong? Then you're really screwed.'"

"That's advice more people should obey. Even me."

I took a seat on the couch as Robin sat in a large overstuffed recliner that resembled an oversized mushroom. "Is there a particular aspect of my investigation in which you're interested?" I asked after a moment of silence. "As I said earlier, I'm looking into Alexis' death, not your sister's. From what I'm told, the book covered that area fairly extensively and the evidence was conclusive against both Alexis and Randy." At the mention of Randy's name, Robin's manner changed and I knew this stroll down memory lane had been a bad idea. I tried to steer the conversation back to our original topic. "Is there any information you could supply about Alexis' death? Is it possible someone from Ravenwood had a hand in her demise?"

"We all wanted to hurt her, from the paper boy all the way to the mayor," Robin replied angrily.

"I can understand that, I really can. I've been in similar situations where I was almost certainly on someone's death list. The difference is so far none have carried out their threats. I'm here. I'm alive, at least for now. Alexis—no matter what you think of her or how she destroyed your family—isn't."

"What about that doctor friend of hers who was convicted?"

"That doesn't mean someone from around here couldn't have

planned her death."

"That's not possible. What you saw at the bar was a typical night in Ravenwood, with a good cross-section of residents in attendance. You were there. Can't you tell we're a bunch of talkers, not doers? We talk a good game but no one would have the balls to actually pull off a murder. We just wanted Alexis to leave, and when she did the town threw a party at the Bud-E Hall-E."

I was confused. "Then why did you want to talk to me?"

"I was hoping that seeing pictures of Patricia and putting a human face to her name, you would reconsider your investigation. Everyone is dead and gone. Patricia, Alexis and Randy—all of them."

"I'm not trying to change history, Robin, and I know I can't bring anyone back to life." As she continued to stare intently at me, I attempted to change gears. "When Patricia was found dead, I'm sure everyone wanted to find her killer."

"And we did."

"But what if Alexis was telling the truth about not being involved in the murder?"

"That wasn't the case."

"What if her only crime was adultery? Should she still be put away for life? My point is, like Patricia, the circumstances surrounding Alexis' death appeared straightforward. The doctor threw her off the balcony and is languishing in prison. However, I think the facts presented at his trial were not necessarily the truth of the case. I'm getting a sneaking feeling he was framed by a killer who is still running around out there. You had valid reasons for wanting Alexis dead but what if you were wrong about her killer? That's what I'm trying to do now—eliminate any doubt."

"There were an awful lot of *what ifs* in that sermon you preached, Mr. Cassidy," Robin said seriously. "What you don't seem to realize is no one around here cares if the Detroit Tigers ball team killed Alexis. She's worm food now and out of our lives forever." She stopped and sighed. "There are so many other important things you could be doing with your time."

I waited for examples—feed the hungry, clothe the homeless—that never came. Robin had finished her little sermon. Amen. I wanted to agree and give her a hug as a thank-you gesture for setting me on the path of righteousness, but I didn't. Instead, I stood preparing to leave. "I'm very sorry about your sister. From the pictures she appears to have been a nice woman."

"She was the best," Robin said, choking on emotion.

"I appreciate you speaking with me," I said, looking toward the door. "I'll show myself out."

As I was about to step into the night, Robin called out, "If you're really looking for someone with a motive for killing Alexis, speak with Lauren Rush."

"Alexis' sister?"

"Oh, yeah. She struck it rich after that fall."

"Did she sue the building owners or Dr. Feldberg for wrongful death?"

"Insurance money," came the blunt reply. "$2 million."

I'm sure everyone in town would hear about the stunned expression that came over my face at this piece of trivia. "All of it?"

"Every last dime."

I stumbled back to my van where I sat for several minutes contemplating the infinite number of new possibilities and partnerships that could make up a kill Alexis cabal, if such a thing ever existed. If this windfall had come from an insurance policy, some questions needed answering. Had Alexis purchased the policy? If so, why for such a large amount? Or had Lauren bought the policy believing some Ravenwood redneck would kill her sister? I found the phone number Paul had given me earlier and called it from a payphone at a small variety store.

"Hi. I'm looking for Lauren Rush. Is she home? My name is Steve Cassidy."

"You're the P.I. looking into my sister's murder," Lauren said.

"Let me guess—you eat at the Bud-E Hall-E, right?"

"Not in over seven years. I'm not allowed in there anymore."

"For real or because you feel uncomfortable when you go there?"

I asked.

"Oh, no, for real. I have a no trespass order against me. The closest I can come to that place is a card store across the street."

"So, you'll be arrested if you step off the curb in the direction of the bar?"

"Yes—arrested again."

"Okay, then a meeting with you close to the bar probably isn't a very good idea."

"Not for another twenty–three years."

"The judge gave you a thirty-year no trespass order?"

"He's the brother-in-law of the owner, whose best friend is my former brother-in-law. Did you follow that?"

"Joe Penney's friend owns the bar and has a relative on the bench who does not like you or your deceased sister."

"You're good."

Lauren gave me her address and directions. Like every residence in town, it was a few blocks away from the Bud-E. After visiting Robin Hannigan's modest dwelling, I was shocked to see Ms. Rush's palatial house, which reminded me of Jarvis' estate.

"I am definitely on the wrong side of the insurance business," I muttered to myself as I walked to the front door. I rang the bell and was met by a black-haired woman in her early 40's who graciously invited me in. *Finally, a little bit of hospitality,* I thought. "Thanks for seeing me on such short notice."

"It's my pleasure," Lauren said as she led me into a large sitting room which could have been featured in *Homes & Gardens* magazine. "Since Alexis' aborted trial, subsequent death, and building this house, I don't get many visitors. Most of the locals hate me."

"I kind of got that impression." I thought she might ask for specifics but didn't. She knew her enemies and had evidently reconciled herself to the situation.

When she left to get some drinks, I had time to look at more family pictures featuring Alexis. These candid personal photos firmly established how attractive she had been in her youth, through her 20's and finally her 30's. She was the type who could turn heads in any

WHEN ANGELS FAIL TO FLY

room and take home any male she deemed worthy. From her wedding portrait, it was apparent she and Joe had married very young—high school sweethearts young.

Lauren returned and sat on the couch across from me.

"You and Alexis look very much alike," I said, pointing to one of the photos on the wall.

"I guess in a way we do," Lauren said, not bothering to glance over to the shot. "As I get older, the resemblance is more pronounced." She let out a laugh, which she immediately tried to stifle. "I'm sorry. I do appreciate the compliment. It's just that throughout our upbringing, Alexis was always known as the pretty one."

"And you were known as what?"

"The older smarter one."

"That's hard to believe," I said honestly.

"I was the older, smarter one. When I told you that with age I'd grown more attractive, that wasn't entirely the truth."

I was puzzled by this. I had only met this woman a few minutes earlier, paid her a genuine compliment and she was now trying to deflect my praise. I began to look more closely at the pictures, and realized the dark-haired, overweight girl with glasses beside Alexis was Lauren. It dawned on me that what she was trying to say was cosmetic surgery and extreme weight loss had more to do with her remarkable transformation than simply growing out of an ugly duckling stage.

"I think I know what you mean—about you and Alexis growing up," I offered, again pointing to the wall of pictures, which Lauren also looked at this time.

"In a way I wish she were around today to see how much things have changed. Of course, most of the changes took place after her death."

Her voice dropped and I wondered if she was feeling a twinge of survivor's remorse. She was only currently living the high life as a result of the insurance payout from Alexis' untimely passing.

"Speaking of that," I said, tactfully trying to address the topic I had traveled to Ravenwood to discuss. "Were you at Max Feldberg's trial?"

"Only for the opening arguments. I couldn't bear to hear all the gruesome details about what happened to Alexis."

So much for her impressions of Max and the evidence. Time for Plan B.

"One of the reasons I'm in town is to see if there was a connection between Alexis' legal problems here and her death in Santana Hills."

I have conducted hundreds of interviews over the years—in homes, businesses, on the street, in alleyways and at the police station—and when a question causes a reaction in the interviewee, a red flag is immediately raised inside one's mind. My inquiry should have been one Lauren had heard many times. It was only logical to attempt to link the two seemingly unrelated events. Lauren, however, lost her composure ever so slightly. It was a miniscule change most people would have missed.

I, of course, am not most people.

Then again, it might simply have been a minor twitch at the corner of her mouth and the squinting of her left eye at an inopportune time. The professional that I am, filed this observation away, but not too far away.

"That's not possible," Lauren finally managed to say. "Alexis got mixed up with a con man out there. It had nothing to do with the murder charges here."

"You're positive of that?"

"Yes, of course."

"What about the book Joe Penney wrote? Did you help with it?"

"That book was mean-spirited and full of innuendo. After reading the first chapter of that trash, I was physically ill. Joe Penney disgusts me! I cannot believe he was ever part of my family. We treated him like a brother and, over the years, turned a blind eye to his faults, which were not included in that stupid book."

"Like what?"

Lauren was now completely absorbed in our discussion. In this town, for her to bad mouth Joe to anyone would probably be a waste of breath. He was the one cheated on. He was the one publicly disgraced. I, however, was an outsider who wanted to hear all the juicy gossip about the poor guy.

"He wasn't the greatest husband in the world," Lauren began. "He was an extremely jealous man. If some man dared to even look at Alexis or compliment her in some way, he would go ballistic."

I recalled how muscular Joe was from his old pictures and from the Bud-E earlier. "I'd hate to be the guy caught hitting on Alexis," I said.

"Why? Joe wouldn't do anything to you. He'd blame Alexis for dressing too sexy or accuse her of flirting. After Joe would leave her stranded somewhere she'd call me in tears to pick her up."

"Some men are like that. They can't believe a beautiful woman chose them, but can't tolerate that other men also find her attractive."

"That's exactly right. They did try marriage counseling, but it didn't work out."

"It only works if both parties are committed to staying together. I know."

"I think Alexis was serious—this was before the affair. It was Joe who wasn't. He actually wore a t-shirt that read *I'm With Stupid* to the first session. Can you believe that?"

"That's a new one," I said, unable to contain a small smile.

"That was definitely not in the book."

"Did he ever hit Alexis?" I asked, hoping her answer might fit into my Ravenwood connection theory.

It didn't.

"Never. Our daddy would have killed him—and I'm not just saying that. You can ask anyone around here."

"Are your parents still alive?"

"No, both are gone. Mom died a few years before all of Alexis' problems began and Daddy passed away last year."

"Sorry to hear that."

"They both had health problems." She paused and looked at a picture sitting atop a nearby piano. "One day her heart finally gave out and he never got over it. After Alexis died, he surrendered to the Lord and just gave up living."

"What was his reaction to her murder charges?"

"Like most of us, he believed she'd been set up by that fool Randy. He's the real killer and he knew he was going away for life."

"Then why take Alexis down with him?" I asked.

"Because he could," Lauren said flatly. "He was a bigger jerk than Joe. Alexis had this type she was always attracted to, and no matter how many times I warned her, she ignored my advice."

"So, you knew about the affair prior to Randy's wife's murder?"

She stared at me as if I had just accused her of setting kittens on fire.

"We were sisters! We talked about everything!" she protested and added, "Next you'll be saying I had something to do with Patricia's death."

"That didn't cross my mind until you said it."

She flashed a wicked grin. "My alibi—unlike Alexis'—is solid. Not that I'm saying Alexis was guilty. She wasn't."

"Fair enough." I felt Plan B was also failing, as it appeared my ally was turning against me. Shifting gears again, I asked, "What happened after the book came out?"

"What do you mean?"

"Did Alexis get any death threats? Was she around at the time of its publication?"

"Just barely. Joe and that court reporter started writing the story prior to the trial date."

"Then when the trial began, they would only have to chronicle those events and the verdict."

"And it would be printed within a few weeks."

"Hit the bookshelves while it's still fresh in the public's mind."

"At least that was the plan," A sly smile passed Lauren's lips.

"I hear Joe has a few copies stored in his basement."

"A few thousand," she laughed. "He thought everyone around here would want a souvenir of the most famous case ever to come out of Ravenwood. That idea went out the window after Randy died in prison and the case was dropped. No one cared anymore. By then the whole town knew all the intimate details of the affair, the arrests and the charges. What they didn't know were the gory details of the murder itself or how Randy and Alexis had purportedly pulled it off together."

"I see your point. Why buy a book when you already know the good stuff?"

"He sold a few, but overall lost his shirt financially. During the past ten years, it's probably the only deal he came up short on."

"Are you saying he should have stuck with real estate?"

"What he should have done was shut up and got on with life. Yeah, Alexis took 50%, but she deserved that money as much as he did. Neither one worked for it. It wasn't as though they had something to do with the auto plant starting up. It was found money."

"To backtrack a bit, did Alexis get death threats or not? I mean real ones, not some local yokel spouting off down at the bar."

Lauren got up and left the room. She returned carrying an accordion-type case, from which she retrieved a manila envelope that she handed to me. "I saved them, in case something ever did happen to her."

The envelope contained several handwritten and typed notes on all manner of paper. "Did you tell the police about these?" I asked.

"Oh, sure," she said hesitantly. "But they'd already arrested that doctor, so they returned them to me."

"Do you remember the officer you were dealing with?" I asked.

"No, I don't."

I sifted through the messages, most of which contained enough grammatical errors to warrant a failing grade. In the end, they were all standard, garden-variety threats more effective at pumping up the writer's ego than scaring the recipient.

"They weren't all bad."

"How so?"

"I remember one—it's on yellow paper—where the writer was very encouraging and told Alexis to stay strong, or something to that effect."

I continued to sort through the notes, until I found the yellow one.

Dear Alexis,

In this life we all face adversity, which we must overcome through the strength of our inner willpower. After buying your husband's very biased book and reading between the lines, I concluded you had been set up for that woman's murder. Although I do not take pleasure in any person's death, the fact that woman's husband died in prison I believe was God's plan and unquestionably a blessing for you in more ways than one. You can now map out a new future for yourself and realize your true potential.

I trust this letter finds you in good health and good spirits.

Sincerely,

Danny Murphy

"Very interesting," I said, as I slid the note back into the pile.

"She even got a few marriage proposals. Can you imagine?"

"There are plenty of strange people out there," I replied. "Would I be able to take these with me?"

"I don't see why not. After all this time, they're just unwanted reminders and clutter."

I put the envelope in my jacket pocket. "From what you've said, I take it you received some sort of insurance money after Alexis' death—which has no bearing on my investigation, mind you. I was curious about Alexis' financial situation at the time of her death. Did she have any of the divorce settlement left?"

For the second time this evening, I sensed an almost imperceptible change in Lauren's behaviour. Granted, the topics of murder and money are not the easiest conversations, especially with a total stranger.

"Do you need to see her bank records?"

"If you have them," I replied. For some reason I don't think she was expecting this answer. "Is that a problem?"

"No," she said, although I didn't believe her. She opened the case and withdrew several bank statements, all in Alexis' name.

I skimmed through the oldest ones first, which revealed that Alexis wasn't a big spender. There were mortgage, car and clothing expenses—none of which were outlandish for a single woman with a lot of disposable income. On the final statement I noted one transaction which stood out: it had taken place on the day of Alexis' death and was for an extraordinarily large amount of money.

"This withdrawal for $150,000—do you know what Alexis had purchased or was going to purchase?" I asked excitedly, recalling the same amount Jarvis Larsh boasted about having only days after Alexis' death.

Lauren took the statement and examined it. "I don't know."

This was not what I was expecting to hear. It was probable Lauren had been not only the sole beneficiary of her sister's insurance policies, but executrix of Alexis' estate. To be unaware of a few hundred dollars missing was one thing. To overlook 150 grand however, was implausible, especially when it was probably withdrawn mere hours before her sister's death.

"Not a clue?" I asked, trying to keep my voice even. "A sports car? A down payment on a condo?"

Lauren did not make eye contact, continuing to stare at the statements as if searching for clues. "I remember that now," she said, several seconds too late to save herself. "We never found out—the accountants, I mean."

"That's an awful lot of money. Do you have any idea what she needed it for?"

This time when she looked at me and said, "I haven't any idea," I believed she was telling me the truth.

"Have you ever heard of a man named Jarvis Larsh?"

In our minds, a thin line divides confusion and fear. Confusion takes the route of *What is he talking about?* On the other hand, fear travels down the path of *He knows! What am I going to do?* It is quite an extraordinary person who can pull off both emotions simultaneously. As I was about to discover, Lauren Rush was one such gifted individual.

"Larsh? Jarvis Larsh? What kind of name is that anyway?" she laughed as she stood, taking her little folding briefcase with her. "No, I can honestly say I do not know such a ridiculously named person," she stated with a nervous laugh.

Oh, she is good, I thought. "What about Derek McDonald?" She stopped and turned to face me. I believe she wanted to display shock or dismay at this new line of questioning. Instead, her expression was that of a stubborn child on the verge of a tantrum in a shopping mall.

"I don't know that person either. Should I?"

"Maybe."

"They're not from around here, so they must be associated with Alexis in Santana Hills. I never visited her there and I didn't know her friends—if she had any."

I was tempted to ask her where she was the night of Alexis' murder, but opted for another tactic. "Have you ever seen the news reports of Alexis' death? Or visited the street where it all took place?"

This seemed to intrigue her. "I didn't go sightseeing," she snapped. "I went to the courthouse and came home."

"Do you have a computer handy?"

"Why?"

"If you're really interested in what happened to your sister, I need to show you something so you'll understand why I'm still pursuing this case." I paused and added, "It'll only take five minutes and then I'll leave for good. Scout's honour."

"Five minutes," Lauren agreed, probably believing I would be the last investigator to travel to Ravenwood to ask questions about her sister. She led me into a large home office, where she logged onto her computer. "All yours."

I took a seat at the desk and tried to remember how Maria had located the clips from the TV station. After a few false starts, I found the two news stories and clicked on the first one, watching Lauren's reaction to the images on the screen.

"What is this?" she demanded.

"A history lesson," I replied.

Only seconds into the live news report, Lauren's face went slack.

"Stop it!" she screamed. "Stop it now!"

I paused the media player and asked, "What?"

"He was . . . he was . . ."

"Who was?" I asked her, not knowing what she was trying to say. She covered her mouth with her right hand and then pointed to the monitor. I refocused my attention on the frozen image. There was nothing, except the reporter in the foreground. I shook my head, trying to adjust my eyesight. Then my depth of field changed slightly and I got the biggest shock of my life.

"That's Jarvis Larsh in the background," I declared, stunned.

"Who?" Lauren gave me another kittens-on-fire look.

"There—in the blue coat," I said, pointing him out as my brain began to race.

Lauren bent forward to examine the shot more closely. "It is, isn't it?"

I looked from Jarvis back to Lauren's now-pale face. "If you weren't referring to Jarvis just now, then who?"

Lauren's shaky index finger reached toward the screen and landed on the face of the man standing next to Jarvis.

"Him. That's Derek McDonald. He was there."

Unable to think straight, I slumped into a chair. I could only stare at the unforgiving screen, wondering what to do next. Lauren had run upstairs, leaving me with thoughts of jumping from the Ravenwood water tower to alleviate the pressure between my ears.

Lauren, however, had a far more deadly plan.

The first bullet grazed my right ear and found the computer monitor, which exploded on impact. The sight of flames slowed Lauren's approach enough that I was able to fall to the floor and hurl the chair in her direction. Luckily, it hit the tip of the gun, dislodging it from Lauren's hand. It was too far away to pick up, so I did the next best thing: I leapt through one of the large, single-paned windows, landing on a row of bushes before hitting the hard ground below. I was directly under the window, camouflaged by thick branches. They couldn't stop an errant bullet, but at this time of night I felt reasonably safe in the darkness.

"It wasn't supposed to end this way," Lauren yelled out the broken window.

The understatement of the century, I mused, hoping this was not going to be how my final chapter was written. As I was unarmed, and negotiating was out of the question, I remained scrunched up in a ball, breathing hard and not moving.

"Alexis deserved to die. She was a terrible daughter, wife and sister. I'm glad they got rid of her the way they did."

I couldn't pass up this moment and crawled on my belly to the left of the window, out of harm's way. "Derek and Jarvis were working together?"

Another shot flew over my head and into the passenger door of my van.

"No—Derek and that doctor. Jarvis had nothing to do with her going over that balcony. He only came around later for the money."

My head began to pound and I felt dizzy listening to Lauren's convoluted tale. "Why would Max want to kill Alexis?"

"Ask Derek. He's the one who set the whole thing up."

"Why would Derek want to kill Alexis? And how are you involved?"

Bullet #3 almost hit the top of my left shoe and embedded itself in the earth below me.

Shorter questions, fool! I chided myself as I shimmied further along the wall on my hands and knees.

"Because he said it was his destiny."

Believing I was out of her vision, I jumped up and made a run for the far side of my van, hoping to climb in undetected. Bullets #4 and #5 took out the front passenger tire and the side door's window.

"Only one of us is leaving here alive, Cassidy," Lauren called out, as I imagined her locating my upper body mass in her sight and preparing to squeeze the trigger.

The sight and sound of cruisers speeding up the long driveway put more pressure on us to either do or die. I opted for do, letting Lauren make her own decision. I picked up two large rocks off the ground and prayed Lauren had not taken the past few moments to reload. I threw one at my van's rear window, which shattered on impact, and then turned to throw the other one through a nearby kitchen window. This unexpected commotion had the desired effect: it scared Lauren, who fired her last bullet, taking out one of the van's mirrors in the process.

I am saved, I rejoiced, as I ran across the lawn ready to surrender to any of the police forces looking for me.

The lead car came to an abrupt halt and the driver flashed his high beams, bathing the entire property in brilliant white. As the lights hit my unconditioned eyes, I heard a popping sound in my head and fell into a heap on the grass.

The last thing I remember was the police ordering Lauren to drop her weapon and a single bullet being fired toward the residence.

It was like the Tecumseh Motel Massacre all over again.

This time however, there would be no banana split melting on the front seat of my van.

Waking up in a hospital bed with your left wrist handcuffed to the metal frame is very disconcerting.

"Well, looky here—he's awake," Officer Kenneth Anderton proclaimed.

"Haven't you done enough damage for one lifetime?" I asked.

"I was about to ask you the same question. I guess great minds think alike."

"I'll tell you next time I'm in a room with one," I said, laughing at my own joke.

Anderton was not amused. "It's too bad that quick mind of yours is going to waste away in prison, ass munch," he barked back.

"Did you call me ass munch? Where did you hear that phrase— the school playground?" I asked, shaking my head. "Now, where am

I and why am I cuffed to this bed?"

"You're the guest of White Plains Memorial Hospital and the Darrien Police," Anderton replied, ignoring my jibe.

I recalled passing White Plains on my way to Ravenwood. "How did I get here? And how is Lauren Rush?"

Anderton got out of his chair and poured himself a cup of ice water, which he proceeded to drink. "You collapsed in that woman's driveway with a bullet wound to your head. The doctor said another quarter of an inch to the right and you would have died instantly. Pity that dead woman was such a bad shot."

"She's dead?"

"Unfortunately for her, the Ravenwood police are crack shots. They told her to put down her weapon and when she refused, they dropped her." A smile swept over his face. "All by the book. No follow-up investigation needed."

It was hard to believe Lauren was gone, although I was certain no one in town would mourn the loss. "You still haven't told me why I'm under arrest."

"Either you have a very short memory or you're plain stupid. Do you realize that in practically every city you've been in lately, you've left behind a dead body? That's just not right—not neighbourly at all. And before you start claiming your innocence, I want you to know that you can't use your bullet hole there to claim amnesia or some other lame defence. I've already consulted with the doctors on that one."

"Hey, fat head!" I yelled. "Stop spraying and start saying. Why am I under arrest? I didn't kill Lauren. I didn't kill anyone."

Anderton took his seat and put his feet on the undercarriage of the bed. "That'll be for a jury to decide. We don't need a body to get a conviction."

"No, but you do need a brain, Sherlock."

"We have your prints all over that house in Sussex, and Linda's blood was found in the bathroom and kitchen sink pipes. You really should have been more careful."

"I didn't kill Linda!" I shouted. "She's alive and you know it."

"That's where we differ, Steve. I think she's dead. It seems to me the only way we'll find out who's telling the truth is if you tell us where you're keeping her or where she's buried." His expression turned serious. "It's a win-win-win situation. So let's stop this charade now."

"I couldn't agree with you more, Anderton," I said, much to his delight. "Nurse!" I called out, while pressing the Help button. "Nurse! I need some help in here, stat!"

Two frantic nurses and a doctor appeared in the doorway and were soon at my side.

"What's the matter?" the older nurse asked. "Unless you're in serious pain, you shouldn't be yelling after surgery."

"My head is fine," I said in a quieter voice.

"Then what is it?" the doctor asked.

"I have a huge pain in the neck and its name is Kenneth Anderton. Can you please remove it before I go into shock again?"

It took them a few seconds before realizing that sarcasm was not a symptom of any ailment and look over at Anderton.

"We'll have to ask you to leave, Officer. This patient needs his rest."

To my surprise, Anderton looked pleased as he stood and walked toward the door shaking his head. "A quarter of an inch, Cassidy. Unbelievable."

Being physically worn out is much different than being emotionally drained. During my hospital stay I got plenty of rest, which took care of my physical aches and pains. However, not being allowed visitors and having Anderton and his clan babysit me did not help my mental state. The worst part of this isolation was worrying about how Dawn and Maria were dealing with this nonsense. Each morning Anderton took great pleasure reading newspaper reports of my escapades aloud, which only depressed me more. According to some chart, sales for *The Murdering Mistress* and *Late For Dinner*—the story of my Barry Jones investigation—had also increased dramatically.

There was one thread that wove its way into each news story: speculation Lauren had something to do with Alexis' murder. It seemed every Ravenwood resident who had ever been in contact with the sisters shared the same opinion: Lauren despised her beautiful sibling and hired Max to kill Alexis due to jealousy. Of course, the details were sketchy, as Lauren was dead, Max was not granting interviews and finally, it was all bunk.

Being handcuffed to a hospital bed—that's reality. Knowing Lauren knew both Derek and Jarvis—that's reality. Not having a clue how I could prove it—that's reality.

Good news finally arrived on the third day of my hospital incarceration. My White Plains attorney, Charelle Platts, fresh from passing the bar exam and pressed into action by the firm's senior partners, won a motion to release me from custody. Her argument was clear: there was no evidence I had harmed Linda in any way. I never denied being at the Sussex house, but there was no proof Linda and I had been there at the same time. As for the blood found in the drains, there was some confusion about Linda's actual grouping. Her family doctor listed her as a type "A" but the Red Cross had her down as a type "O" donor.

"I believe something happened in that house," the judge had declared to the packed courtroom. "However, I'll need more proof to keep Mr. Cassidy in custody." He looked down at Anderton and added, "Bring this to me when you've found that missing link. You're close. Just not close enough."

Anderton didn't have the stones to return to the hospital, letting a rookie set me free instead. "Tell your boss he's a coward," I said, as I massaged my wrist.

After a final medical examination, I retrieved my belongings and checked out of the hospital. For my safety and insurance concerns, to avoid the throng of reporters outside, a paramedic put me on a gurney and drove me out of the area in an ambulance, lights on and siren blaring. Several blocks away, he dropped me off at a house where my lawyer had parked my van in a friend's driveway. "Thanks for the lift," I said to the driver.

"Not a problem. If you need anything else, call me day or night," he said, handing me his business card. "I gotta go. Sick people need this wagon as much as private eyes. Can't keep them waiting."

With lights and siren going, he blasted out of the area as if racing to a hundred-car pile-up.

I climbed into my van and turned the radio on, cranking up the volume to render useless any listening bugs the police might have hidden when collecting their evidence. To me, it seemed like a waste of time to take hair and fiber samples because Linda had been in the vehicle almost daily for several months.

I called my message centre, which was full. I didn't know how many calls could be stored and dreaded having to listen to a hundred requests for interviews. As soon as I heard the words, "I'm from the Tribune/Sun-Times/Herald," I hit the delete button. This went on for several minutes until I recognized a reporter's voice whose message was worth hearing.

"Hey, Steve, it's Sabrina Howell from the Standard. Sorry to hear about your trouble in Ravenwood. I'm sure everything will be cleared up soon and hope you're feeling better. Nothing ruins your day like a bullet to the head—at least that's what the coroner has always told me. Anyway . . . I learned what the paperwork problem was with Suite 2418 at the Indelible Corporation Building. Apparently Derek McDonald signed the sublease under the name Danny Murphy. Before head office discovered the discrepancy, the lease was up and they didn't think twice about it—until now, of course. So when you're finally up and about, give me a call even if it's collect from the clink," she said with a small laugh.

"There it is!" I yelled jubilantly, feeling like a chess player who sees an opponent's mistake and knows victory is ten moves away. I saved Sabrina's call and while continuing to listen to my messages, dug into the plastic bag containing my personal items. My hand found the envelope Lauren had given me before she went ballistic. I poured the numerous death threats and marriage proposals onto the passenger seat and looked for that one special letter written on yellow paper.

"Mr. Cassidy, this is Jenne Rendall of the Franklin Bulletin . . ."

Delete.

"Hi, my name is Clarence Marchman of the Delaware Chronicle and I . . ."

Delete.

As I used my left hand on the phone's keypad, my right continued to sift through the pile—some letters falling onto the floor in the process. "Come on. Where is it?" I asked the invisible mail sorter in my head. When I saw the corner of my desired prize I began to smile, but only for a second.

"Steve. It's Maria. Linda called me and she sounded frightened. Please get back to me as soon as you get this."

Check and mate.

TWENTY THREE

"When did she call?"

"Two days ago, around ten."

"In the morning?"

"No, at night."

"And she sounded frightened? Did she say by what?"

"She was talking very fast . . . and, I don't know . . . sounded scared to me," Maria replied. "She wants to talk to you."

"I've been held against my will in a place called White Plains."

"I know. The newspaper and TV station ran stories on everything. I think maybe that's why Linda contacted me."

"Is she waiting for my call? It's already been a couple of days. I don't want her to think I'm ignoring her."

"She's going to contact me today and then I'll call you."

"You didn't happen to get the number she was calling from, did you?"

There was a brief silence before Maria said delicately, "Even if I had, Steve, I don't think it would be my place to give it to you."

"I understand. At this point, I wouldn't trust me either," I replied. "Give me a shout later then and tell Linda I'll meet her anywhere, any time, any place."

"I'll do that." I thought Maria was going to end the call until she asked, "Are you okay—I mean with the bullet wound and everything?"

"I am. I was more grazed than actually hit," I admitted. "They wanted to make sure my hearing and motor skills were okay. I'm fine though, really—just another battle scar. Thanks for asking."

"That's good to hear," she said. "Well, I should keep this line free. Take care of yourself and I'll talk to you soon."

Deciding it was time to get out of White Plains, I headed toward the highway, checking my mirrors constantly, looking for followers. I had mixed emotions about Maria's phone call. I was extremely happy to learn Linda was alive, even if her mental state was unknown. That was the good news. This planned meeting had me worried, though. Was it some kind of set-up? With all the false allegations about the insurance policy, and the house in Sussex, to my own suspicions about the hidden house key, I had good reason to believe our get-together might end with me in handcuffs—or worse.

I tried to push that idea aside and focus on things that needed my attention. I buzzed through the remaining voice mail messages and did not find any other verbal landmines. I then placed a call to Sabrina.

"Had I known you were a fugitive, I would have called the cops and collected the reward money."

"Trust me, the cash payout wouldn't cover the cost of a cup of coffee."

"Are you feeling better? When they were fishing around in your skull, did the doctors find any other neurological problems?"

"Nothing a bottle of Jack Daniels couldn't cure."

"Make sure you call me first because you should never drink alone." After our laughter died down, she asked, "I take it my little piece of sleuthing helped?"

"It connected one dot to another, that's for sure. Are you near a computer?"

"I'm at my desk now." I told her to go to the television station's website and watch the news reports. "What am I looking for?"

"If I told you, it would spoil the fun. Here's a hint: keep your eye on the sidewalk crowd."

For the third time, I heard the desk anchor throw to the street reporter and hoped one of Lauren's final declarations was true.

"What in the world was Derek McDonald doing down there that night?" Sabrina asked.

I wanted to make sure we were talking about the same person. "The man to Derek's right is wearing a coat. What colour is it?"

"Blue. Why—who is that?"

"Jarvis Larsh."

"And who is Jarvis Larsh?"

"We are about to find out, Sabrina."

I called the airport to learn when the next flight to *Jarvis Country* was scheduled. I then spoke with Charelle to confirm I had no travel restrictions.

"Technically, you have nothing pending in any jurisdiction, although I think Darrien Police will re-file the kidnapping charge."

"I'm not too worried about that one," I said, vaguely.

"And why is that?"

"I don't know the details yet, but I have it on good authority Linda is alive and well."

"And your source would be?"

"I can't say, Charelle. When I know more, you'll be the first person I call."

"I don't like the sound of that."

"Neither do I. Unfortunately, I don't have a choice in the matter."

"Okay. So, why did you want to know about travel restrictions? Are you planning a trip to the Caribbean?"

"Not quite. I'm heading back to Santana Hills."

"Oh, come on, Steve. What's going on?" she pleaded. "If you thought I was worried about you a second ago, I'm even more scared now. Why go back there? Haven't you had enough punishment from that town already?"

"Punishment is a good word but I think there's a connection between members in my cast of dysfunctional murder investigation characters."

"The one that was solved five years ago?"

"That's it," I replied. "Now that I have clearance to fly, I've got to catch a plane leaving in two hours. Thanks for the lawyerly advice. Just add it to my bill."

I heard Charelle sigh. "If your next interview subject has better aim, it won't matter how much the bill adds up to, will it?"

"I'll be careful."

"Sure you will."

While waiting for my flight, I updated Sabrina on the Jarvis-Alexis-Max-Derek/Danny debacle I had uncovered. By the time I was to board the plane, Sabrina and her editor had agreed the newspaper would only publish the story on my say-so. As the investigation was largely conjecture, they had no problem with this arrangement, knowing if everything panned out, they would have an exclusive.

Sabrina met me at the airport and was not what I had expected at all. She was in her late 30's, kind of tall, with short blonde hair, huge green eyes and a thousand-watt smile. What impressed me most was that she was wearing a black Coyote Ugly t-shirt, strategically ripped blue jeans, cowboy boots and a leather jacket which looked like it had survived flights over Germany during the last world war.

One very cool chick, I thought. "Casual Friday at the paper?" I asked when she introduced herself in the terminal.

"Paul told me to watch myself around you," she replied.

"How is he these days? Did he give you *The Murdering Mistress* to read?"

"Oh, yeah," she said, as we made our way to the parking lot. "That and your tour-de-force, *Late For Dinner*."

"I'd actually like to see that one. Is it any good?"

"*The Murdering Mistress* or *Late For Dinner*?"

"*Late For Dinner*. I've only read the back cover."

"You're kidding me, right? I figured your fingerprints would be all over it."

"I had nothing to do with it. I can't imagine any book written by a private investigator being very good, but who knows—there might be a few talented enough to pull it off," I said. "The *Late For Dinner* author never even contacted me, although I have heard I come off pretty well."

"Sure, if you skip the whole police corruption scandal and the shooting of the Chief of Police—yeah, you come off like a saint."

312

I was about to answer her backhanded compliment when I saw the wry smile on her face and knew she was simply busting my balls. Soon we were sitting in the front seat of a vehicle marked with the words *Santana Hills Sentinel*.

"So, Mr. Cassidy, the paper has entrusted this lovable Cavalier to me for the purposes of tracking down the story of the decade. Where's our first stop?"

"You're going to love this," I said. "The Shakin' Pussycat Bar."

"Are you serious?"

"You betcha."

"You didn't tell me your informants were working there. I know a few of those girls."

"Interesting," I replied, not quite sure how to react. "Well there is one person who can help unravel this mess and I'm hoping she's on duty."

"It's three in the afternoon. What if she doesn't come in until later tonight?"

"We wait. Why—do you have a problem with seeing naked women dance for horny losers?"

"Not at all," Sabrina shrugged. "I'm just wondering how much the paper allows for expenses incurred at a strip club. I'm pretty sure they'll cover my bar tab and meals, but I don't think the girls give receipts for dances."

"I don't know either," I chuckled, as Sabrina drove downtown. "If we run into that situation, I'm sure we can come up with some creative accounting entries."

Twenty minutes later, we were walking through the doors of the club. My bouncer buddy Dillon was nowhere to be found, replaced by another steroid-enhanced hulk of a man. We went to the bar where I ordered a beer and Sabrina a whiskey on the rocks.

"You're the designated driver, right?" I asked with a grin.

"It's one little drink," she protested. She picked up her drink off the bar, gulped the ounce of hard liquor in one fluid motion and slammed the glass back on the counter. "Hey, barkeep. I need this refilled—only with cola this time." She gave me a quick grin and said, "Because apparently I'm the designated driver today."

"We do have a free shuttle service," the bartender said, as he filled the glass with pop. "Everyone gets home alive."

"I'll take that under advisement," Sabrina said, taking a sip of her beverage. "What now, Cassidy?"

"I'm waiting."

"For what?"

"For whom," I corrected her. "We're here to talk to the dancer on stage."

Sabrina turned her attention to the front of the club and watched for a few seconds. "We're here to speak with Melissa? Why didn't you say so earlier? Barkeep—two more whiskeys. One for me and one for Destiny Rose—when she's done swinging her stuff around up there." Sabrina then pointed to the table I had during my previous visit and said, "I'll take both now. Have Destiny come to that table over there for hers, okay?" Sabrina looked at my shocked face. "This is a very small city, Steve. So, no matter what field you work in, if you're a star, eventually the paper will run a story about some good deed you've done."

"I'd heard Destiny Rose was a big deal, but how is her ability to bring joy and pleasure to businessmen newsworthy? What kind of paper do you work for anyway, Sabrina?" I asked, not having seen the publication.

"Get your mind out of the gutter," she replied as she scooped up the beverages and walked to our table. "Every summer she holds a car wash for cancer benefit. All her friends show up and hand wash vehicles in the skimpiest bikinis allowable by law. They raise more money in three hours than most organizations do all year selling crappy cookies and pies at bake sales."

"And let me guess—you were assigned to cover this major civic event?"

"Assigned? I volunteered."

Hanging around women wearing little or no clothing was not a problem for my new friend or for me. As I was about to speak, the club's speakers went quiet and there was a smattering of applause from the males and one female in attendance. We watched Destiny Rose gather her belongings and go into the back room. A few minutes later, she re-emerged and found her way to our table. When she saw her fan was Sabrina, a big grin crossed her face. The smile disappeared when she noticed I was also at the table.

Sabrina stood and gave Destiny Rose a friendly hug. "It's been awhile," Sabrina said. "How have you been doing?"

"I was doing fine until I saw him."

Sabrina turned and waved me off. "Steve? He's harmless. Just a bit . . . you know, rough around the edges."

"If you say so," Destiny Rose replied, as she took the seat furthest from me. "We have some history and I'm worried it's about to be dug up again."

"Well, regardless of how you feel about me, it's nice to see you again, Destiny," I said apologetically. "I didn't plan to have our relationship end the way it did."

"I bet."

"For whatever reason, it seems you two don't like one another," Sabrina broke in. "What's important, however, is putting aside your differences and assisting me with the story I'm writing."

I sat in awe as Sabrina then laid out what we needed from Destiny Rose, claiming it had been her idea from the start. This way, Destiny Rose felt obligated to help an old friend, convincing herself she was not helping me.

Brilliant.

After Destiny Rose signed up to help, Sabrina and I went to the police, where I laid out my findings regarding Alexis Penney's murder. Unconvinced at first, the detectives' interest in the case slowly grew, as it became evident there were too many coincidences to be explained easily.

Arresting and convicting the wrong person is bad—even when that individual was a sleazy con man. To mistake the identity of the killer though, is even worse, and bad for morale. With my awesome oratorical skills, I convinced the unit we could rectify the situation quite easily. That was the hope, at least.

If only Jarvis would co-operate.

With the first part of our strategy in place, I reached out to another local admirer of my work: Sergeant Garelick. He may have been assigned to the courts when I was last in town, but after listening to my tale of murder, he was sent to the detective unit to run a very special operation.

The official surveillance of Jarvis Larsh's residence began before sunrise the following morning. Destiny Rose had told us Jarvis made a regular Saturday morning stop at the club, as well as a Sunday evening visit. She had changed her schedule to anticipate her best customer's arrival.

Due to the nature of this investigation, the police would only allow their officers to work ten hours total on surveillance. This meant if Jarvis didn't head downtown this weekend, there wasn't much hope my plan would work—at least not with police participation. In the course of my recitation of the facts, I learned Lauren had never sent the package of death threats to the Santana Hills Police for follow up. Why muddy the waters when her beloved sister was already dead and she was richer for it?

"We have two teams working right now—one on Jarvis' street and another positioned in the area to follow him when he departs," Garelick told me. "And I want to make one thing crystal clear, Cassidy— when he leaves you are not to follow him. Do you understand?"

What was there not to understand? Given my shady dealings of late, the last thing the local force wanted was trouble because of me. This was their show. "Yes, I understand and will try to behave myself, Sergeant."

"Do you really think Destiny Rose can pull this off?" Sabrina asked me, as we stared out the window of the paper's Cavalier, which we'd discreetly parked in the neighbourhood.

"At this stage you go for broke," I replied. "Jarvis isn't going to talk to me again, and because there's no concrete proof linking him to

Alexis' death, the police will also continue to drag their feet. Destiny Rose has a way with men—I've seen it first-hand. After all these years of silence, I know Jarvis is about to burst. He wants to tell someone how smart he is, but who would listen—his wife? Don't think so."

"I'm just not convinced Destiny Rose possesses the qualities needed to garner a confession from him."

"To impress women, men do an awful lot of irrational things," I countered with a smile. "He's been trying to impress Destiny Rose for a very long time. We're like his wing men today—paving the way for him to have a few minutes alone with his dream girl."

"He's had plenty of opportunities to speak with her at the club. Do you really think this morning will be different?"

"Definitely," I declared.

Three-and-a-half hours later, it appeared we would learn just how good our stripper friend was when Garelick's booming voice came over the radio.

"Jarvis is on the move and he's alone. Both teams proceed with caution. We don't want to get burned."

Sabrina started the engine and we waited patiently for Jarvis to come into view. A few moments later, he turned out of the subdivision, followed discreetly by the police vehicles and the Papermobile, as we had affectionately dubbed the Cavalier.

"How is it people never know when they're being stalked like this?" Sabrina asked, as we merged into traffic. "Don't they look in their mirrors?"

"They do. They just don't register the same blue van behind them or beside them. Even if they do, their minds automatically assume it is everyday traffic conditions and discard the information."

"Still . . ."

"Of course, the mind isn't dumb—or at least that's what it tells itself all day. If you see a blue van at a stop light, you think nothing of it. If you see the same van at the mall you've driven to, again you think it's a fluke. However, if you see that same van with the same creepy driver sitting on your street, your mind begins to scream, 'Hey, wait a minute here,' and you call the cops."

317

"And then you're done for the day?"

"Pretty much. You give buddy a week to calm down and go back on him using a different vehicle. Nine times out of ten, he's completely oblivious the second time around."

"Because he's still watching for that mysterious blue van, right?"

"Precisely," I replied. "The other big factor is most people have no reason to believe anyone would be interested in following them. Take Jarvis—he had a good night's rest, some eggs for breakfast with his wife and is heading to a strip club to feed his one weakness. This is a typical Saturday morning for him."

"And for you, right?"

"Sort of. The only difference is I'm usually in the driver's seat."

"Oh, poor baby," Sabrina said sarcastically. "But regulations state only employees of the Standard can operate these vehicles."

"It's always something with insurance companies. If they aren't paying out huge death benefits to murderers, they're giving hard-working blokes like me the shaft."

Sabrina looked over at me, trying to decide if I was being serious or not. "Too funny," she finally said, as we continued to roll into the downtown core with Jarvis and his police escorts.

"He's parking on Linderlost Crescent, behind the club," one of Garelick's men barked over the radio. A few seconds later, a second transmission came across the airwaves. "He's in."

I glanced at Sabrina and smiled. "Phase One complete."

Garelick came on again. "Okay, Unit One, stay on the car. One of you lucky simpletons gets to go inside and watch for any trouble. I don't care who it is, flip a coin or something. Unit Two, head over to the apartment. Cassidy and Howell will meet you there in a few minutes. Get set up and wait for my call. If this guy is as horny for this dancer as she claims, we'll all be making our way over there very shortly."

After everyone 10-4'd the Sergeant, I said, "You heard the man, Sabrina. Let's rock and roll."

"The fact I'm in the driver's seat doesn't mean I'm your chauffeur," she replied, as we headed out of the area.

"What if I climbed into the back seat?" I said with a grin.

"We'd still be a team. I just wouldn't have to listen to your inane topics of conversation. I mean, really—who cares about your theories on World War II or the best stripper song of all time?"

"You weren't listening to me. The topic was, What was the best stripper song *during* World War II?"

"You're right—I wasn't listening then or now," she laughed. "Which way do I turn at the lights?"

"If you're listening, turn left. Garelick said the name of the apartment building is St. Clair Towers."

"Really? I think I used to live there," Sabrina replied.

"Was that before or after the drug dealers took it over?"

"During, I think."

"Cool."

WHEN ANGELS FAIL TO FLY

TWENTY FOUR

Most sting operations take weeks of planning and once set in motion could last for months or even years. This had been the case when the Santana Hills Police and other federal agencies set up a fake distribution centre in the heart of the city's drug district. From all accounts it had been a huge success, and once the bad guys were put away the area began to prosper. For reasons never fully explained, the three-bedroom apartment which had housed the fake drug dealers and the unit next to it, where we would be observing all the action were still under lease to the local police. My guess was that after the extensive renovations—walls knocked down, two-way mirrors installed and electronic hook-ups—it was still occasionally used for other covert operations.

This was to be one of those occasions.

Today the high-tech pad would masquerade as Destiny Rose's friend's personal residence—a kind of ultra V.I.P. room. That Sabrina and I had convinced her to take part in this cockamamie scheme was a testament to her sense of civic duty. After explaining how Jarvis may have had a hand in Alexis' death, she wanted to help put the little creep away.

When I asked if she was scared, she said, "Scared? Of him? I'm doing this for my own reasons. If this works it will be the last time I'll ever be in the same room with this pervert." Once we had the police lined up, Destiny Rose was even more eager to make our plan work. "Guys tell me stuff all the time, because they know I'll never pass along the information. Who would I pass it to anyway?"

I tried not to coach her too much, giving her the basic areas needed to be explored, such as the source of Jarvis' wealth, his involvement with Alexis' sister Lauren, and most importantly with Derek/Danny.

"Get me alone with him and he'll be confessing to being a male prostitute in a former lifetime—and loving it!"

No one could ever accuse Destiny Rose of low self-esteem or a lack of confidence.

"They're coming out," the call came over our radio, "and getting into Larsh's car. Here we go."

"Phase Two complete," I said to Sabrina.

"How many phases are involved in this thing? Should I cancel my dinner plans?" she asked. "I don't remember an actual number being discussed at our meetings."

I pretended to ponder her question and replied, "Phases are like waves in the ocean," trying to sound very philosophical.

"So, you don't have a clue, right?" she said bluntly.

"I don't have a specific number, no. You can't, because the circumstances involved in one phase leads into the next phase and . . ."

"And those two phases tell two phases and so on and so on. I get it."

En route to the apartment building, we heard Jarvis had zipped into a liquor store to buy a large bottle of whiskey, which caused much consternation in our apartment hideout.

"You told her we needed both of them to be sober, right?" Garelick asked me. "And no drugs."

"I told her—I swear," I lied. "However, I didn't have time to talk with Jarvis about it. Maybe we can speak to him in the hall before he enters the apartment."

Garelick let out a loud sigh. "If Jarvis or your stripper friend gets wasted or snorts some cocaine, any confessions are going to be thrown out and we'll be standing around with our dicks in our hands."

"Speak for yourself, Sergeant," Sabrina interrupted him.

"You know what I mean," he snapped.

"Melissa doesn't do drugs," Sabrina said.

"Did she tell that to all the girls at the weekly Sparkling Gems group sleepover or only you?"

"I think it was just me," came the caustic reply. "We've been best buds since kindergarten."

"Why is she here again?" Garelick asked me.

"Comic relief? How should I know?"

"You two better not screw this up."

Sabrina and I looked at each other and started bickering like kids.

"You heard him—*you* better not screw up!"

"No, *you* better not screw up!"

"Larsh is parking on the street. Get ready, here they come."

This announcement put an end to our foolishness and everyone was again very serious.

"Roll cameras and audio," Garelick ordered the two officers in the room. "And for those of you new to this location, you have to be completely quiet, as the walls between apartments are not exactly thick.

"What about the two-way mirror—is it shatterproof?" Sabrina asked.

"Bulletproof," Garelick said with a smile. "The irony is if someone fired a gun, the bullets would bounce off the glass but penetrate the surrounding wall—most likely killing one of us."

"You say that like you have one of us in mind," I said.

"If Lauren Rush had done the job right the first time, none of us would be in this room risking our lives," he said with a smirk.

"They've entered the elevator. They're all yours."

Sabrina turned to me. "Let me guess—Phase Three complete?"

"Otherwise known as Showtime."

The following several seconds passed in silence, broken finally by the key in the deadbolt and Destiny Rose's voice.

"My friend Josie Glengyle has a sugar daddy who rents this place for her. She's out of town and asked me to check on the place. This isn't the best neighbourhood in the east end."

"I've never been through this area of the city," Jarvis said, as they came into our view. He then relocked the door and for a moment I was worried about Destiny Rose's safety.

"We're right here," I said under my breath, as I watched the two of them head toward the couch.

"Got any glasses and ice for a drink?" Jarvis asked, looking to the kitchen.

"She must someplace," Destiny Rose said, as she took the bottle of whiskey from Jarvis. As she walked into the kitchen, Jarvis' eyes watched her cheeks sway to and fro inside her tight jeans.

"Why today?" he asked.

"Why today what?"

"All this? You and me, away from the club. You've never even allowed me in the V.I.P. area."

Destiny Rose returned carrying a glass containing ice and whiskey and a glass of what appeared to be juice. "How old is that stuff?" I whispered to Garelick, knowing this place wasn't used often.

"It's orange juice. It never goes bad," he replied.

"You're paying her hospital bill if it is."

Jarvis took his drink and then stared at the contents of the other glass. "I hope you found some vodka in the cupboards."

"Sorry," Destiny Rose said demurely. "A vodka and orange juice would be amazing right now. Unfortunately, last week I fell on stage—some idiot sitting in pervert's row spilt his beer and I didn't notice. My doctor prescribed some pills and gave me strict orders not to drink alcohol with them."

"A couple of sips won't hurt you."

"Better safe than sorry, Jarvis." The mention of his first name had the desired effect, softening Jarvis' features. Even his body language changed. Then Destiny Rose played her final card and sat next to her quarry on the couch. "Drinking dulls the senses. You don't want dull senses around me, do you?"

For all his tough talk and bravado at the club, Jarvis Larsh rapidly regressed to the scared, geeky teenager he had been before money and a feeling of entitlement had overtaken him. Here he was being propositioned by the girl of his demented dreams and had no game to pull it off.

As someone blessed with the gift of gab and plenty of game, I almost felt sorry for him.

"No, not at all," Jarvis stammered, placing his drink on the coffee table, while watching Destiny Rose seductively stir her drink with a swizzle stick.

"To answer your question, I thought you and I might hit it off

324

better away from the Pussycat. It's not the best place to talk, plus the lighting is atrocious." She leaned back into the couch, kicked off her open-toed heels and placed her feet on the table. With her body now almost horizontal to the floor, every part of her appeared to be in a completely relaxed state.

Well, almost every part of her body was horizontal.

The two large mounds on her upper body appeared to defy gravity and remained vertical—something Jarvis had a hard time not noticing.

"What is it with guys and breasts?" Sabrina asked no one in particular, as we all continued to stare at Jarvis as he continued to stare at Destiny Rose's chest.

"It is what it is. Now shut up," Garelick ordered, which produced a roomful of amused smiles. With his mind apparently still focused on Destiny Rose's assets, he asked me, "She knows she can't flash those puppies or have any sexual contact with him, right?"

"Or his confession will be thrown out, yeah, yeah, yeah," I replied.

"It certainly is brighter here," Jarvis said. "You look much different than at the club."

Destiny Rose turned her head, allowing her flowing red hair to fall ever so slightly across her left cheek. "Is that a compliment?"

"It is," Jarvis declared. "What I meant was . . . well . . . it's kind of weird to see you like this. It's like sitting down with a movie star you've seen on the big screen and in interviews but never had the opportunity to sit with them to . . . ah . . . talk. You know—get to know them as a person, not as a performer."

"Do you like what you see so far?"

"Of course. How couldn't I?"

"Some men don't. I knew you were different. Most men only see me as some sex object and fantasize about doing all kinds of dirty things to me—not with me—*to me*."

"Those guys are fools."

"They tell me their deepest, sickest thoughts when we're back in the V.I.P. room. I want to have a shower at the end of each session."

Destiny Rose then batted her eyelashes in Jarvis' direction. "But you're not like that, are you?"

"Is that why you never allowed me in the back?"

"This guy is a moron," Sabrina piped up. "Tell me he doesn't have any kids running around this planet. Please? Someone?"

"I was thinking the same thing about you," Garelick shot back. "He has no kids. Now be quiet."

"Yes, it is," came Destiny Rose's soft reply. "I know you're married but you and your wife must have some kind of arrangement. Otherwise, you would never be allowed to come visit me so often."

Jarvis was thinking so quickly you could almost smell the wood burning between his ears. "We even had the arrangement prior to getting married," he said coolly.

"What about your first wife?"

"Phase Four begins," I whispered in Sabrina's ear.

"My first wife?" Jarvis asked, momentarily confused.

"Yeah—what was her name? Ally? Alison?"

"Do you mean Alexis?"

"That's right, I remember now," Destiny Rose said with a slight nod. "Did she let you visit strip clubs or were you just being naughty?"

"Well . . ." He stopped, having to think this over a little longer. Several seconds later, however, a suave smile crossed his lips. "I was about to bring the open marriage idea up when she passed away tragically."

Even I couldn't believe he was playing the "widower pity card" this soon. I glanced over to Sabrina, who was pretending to make herself vomit by putting an index finger in her mouth and leaning forward.

"That's awful."

"It was dreadful."

"Was it a car accident or an illness?"

The questioning started to make Jarvis squirm. He was here to get it on with his favourite stripper and all she wanted to talk about was a dead woman.

"She was murdered and I really don't want to talk about her."

He placed his left hand on Destiny Rose's right knee. "I'd rather talk about us. The here and now."

"That's terrible," she said, ignoring his advance. "I had a friend involved in a murder a few years ago. He was my therapist. His name was Dr. Max—"

"Feldberg," Jarvis said, finishing off Destiny Rose's sentence and looking at her apprehensively. His left hand returned to his lap. "He was a friend of yours?"

His transformation from smooth-talking stud to sociopath was absolutely seamless. His eyes narrowed as his brow furrowed into a "V". His body tensed in increments, starting at his shoulders and slowly working down to his legs. He adjusted his position on the couch, moving slightly away from Destiny Rose. He then pursed his lips tightly, as if to hold back a stream of words for a few moments longer—until she answered his question.

From her manner and relaxed body language, it was clear Destiny Rose had not perceived any change in Jarvis. She was still in flirting mode and intentionally avoiding eye contact with her guest, portraying herself as the shy schoolgirl type.

In the next room, we had all witnessed Jarvis' disquieting make-over and were immediately troubled by what we saw.

"Unit One, I need both of you outside the door for a possible violent takedown," Garelick spoke quietly yet decisively, into the radio. "The door is locked, with Larsh and Destiny Rose sitting on the couch in the living room. We have a situation that looks like it might go sideways. Get up here now—and be extremely quiet. On my command, enter with your guns drawn." He glanced over to me. "I hope your girl knows what she's doing, because if she doesn't . . ."

The unpleasant implication hung in the air.

"She'll be fine. She deals with scum with attitudes every day at the club," Sabrina spoke up. "Once she sees what's going on, she'll adjust her approach with Jarvis. Just watch."

And we did. We had no other option.

While I had been prepping Destiny Rose, she confessed to being one of Max's patients, although she didn't admit to losing any money as her friend had indicated. I thanked her for her honesty and told her to mention Max's name in conversation, believing she and Jarvis might bond further due to their shared experiences as patients. Watching Jarvis' physical reaction to Max's name, however, I realized this had been the wrong path to take.

"Not really a friend," Destiny Rose said casually. "We used to talk a lot."

"Where?"

"At his office," she replied, following my instructions, trying to befriend Jarvis and get him to speak freely about his past. Then she added one word, which set our fragile little house of cards aflame. "Wherever."

"At his office or *wherever*? Is that what you said?" Jarvis reminded me of a wolf preparing himself for the kill. He stood and began to pace the room. "When I wasn't around, did he ever come and watch you at the club?"

I could see the confusion on Destiny Rose's face as she tried to decide how to answer this loaded question. Still believing in my misguided plan, she replied, "Sometimes—I think," hedging a little. "It was a long time ago."

"Did you dance for him in the V.I.P. room?" Jarvis demanded, his face beginning to turn scarlet.

"He's about to blow," I said to Garelick. "Are your guys in place?"

Garelick confirmed they were ready to enter at any moment. "Stand down until I give the word."

At long last, Destiny Rose clued into the dangerous situation she was in and sat upright on the couch. A flicker of terror flashed across her features. "Like I said . . . that was years ago, Jarvis." This time the use of his name had a very undesirable effect.

I heard Garelick tell his men in the hall to remain in place, at least for another few seconds. With no obstacle between them, Jarvis started toward Destiny Rose, his arms outstretched and his hands reaching for her neck. What he hadn't counted on was her cat-like reflexes. From her seated position, she landed a solid kick to his midriff, and rolled over the back of the couch to establish a barrier.

"You're like that whore Alexis," Jarvis screamed. "To get cheap therapy, maybe I should have screwed Feldberg too. I could have saved the health system a few bucks."

"I don't know what you're talking about," Destiny Rose yelled back. "I didn't have sex with him."

"You lie. You'll do anything for cash and even more to keep your hard-earned money." He laughed at his own observation. "Hard-earned! What's so hard about flashing your titties to a bunch of strangers or spreading your legs for a few minutes in a back room?"

"At least I work for my money," Destiny Rose replied. "I don't kill people for it."

From his reaction, you would have thought Jarvis had been hit in the chest with a cannonball. "Oh, you are so wrong, sweet Destiny Rose. I'm going to kill *you* and you don't have any money," he snarled.

"Why would you do that?"

"The same reason I killed Alexis—she was cheating on me."

Sabrina and Garelick both gave me quizzical glances.

"You knew about this?" Garelick asked.

"Hey," I protested, "this is news to me."

"Right," Destiny Rose spat out with a mocking laugh. "As an act of revenge, you threw her from the balcony? I doubt that. We both know it was for the $150,000. And you have the nerve to call me a liar."

Confused, Jarvis cocked his head to one side, like a dog does when you utter the word *walk*. "How did you know about the money? Who told you?"

"Trade secrets, psycho." Destiny Rose began to walk toward the door but stopped at the sound of breaking glass. She turned to see Jarvis running toward her, his broken drinking glass raised above his head, ready to drive it into her.

He almost made it happen.

At the sight of Jarvis smashing his glass on the corner of the over-turned coffee table, Garelick ordered his men inside. As Jarvis ran toward his victim, it became apparent they wouldn't arrive in time to save Destiny Rose from serious harm. I watched helplessly as she screamed for help.

Racing out of the observation apartment, I passed a TV monitor and saw Jarvis leap onto Destiny Rose, both of them collapsing on the floor. As he raised his weapon a second time, I heard two gun blasts and turned to see Garelick down on one knee, his service revolver in both hands. Jarvis cried out in pain as one bullet caught him in the upper arm and the other found its mark in his right knee. Suddenly there was blood spraying everywhere. Unit One finally came into view with their weapons drawn and aimed at Jarvis' head.

For a moment the entire scene confused me, until I noticed the two small holes that now decorated a portion of the drywall beneath the two-way mirror. "If bullets could enter this room through the walls," Garelick said as we all sprinted out the door, "I figured they could exit the same way."

In the few seconds it took us to run down the hall, things had changed dramatically in the other apartment. Instead of entering a secured crime scene, we found ourselves in the middle of a hostage negotiation.

"Put the glass down—away from her neck," one of the officers ordered, his gun barrel still trained on Jarvis' sweaty forehead.

"Go ahead and shoot. I'm going to die anyway," Jarvis cried out. "I think you hit an artery."

Jarvis and Destiny Rose remained on the floor, squeezed into a corner of the kitchen. Jarvis was against the wall, using his good arm to keep Destiny Rose in place on top of him, creating a human shield. In his right hand, he was holding the broken lip of the glass against her throat.

"Let her go, Jarvis. It's over."

Jarvis' confusion was evident once more when he asked me, "You did this?"

"No," I corrected him. "You did this. You and Derek McDonald."

"Derek McDonald is a ghost."

"How so?" Garelick asked, his gun pointed between Jarvis' eyebrows.

I was hoping this statement was literal and that Derek was actually dead. One less body to find.

"After he set me up, he vanished."

"He didn't set Max up?" I asked.

"He set both of us up—I just didn't know it at the time. I thought we were partners."

"But why Alexis?"

"Apparently he was on some sort of an eye-for-an-eye crusade."

At this statement, everyone in the room except Jarvis seemed lost.

"No one knows what you're talking about," I addressed Jarvis. "Plus, if you don't get medical attention you'll never get to tell your side of the story. You wouldn't want that now, would you?"

His face did appear to be losing colour. What he didn't know was he was merely a bleeder and that no artery had been severed. He was losing a lot of blood and it was making him weaker—which was in our favour.

"So let Destiny Rose go and we'll help stop the bleeding," I said.

"What about the money?" he asked, lowering the glass a couple of inches.

"What money is that?" I inquired innocently.

"In my bank account. If I die, what happens to it?"

"What's so special about this money?" Garelick asked.

"It's blood money isn't it, Jarvis?" I spoke up. "You got it from Alexis' life insurance payout. You and her sister Lauren were in on this thing from the beginning."

"Like hell we were!" he howled. "I didn't even know Alexis had a sister until after."

"Go on," I said. "After what?"

"After Alexis' death. One day out of the blue, Derek contacted me and said I should go see Lauren and shake her down for some cash."

"Let me get this straight. You and Derek murdered Alexis, framed Max and went after Alexis' sister for what—hush money?"

"Yeah, we did those things, but the money wasn't hush money," Jarvis argued, clearly not realizing what he had just admitted.

331

Garelick and I made eye contact, silently acknowledging we had achieved today's goal to get Jarvis to confess to murder. I looked toward the two-way mirror, imagining Sabrina on the other side smiling at us and taking notes for her exclusive.

"Then what was it?" I asked, feeling more confident now.

"It was blackmail money," Jarvis replied. "I told her if she didn't give me some of the insurance money, I would do to her what I had done to her sister." He started to laugh uncontrollably. "You should have seen her when I began to tell her details only the killer would know. I remember how her hand was shaking at the bank when she filled out a cashier's cheque made out to cash."

"For how much?"

"$400,000."

The amount would explain the house purchase and his opulent lifestyle. "What about the $150,000 Alexis withdrew on the day she died? Or had you threatened her and gone to the bank to watch her hand shake as well?"

"And if she paid you—why go back on your deal and kill her?" Garelick asked.

"Have any of you heard the phrase *found money*?" Jarvis asked with a roguish grin. "It's usually when you find a ten-dollar bill in a pocket and decide to splurge on take-out food that night."

"You found $150,000?"

"Call Ripley's Believe It or Not, because that's exactly what happened. After I hit—" he stopped himself, then continued without the gory details. "I found a cheque in Alexis' wallet made out to cash. I figured there was no use letting some copper slip it into his pocket when no one was looking. So I took it and cashed it a few days later."

"That's when you flashed your bank statement at the club," Destiny Rose said in an unsteady voice. Still in Jarvis' grip, she now appeared to be more disgusted with than frightened of her captor.

"Probably," Jarvis admitted, with an odd smile.

Knowing these confrontations never end well and with officers aiming their weapons at Jarvis, I needed to bring this investigation to a close.

"Did you know Lauren is dead?"

This prompted a double-take from Jarvis. "Really?"

"A couple of days ago."

"Are you also going to try to pin that one on me? Because I have an alibi."

"I'm sure you do. You were probably at home watching TV with Chantal." Earlier, he had been worried about his money, but what really scared him was that his wife might lose everything. I believed he had somehow found peace with her and knew she'd be devastated when she learned the truth about him. I had to exploit this for all it was worth—and soon.

"Leave her out of this," Jarvis said sternly, even as his eyes were beginning to close.

"I will if you answer this question: How did Lauren and Derek know each other? Before she died, she identified both of you on the sidewalk behind a TV reporter. You said Derek was on some kind of mission—a crusade. How did it involve Lauren?"

Jarvis stretched his neck and tried to reposition himself and Destiny Rose. "He went to Ravenwood to find her."

"Lauren?"

"No, Alexis. He was looking to find her and kill her."

"You've lost me again."

"His crusade, you moron! He saw himself as some great do-gooder vigilante, righting wrongs, especially when it involved people getting away with murder."

Even though I was pretty sure I knew the answer, I asked the obvious question. "How did he pick his victims?"

"You're going to love this. He read about them in true crime books," Jarvis said, as he let out a wheezing laugh. "Is that insane or what? If he believed someone had got away with murder and was roaming the streets, he'd track them down—"

"And kill them?" I interrupted. "All because some dopey author wrote they *might have* been involved in a murder?"

"Insane, right?"

This from a killer of imaginary girlfriends. Astonishing, I thought.

333

"Getting back to Ravenwood," I interjected. "Are you saying Derek talked with Lauren about killing Alexis for the insurance money?"

"Maybe," Jarvis said before he added, "I'm pretty sure that was Lauren's motivation."

"Why did it take so long to implement his plan then?" Garelick asked.

"Because Lauren didn't know where Alexis was living."

"She told me they were very close," I countered.

"Then she lied. Derek said it took him months to track Alexis down. She was keeping a very low profile after her escape from justice."

"If you got $400,000, then how much did she pay Derek for all his hard work? Half a million?"

"Not a dime."

"Again, that's kind of hard to—"

"The crusade. Why do you keep forgetting that part?"

A pained look came over Jarvis' face and his right arm twitched, causing the jagged edge of the glass to nick Destiny Rose's chin. She let out a small cry and began to breathe heavily. All the officers present were immediately recharged and refocused.

"I didn't mean to do that," Jarvis said. "My arm moved on its own. You saw that. I wasn't going to hurt her."

Though we hadn't noticed, Jarvis had loosened his grip on Destiny Rose. As he continued to plead for our understanding, she made her move, grabbing his right wrist and ramming it—and the broken glass—into his upper thigh. She rolled off Jarvis and stumbled toward one of the officers at the door.

Meanwhile, Jarvis let out another high-pitched shriek, falling on his side, both hands instinctively putting pressure on his leg which only caused more pain. Garelick was the first to jump on him and jam his face into the carpet. Another officer was immediately at his side, pulling Jarvis' arms behind his back and cuffing him. I went to Destiny Rose to give her a hug as tears started to cascade down her face and she began to shake uncontrollably.

Sabrina entered the room as a screaming Jarvis was shoved against a wall.

"And what phase would this be, Steve?" she asked in a semi-serious tone.

"Hopefully, the final one," I said, as I transferred Destiny Rose to Sabrina's shoulder. I walked over to Jarvis Larsh and said, "One last question. What is your involvement in Linda Brooks' disappearance in the city of Darrien?"

The question produced a puzzled look.

"Who's Linda Brooks and where is Darrien?" he asked.

With everything that had happened and the pain he was in, his response was what I had expected: honest.

TWENTY FIVE

LINDA

It had all started with a phone call on an idle Wednesday evening. Steve was out of town on a case with Samantha and Linda was home alone—again. When she had decided to move from Delta to Darrien, it was an exciting adventure. New city. New job. New opportunities. A life with Steve. Everything felt right. Over a period of a few months, Steve had convinced her there was more to life than what a one-stop-light village could offer. "You're a cosmopolitan young woman stuck in a dead-end farming community," he had declared.

In a way she agreed, but from time to time doubts would creep into her mind. She feared her new boyfriend would soon find she really was just a typical small-town girl, with no aspirations of becoming a metropolitan, career-oriented woman. Steve claimed he was still a small-town boy at heart and no longer interested in the sordid city activities that caused him so much trouble in the past. "Been there, bought that t-shirt," he once said.

With any major life change comes stress, whether the change is positive or negative. From the start, Linda discovered that navigating the city streets and trying to fit in with her new co-workers were both extremely depressing. Then there was life with Steve. When entertaining friends, his stories of late nights, long days and an unpredictable work schedule had been a source of amusement to anyone willing to listen. After dinner conversations would focus on tales of catching subjects cheating on their spouses or milking an insurance claim. "I nailed this one guy who was claiming a back injury, landscaping a huge yard at a friend's house and then fooling around with his buddy's wife in the swimming pool! It was unreal."

As Linda soon found out, it was unreal. Not all of it, of course. Although Steve's stories were factual, they were told with what he liked to call *embellishments*. Yes, he videotaped a subject landscaping but not having sex with his friend's wife—that was another subject on a different day. "What does it matter?" he asked when she had raised the subject. "They're only stories. It doesn't matter when they happened. It's not as though anyone is going to ask me for proof." When he put it like that, she was inclined to agree, since his yarns were entertaining and provided endless enjoyment for their guests. *There is nothing better than sitting in a room filled with laughter,* she'd once thought after a particularly good time out.

Prior to moving these exotic P.I. stories were just that—stories. As his own boss Steve could usually set his own schedule, meaning work did not interfere with their plans while they pursued a long-distance relationship. A weekend together meant a weekend together.

During her first week in Darrien, he had put files off to help her adjust and soothe her nerves when they got the better of her. These arrangements, however, could not last indefinitely. Bills had to be paid and files were piling up. As the weeks passed, Steve's hours became more erratic and plans often had to be rescheduled at the last minute—exactly as he'd warned her they would.

Timing is everything in life. If you're involved in a car accident, you wonder if hitting the snooze bar might have prevented being sideswiped on the way to work. The same applies to relationships. You can meet the perfect person, only to learn they are too busy to date. Try again later. After two very trying months of transition that caused tension between her and Steve, Linda was finally looking forward to mending some emotional fences. She believed she was in the right state of mind to get their relationship back on track.

Then Samantha was hired.

"For some reason I'm getting more and more marital cases and need a female investigator," he had said one night after dinner.

In the beginning, Linda had no qualms about this. She knew that to stay competitive in the investigations business, having a woman available for these files would be useful.

"I have no problem with that, Steve," she had said. "Just make sure any investigator I hire doesn't get compromising shots of the two of you at some cheap hotel, working off the clock."

"Strictly business," he'd promised with a laugh. "Besides, the girl I have in mind is getting married next August."

A week later, Steve proposed at a fancy restaurant owned by a former client. "Linda, I want to spend the rest of my life with you," he had declared.

After learning about Steve's affair, Linda wondered if he had ever really loved her or if his proposal had been a way of overcompensating for cheating.

"Hello, I would like to speak with Linda Brooks."

She was initially suspicious, as no one except Maria ever called to talk to her. "This is Linda Brooks," she answered slowly.

"I'm calling about your boyfriend, Steve Cassidy."

"Is he okay?" she asked, imagining the caller was a police officer or doctor.

"Is he home?"

This puzzled her. "Who is this, please? Has something happened to Steve?"

"My name is not important, Linda. I knew Steve from his police days."

She didn't like how this call sounded. "Well, he's not home. Can I take a message and he'll call you back?"

"After this conversation, I doubt he's gonna want to talk with me."

"We're not having a conversation," Linda said, getting more irritated with each second. "What is it you want exactly? I'm about to hang up."

"Please don't do that. This may be important to you. Hear me out."

"You have very little time, whoever you are."

"Do you know Samantha Jennings?"

Linda's skin began to crawl.

"Yes," she replied tentatively. "She works with my fiancé."

"It's fiancé now? Congratulations, I guess. I never figured Stevie as the marrying kind, especially after the way his first marriage blew up. But hey—maybe you'll be the woman who can straighten him out." He waited for a response. When he didn't get one, he continued. "I can't give you my name. I will say that I work in the same field as Steve and this phone call is highly unethical."

"What do you want?" Linda asked, exasperated by the man's preamble. "I know the business. If you are a private investigator, you've been hired by someone. Either tell me who that is or how your business involves Steve. Your time is almost up. I'd make it quick if I were you."

"Does the name Richard Park ring any bells?"

"No."

"He was Samantha's fiancé."

"Oh, yes—I might have heard his name before," Linda acknowledged uneasily, a knot beginning to form and tighten in her stomach. "They broke up a few months ago after he cheated on her."

"Richard admits that, but claims there were other factors prior to getting *involved*, as he puts it, with another woman."

"Again—what does any of this have to do with me? I wasn't the other woman in their relationship, if that's what you are implying."

"But Steve was the other man."

"You're lying and so is Mr. Park," Linda exclaimed. "Your client is angry he got caught and needs someone to blame for his stupidity. Steve is the obvious target."

Though her words carried conviction, deep down she was beginning to unravel.

This cannot be happening, she thought

"I have videotape of them together, Linda."

"No, you—"

Yes, he does. Ohmigod, he has tape of Steve and Samantha.

"Yes, I do."

Linda walked unsteadily to the couch and fell into the cushions.

"Why are you saying these hurtful things?" she asked weakly. "During his police career I know Steve made plenty of enemies, but he's changed. I know he has," she added, as her gaze fell on a stack of love letters on the fireplace mantle.

I'm just like all the others. To be used and discarded.

"Zebras can't change their stripes, no matter how hard they try."

"I don't know how to react to this," she said, wiping the first of many tears from her cheeks. "Steve's not here now. When he gets home—"

"From Hadfield."

"How do you know he's in Hadfield?"

"Because that's my job, Linda."

"Stop calling me by my name! Only my friends call me that," Linda snapped.

"Fair enough, Ms. Brooks," came the calm reply. "Honestly, this is only a courtesy call—off the record. Until three days ago, I hadn't thought about Steve in years. Then this file landed on my desk and presto, past and present collide. When I discovered he was still fooling around on the women who love him, I wanted to make amends for past wrongs."

"His or yours?"

"Mine. You see, I knew his wife and know how much his infidelity hurt her. We all knew about it but didn't tell her—like it was some macho guy code none of us wanted to break. I was fine with that until I learned everyone also knew my wife was cheating on me." The mystery caller paused and said, "You can believe me or not—I just have a gut feeling that, for whatever reason, you and I have been brought together. I know Steve and Samantha are in Hadfield because I'm in Hadfield. I'm sitting in a parking lot across from their motel room, which has only one queen-sized bed. If you want to see for yourself, I'll give you directions. You can also watch the video footage I've shot so far."

He's going to be very sorry if this turns out to be true, she concluded, staring at her engagement ring.

After much debate, she wrote down the address where Steve and Samantha were allegedly sharing a room—something he swore would never happen. "Linda, the only person going to be seeing me naked for the next fifty years is you," he'd promised.

Her hour-and-fifteen minute drive was excruciating; there were simply too many miles to contemplate Steve's betrayal. She met her mysterious contact in a plaza parking lot and when she climbed into his van, he silently handed her a video camera and pressed Play.

"It runs about five minutes," he said, as they watched the happy couple holding hands and occasionally kissing in various locales. "He hasn't changed much since his days in the service."

"Do you mean in appearance or in moral conduct?"

The P.I. laughed at her question. "Both, I guess. Like I said before, Linda—I mean, Ms. Brooks—a zebra can't change its stripes."

"Apparently not," she said, turning the camera off. "And please, call me Linda."

"I thought only your friends called you that," he said.

"I did and I meant it," she said. "Call me Linda from now on. Would you mind if I stayed awhile?"

"As long as you stay hidden in the back. Being a P.I. is pretty lonely, sitting for hours by yourself, watching for cars to leave driveways."

"Yeah, I know. I've heard all about it," Linda said, as she climbed into one of the rear seats and made herself comfortable.

When the lights in the motel room went out, Linda proclaimed she was going to knock on the door and confront the two of them.

"That never works," her new friend advised. "It's dramatic and all, but only lasts a few explosive minutes, and then burns out. The only thing you accomplish is raising your heart rate and causing more pain—which you definitely don't need right now. What you want to do is drag this thing out a few days. You know—cause Steve some heartfelt pain."

"I don't follow," Linda said, her eyes burning a hole in the motel room door.

"They're in for the night. Do you know where they'll be tomorrow? Are they going back to Darrien?"

"Steve has another marital file he says is out of town—surprise, surprise—but who knows, it could be right in Darrien. I don't remember the details aside from the fact some plumber from Plymouth is suspected of cheating on his wife. In any case, Steve and Samantha won't be back for two more days."

"Excellent. That will give you plenty of time to pack things up and disappear for a few days."

"What do you mean, disappear?"

"Just get away for a couple days. Make him sweat."

"When do I confront them then?"

"Once we have your vacation plans in place, you'll knock on their door at the next motel. You'll have your argument with Steve, call Samantha a few choice names and then be gone."

"Gone where?"

The P.I. turned to Linda. "When I found out about my wife and her Traffic Unit lover, I conceived an elaborate plan—the one I'm proposing to you—but didn't think I could pull it off alone. Between the two of us though, I think it could work." He paused, waiting to see some sign of interest on Linda's face. "Of course, the decision would be all yours."

"I'm listening," she replied through clenched teeth. "If it's going to cause Steve pain—physical or otherwise—I'm all ears. Because at this moment, all I want to do is kick down that door and beat them both senseless with a table lamp."

TWENTY SIX

"Do you believe a word he said?" Garelick asked, as we left the apartment.

"Most of it," I replied. "What about you?"

"It doesn't matter what I think. Criminals will confess to anything when a gun is aimed at them. Then later their lawyers will claim their clients were under undue stress, fearing for their lives. It's a no-win situation."

"Do you think Jarvis will do that?"

"For sure. He's not stupid and he doesn't want to lose that big house or his wife. Plus, he can afford the best defence team in the city." We walked out into the fresh mid-morning air and each took a deep breath. "But that doesn't mean he wasn't telling the truth."

"That's also my feeling."

Garelick stopped at the side of the Papermobile where Sabrina was in the driver's seat, going over her notes. "We got the confession, and like everything else in the criminal system, that's nine-tenths of the law." He extended his hand to me. "That was good work in there, Cassidy. It's not often I get to watch a pro in action."

I shook his hand. "Thanks. I was about to say the same."

"Sure you were," he said with a smile.

"Are we following you to the station?" Sabrina called out to Garelick.

"Might as well. There are a few reports we'll need your help filling in."

"While we're there, maybe we can run Derek's name through the database and get a hit on where he's living these days," I said.

"Paperwork comes first."

"Of course," I replied.

Unlike a regular police report, when a suspect is shot the number of boxes to be filled in triples. There is actually less paperwork when the suspect is killed during an altercation. As I watched Garelick slave over his account, I'm sure he cursed the fact that bullet-proof mirror had not allowed him a clear shot. As for Jarvis, despite his whining, he came out of surgery no worse for wear. As it was, his arm wound was superficial, and the surgeon thought the knee would be healed in a couple of months.

When I found the time, I placed a short call to the Farmington Penitentiary to request a call from inmate Max Feldberg. A short time later, I was advised to be near my telephone the following day between 4:45 and 5:00 p.m. Figuring Garelick and the others wouldn't miss me for a few more minutes, I gave Maria a quick call.

"Did Linda get back to you yet?"

"Yes. She wants to meet you tomorrow at noon at the park near Darrien Beach."

"How did she sound today?"

"Better," Maria replied. "I still don't know what's going on with her or where she's been. She just said I'd know shortly."

"Sounds ominous."

"That's what I thought. Maybe you can get more answers out of her tomorrow."

"I'll do my best to put this nightmare to rest once and for all."

"Good luck."

"Thanks. I think I'm going to need it."

By the time the sun had set, most of the detectives were exhausted and wanted to go home. In spite of that, Garelick and Sabrina hung around as the search for the elusive Derek McDonald/Danny Murphy began. As the dust of this investigation began to settle, it became clear this man was the mastermind behind Max's frame job and Alexis' untimely death. In all likelihood, he was still out there, reading new true crime novels and selecting his next victim. If he were ever apprehended, I was certain the reasons for his murders would be anything but rational. Serial killers' motives are never simple. Even in this case, I had pursued the theory a man was targeting red-haired women because he had Mommy issues.

One of Garelick's men entered the office and said, "I think we found him, Sarge."

Garelick took the folder from the detective. "Please tell me he's already dead or locked up on another charge."

"Afraid not. He's been on the run since 1990."

"For what?" I asked.

"Murder. The authorities up north think he killed his wife."

"Unbelievable," I said, as I flopped into a chair.

"Both Derek McDonald and Danny Murphy are aliases."

"His real name is Donald Henry Monroe," Garelick read from the file. "His wife was bludgeoned to death with a baseball bat in '89."

"Was he the only suspect?" Sabrina spoke up. "Did they charge him?"

Garelick continued to read.

"Do they have a picture of him in there?" I asked, leaning toward the desk. Garelick threw me a poorly photocopied driver's licence. Sabrina examined the picture and said he was the same man who testified at Max's trial. We agreed he was the man standing beside Jarvis in the news footage.

"They charged him and then dropped it a day later. The police went after his brother for the crime," Garelick said. "Apparently the brother and the wife were having an affair at the time."

"So the brother is in jail?" I asked as I turned to Sabrina. "Maybe we can interview him."

"I hate to be a wet blanket. The brother was never convicted because while awaiting trial he committed suicide."

The expectation of going on another investigative road trip disappeared from Sabrina's face. "Then why is our guy on the run and murdering people from the bestsellers' list?"

"It looks like he was the killer all along," Garelick answered, flipping over another sheet of paper. "The brother committed suicide not from guilt, but because he couldn't bear the idea of living without his lover— his sister-in-law."

"She must have been one helluva a woman," I remarked. "Getting both brothers like that."

"Why didn't the case die with the brother's death?" Sabrina asked, ignoring my comment.

"From what I can tell, his suicide note left several clues, leading authorities to the real killer—his heartbroken brother."

"Aren't families great?" I said with a laugh. "Obviously he slipped through the locals' hands and fled. How do they know about his aliases?"

"From fingerprints found at other crime scenes. When the police questioned witnesses, they discovered he had used the aliases Darren Millhouse, Deacon Morrissey and Danny Murphy."

"The name he used on the office lease," Sabrina said with a knowing nod. "I wonder where the name Derek McDonald came from—aside from the initials being the same as all the others."

"It's easier to remember a fake name that way," I said, as I threw the picture on the desk. "If I were picking an alias, it would be Sam Cleary or Stanley Coles—anything with the initials I've used all my life."

"So, where do we go from here?" Sabrina asked.

"Well . . . with Larsh's confession to killing Alexis Penney, I think we can wrap up that case." Garelick glanced up at me. "On the way to the hospital, he admitted taking ten grand from Derek for the murder, which should also help us get a conviction."

"Hey, that's $9,999 and not a penny more," I said. "I can see his lawyer arguing over that last dollar until he's blue in the face."

"I'll make a note of that," Garelick replied sarcastically.

"What about your friend in the penitentiary? What happens to him?" Sabrina asked me.

"Nothing, I guess. Not until there's a conviction in Alexis' death. I'm going to talk to him tomorrow."

"Why not go up there? It's only an hour away."

I smiled and said, "Because if we ever came face-to-face, I would be the one staying behind and he would be the one leaving—in a body bag, mind you—but leaving all the same."

"Oh," Sabrina said. "Never mind then."

"Back to the great impostor for a second, Sergeant. What happens next?" I asked.

Garelick put the folder down amid other files strewn across his desk. "You know the drill, Cassidy. I'll put our findings on the national database and hope he slips up sometime. At this point we're five years behind him, which means someone will probably have to die before we catch up with him."

The statement put everyone in a somber mood.

"I suppose we're finished here then," I said, standing to shake Garelick's hand. "It's been a pleasure. I'm sure we'll all be together again for Jarvis' trial, whenever that is."

"I can't wait," Garelick said, as he also shook Sabrina's hand.

"In your article, make sure I come off as some brilliant, crafty, investigative genius. I'm due for retirement in five years and would love to coast on the coattails of this one case."

"I'll try my best," Sabrina laughed, as we walked out into the hall-way.

"Hey, Cassidy," Garelick called out. "You'll never guess what Monroe did for a living?"

"A cop?"

Garelick let out a loud laugh and said, "Are you kidding me? He's too smart to be a cop."

"Then what?"

"A part-time librarian. Shocking, huh? Maybe he's still in the business and working alongside your missing fiancée. Now that would be the kicker, wouldn't it?"

After all the goodwill we had shared over the past twenty–four hours, I had no idea why he would say such a mean-spirited thing, but decided to let it slide.

"Yeah—a kicker, Sergeant," I said.

Once in the Papermobile, Sabrina asked, "What are your plans now?"

"Return to Darrien first thing in the morning," I said.

"Don't want to stick around to do media interviews, like you did after solving the Barry Jones case?"

"Ah . . . no. I learned my lesson after that one."

"Have a hot date when you get back?"

Thinking about Linda, I said, "I do have a date, although I don't think the sparks will create the heat you're talking about."

The early-morning flight was uneventful and I went straight home. I called Dawn who said she would drop by after her shift and bring some dinner from the pub.

"Are you craving anything in particular?"

"As long as it's not hospital food, whatever you bring will be great."

With some trepidation, I left for my rendezvous with Linda. *High noon, how appropriate*, I thought. I no longer believed this meeting was a set-up or that I was in any danger. A huge public park is not the place you take out your enemy. Although a specific location hadn't been named, I walked to a bench we used to sit on when in the park. On the back of the bench was the inscription, *Henry and Tina Cole – True Love Lasts A Lifetime.*

"In fifty years maybe someone will purchase a bench for us," Linda had said one night.

"I'll speak with the works department tomorrow and reserve a spot near the monkey bars where our kids will play," I'd replied.

A half-hour after my arrival, I was worried this was a hoax and that Anderton's men might swoop down from the trees to take me by surprise.

"Steve."

I turned and saw Linda standing alone behind the bench. I stood, keeping the bench between us as a barrier, which reminded me of Jarvis' and Destiny Rose's positions the previous day.

"You remembered," she said slowly, reaching out to touch the top board of the bench. "It's sad that all the good memories I associate with this place are now tainted with bad ones." She looked me in the eye. "But I guess that's life, right?"

I was about to offer her an apology, but realized the time for that had passed. She wasn't here for empty words and sentiments. "It's good to see you again," I said.

"Alive and well."

"The police and your friends will be glad to know that."

"They will—tomorrow."

"Why tomorrow?"

"Because it's not today," she said. "I can't handle any more stress today, so everyone will just have to keep believing I'm missing for one more day."

"At least Maria knows, so Wayne and Trudy probably do as well. I'm sure they'll keep your secret for another twenty–four hours."

"You know—I don't even know why I'm here," Linda said, taking a few steps back as if planning to depart. "After you publicly embarrassed me like that, I should never speak to you again. Stupid me, though, I still have a place in my heart for you. Plus, I didn't want anyone causing you more trouble."

"Are you talking about the police? I can handle Officer Anderton," I said matter-of-factly.

"I wasn't referring to him. I was talking about someone you used to work with."

"I . . . I don't understand—"

Linda cut me off. "Of course you don't, because you never realized my vanishing act was executed like a military operation."

The idea a former colleague had taken vengeance wasn't as shocking as knowing Linda had been in on it.

"And I was the target?" I asked.

"You and your reputation."

"I must say you did an excellent job. I've been hunted by police in three jurisdictions, all wanting to know where I had dumped your body."

A cold smile crossed Linda's lips. "I wish I could empathize with you. However, you got everything you deserve."

"Except I'm not rotting away in prison. Wouldn't that have been the ultimate revenge?"

"Trust me, when I first saw video of the two of you strolling around Hadfield like lovers on their honeymoon, the idea of your slow, painful death was on top of my list."

"Hadfield?"

"What—you don't remember staying at the Day & Night Motel on Kennedy Street? Or your steak dinner at Julia's Bistro on Creekbank Road? I think Samantha had the chicken penne and a nice Merlot." She paused and then spoke in a low growl. "Still in the dark, Steve?"

"I remember Hadfield," I stammered, knowing now how my subjects must feel when confronted with evidence disproving their claims. "So, you hired a private investigator to follow me?" I asked, trying to sound confused.

"Not exactly, although the thought had occurred to me during the past month."

"Okay . . . go on."

"You know how you always say coincidences don't exist—that everything is connected somehow?" She waited for me to nod. "I never believed that until I got a call from a P.I. who said he had proof you were cheating on me."

"Out of the blue this guy calls up? That's kind of hard to—"

"He'd been hired by Richard Park," she interrupted me. "You remember Richard, don't you?"

"Loaded with money. Too dumb to see . . ." I didn't finish the sentence, as my foot was now firmly lodged in my mouth.

"Too dumb to see what a lovely young woman Samantha had turned out to be? Was that what you were about to say?" I said nothing. "It appears you and Richard have the same character flaw. The difference, of course, is he's rich."

I held my tongue. This friendly meeting was not about continuing a war but attempting to come to a peaceful resolution. "So, cleaning everything out of the house was my former colleague's idea?"

"That, the videotape taken at the Tecumseh Motel and the empty house in Sussex." She let out a peculiar laugh. "Remember pregnant Tamra? You can see her next performance this Christmas at the Capitol Theatre. She'll be playing Mary and her little boy will be the Baby Jesus." She gave me an *And you think you're so smart* smirk, before continuing to knock me down peg by peg. "The part I liked the best was the life insurance policy, though it didn't work quite the way we'd hoped. You were supposed to follow up on it and go to the address on the letterhead."

I only half heard what she'd said, as my mind lit on an entirely different possibility. "I don't know what Casey Ellerby told you, but I never worked with him on the force."

A puzzled look crossed Linda's face. "Who is Casey Ellerby?" she asked slowly.

"He's your P.I. friend—the one who leaked the insurance policy to the press and police."

"No, he's not. You're wrong," she said, after a few confused seconds. "He must have been hired for the job or something."

"If this great planner wasn't Ellerby, then who?"

"His name doesn't matter and if you ask me again, I'm walking out of here for good—and I don't just mean the park."

"It doesn't matter. Don't go," I pleaded. "You said something about not visiting the address of the insurance company. Why was that so important?"

"Because like at the house, you would have walked in and found it empty."

"But I would have left evidence behind," I said, grasping the basics of the clever plan. "Then what—you tip the cops, who then find your blood in a back room?"

"And your fingerprints—mysteriously placing us both at yet another place."

"The flaw—aside from the fact I didn't go—was that it would be difficult to prove we were there at the same time. Officer Anderton found that out the hard way."

"We knew that going in. The hope was to have our joint DNA and fingerprints found at four or five random spots. That we were never seen together wouldn't nullify the impression that you were moving me—dead or alive—from one place to another."

Like the last tumbler falling into place, this final piece of information unlocked a long-forgotten memory. I knew the identity of Linda's co-conspirator: Jason Lawrence. Years earlier I had heard him describe almost identical plans to disgrace his wife and her lover, a fellow officer. During my corruption trial, this sad and broken man suffered a nervous breakdown and took early retirement. That he was now working as a private investigator was, as Sabrina would say, *Too funny.*

As much as I wanted to spring this knowledge on Linda, I showed unbelievable restraint and said nothing. In high school Coach Kigar would tell his young football players that half the battle is learning how your opponent operates. "Once you understand your enemy, you know how they'll react." Using this logic, and thankful for a good memory, I recalled how my old friend's plan was to end: after several days in hiding, he would resurface claiming amnesia, not recalling where he'd been. However, I did not remember a one-on-one confrontation with his wife prior to his reappearance.

"Why stop now?" I asked Linda, not wanting to go into further detail. "No one knows where you are and the police are still focused on me."

"Like I said before, it's because I have a heart—unlike you, Richard, and other cheating bastards out there," she said. "When I heard about the shooting, the only thing I could think of was you dying on the operating table and not having the opportunity to set things straight—no matter how painful that would be. I realized in my blind anger I had foolishly become caught up in a sick game and that it was time to end it. I had made my point and I wanted to get on with my life. That's why I'm here today. This is my closure."

I stood speechless for several moments. "I'm sorry about what happened. I thought I was ready for a committed relationship. Obviously I was wrong and—"

"It's hard to believe you couldn't have been truthful with me," she said, cutting me off. "You knew how much my ex-husband's cheating hurt me. Was being with me and only me really that hard?"

"Of course not, Linda," I proclaimed. "Being weak is my problem, not a reflection on the hope and joy you brought into my life. I wish I could change the way I have behaved lately, but I'm afraid in time we'd only find another awful person lurking under the surface."

It was hard to tell if she believed me, and we stood in awkward silence several more moments, the bench still between us. There would be no farewell hugs on this or any other day.

"I have to go," she said finally. "Tomorrow I'm going to walk into the police station and tell them to call off the dogs."

"What will you say when they ask where you've been?"

"The truth. That after moving into a new place in Sussex, due to the stress caused by my cheating fiancé, I took a vacation."

"I can see the headlines now. Anderton will not be happy."

"The way you operate, Steve, I'm sure you'll give him another opportunity to arrest you in the near future." She reached into her pocket and threw me a small jewellery box containing her engagement ring. "Almost forgot."

"Thanks," I said sadly, as I slipped it into my coat pocket. "You should have kept it."

"No," she said, as she prepared to leave. "I figured you'd want to give it to your new friend Dawn. Maybe she'll have better luck with it than I did." She then turned and said, "Goodbye, Steve Cassidy."

"Goodbye, Linda Brooks."

As I watched her walk away, it hit me my police college instructor was wrong. Coincidences do occur in real life. There was simply no other way to explain the initials "J.L." on the mover's and Ellerby's contracts stood for Jason Lawrence, not Jarvis Larsh.

I left the park wondering what other mistakes I had made carelessly following another man's beliefs instead of thinking for myself. Linda was right when she said I would make similar mistakes in the future.

That's just who I am.

After going through the operator and dutifully pressing 1-1 on the phone keypad, my conversation with Max was short and to the point. Through the penitentiary's grapevine, he'd already heard of Jarvis' arrest and confession.

"Don't pack your bags yet. That trial and subsequent appeal is going to take a few years, Max."

"Better than a few decades. My lawyer said if Jarvis is convicted, I could be out on the street the next day, with good behaviour and time served."

"I can't say that thrills me," I replied. "I do have a question about your fraud schemes however. Was Alexis bringing you a cheque that night?"

"Yeah—$150,000. I never saw it though."

"Unfortunately, Jarvis did."

"That loser stole my money!" Max exclaimed.

"Again—I can't say I share your moral outrage."

"This call will terminate in one minute."

"I have a couple of other questions I need answered, Max."

"Shoot."

"At the end of our last conversation, you implied both Maria and Linda would be in danger if I didn't help you."

"Did I say that?"

"Yeah—you did."

"I don't recall that . . . but maybe I did in the heat of the moment. You know I would never hurt Maria. She was the hottest girl in school."

"What about Linda?"

"I didn't even know she existed until Maria mentioned her when she returned my call."

"Unreal," I muttered to myself. "Okay, last one. Who spoke to me on the phone and left packages on my back porch?"

"I can't give you a name. He's a guy who owed me a favour."

"Tell him to move on to his next job and leave me alone."

"I did this morning, right after talking to my lawyer."

"So, we're good, right? You got what you wanted."

"Oh, yeah. You did real good work, Steve."

"Great," I said. "Also make sure your friends at the Pro-Justice League leave me alone."

"Sure, sure. Done."

"Excellent. I think that takes care of our arrangement. I'm going to hang up now."

"We still have a few seconds left," Max said frantically. "Have you spoken with Wayne lately? I can't believe he—"

With great pleasure I terminated our call, hoping never to have contact with Max again. If another call ever came from the penitentiary, I would unquestionably press 2-2 at the prompt, permanently removing my number from Max's approved call list.

Recalling Linda's remark about closure, I carried Max's box of "evidence" to the back yard and emptied its toxic contents into my fire pit. When I re-entered the kitchen for matches, I found Dawn unloading bags of take-out food onto dinner plates.

"I hope wings, mashed potatoes and honey garlic ribs are okay," she said with that smile that had so entranced me that day at the beach.

"Sounds good," I said, as I began to open and close drawers.

"Whatcha looking for?"

"Matches. I want to start a fire in the pit."

"Here," she said, reaching into her pocket and producing several Sunsetter Pub & Eatery matchbooks.

"Thanks." As I took the matches, our fingertips briefly touched. "You're going to make an excellent wife for some lucky guy."

She picked up our now-overflowing plates and rose on the tips of her toes to kiss me on the cheek.

"I know," she said with a laugh as she walked out the back door. "That's what all my boyfriends tell me."

.

TWENTY SEVEN

As he put down the phone, Donald Henry Monroe could only reflect on one thing: that breaking up was really hard to do. The fact his "girlfriend" had not taken the news well only complicated matters. In this instance though he knew it had to be done.

It was out of character for him to have become emotionally involved with someone close to a potential victim. In the past he might have befriended someone to gain information on his target's whereabouts. That had certainly been the case with Lauren Rush. After reading *The Murdering Mistress* he had gone to Ravenwood, believing Alexis Penney would be easy to find and kill. When her body was discovered, he fantasized the entire community coming under suspicion, allowing him to slip away. No one would remember the freelance journalist writing a piece for an unnamed magazine. To say he was disheartened that Alexis had fled to parts unknown would be an understatement. All his previous targets had had the good sense to stay put. Evidently this chapter in his divine crusade would take a little longer to complete.

From the moment Lauren opened the door of her rundown house, Donald had felt a kinship with her. In her late 30's, she had a drab look: stringy bottle-blonde hair, bad skin and fifty unwanted pounds. She invited him in and they sat in the living room, which was cluttered with garage sale knick-knacks. The furniture was old, as though her parents had passed it down to her only after they'd tired of the dull floral print. He believed she felt a connection with him as well, but as their conversation about Alexis' murder charges continued, he concluded she was more interested in the money she would receive from the magazine.

"I haven't talked to anyone about my sister. Not even for my former brother-in-law's trashy book," she had said. "However, I would give you an exclusive. I could also be a consultant, if you ever got a movie studio interested in making a film."

"That's a long way off," he'd said with a laugh, "but you never know. Right now, I'm not being paid for this research. Everything is coming out of my own pocket."

Their budding friendship almost ended there, as Lauren became angry at this news and started to usher him out.

"That bitch kills someone, then walks away with almost half a million dollars, and I'm stuck in this hole without a dime to my name. I was the smart one!" she proclaimed.

Donald had halted his march toward the front door and turned to her. She was, without a doubt, mentally unstable, which he knew he could use to his advantage. Before long he had coaxed her back to the couch, where she continued to vent about her younger, more beautiful sister. She was a woman in pain, no doubt about it. During their long one-sided conversation, he determined Lauren's hatred for Alexis was genuine and, more important, deep-rooted. It was then he gave her a piece of advice which he believed would change her life.

"Buy life insurance on Alexis," he said.

"Why would I do that?" Lauren had questioned. "She's going to outlive all of us. That's the way it always turns out. The most despised person in any family will be around for the rest of your natural life, and then continue to torment you in the afterworld."

"If you help me locate her, I believe I can assist you and your family." He didn't dare share his motives, as that would only confuse matters more.

"What exactly are you saying?" she'd asked him. "What are you asking me to do?"

"Two things," he'd said. "Buy life insurance on your sister and help me find her for the article. That's all."

The first part had been easy, although the $2,000,000 policy did concern him, as it might cause unwanted attention later on. The second was a little more difficult, due to Alexis' decision to stop speaking to anyone in Ravenwood. To keep himself active during this time, he'd tracked down and killed two additional criminals roaming free, honing his skills each time. When Lauren called to say she'd received a birthday card from Alexis with a Santana Hills postmark, the hunt was back on.

Meeting and starting a relationship with Maria Antonio had happened in much the same manner as with Lauren, more by chance than design. The difference was Maria was the bond of attraction, not vindictiveness. Since the death of his wife Alicia, he'd been alone in the world—not counting the infrequent hookers and strippers who kept him company for an hour or two here and there.

When he arrived in Delta he was drained and vulnerable. His last victim had been a factory worker who had killed his father because he wouldn't help him purchase a truck. After reading *The Family That Kills Together*, which outlined how the case was dismissed due to contaminated medical evidence, he knew something had to be done. As poetic justice, he'd shot the son in the head with an arrow as the man sat in the front seat of a new pickup.

Problems arose during the getaway when he'd been caught with the stolen credit card he'd used to buy the bow. As the store clerk called the card company, he'd bolted from the shop and narrowly missed being picked up by the local police. As a precaution, he decided to lay low for a while, and began a cross-country trek to clear his head and reassess his mission.

In his youth, Donald had been an avid murder mystery reader. One summer he had read only classic Agatha Christie novels and become fascinated with how to commit the perfect murder. In her books, however, a smart detective or nosey old woman always caught the culprit. It wasn't until he stumbled across the True Crime/Unsolved Mysteries genre he learned that ordinary individuals had not only attempted the perfect murder, they had got away with it.

Years later, when he found a love letter written by his wife to his brother, his obsession with these stories became more like research. Borrowing his brother's aluminum baseball bat was a cinch, and he found repeatedly hitting his wife over the head almost therapeutic. As the grieving husband, he'd been arrested for the murder. However, when the affair came to light and his brother's fingerprints were found on the bat, all charges were dropped. His brother, who was now facing life behind bars, apparently found this prospect too hard to bear. The next morning they found him hanging lifelessly from a bed sheet around his neck.

Case closed.

Except for the damning suicide note he'd left behind.

> *Taped behind Alicia's nightstand there is a voice-activated recorder. She felt Donald knew about us and was worried when they were alone he would threaten her and she wanted proof of it.*

After days on the run, with guilt eating away at him, a remorseful Donald decided to turn himself in. He had even contemplated taking his own life. However, when he arrived at the police station his melancholy mood passed, and he no longer felt the need to surrender.

What good would come from me being locked up for the rest of my days? he'd thought. *I can be more useful outside prison bringing other criminals to justice.*

Envisioning himself as some sort of equalizer, Donald returned to his love of reading and discovered a wealth of helpful information was at his fingertips: true crime books, documenting people who had gone unpunished for their crimes. To further assist him in his new role, each book firmly established the facts of the case: criminal charges had been laid; a trial had been held; and a killer had been released to kill again.

These people must be stopped, he thought

And so it began.

Although numerous books chronicled the murderous deeds of upstanding police officers, Donald didn't pursue these. He figured those individuals bent on killing cops for revenge would do so in time. Then he'd picked up *Late For Dinner* and felt it was time to reconsider his previous stance. The problem was the book's main character, Steven Cassidy, was an ex-cop. Although there were no reports of Officer Cassidy killing anyone while investigating a case, an unsettling incident had occurred and an innocent man was killed.

What intrigued Donald was that the dead man was the Chief of

Police and that his untimely death had taken place outside Cassidy's jail cell. To be thorough in his research, he spoke with the grieving service's Acting Chief, who was adamant Cassidy had gotten away with murder.

"He was taunting Chief Gordon at the time of the altercation," the man had said.

Although another officer had fired the fatal shot, everyone seemed to be convinced the P.I. was equally responsible for the tragedy. As tenuous a connection as this had to his new undertaking—Cassidy could not have planned the shooting—he was *one of them*. He may call himself an investigator these days, but police blood still coursed through his veins.

Not totally convinced killing a cop was worth the karma it would cause, Donald elected to continue his research on this matter a little more closely.

Plus, the town of Delta was on his way to somewhere as yet undetermined.

No harm in taking in the sights, he thought.

He'd done a preliminary tour of the village, getting a feel for the surroundings and locating some of the landmarks described in the book. His first stop was the post office, believing that all gossip filtered though there. The postmistress was very helpful and gave him a list of people he should interview for his article.

"Growing up, Steven was a real nice boy," she'd told him. "Now I don't know anything about all that bad police business he got wrapped up in, but the people around here were sure glad when he came home to look into that Barry Jones case. He's kind of a hero to a lot of us. We wish he had stuck around a little longer."

"Where did he go?"

"I'm not sure. The first person on that list will, though. Maria runs a flower shop up the street. She and Steve were real close in high school. I'm positive she could get hold of him."

At first he was disappointed to learn his intended victim had already moved on. However, the moment Maria walked out of the back room of the shop, this letdown vanished.

"Can I help you?" she had asked with a wonderful smile.

He stammered something like, "Ah . . . I hope so." All of a sudden the idea of killing went out the window. He regained his poise briefly and gave her his prepared line about being a journalist, but instead of bringing up Steve Cassidy, he said he was writing an article on small-town life. Lying to such a beautiful creature didn't feel right, however, and he quickly ad-libbed he was really a traveling salesman who wanted to be a writer.

Their conversation was short, as he was uncharacteristically uneasy in his new role as killer/journalist/salesman and needed time to regroup. He did stay long enough to ask Maria if she would like to have coffee during her lunch break. He was as surprised as he believed she was, when she'd said, "Yes," in a nervous, yet optimistic tone. By the end of their noon hour get-together, he felt secure enough to inquire if he could call her in a few days. When she again replied, "Yes," he was elated. He walked her back to the shop and shook her hand on the sidewalk.

"It was very nice to meet you, Miss Antonio," he'd said. "I look forward to our next meeting."

"So do I, Mr. Murphy," she'd replied warmly. "And good luck with your sales in Kelsey Lake."

As he headed unsteadily to his car, he made a mental note to remember he had used the name Daniel Murphy. It was yet another variation of Danny Murphy, an alias he hadn't used in some time.

Driving past the *Thanks For Visiting Delta!* sign, he began to feel guilty about his flirtatious behaviour. Unlike his wife, he had never cheated, although the opportunity had been plentiful in his line of work. Employed as the sole male librarian at a city library, he had access to single female employees as well as the endless stream of mothers with young children and bored housewives who regularly frequented his branch. Yet, he never "checked out" so to speak, any of them outside the library. That was not his style and besides, he was happy in his marriage. He thought Alicia was also, until he found that racy note.

The idea of killing his wife started as a slow burn which escalated into a bonfire over a two-week period. He must have emitted some air of knowing around her, as they both began acting differently around the other. Their dinner conversations became strained and awkward. How she'd figured out he knew about the affair would remain unknown. She had though—hence, the voice-activated tape recorder. Had she not been asleep when his brother's baseball bat crushed her skull, he might have asked her.

Even after all these years eluding the authorities, he remained strangely loyal to Alicia and his marriage vows. Whenever he placed their wedding picture on a nightstand or office desk he thought, *People would think this is crazy.* Yet the ritual continued in each new town.

There was something about Maria that changed everything. After their lunch, when he did finally check into a hotel room, he hadn't taken the sentimental photo out of his suitcase. He wondered if this decision was due to his newfound feelings for Maria or the realization his marriage was over and it was time to move on. As the days passed, this troubling debate invaded every waking moment and caused him to lose sleep. In Kelsey Lake, his research on Steven Cassidy's character came to a standstill.

Unsure of his feelings for Maria, he made excuses for constantly having to leave the Delta area, although he remained sequestered in his Kelsey Lake hotel. He was paralyzed—move forward with this flower shop owner or move on to his next target? The decision was made for him when Maria received a call from a mutual friend, Max Feldberg. When she recounted the unusual conversation, his first reaction was to run, as he was a firm believer in predestination. Staying around Delta under these circumstances was just too risky.

This time though, he took Max's phone call as a sign his journey was nearing a conclusion. *All good things must come to an end,* he'd decided. Nevertheless, he was fascinated to see how this development would unfold and couldn't imagine not seeing this final chapter through.

A front row seat to the investigation of a crime for which he was responsible was too intriguing to pass up.

He'd gladly given Maria his blessing to travel with Steve, on the condition she keep him updated on their progress in Santana Hills. Her premature return to Delta a few days later was troublesome, especially under the circumstances. Luckily, a planned "business trip" had been postponed and he was able to meet her at the airport. When she ran to give him a passionate kiss, his world turned upside down. On the ride home, she told him how Steve would never change his selfish ways and how angry she was with him.

"Then stop talking to him," he'd said flippantly, hoping there was still a chance they could forge a future together without her meddlesome ex-love in the picture. "Drop him like a hot potato."

Her quick answer had clarified his dilemma, but not in the manner he'd expected.

"He's an ass, for sure," she'd said slowly, continuing to stare out the front window, "but a part of me will always care for him. And when he finally matures, I still want him to be part of my life." She turned to him and added, "I'm just hoping that won't take too long, because I really want him to meet you."

"That may not happen for some time."

"I know," she'd replied, taking his hand in hers, resting them on the seat.

They returned to her house and it was apparent from the moment they'd stepped inside she wanted to take their relationship to another level, leading him directly to the bedroom.

But it was not to be. Not now. Not ever.

Telling Maria the timing for such an intimate act wasn't right would only cause confusion. Yet sadly, he knew it was the only way as there was no hope of a future together. He couldn't keep up the businessman façade forever, and once she discovered the truth they would be finished.

Short-term pain for long-term gain, he thought.

She had not taken his rebuff kindly and blamed herself for running off to play girl detective. In a stroke of genius, he agreed and said, "I want our first time to be special—not a reaction to a trip that went poorly. Right now you're angry with Steve—as you should be—and it feels as though he's somehow part of this decision."

"No," she said. "That's not the case. I really do want to make love to you," she pleaded.

He sat beside her on the bed and kissed her forehead. "I want to make love to you too, Maria, but the saying, 'two's company, three's a crowd,' was coined for moments like these. I can't express how much you mean to me," he'd said tenderly, lightly kissing her cheek. "You're incredible and I want our first time to be just as incredible. You can understand that, can't you?"

She'd sobbed softly, then smiled, then laughed, and then they embraced, falling backwards onto the bed. "Next time we're together then? How does that sound?"

"I can't wait," he'd said. "When I return from my next trip you and I will have a night to remember."

While away, Maria had kept him updated on Steve's investigation and its surprising conclusion.

"You'll never guess one of the aliases this psychopath used," she'd said with a laugh.

Want to bet? he'd thought sorrowfully. "Steve Cassidy?" he'd replied, knowing what was coming next.

"No, Danny Murphy! Do you believe that?" she'd asked. "Isn't that hysterical—and a bit creepy? I mean, what are the odds this freak has the same name as my boyfriend?"

Like many of their recent firsts as a couple, this was the first time she had referred to him as her boyfriend. As much joy as this must have given her to say, it could only be equalled by the pain it had caused him.

After several awkward moments of silence on the line, he finally found the courage to say, "Maria, there's something I have to tell you."

Dear Mr. Cassidy,

Although we have never met, you and I have much in common, both in life and in love.

We have shared the extraordinary company of Miss Maria Antonio and are both extremely fortunate for the experience. When I recently informed her I was married and could no longer continue our relationship, she sounded as devastated as any woman could be, as yet another man had seemingly toyed with her emotions and walked away, leaving her alone once again. This is a repulsive trait you and I also share.

I am ashamed of my actions. Are you?

In the book 'Late For Dinner' your lawyer stated one of your guiding principles is that there is no such thing as coincidence. I too believe in this concept. The idea that while planning to kill you I fell in love with the one person in this world who could stop me is not merely a coincidence – it's FATE.

And we all know what they say about tempting that, don't we?

After I hung up the phone with Maria it occurred to me that from the first time we had held hands, she was actually leading me toward another life path – a route I had forgotten existed.

As I have stated earlier, my time with Maria has made me a better man, and by extension, a better human being – another quality I have sorely lacked since my wife's and brother's deaths.

By now Maria has no doubt forgiven you for how you treated her in Santana Hills, and has informed you her "boyfriend" turned out to be married. If you have not received such a call, I would advise that you reach out to her, as it's obvious you inexplicably remain a kind of rock she clings to during rough periods.

That last point is the real reason for this letter. Maria now believes she is cursed or unlovable, which we both know is not the case. She has simply fallen for the wrong men. As the causes of her heartbreaks, neither of us can fix this now. We've damaged her enough. All we're left with is the ability to make sure it never happens again. She deserves better.

As it is unlikely I will ever speak with Maria again, I am offering you this once-in-a-lifetime, non-negotiable deal: From this day forward, you will act as Maria's guardian angel and help her regain the self-confidence we've helped to destroy. How you accomplish this, I am not certain. What I am sure of, however, is not attempting to help her would be a deadly mistake on your part.

The second condition is that during any future discussions with Maria, you will never reveal my true identity. Not to her nor anyone else for that matter. This is a private arrangement between us. Think of us as Siamese twins who will take this secret to our graves.

The final condition is equally simple: if I contact Maria in the days, weeks or years ahead, by phone or in person, and she exhibits any sign other than disgust with me for lying about my marriage, I will conclude you've broken our agreement and will track you down and kill you where you stand. The same punishment will be carried out if I ever hear a word about my involvement with Maria in police circles. Unlike you, I have a surprisingly large number of friends still in law enforcement. They may know me by other names but they're friends all the same.

I don't want you to believe this pact is one-sided, with the burden of responsibility resting solely on your shoulders. In the name of love, so to speak, I will also be making a personal sacrifice, and promise to abstain from dealing out my brand of righteous justice, as I did with Alexis Penney. However, I will be leaving one name on my hit list: Steven Cassidy.

In closing, I'm not clear where this new path will lead me. I trust it will not be to your front door.

Please take care of Maria, as if your life depends on it.

Sincerely,

D. H. M.

THE END

PRAISE FOR JOHN SCHLARBAUM'S
Inspirational Books

THE DOCTOR'S BAG
A Sentimental Journey

The Doctor's Bag: A Sentimental Journey is the heartwarming tale of the life of Thomas Sterling and his son Robert. Readers will become enthralled with *The Doctor's Bag* as the intimate story between father and son unfolds, giving new meaning to the actual doctor's bag itself. As the doctor's bag acts as the metaphor between healing and pain from year to year, *The Doctor's Bag* leaves the reader with an enlightening message of life, love and hope. *The Doctor's Bag* is strongly recommended to the general reader and those searching for a gentle, touching, and life changing read.

- THE MIDWEST BOOK REVIEW -

AGING GRACEFULLY TOGETHER
A Story of Love & Marriage

Aging Gracefully Together: A Story of Love and Marriage is an intimate autobiographical account of one couple's undying love from the time of their engagement through their fifty years of domestic partnership. Captivating readers from first page to last, the story of Henry and Tina Cole's hopes, dreams, joys, heartaches, struggles and triumphs is an inspiring story of love and marriage. *Aging Gracefully Together* showcases a thoughtful and caring relationship and is very highly recommended reading - especially for those who are themselves about to embark upon a lifetime matrimonial journey together.

- The Midwest Book Review -

For more information on these titles and to order your books and CDs, please visit: www.scannerpublishing.com

PRAISE FOR
BARRY JONES' COLD DINNER
A Steve Cassidy Mystery

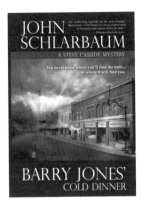

Go Back To The Beginning
– The First Mystery

"An enthralling mystery all the way through. *Barry Jones' Cold Dinner* is a finely crafted work of the genre and a great choice for fans."
– THE MIDWEST BOOK REVIEW –

"Barry Jones' Cold Dinner has sturdy traditional crime bones. Schlarbaum isn't lacking in wit or an attractive protagonist."
– SUN MEDIA –

In March 1990, after kissing his wife and boys goodbye, Barry Jones departed his small town home and headed to work in the city. He never arrived. Now seven years later, his wife wants the courts to declare her absentee husband dead once and for all.

Enter P.I. Steve Cassidy – a disgraced ex-cop with a broken soul and looking for a second chance. Hired to take a fresh look at this cold case, he must try to uncover new clues to Jones' disappearance.

With the court date looming, Cassidy knows he only has one shot at redemption and can blame no one but himself if he fails to solve his first big case.

Watch the Book Trailer at: www.youtube.com.
Keywords: John Schlarbaum

**For more information and to place your order
please visit: www.scannerpublishing.com**

About The Author

John Schlarbaum was raised in the small town of West Lorne, Ontario. He began his professional writing career working as a Writer and Field Director for several nationally syndicated television programs. After a fifteen year career as a Private Investigator, he is now operating and is co-owner of the Page 233 Bookstore in Amherstburg, Ontario. He is also writing his next mystery novel.

The first Steve Cassidy Mystery - *Barry Jones' Cold Dinner* - was released in 2008.

233 Dalhousie Street, Amherstburg, ON